CW00921453

DECKER

EDEN SUMMERS

DEDICATION

To love so pure it's dangerous.

Cover Design by Letitia @RBA Designs

PROLOGUE
DECKER

I STARE AT THE BLOOD ON THE FLOOR, THE LIQUID soaking the carpet and bathing my soul in sins.

I didn't cause the death at my feet, but the guilt taunts me regardless.

This isn't the happily-ever-after I expected for this meeting. I only wanted to help Hunter. And in return, I'd be helping the woman who has made a remarkable change in him. The same woman he knocked out minutes ago for her own safety, then watched in livid rage as Torian, the psychopath we're now indebted to, carried her from the scene of the crime, leaving us to deal with the aftermath.

I can't think straight through the whiplash.

One minute we had the upper hand, the next that same hand is shoved up our asses and Torian is playing ventriloquist with our lives.

It's a fucking disaster with consequences set to haunt me to my dying day, because now I'm trapped. Not in this office in the back of a prestigious restaurant, but in this world.

I'm no longer a spectator, dabbling from the sidelines.

Now I'm in the thick of it.

"Keep your mouth shut." Hunter gets in my face. "Neither of us saw what happened. We were talking. They were arguing. Then hell broke loose. You got it? If they ask for specifics, tell them you can't remember. Shock has fucked with your head."

I nod, because, seriously, shock *has* fucked with my head.

"*You got that?*" He grabs my bicep and gives me a shake.

"Yeah." I yank my arm free. "I've fucking got it."

The police close in, their indecipherable instructions booming from a loudspeaker near the front of the building.

"This is going to get messy." Hunter's comment is serious. Not one hint of a joke.

My attention drifts over the frontal lobe splattered across the floor before I drag my gaze to his. "Somehow I think we're past that point."

We predicted a mess. We knew getting out of here wouldn't be easy. But this... *This*—the lifeless bodies and the taint of gunpowder in the air—this shit is a whole different dimension from mess.

This fucked up disaster is beyond repair, and certainly beyond salvation.

It's the hole that keeps on digging.

The shitty gift that keeps on giving.

"*This is the police*," a voice shouts. "*Is anyone in here?*"

"Yeah. Back here." Hunter jerks his head at me, silently asking if I'm holding myself together.

I nod, pretending this crap happens on a daily basis.

It's no skin off my nose.

I lie to the cops about double murders all the damn time.

Piece of cake.

The squishy crap on the rug that looks like brains isn't going to haunt me for years. Nope. I've already resolved that shit.

I'm chill.

Hunter narrows his eyes, and I can practically hear his thoughts. He's well aware one slip will land us both in prison where we'll have to hold our ankles during shower sessions until we're old and gray.

"We've got this," he murmurs. "Torian has cops in his pocket. He's not going to let us fry. So man the fuck up and keep it simple."

2

Eight hours later...

"They questioned you for a lot longer than they did with me." Hunter's stare pins me in place from the other side of the dining table. His words are a harsh accusation despite the lazy way he cradles the beer in his hands.

"Excuse me?" I take a sip of scotch and mimic his relaxed demeanor even though there's so much shit churning in my head I swear I'm a few brief contemplations from a stroke.

"The police station," he clarifies. "Your interview took twice as long as mine. Did you keep your mouth shut like a good little boy?"

"Yeah, I kept my mouth shut," I sneer. "But rumor has it that you didn't. The cops mentioned something about you sucking pole like it's going out of fashion, just so you could get out before dinner."

He grins, but it's not kind. It never is. "You're edgy. Did little Deckey sing like a canary?"

I glare and down a gulp of alcohol to stop myself from reaching across the table to smash his face against the thick polished wood. "Question my integrity one more time, asshole, see how far it gets you."

I didn't squeal on Torian. If I did, I would've been long gone hours ago instead of sitting in an unfamiliar house with the asshole breathing down my neck, claiming I'm his new poster boy for criminal activity.

Apparently, I work for him now.

I no longer report to Hunter. I'm not the big teddy bear's faithful sidekick who tags along on the occasional stakeout or hacks into some random joe's personal information.

I'm balls deep in Cole Torian's pocket.

His pathetic little bitch.

Yay, me.

Hunter leans forward and shoots a quick glance over his shoulder, checking on the man of the moment, who talks on his cell. Torian seems to be relaying the same fictional story to everyone in his employ—Jacob, aka his out-of-town drug runner, fatally shot his number one goon, Carlos, moments before the now-dead-guy inflicted a fatal shot of his own.

Implausible? Hell yes.

Will anyone dare to question him? Fuck no.

Nobody who knows his power and reach would be that stupid.

Hunter meets my gaze, his eyes intense as he murmurs, "Are you sure this is the life you want?"

"Oh, yeah," I seethe. "This shit is right up my alley."

I roll my eyes then return my scowl toward the living room. This house is dripping in dirty money—the artwork, the furnishings, the architecture. And it's not even Cole's house. It's his older sister, Layla's. The same sister who listened to the fictional murder story and didn't question its lunacy. Then she nodded like a good little puppy when her brother told her to go get her kid from a friend's house.

She's either scared out of her mind, or an obedient little doll.

I don't know which is worse.

"Have you thought about running?" Hunter whispers.

"Of course I have." I keep my voice low, making sure not to disturb the psychopath in the room. "But waiting for a bullet in the back of my brain for being a traitor isn't something that fills me with giddy excitement, ya know?"

"I'll help you run. You're stupid if you stay."

I scoff. "Jeez, Hunt, you always know how to make a guy feel special."

"I'm not joking. If you want out, say the word. It's now or never."

Maybe I should take him up on the offer.

Walk away. Start over someplace new.

But I'd have to leave all this behind. Every little bit. And not just the money. I'd have to forget what I've seen. What I've done.

I came looking for trouble. I wanted destruction.

Well, maybe not to this degree.

Back then I wasn't entirely stable. I wanted to be a part of this stupid game of chicken. Now I don't know what the hell I'm doing setting down roots in the middle of a minefield.

Torian falls silent, taking a gulp from his glass of gin and tonic before starting another call.

"Let me think on it." I push from my chair, grab my drink, and stalk outside the glass doors to get much needed fresh air on the back deck.

Hunt's right. If I don't jump ship now, I never will. Not unless it's in a body bag. And I guess that doesn't really matter much anymore, either.

My life doesn't have a high value these days.

I've got nothing. Nothing but this.

Yes, my family is out there somewhere—my parents are traveling the country in their camper van, trying to outrun their nightmares. My brother is living in the middle of desolate-as-fuck Oregon, basking in seclusion. And my sister is...

I huff out a breath.

I lost sight of Penny so fucking long ago. She's God knows where, doing God knows what, with God knows who. It's the unknown that kills me.

Nobody is waiting for me to drop by.

This, right here, right now, is all I have.

I lean against the wall of the house, one foot cocked against the brick while I drink the last of my scotch and curse myself for the stupid decision to give up smoking twelve months ago.

I'd give anything for a nicotine boost right now. And more scotch. And less of a death wish.

The slam of a door brings me to my feet, and I turn to find a woman stalking through the living room. Another Torian. I've seen her picture online. I've read about her in the papers—Keira, the youngest member of the crime-riddled family, at least before Layla's daughter, Stella, was born.

I cock my head, trying to hear the vehement words from the slim brunette, but I can only make out the vicious tone.

It's a showdown. Unhinged Barbie versus Satan in a suit. Not that it's a fair fight. Satan is entirely unfazed by the confrontation, while Barbie has blushed cheeks and disheveled hair, as if she's trekked her fingers through the long, dark strands a thousand times.

I step forward, not willing to miss a moment of the theatrics, and slowly inch the door open. There's the softest squeak of the hinge as her aggression batters the room, but she hears it, those rage-filled baby blues snapping in my direction.

She tries to stare me down, her petite frame so tightly wound I bet I could twist a stick up her ass and hear a music box melody come to life.

"Hey, sweet cheeks." I give a derisive finger wave. "Don't mind me. I couldn't hear the drama outside. It's much better from in here."

Torian ignores me. He should know me well enough by now to understand I'm not going to stop being a smartass just because he's got my balls in his fist.

He may own me, but he sure as fuck won't control me.

"Who is *he*?" Keira's gaze snaps to her brother.

"Decker," Torian mutters. "He works for us now."

She scoffs, the burst of menace turning into a bitter laugh. "And I bet he found out before I did, too."

"He was there, Keira. It's pretty hard to tell you about the incident before someone who witnessed it."

"Don't talk down to me, you smug piece of shit. I had to hear about a fatal shooting in my own family's restaurant on the *damn radio*. And when I tried calling you, *numerous times,* all I got was your message service."

"This is business. I had to make some calls before—"

"Oh, I know." Her eyes narrow to spiteful slits. "I got in contact with ten people in between my calls to you. *Ten people, Cole.* And all of them had already spoken to you. How can you keep me in the dark like this? You're risking my safety."

"I'm not risking a damn thing." His tone is sinister. "This had nothing to do with you. So, if or when I finally got around to calling, it would've been out of courtesy, not necessity."

"Courtesy?" Those pretty ruby lips flatten into a straight

line. Her jaw ticks. "Who are you, Cole? I don't even know you anymore."

He inclines his head. "It's better that way."

She retreats, her face crumpling as she wraps her arms around her middle. Moments of heated silence pass, the tension building while Hunter and I watch in avid fascination.

The woman has brass balls, that's for sure.

As if hearing my thoughts, her gaze meets mine, those deep blue eyes shimmering with emotion, before she glares and focuses out the window. "Where's Layla?"

"She went to get Stella from a friend's house."

"Under your instruction, of course." She sniffs. "I bet you put her on lockdown, too. Are you the reason she wouldn't answer my calls? I swear to God, since Dad left, you've lost your fucking mind."

Torian takes a threatening step forward. "Watch your mouth. I'm growing tired of your bullshit."

"Fuck you, Cole. You can't tell me what to do."

"Can't I?" In a flash, his hand wraps around her throat.

I shove from my chair, and Hunter follows suit.

She doesn't flail. She barely reacts. Apart from the high tilt of her chin, nothing has changed. Venom still shoots from her gaze. There's no fear. No retreat.

"Let her go, Torian." I step toward them.

He gets in her face. "Pull yourself together," he repeats, this time softer, under control, as he releases his grip.

She doesn't whimper. There's barely a sag in her shoulders. Instead, she seems to take his demand on board, pulling her crazy into check.

"I'm getting another drink." Hunter starts for the kitchen, his leveled words and casual pace creating a calming buffer. "Who wants one?"

"Make mine a double." Torian turns his back on his sister and grabs his empty glass from the coffee table.

Life returns to normal.

Well, as normal as this fucked up existence can be, but I can't drag my gaze away from her. I can't stop waiting for the moment where she weakens. Where she breaks.

She doesn't.

It's fascinating.

She's fascinating.

She's also beautiful and strong, yet obviously harboring the same death wish that has coiled around my soul.

Her rampant breathing lessens, the warrior vanishing, and a picture of vulnerable perfection takes its place as she glances my way. This time when our eyes meet, she doesn't glare. There's no menace or spite in her gaze. I see confusion in the deep furrow of her brow.

But most of all, I see appreciation.

I see her thanks.

And it's the only reason I need to make me stay.

1

KEIRA

FOUR MONTHS LATER

I GLANCE AROUND MY FAMILY'S RESTAURANT, OVER THE standing guests who mingle and laugh between each guzzle of expensive alcohol. They exude joy in their tailored suits and stylish dresses while filling their bellies with the finest cuisine.

It's what we do.

All part of the show.

I paste on a grin, playing my role. I appear humbled by their presence. Blessed by their support as I saunter around the room flaunting a halter-neck gown worth more than most people earn in a month.

I'm acting.

But so is my audience.

Their kindness is a facade. Their friendship a lie. Their happiness a bluff.

I don't doubt that each and every man in attendance would slaughter me and mine in a heartbeat if they thought they could get away with it. If they thought, for even a second, they could bring us down.

The women aren't any better. Their polite questions are made with sinister intent. Digging for information. Scrambling for leverage with every softly spoken word.

They're fake. From their personas to their smiles—none more so than mine.

"Can I have your attention, please?" I raise my champagne flute, my mask of charm perfectly in place as the chatter lessens. "I'd like you all to join me in a toast."

My focus strays to the reason for the engagement party— Hunter and Sarah—and for a moment I don't have to feign happiness, even though the man in question scowls at me.

The love between these two is one of the very few *real* things in my world. Their relationship isn't about rainbows and butterflies. It's dark and gritty. Pure and honest. At times, it's honestly fucking scary. But honest nonetheless.

They've created an unbreakable partnership amongst the threats and betrayal surrounding us. They beat the odds and have earned my admiration, along with the slightest case of jealousy.

"To Hunter and Sarah, may your upcoming marriage be filled with peace—" which is non-existent. "Love—" that will make you vulnerable. "And friends and family—" who can easily stab you in the back.

"To Hunter and Sarah," the guests echo, raising their glasses to drink away my poor excuse for a toast.

Finding the perfect sentiment to describe this moment is something I gave up on nights ago. We don't do perfection. We do manipulation and lies. Deceit and danger.

There are no fairytales here. Only wealth derived from the death of many and the demise of more.

A presence approaches behind me, making me stiffen.

A man.

No, *men*.

There's more than one, their proximity raising the hair on the back of my neck. But I show no fear. I can't. Not in a room filled with security and people I'm supposed to cherish.

I have to pretend I'm safe. Although we all know safety is another illusion.

"You're off your game, sis." Cole gives a friendly nudge to my elbow, washing away my discomfort with his gruff voice. "I thought you would've bored us for hours with a gushing speech about love and commitment."

I raise a brow in offense and wave a hand for him to continue forward. "Why don't you show me how it's done?"

He smirks, and for a moment I glimpse the devil. The determination and unwavering confidence in his gaze is unfathomable. But there's sterility, too.

He's not entirely present. He hasn't been for a while.

"I will." He strides ahead, wordlessly demanding everyone's attention.

Conversation dies a quick death under his muted authority. The crowd becomes enraptured, acting as if this man is their savior instead of the one threatening them to remain loyal.

"Thank you all for being here tonight." He indicates the not-so-happy couple with a tilt of his chin. Hunter glowers, his irritation unrestrained, while Sarah glares, her eyes narrowed to spiteful slits. "Although neither of them were enthusiastic about having an engagement party—"

"Slight understatement," the man at my back murmurs near my ear.

A shiver skitters down my spine. I know that voice. I've grown accustomed to the way it makes my pulse quicken.

No man has ever intrigued me the way Decker does.

"But through their adamant disapproval," Cole continues, "I knew this would be the perfect opportunity to bring us together. All of you were invited today because you're a part of the family. And right now, with our uncle still fighting for his life in hospital, we need to remain close."

My heart snags beneath tightening ribs. The flash of Uncle Richard's bruised and swollen face assails my mind. The broken arm. The cracked skull. The unrecognizable form in a crisp white hospital bed littered with cords and IVs.

It would've been more humane if he'd died. No man should've survived his injuries.

"Not only was his attack a blatant display of what others will do to try to tear us apart, it's also an act I can't ignore. I will fight for what's mine, and I will find everyone involved."

For the naive, Cole's speech could be considered protective and inspiring. To those who know him, it will be heard for the threat it is. It's a reminder to those in this room who have contemplated betrayal. A clear warning to anyone questioning their loyalties.

Remaining devoted is the only option for anyone who values the breath in their lungs.

At one time the sentiment frightened me, back when I was a child and the harsh words of a heartless father were something I whimsically hoped he'd outgrow.

I'm the one who outgrew the whimsy.

I adapted to my circumstances because there was no alternative. The weak don't survive here.

Mentally or physically.

"I will not stand idle and watch my family be destroyed. With Hunter and Sarah's engagement, we become stronger. We show outsiders how powerful we are when we work together."

I drown out my brother's words with another sip of champagne and scrutinize the vultures eagerly waiting for the scent of blood. They want Cole to expose a weakness. The slightest flaw.

"For a powerful man, Torian sure talks a lot of shit, don't you think?" Decker mutters.

I stifle a chuckle, my morbid thoughts being ripped away by his comic relief. "You can leave at any time," I murmur over my shoulder, not willing to make eye contact.

I know what I'll find in his expression, and it won't be the cold calculation I see from everyone else.

"Yeah... sure I can," he drawls. "With a bullet in the back of my skull as a parting gift."

I cringe, the visual hitting with vivid clarity.

"Besides, I couldn't leave you behind. You'd die of heartbreak. Sarah, too, for that matter. How could I live with the guilt?"

I roll my eyes. "Does your best friend know his fiancée is the only reason you stick around?"

"Of course. I tell him often."

I snort, earning the attention of my brother, who pauses mid-speech to shoot me a glower.

"*Sorry*," I mouth.

Cole's hard gaze slips over my shoulder, his stare intensifying for a threatening moment, before he turns back to the crowd and continues his dictatorial speech.

"You're a bad influence," Decker mutters. "Nothing but trouble."

I bite my lower lip, my neck tingling with the need to face him.

I'm dying for another glimpse of that spectacularly fitted suit. The chocolate hair styled to perfection. The shadow of stubble along his jaw that begs for my touch, and eyes so dark and deep I could lose myself.

Sometimes I want to lose myself.

Instead, I have to ignore the escapism that comes when I'm around him. The playfulness. The banter. Getting mixed up in him isn't smart.

And I'm always smart.

"Stop playing games," I murmur.

He chuckles, the subtle sound smooth and too damn cocky. "Life is a game. If it isn't fun, what's the point in playing?"

There's a beat of silence where my heart lodges in my throat, then the crowd raises their glasses in unison. "To Hunter and Sarah."

I follow suit and take another sip of champagne, this one longer than the last.

Decker's scotch glass grazes my peripheral vision then disappears from view. I imagine his throat working over the liquor. The swipe of his tongue against his lower lip to lick away the moisture.

My mouth dries.

My skin prickles.

This man stokes to life a sexual appetite I've deliberately kept starved for years.

"I'm going to speak to the happy couple." I hold my head high and saunter away, not wanting to test myself more than necessary. His warmth fades, leaving me chilled. My fake smile returns, and the sterility of my existence along with it.

"You're hating every minute of this, aren't you?" I ask Sarah in greeting.

"Yes." She crosses her arms over her chest, fending off well wishes from guests with her hostile expression. "Do we look like the type to get giddy over an engagement party full of thugs?"

I cock my head in mock scrutiny. She's beautiful, and not merely in physical form. She can be brutal and kind in the same breath. Vicious and caring. This woman is truly remarkable. "Will you strangle me if I say you're not the type to get giddy over anything?"

Her lips twitch. "I'm not going to strangle you for an accurate assessment. But this—" She jerks her chin at the vultures. "This is in no way a reflection of what I'd like to be doing to celebrate our engagement. I have far more important things on my mind."

"She means fucking," Hunter adds, deadpan.

I grin. "Yeah, I figured."

"Torian is right, though." He pivots away from Sarah to watch my brother approach the bar. "Tonight was a good opportunity to get everyone together. We need to lock this shit down before the whole operation unravels."

He's referring to the attack on my uncle and how it makes our family hierarchy appear fragile. Especially when my father hasn't shown his face in months. We're teetering on shaky ground, but this isn't the first time. And it won't be the last.

"Has there been any news on who ran him down?" I hedge. "You know Cole doesn't tell me much."

"And that's for your own safety." Hunter's response is gruff. "He'll tell you what you need to know. *When* you need to know."

My pulse increases with the placation. I despise being seen as the clueless little princess. But perception is everything. "Would your fiancée accept that type of overbearing protection?"

He holds my gaze, his eyes narrowing.

We both know Sarah would demand complete transparency. If kept in the dark, that woman would create havoc. I'd love to hold a fraction of her warrior's reputation. To be known for strength instead of weakness. To be seen as an asset instead of a liability.

We are regarded in entirely different light, but in reality, we aren't all that different. At least, that's what I'd like to believe.

"I don't like secrets, do I, handsome?" Sarah places her hand on Hunter's chest and winks at me. "Don't worry. If I hear anything, I'll let you know."

He snags her wrist in a tight grip. "If you hear anything, you'll keep your mouth shut, woman."

She smirks. "Now you're just turning me on, big guy. Do you want to take this macho bullshit some place private?"

His nostrils flare.

"Speaking of being turned on..." Decker appears beside me. "Have I told you ladies how gorgeous you look tonight?"

Hunter releases Sarah's wrist and clenches his fist. "Don't push me, *Deck*."

"What did I do?" Decker holds up his hands in surrender. "It's not like I told them I'm going to be picturing them while I'm all alone in the shower. I actually restrained myself this time. What more do you want from me?"

Sarah rolls her eyes, and yet again, I can't help appreciating the lack of apprehension I feel around the joker beside me. Decker is a loose cannon. He's the guy who eases tension with his endless sarcasm. He's also the guy who will get himself killed for running his mouth.

I'm still trying to learn who he is. Piece by piece. Day by day.

I've witnessed a glimpse of honor and protection. But like all the others in this room, his actions could be for underhanded reasons.

"I want your respect," Hunter grates.

"I respect you, buddy. Otherwise I would've taken off with your girl a long time ago."

Sarah laughs. Long and loud. The sound is contagious. "Decker, you wouldn't know how to handle me."

"Maybe not, but I'm willing to learn." He waggles his brows.

"I'm going to fucking kill him." Hunter takes a threatening lunge forward.

Sarah grabs her fiancé's hand and entwines their fingers. "You touch him and it means we have to stay here longer explaining the bloodied mess to Torian."

Decker clucks his tongue in another taunt. "That's a good puppy, *Hunt*. We all know Torian is as forgiving as I'm—"

"Intelligent?" Hunter interrupts.

"Sophisticated?" Sarah adds.

I want to add a sarcastic contribution and say unattractive, because God knows this man is as sexy as he is comical, but instead I offer, "Socially aware?"

"Jesus." He retreats, and from the corner of my eye I see him slap a palm over his chest. "You don't understand how much your words hurt."

"My fists will hurt a lot more." Hunter cracks his knuckles.

I smother a laugh under an unconvincing cough. "I'm going to get another dr—" My sentence is cut short by a burst of noise.

Glass shatters. People scream. *Pop, pop, pops* echo from the street, and I stand frozen as gunfire peppers the night like rain. Guests scatter, running, shoving. The lights go out, bathing us in darkened madness.

Decker barrels into me, knocking me to the ground, stealing the air from my lungs. I gasp for breath and fight to break free.

"Don't move." He shields me with his body, his head low, his gaze darting around the room as he pulls a gun from beneath his suit jacket. "Hunt, you good?"

"We're good," Sarah replies.

"*Torian?*" Hunter yells.

There's no response other than women hysterically wailing and men shouting.

I struggle to get out from beneath Decker's hard body, his

weight becoming heavier. I'm trapped while my siblings could be lying in a pool of blood mere feet away.

"*Torian*," I scream. "*Layla*."

A shadow rushes toward us, my brother's face coming into view. He's panting, his gun in his hand. More pops ring out, but they're different. Maybe our return fire.

"Get her out of here." He doesn't look at me as he pulls something from his pocket and hands it to Decker. "Guard her with your life or risk losing your own."

2

DECKER

I clench the car fob in my left hand, my gun in my right, and scramble into a crouched position.

"No." Keira shakes her head. "Not without Layla."

"I already told her to run. Now get moving." Torian rushes toward the shattered windows of the restaurant, Hunter and Sarah following close behind.

"You heard the guy." I hold out a hand. "Let's get out of here."

She rolls onto her stomach and scans the room. "I can't leave without seeing Layla first."

"You can. You will. And you are. Either on your feet or over my shoulder. It's your choice, pumpkin." I grab her wrist and tug. "You don't want to be here if the shooter comes back."

She struggles to her feet in the long evening dress, the tight material restricting the movement of her legs. Once upright, she continues to scan the darkness, the streetlights from outside the only illumination. "*Layla.*"

I pause, waiting for her sister's shout, but there's no reply. Only the sound of panic and hysteria as guests scramble like mice.

"Come on." This time I yank her hard, pulling her into my side and trapping her there with an arm around her waist. I drag her toward the back of the restaurant, ignoring the trail of blood on the floor.

Keira remains strong, a mere shudder of breath and wide eyes her only show of fear.

"Keep walking." I hold her against me and push through to the kitchen where women huddle in corners and hide beneath steel counters. "Get out of here. Escape out the back."

They rush to follow my command, eager for any leadership.

"You okay?" I murmur near Keira's ear, not appreciating her silence.

"Yes." One word. One syllable. No emotion.

I can't tell if she's totally badass or so tightly wound she doesn't know how to express the fucked up shit running through her head.

We make into the fresh air as the small crowd of females flee the employee parking lot in a mass of sobs and clicking heels.

It's then that Keira plants her feet and turns in my arms. "Layla wouldn't have run without me. I need to go back."

"I'm sure you're wrong. Fear does crazy things—"

"There's no more gunfire. I'm going back."

She takes a step, and I block her path. "It was a drive-by. How hard do you think it is for them to turn around and go for round two?"

She narrows her eyes on me, her pupils almost eating up all the pretty blue. "Who's to say they're not trolling the back streets trying to gun down those who escape through the alley?"

Good point. Unfortunately, not good enough to convince me to let her go.

"That's a risk we're going to have to take." I drag her to the black Porsche parked a few feet away and unlock the doors with the fob Torian gave me.

I don't even get her door open before the unmistakable wail of police sirens poisons the air.

The sound is close. Too close.

They were watching.

Fuck.

19

"We need to move." I yank open the passenger door and wait.

She blinks at me, her breathing labored. "Please, Decker, let me stay." She tries to wear me down with puppy dog eyes, her master manipulation working for more seconds than I care to admit.

"Get in the damn car." I pull her forward and have her huddled inside before she can pummel me with another protest. Then I'm sliding into the driver's seat, placing my gun in her lap, and starting the engine while red and blue flashes through the sky.

I don't turn on the headlights. I drive down back alleys in darkness until we're blocks away and I can risk returning to the city streets.

I have no clue where I'm going, I just drive, her constant anxiety-riddled glances out the rear window a torturous companion as adrenaline pulses through my veins.

I check the mirrors and don't find anything suspicious to worry about. "We're not being followed."

"How do you know?"

I pull to the curb and let all the vehicles in the vicinity pass. Then I take the next left down a side street. "See." I jerk my chin at the mirror. "Nobody is tailing us."

She keeps her focus on the rear window, poised to prove me wrong even after I turn left along a desolate road, then right down another.

"You okay?" I switch on the radio, letting the soft murmur ease the tension.

"Stop asking me that." She settles into her seat, her hands delicately stroking the barrel of my gun.

My gaze keeps returning to her fingers, the nails polished in a feminine light pink to match the darker color of her dress. "Do you know how to use it?"

Her movements pause, those soft hands shifting to her thighs. Her nails dig into the shimmering fabric along her legs, betraying her tightly guarded distress. She doesn't answer. Doesn't give me an inch.

"Would you prefer to talk about the weather?" I lean

forward and check the night sky. "It's clear out. Not a cloud in sight. I thought they predicted rain."

Again, it doesn't seem to be the best conversation starter if her silence is anything to go by. Unfortunately, comfort isn't something I excel at. My verbal expertise is in the range of politically incorrect jokes and inappropriate comments. This close and personal shit usually gives me hives.

"I promise you everything will be all right." My placation is useless at best.

"Don't insult me, Decker. I'm not a child."

"Okay... Then let's discuss it. Who do you think is responsible for pulling the trigger?"

She turns to me, her brows tight in confusion. Those blue eyes scrutinize. Questioning. Searching.

"What?" I ask. "You don't want to talk at all?"

"No. It's not that." She shakes her head. "It's just that nobody has wanted my opinion before. I've never been asked to contribute my thoughts."

"Well, here's your chance. What do you think happened?"

She narrows her gaze, and for a brief second I think I've crossed a line. I've pushed. I've pried into the inner workings of the most notorious family in the state. Then, as quickly as her scrutiny arrived, it retreats.

She wraps her arms around her waist and returns to her silence.

"Keira?"

She sucks in a long breath. "I don't know." The response is tortured, the words pulled from a place etched in pain and suffering.

"I don't think anyone will for a while," I offer. "Whoever is playing games knows how to cover their tracks. Just like with your uncle."

Her arms fall, her hands moving back to her thighs, the nails digging deep.

"I bet you're worried about him."

"Of course." She scowls at me. "He's my uncle."

Her statement is a question on my intelligence. The Torians value family above all else. But the comment is also a deliberate deflection. She's keeping herself locked tight, the vibrancy in her eyes betraying strong emotions.

She's known as the weak one. The vulnerable, emotional Torian. Although, clearly, her strength under pressure proves she's much more of a woman than the average man could handle.

Despite her fortitude, I've wanted to save her since the first night we met—from her brother and this life—but I'm yet to determine if she wants to be saved. I'm also clueless when it comes to her moral compass.

"Sorry. Stupid question." I drive for long minutes, sticking to the speed limit, determined not to give any cop the excuse to get up close and personal. A speeding ticket is the least of my worries at the moment, but it's also a hassle I don't need. "Do you have anywhere safe we can go?"

"Home," she whispers.

"That's not happening." With her uncle down, this additional attack seems like an attempted family assassination, and I don't want her dying on my watch. "What's option B?"

She sighs, giving in to my protection without a fight. "Cole has a place." She opens the glove compartment, brushes aside a gun and numerous documents, before pulling out a blank security keycard. "I don't even know if this is the right pass to get through the gates. Mine is in my car at the restaurant."

"Well, we're not going to your house, or back to the restaurant, so it looks like we're giving the card a try."

"I assumed as much," she drawls.

I grin, enjoying her hostility a little too much. "Where are we headed?"

"Westport."

Westport? A ninety-minute drive.

"Second-guessing letting me go home yet?" she taunts.

Hell no. I don't want her going anywhere familiar. "Westport is a great idea. Once we arrive, we can call your brother and get an update."

"We can't call him sooner?" Her question is almost a plea.

"He'd have a swarm of police up his ass by now."

"What about Layla? Can I use your phone to call her? I

22

left mine with my purse, and as you can probably guess, they're back at the restaurant, too." She blinks those long lashes at me.

"Sure." I lean to the side, pull my cell from the back pocket of my suit pants, and hand it over.

She's dialing in seconds, the ring tone a faint hint of sound.

It doesn't take long to figure out her sister is unavailable. There's no answer. Not on the first, second, or third time she calls.

"She's probably still running," I offer, hoping to calm the growing tremble in her hands. "I'm sure she'll get in contact when she can."

She gives back the cell and stares at the gun in her lap. "I don't even know where she was when the bullets hit. What if she was right near the glass? What if—"

"I'm sure you would've heard by now if something went wrong. Bad news always travels faster than good."

"That's comforting," she mutters. "Thanks."

"Just trying to be honest." I flash her a half-hearted smile. The expression isn't reciprocated. Her face is solemn. Pained. She fills me with guilt because I have no fucking clue how to help her. "Seriously, if something happened, I'd have Hunter and Sarah blowing up my phone by now. The silence is a sign the worst is over."

"Maybe."

I don't push the conversation further. I'm familiar with the adrenaline high. She probably thinks her mind is clear and sharp, when inside that head of hers would be a fucked up mess.

If gossip can be believed, her brother keeps her sheltered from family business dealings. She's supposed to be kept in the dark from the brutality and criminal activity. If those rumors are true, tonight would act as a bitch-slap of reality.

I leave her in silence to deal with her thoughts, keeping my mouth shut as we travel out of Portland. I should've been subtle in my concern over taking her home. It's obvious her life is under threat. But on the other hand, I doubt she would appreciate me coddling her.

The closer we get to Westport, the more I notice the stiffening of her posture. Her unease is growing instead of dissipating. I glance at her every few seconds. With each visual pass, I latch on to the fingers trembling more and more against the gun seated in her lap.

"Keira," I say softly, "I know you don't want me asking, but are you still doing okay?"

She doesn't respond. Her focus is glued to the darkness outside the window. She's not ignoring me. There's something more to her lack of communication. She's lost, her beautiful skin devoid of color.

"Keira?" I touch her wrist, my fingertips connecting with cold skin which sends my pulse skyrocketing. "*Christ.*"

She's in shock.

I swerve off the road, her gasp hitting my ears. I kill the engine and rush from the car to round the hood and pull open her door.

"What's going on?" She turns to me, her lips parted.

Shit. Her eyes are wide, but the pupils are no longer dilated. She's present under her concerned stare. "You're pale. And cold. I thought you were tapping out on me."

She rubs her arms. "The air-conditioning is freezing in here. Cole always has it too low."

"I was calling your name..."

"I didn't hear you. I must have been lost in thought."

Fuck. I retreat and run a hand through my hair, trying to calm my breathing. I'm being a pussy. A tight, wet snatch with all this coddling bullshit.

"Decker?" Her voice is timid as she unclasps her belt.

"Don't." I shove my open palm in her direction. "Just sit the fuck down. I need to get us out of here."

She jerks back as if I swung more than my frustration at her. And yes, the pain in those baby blues makes me feel like a ripe asshole deserving of an unlubricated fuck.

"I'm sorry," I lower my voice, "I didn't mean to snap."

She refastens her belt and scowls straight ahead. "It's fine."

Fine—the most cringe-worthy syllable known to man. With one word, my crappy night becomes a whole lot

24

crappier. "Okay... Well... There's not much further to go until Westport. Can you focus for me so you can start giving directions?"

She raises her chin, her lips tight. "I'm focused."

"Good." I gently close her door and round the hood, cursing my stupidity with each step.

Minutes ago, I thought one of us was losing our mind.

Turns out, it's not her.

3

KEIRA

THE SECURITY CARD WORKED ON THE GATE AND AGAIN ON the panel to unlock the front door, allowing us access to the house I once knew as a family vacation home.

It was never a holiday for my parents, though.

As I reached my teens, I realized our trips here were out of necessity, not relaxation. We only visited this house because our lives were threatened. Not due to my dad's desire to bond.

"Once you're settled, I'm going to take a walk outside to check the yard." Decker hovers over my shoulder as I disarm the alarm in the foyer with my fingerprint.

"Okay." I flick on the lights and lead the way down the hall, the familiar space filled with tarnished memories that threaten to overwhelm me.

Despite the reasons for our visits, my mom used to love it here. She would bake all day and watch movies with us all night. We'd chat and read for hours. And now she's gone, taken by a bullet through the chest, her life stripped by the insanity that still surrounds us.

I shake away the grief and focus on the change in decor as I walk down the hall, determined to pull myself together despite the nightmares nipping at my heels. The paintings are different, the floorboards replaced with elegant tile, and the color scheme lighter than the peach walls I remember.

As I lead the way into the open kitchen and living area,

I'm not surprised the main room has also been updated. It's fresh and new. It's better this way. But even with the vast changes, my limbs prickle as if ghosts stroke my skin. It's unsettling. Almost panic-inducing with the way my stomach hollows.

"Are you sure nobody else knows about this place?" Decker swipes his finger over the kitchen counter, the trail leaving no mark due to the lack of dust. "I could eat my dinner off the marble."

"Cole would use an agency to arrange cleaning and gardening staff. Nobody should know who's doing the hiring and firing."

"Good." He nods. "Are you all right if I go outside to check the perimeter?"

"Yes. Please go." My response is quick. Enthusiastic. I'm desperate for space to pull myself together.

He raises a brow, seeming to take offense.

"I'm sorry." I shake my head. "I just need time alone."

His lips kick in a sad smile, the gentle affection reaching his dark eyes. "I get it. You've been through hell tonight."

"I'll be fine."

"There you go again with that word." He chuckles. "I don't think it means what you think it means."

He winks and walks for the front door, disappearing from view while I wonder if he deliberately dropped a line from a cult classic romance.

He's such an anomaly to me. A contradiction.

There's darkness and light. Aggression and charm. I've always struggled to determine the real from the fake, but tonight it's worse with my head a tangled mess of madness.

I've never been close to death. Not like this. I haven't had the misfortune of seeing my past transgressions flash before my eyes. And that wasn't the worst of it. The thought of my niece, Stella, being at the party hours before still leaves me in a cold sweat. That little girl means the world to me. There's nothing more important than her safety.

Not one damn thing.

Yet I'm responsible for putting her in harm's way.

I created the danger.

Nausea inches up my throat, my self-revulsion warring with remorse.

I stagger forward and press my hands to the polished marble counter, sucking in breath after breath. I need to find calm. This isn't the time for strategy to take a back seat. But I'm struggling to regain control.

Screams echo in my ears. The sight of petrified faces haunt me. I can still feel the shattered glass pinching into my palms and the weight of Decker's body on mine.

He'd been selfless in his efforts to protect me. Entirely without fear. Wholeheartedly negligent toward his own life.

Maybe joking about him having a death wish isn't such a joke after all.

I release the air in my lungs then fill them to capacity, repeating the ritual over and over.

Breathe in. Breathe out. Focus.

I drag my gaze around the room, trying to distract myself, but the only replacement to the recollection of gunfire are the childhood memories making my throat tighten.

Sparks of nostalgia flicker to life like a movie, the images from my younger years becoming clear and crisp. I used to sit here for breakfast. For lunch, too. My mom would braid my hair, and I'd complain about how long it would take. I can vaguely remember the subtle tug, tug, tug as she tried to tame my unruly lengths.

An uncomfortable ache nips at my ribs.

She died too young. Too beautiful.

One day she was reading bedtime stories and apologizing for the way my dad avoided his daughters. The next we were dressed in black and crushed under suffocating grief.

That same grief assails me now, stealing the oxygen from the air.

She wasn't made for this world. *Our* world. The one with deception, betrayal, and murder.

She'd never been flawed like my father. Her love had outshone his neglect. She was the mesmerizing smile through a crowd of scowls. The virtue surrounded by sin.

For that reason, I'm certain she would hate who I've become.

I'm guilty of horrible things. The skeletons in my closet are so tightly compacted I swear one more deceitful action will bring them toppling out.

"Stop it," I demand aloud.

The panic is increasing, my pounding heart struggling with the building mania.

I shove from the counter and kick off my heels to pad toward the tinted windows. The black of night stretches before me, lonely and cold.

I greet my reflection with a wince—the disheveled hair, the haunted eyes. I can barely stand to look at myself, not because my lavish makeup is betraying me, but because I'm disgusted by my actions.

My nose burns, the overwhelming tingle announcing a potent fragility that sickens me. It's pathetic. *I'm* pathetic.

I pivot on my toes, poised to run from my reflection, only to pause at the glimpse of an abnormality on my cheek. I tilt my chin and narrow my gaze on the darkened mirror. Spots cover the right side of my face, all shapes and sizes freckled along my jaw and down my neck.

I swipe them, the rough, dry patches scraping my fingertips.

My heart stops.

My throat clogs.

"Oh, God." It's blood.

I touch everywhere—my face, my shoulders, my neck. There's no tender areas. Not a single cut, or bruise, or scrape.

The spots aren't from me.

A stranger's blood marks my skin like a brand.

I wipe them with an open palm, the gentle swipe having no effect. I quicken the pace and severity, scrubbing over and over, my arm trembling with each movement.

I glance further down, glimpsing tiny stains on the strap of my dress and along the bodice. More splotches taunt me. The liquid is engrained.

"It's everywhere." My voice cracks as I use my nails, clawing at my cheek, my jaw, my neck.

My pulse grows frantic. I can't get enough air.

I can't breathe.

The room darkens, my vision blurring over everything else except those spots that become crystal clear. I tug at the bodice and struggle to reach behind me to release the zipper.

"Keira?"

A door slams. Faint footsteps reach my ears as I scrub, scrub, scrub.

"*Keira.*" A tight grip grabs my wrist.

"*Get it off,*" I scream. "I need to get it off."

I use my free hand to scratch my neck, only to have Decker swirl me around to face him.

"Let me help you." His eyes are wide, his concern only increasing my panic.

I'm shaking. My arms tremble in his hold.

Tonight was my doing. *I've* caused this. *I'm* responsible.

"It's all my fault." The admission bubbles up my throat without permission.

"No, baby. It's not." He leans closer, getting in my face. "That's the adrenaline talking."

I try to tug my wrists away, but he holds tight. He won't let me go, and there's comfort in that. There's reassurance he won't allow my demons to take over. Only there's fear, too. More hysteria with the restriction.

"Keira, this isn't your fault."

His seriousness is foreign. He's always the life of the party, no matter how much my brother despises his antics. But this... This strong, caring man breaks me, cracking my foundations.

Muscled arms engulf me, leading me away from the window and down another familiar hall. "Is the bathroom this way?"

I don't answer, just keep dragging my numb feet in the right direction as the dried blood sinks under my skin, making me itch.

He stops before the alcove with the basin, vanity, and mirror. The door to the toilet is behind us, another to the main bathroom by our side. He yanks open drawers and cupboards until he finds a cloth, then runs the material under water and squeezes out the excess.

It won't help.

It's not enough.

The stains are marrow deep, now marking my soul.

I step away, opening the door at our side to escape toward the shower. I flick on the light and lunge for the taps.

I don't wait for the water to warm. I climb inside, needing to cleanse my soul, the cold spray hitting hard. I scrub and scrub, not stopping until the rough patches turn smooth, then disappear completely.

It's still not enough.

I tear at my dress, yanking, tugging, until the heavy, sodden weight falls to my ankles.

I stand in my underwear, head bowed, the soaked mass of my hair curtaining my face like a shield as I stare blankly at the floor.

I can't be like this. I have to pull myself together. There's no alternative, but my body won't comply. I succumb to the burning in my eyes. I cry, the tears flowing silently, the sobs wracking my chest as I brace a hand against the cold tile and purge every last drop of self-loathing.

I surrender to fragility for long moments. Maybe minutes. Possibly hours.

Nothing breaks through until him... Until Decker's shoes come into view at the entrance of the shower.

"Keira..."

His voice wraps around me, making everything worse and somewhat better at the same time.

I don't know how to react. I never do with him.

I suck in a breath and straighten, swiping the hair from my cheeks.

Strong hands reach out before me, shutting off the water. I stare at those fingers, the tanned skin.

I summon the strength I need. I create it, building from the inside out. I have no choice. I can't be fragile around him.

I turn to find him holding a plush white towel, his

expression tight. His eyes have lost the taint of concern. They're different. The comforting depths now portray something I don't appreciate.

"I'm not weak," I blurt.

"I know, tiger."

"Then don't look at me like that."

He frowns. "Like what?"

"Like you pity me." I step out of the shower, my limbs numb as he wraps me in the thick material. Despite my request, I can't help letting him dry me like a child.

"I can leer at your tits if it will make you feel better."

Something squeezes inside me. Not my stomach. Not my lungs. It's bigger. All encompassing. I guess it's appreciation.

Again, his infusion of humor has endeared me.

"What's option B?" I repeat his question from earlier, earning a slight tweak to his gorgeous lips.

"While you were..." He waves a hand at the shower, wordlessly referring to my psychotic break. "I did a quick search of the house and couldn't find any spare clothes." He wrings my hair, a mass of water droplets hitting the tile at my feet. "You'll have to wear my shirt." He wraps the towel around my back, holding the ends out for me to take. "Can you grab this for a minute?"

I clutch the offering in both hands, clinging tight.

He shucks his tailored jacket to the floor, then begins to unbutton his white long-sleeve shirt. I should stop him. I'm sure I could find a robe or a blanket; even a sheet would do. But I keep quiet as he exposes a chiseled chest, muscled arms, and a haunting mass of inked skin.

The art on his arm is a collage of ominous images—a woman in tears, skulls, a chessboard, skeletal trees. I commit the eerie images to memory, none more so than the beautifully written script on his left pec. Delicate text is written above his heart, my gaze skimming over some of the words—*gentle, rage, dying, light.*

"Please don't look at me like that," he drawls, each syllable dripping with cocky menace.

A breath of delirious laughter bursts from my lips.

Through all this insanity, he provides a distraction. This man… He's crazy. Ridiculously so. And I can't help the extra hard thump that hammers in my chest as I look at him. Nobody speaks to me the way he does. He's different, his anomalies always strumming my curiosity.

"I'm sorry." I clear my throat. "How would you like me to look at you?"

His mouth twitches, the hint of a smirk breaking through. "I'm just kiddin'. You can ogle all you like. In fact, if you've got some dollar bills, I can put on a show."

And just like that, my mental break is forgotten. He doesn't judge me for losing my shit. Doesn't even acknowledge it happened.

"Here." He hands over his shirt and takes the towel, diverting his gaze as I pull the material over my shoulders and button up.

His scent envelops me, the delicious cologne masculine and woodsy. It strengthens me, makes me feel stable again. I tilt my face to the side, craving more, and take a subtle inhale against the collar, dragging him deep into my lungs.

The comfort engulfing me is ridiculous, I know that. He's not a man I can trust. And still I wrap his shirt tighter, stealing all I can get, wanting the material to cling to me like a second skin.

I close my eyes for a brief second, take another deep inhale, and blink to find him staring at me. Watching. His ravenous gaze freezes me in place.

I no longer see an ounce of his pity. His humor is nowhere in sight. What bears down on me is narrowed intensity.

Ferocity.

Lust.

"Decker—" The flare of his nostrils cuts off my sentence, and I tremble, caught between responsibility and potential stupidity.

4

DECKER

SHE SMELLS MY SHIRT, AND EVERY HAIR ON MY BODY rises. Those wide eyes slay me, or maybe it's the perfect body I couldn't steal my gaze from moments ago.

"I'll check to see if there's any food in the cupboards." My voice is deep, the pitch an unintentional Darth Vader imitation. The only thing missing is the heavy breathing.

"Okay..." She nods. Swallows. Looks entirely flustered. "I'll be out in a minute. I need to fix my hair."

I stalk from the bathroom, snatching my suit jacket off the floor along the way, shoving my arms in the holes as I escape down the hall. I clench my fists. Clamp my teeth. I try hard to ignore the multiplication of my perverted thoughts when I usually allow those fuckers free rein.

She just survived a shooting, less than two weeks after her uncle escaped a warranted assassination attempt in the form of a hit and run. And here I am, drilling holes through my pants like I'm a perverted teen.

Seems my dick has a death wish, too.

If only Hunter could see me now. That prick would be laughing his ass off. Torian's reaction wouldn't be as funny. I'm almost positive he would hang me from the ceiling by my cock.

I palm my cell and play phone-a-friend to get my thoughts back on track. Hunter answers on the first ring.

"You safe?" he asks.

"Yeah. I think we're in the clear. We got out of Portland."

"Good. The cops are chasing their tails here. We're going to be stuck at the scene for a while."

I walk into the open living area and head for the kitchen. "What was the end tally?"

"None for none. All the bullets lodged in the roof. Nothing came close to striking distance."

"You sure?" I frown. "Keira was splattered with blood."

"That shit is everywhere because of the shattered glass. If you took a look at the scene, you'd think those stupid fucks were rolling around in it for all the mess they've left on the floor. But no, no bullet injuries."

I start opening cupboards above the counter. The first is empty. The second and third, too. Then the fourth holds canned goods—vegetables, soup, pickles. "So, whoever did this is either a really shit shot or—"

"Or it was a warning."

"For what?"

"Who knows. It could be anything. But once Torian finds out, heads will roll."

"How's he handling the drama?"

"He's an angry fuck at the moment," Hunter grates. "He's got a lot going on, and I'm sure I don't know the half of it. But one of the biggest issues is the cops. They got here too quick. Either the informant is handing out information like flyers on a street corner, or the pigs heard something was going down and decided to leave us out as bait."

My pulse rises, my anger building. "Do you think they'd leave women in the firing line and not give us a heads up?" Kids had been at that party earlier in the night. Keira's niece, for one. "I don't think the authorities would be that callous. They can't be."

Hunter scoffs. "You got a sweet spot for the men in blue all of a sudden?"

"Oh, yeah, baby. You know me." I open a fifth cupboard— the holy grail. The two shelves are filled with liquor bottles begging to be consumed. "I'd roll over in a heartbeat for a Taser and a pair of cuffs."

"You'd roll over for half a bagel and a used cigarette, asshole."

"Yeah. I guess." Although, I haven't smoked in a lifetime. Not since I started working with Hunter and my potential lifespan shortened by a fuckton. "So, what's the plan from here? What does the bossman want me to do with Keira?"

"Hold tight for a while. With her sister in the hospital along with her uncle, we're already too vulnerable."

"Her sister?" My pulse hammers.

"It's nothing serious. She got caught up in the glass. But we don't want anyone knowing another Torian has temporarily been affected."

Shit. "Keira will lose her mind." Again. "What's the damage?"

"Nothing major. A few stitches to the side of her face, and some in her arms."

Great, relaying the third-hand information is going to be super fun. "And I guess I'm supposed to babysit until this blows over?"

"Yep," Hunter quips. "Enjoy."

"Thanks." I pull a scotch bottle from the cupboard, stroke the frosted glass with reverence, then put the treasure back because there's no way I can succumb to my hearty thirst until this bullshit blows over. "Keep me updated."

"Same. I'll call you later."

I close the cupboard, disconnect the call, and place the cell in my jacket pocket. That's when I feel her. Keira's presence hovers close.

"I don't need a babysitter," she mutters.

I sigh and stare at the fifth cupboard, eyeing the door, wishing I could crawl in among the goodness. "I know." I turn to face her. "I was playing the macho card, hoping to make myself seem tougher than I really am. Did it work?"

I force myself to hold her gaze. I can't lower my attention. I fucking won't, no matter how much exposed thigh taunts me.

"I'm not joking, Decker. If you want to leave, then leave. I'm safe here."

I lean back against the counter, cross my feet at the ankles and my arms over my chest. "One minute you're ogling my body like a starved beast, the next you're kicking me to the curb? That hurts, shortie."

She rolls her eyes. "Don't even start. Who was on the phone?"

"Hunter."

"What did he say?"

I pause, pondering my answer. It would be easy to keep her in the dark, just like her brother does. Or I could earn her trust. "Not much."

Her chin hitches. "Decker, please."

The plea on those rosy lips is a test to all my senses. She's too gorgeous for her own good. Possibly the perfect weapon in her brother's arsenal, if the guy understood her potential.

My gaze lowers without permission, taking in every inch of the seductress. My shirt clings to her chest, the damp patches over her breasts making her bra visible. Then there's her legs. Those fucking tempting thighs with their perfectly tanned skin. If the material hanging off her was two inches higher, I'd be able to get another glimpse of that lace G-string.

"You were right," I admit. She hates being kept in the dark, and I'm going to brighten her surroundings a little. "Layla didn't get out before us."

Her eyes widen. Her lips part. "Is she okay?"

I nod. "She got into a fight with some shattered glass and came out second best. But it's nothing to worry about."

Her gasp splits the air, a shaky hand moving toward her mouth before she stops and drops it to her side. She gains control, reclaiming her strength, even though the fractures still show.

"Don't panic. Hunter told me she's already stitched up."

She steels herself, her shoulders straightening. "Do you promise?"

"I'm not lying. I swear." I paint an imaginary cross over my non-existent heart. "You can try calling her again if you like."

"She won't answer. Cole would have her on lockdown. No communication in or out apart from directly through him until he has the situation under control."

I bite my tongue, determined not to pit brother against sister. It's not in my best interests to fuck with Torian. "He's trying to protect you."

"From what?" She scoffs and pads toward the dining table, grabbing the back of a wooden chair in a tight grip. "Ignorance is no way to shield someone."

"Being in the dark is for the best. He deals with some pretty heavy shit."

"Believe me, I know. I watch the news. I read the papers. And as if that wasn't enough, I hear the whispers, too."

Pfft. The media knows jack shit about her brother's criminal activities.

But her cluelessness is a good thing. It means I don't have to feel guilty for the respect I have for her. The attraction, too. "Earlier, you mentioned tonight was your fault. Why?"

"I don't know." She shrugs and lowers her attention to the table. "I guess it was like you said, the adrenaline messed with my head. I kinda lost hold of reality for a minute."

"You sure?" I scrutinize her, trying to determine if she's lying or I'm paranoid. Something about her response doesn't seem genuine. "I don't want you thinking you're responsible."

"That's sweet. But I'm over it now."

"Are you lying to me, lemon drop?" I walk toward her, stopping a few feet away. "You were adamant before."

She meets my gaze, the connection between us growing potent for long moments until she shrugs. "I came up with the idea for the engagement party. I'm the reason we were all there." She gives a bitter chuckle. "I wanted us to have something nice to celebrate. Something normal."

I raise my brows, unimpressed. "That doesn't make you responsible."

"It is what it is."

"What it is," I drawl, "is some truly fucked up logic."

She sighs and rests against the dining table, her long lashes

38

batting with gentle lethargy. "You have a way with words, Decker. You're rarely serious."

It's my turn to laugh without warmth. "This job is morbid as fuck. If I didn't have my sense of humor, I would've offed myself long ago."

Her eyes pin me, calculating, as if trying to determine if I'm capable of taking my own life. For once, I don't enjoy her attention.

"If you can't have fun with life, what's the point?" I add.

"You've said that before." Her voice is almost a whisper as she glances to the left, staring out the window.

I push from the counter, not liking her rapid descent into deep thought. "Is it time for a drink?"

"No." She shakes her head. "I might borrow your phone again, though, if that's all right. I want to call Cole."

"No problem." I grab my cell from my back pocket. "You're not going to rat on me for telling you about Layla, are you?"

"Rat on you?" She rakes her teeth over her lower lip and pushes from the table to pad toward me, her hips holding enough sway to trigger a reaction from my dick. "You expect me to cut loose the only person willing to tell me the truth? Not likely. If anything, you and I just became soul mates."

"Don't tease, gorgeous." I smirk, adding a thick layer of cocky arrogance to mask the way she's hypnotizing me. "You'll only break my heart."

"Not teasing. But I do want to call Cole to see how long you have to *babysit*" she snips, dealing the backhanded blow with effortless precision.

"Now, now. Don't get those panties in a twist. They're the only thing protecting your modesty."

She chuckles, and it brightens her face enough to increase my pulse. The light blush warming her cheeks doesn't help, either.

I can't afford to lose my focus around this woman, but I can see it happening. I can feel it, too.

She stops in front of me and takes the cell from my

outstretched hand. "I'll try my best not to get you into any trouble."

"Great." I nod. Slow. Measured. Panicked. Because she sure as shit made that sound like more of a threat than a promise.

5

KEIRA

I palm Decker's cell and walk from the room, needing privacy and distance. One more than the other, although I'm not entirely sure which is more important at this point.

I dial Cole's number then bite my tongue as he barks, "What is it?"

"It's me." I keep my voice low.

"Keira? How are you? *Where* are you? I tried calling—"

"I left my cell in the restaurant because some jerk shoved me into the arms of one of his goons and demanded I leave."

"That jerk was trying to keep you safe."

I roll my eyes. "I can keep myself safe, brother."

He sighs. "I don't have time to argue with you right now. Hunter said you're out of town. Where, exactly?"

"The safe house."

"Which one?"

"There's more than one?" I accuse. "Since when?"

"*Fuck.*" His frustration echoes down the line. "We'll discuss details later. Just as long as you're safe, that's all that matters."

"I am. Decker has everything under control. He's been perfect."

"Perfect?" The disapproval in his voice is loud and clear. "Is he close by?"

"In the kitchen. Do you want me to get him?"

"No, what I want you to do is be careful."

I continue down the hall, toward the far end of the house, glancing over my shoulder every few steps. "Yeah, I know. You don't have to warn me."

"He's still new. And reckless. And a motherfucking smartass. His attitude doesn't sit well with me."

"So why make him my white knight? I should've stayed with you."

"It was good timing and the perfect opportunity."

My pulse increases. "The perfect opportunity for what?"

"Keeping an eye on him. Getting inside his head."

I clench my jaw, unsure and a little disturbed at how my brother could've thought about strategy while bullets were flying and people were screaming. "He's been good to me, Cole."

"Good or cunning? Don't be naive, sis. You know he can't be trusted."

The intensity in his voice puts me on edge. "Am I in danger?"

"From him? No. I wouldn't have sent you with him if I thought he was capable of hurting you. But is he capable of hurting this family? I'm not sure. He's yet to prove his worth. And until he does, his intent will remain questionable."

"What do you expect me to do?" I ask.

"Nothing. Not yet. Just remain open to testing him if you get the chance."

"Testing him?" I hiss under my breath. "He's supposed to be on our side."

"What's supposed to be and what usually happens are two different things. You know we're both paranoid for good reason."

He's right, even though judging Decker as the enemy feels entirely wrong.

"Be smart, Keira. Be safe, too."

I nod. "I will."

I'm not going to plead Decker's case. Not yet. I'll take more time to come to my own conclusion first. To cement my

42

assumptions. "Do you have any news on who's responsible for tonight?"

"There's nothing to go on. Not yet. But I'll find out sooner or later."

Nausea swirls in my belly. The slightest tremble works its way into my hands. Knowledge isn't always a good thing. Sometimes ignorance is most certainly bliss. Especially when knee-jerk, death-causing reactions are likely. "Don't do anything rash, okay?" I beg. "You, more than anyone, need to keep a level head."

"You know me, Kee, I'm nothing if not level."

His sarcasm is scary. I'd laugh if I didn't want to crumple.

"Look, I've gotta go." His tone turns dismissive. "It's not a great time to talk. I'll call you tomorrow."

There's a pause, and for a moment I think he's already disconnected. "Cole?"

"Yeah?"

I swallow over my drying throat. "How's Layla?"

"She's fine." His response is instant. Without thought. "She got out before you did."

My brows rise at the placating lie.

"Right..." I suck in a calming breath and let it out slowly. "Well, can you let her know I lost my phone in the restaurant? I have to use Decker's, and she's not answering my calls."

"She's probably screening and doesn't recognize the number. I'll pass on the message."

Liar. Liar. Liar.

"Thanks."

"I'll speak to you soon, Kee. Make sure you lay low until I call."

"I will." I hang up and stare out the window at the far end of the hall.

Cole is playing a dangerous game by distorting the truth in an attempt to keep me calm. All our enemies need is a weak spot. Just one. That's it. Then, *bam,* we're vulnerable.

But I get why he lied. We all have secrets. Some are made to protect those we love.

He thinks he's doing the right thing.

He doesn't want me to worry. And yet the intent has had the opposite effect.

I'm concerned as hell. About being alone with Decker. About my mental stability. About Cole reacting without thought when he finds out who's responsible for the drive-by.

I can't hold tight to the strength I usually cling to. Adrenaline has zapped my common sense.

Come on, Keira. Pull yourself together.

I tread lightly down the hall and pause in the shadows. Decker is still in the kitchen, now eating from a can of corn with a spoon. He isn't doing anything sneaky or covert. He's relaxed, his jacket gaping to expose his inked chest, his dark hair mussed and falling around his forehead. There isn't a glimmer of deception ebbing from him, but I know there shouldn't be if he's an accomplished manipulator.

Deceit is rarely obvious.

I inch into the living room, my gaze never leaving him as I stop a few feet away from the kitchen counter. "That looks appetizing."

His lips kick, his face the very definition of cocky arrogance.

"I was talking about the corn," I clarify.

"Sure you were." He tilts the can in my direction. "Want some? We don't have a lot of options where food is concerned."

"No, thanks. I don't think my stomach could handle it at the moment."

He shoves another spoonful into his mouth, his chiseled jaw working overtime. "How's your brother?"

I shrug. "He's the same ol' Cole. Nothing changes."

He pauses, his eyes narrowing. "Something's wrong."

It's not a question, it's a statement that catches me off guard. He can already sense my mood, can already decipher my expression. The realization fills me with apprehension and appreciation in equal measure.

"No. Not upset," I lie, indicating my face with a swirl of a finger. "This is a look of annoyance. He lied to me again."

"I'm sorry to hear that."

"I should be used to it by now, right? To be honest, I'm surprised it still bothers me."

He throws up a hand in a what-are-you-gonna-do gesture. "You've had a long day. Maybe you should get some rest."

"Yeah. That's the plan." After getting off the phone, I've gained a few new layers to my exhaustion. Only I'm finding it hard to walk away. Maybe I should test him. Not to claim answers to Cole's doubt, but to prove my instincts about Decker are right. "Will you be okay finding a room of your own?"

He spoons a few more kernels of corn into his mouth. "I'll crash on the sofa if I have to."

"If you have to? You don't plan on sleeping?"

"I might doze a bit."

"Why? We're safe here, aren't we?"

"Yes, of course." He pulls out the garbage drawer and throws the can into the trash. "I'm only being cautious."

I don't want to believe him. I can't. One, because trust is a personality trait I rarely indulge in. And two, because the thought of him giving up sleep for me makes my stomach twist in knots.

"Keira, if there was something to worry about, I'd tell you." He leans forward, arms spread along the counter, gaze intent. "Go. Get some rest. We can figure out our next move in the morning."

I nod.

Despite Cole's warning, I do agree Decker is no threat to me personally. I can't picture this man hurting me. I can't see it at all. And I'm more than aware betrayal can come from a friendly face. "Good night, Decker."

"Night, kitten."

I drag my feet down the hall, while my thoughts stay with him in the kitchen. I don't want to be alone, and it's not because of his flirtation and dripping innuendo. I crave the truth. I need answers. I want them so much my neck prickles with anticipation.

I reluctantly close myself into the master bedroom and stare at the door handle for long heartbeats. I should lock it, even though I'm not scared of the gorgeous thug protecting me. It's the smart thing to do if I plan on getting even a lick of sleep...which isn't highly likely anyway.

I gently flick the lock, hoping the sound doesn't resonate down the hall, then do a visual sweep of every inch of the room before turning off the light and climbing into bed. I lie on my side, his shirt bunched at my shoulders, my nose nestled against the material.

His scent fills my lungs, and I struggle to recount a moment with him that could've held questionable intent.

He's proven himself to me tonight. He showed his loyalty by shielding my body with his own, and in every other action afterward.

But then again, he had proven himself to me all those months ago when he confronted Cole. My brother's hand had been wrapped around my neck, the squeeze light despite the rage in his eyes.

With one sentence, Decker stood up for me. He showed sincerity and promise.

Cole would've seen it as defiance. Not me, though. I appreciated the honor. The morals.

The outburst doesn't mean he's worthy of trust. But leniency? Yes.

He deserves to be given a chance.

I try to build on my convincing argument, tossing and turning for hours as I analyze every moment I've spent with Decker—the playfulness, the protection, the lingering lust he keeps tightly leashed.

And he told me the truth about Layla's injuries. That, by far, is the attribute I cling to for dear life.

But it could be a game. I know better than anyone that deception comes from those you least expect. I seriously can't let down my guard. No matter how much I want to.

Each minute that ticks by brings more madness to my exhaustion. I start to lose grip on my thoughts, and waking nightmares hover close.

The flashback of shattering glass enters my mind. The rapid gunfire. The screams. The panic.

I try to douse the flames with the memory of Decker's hard body atop mine. The frantic way he pulled over on the highway. The gentle hands that dried me after the shower.

Don't be naive, sis. You know he can't be trusted. My brother's words haunt me.

As if I didn't have enough to worry about without adding mixed feelings about Decker to the list.

I throw back the covers and slide from bed.

I stalk from the room, my feet slapping against the hall tiles as my pulse pounds in my throat. The house is bathed in shadow, the glow from the muted television the only illumination as I enter the living room.

I stop at the foot of the sofa, staring down at his sprawled body, his chest bare, his arm slung over his face, covering his eyes. He's peaceful, and trustworthy or not, he's truly magnificent to look at. For long minutes I peer down at him, stalker like and entirely unapologetic.

The woman tattooed on his bicep stares up at me, her beauty ethereal and haunting as a tear streaks down her cheek.

"Can I help you?" he mumbles.

My heart shoots to my throat at the sudden break in silence. "*Christ.* I didn't realize you were awake."

"I figured." His arm falls to his side as he blinks up at me. "What's wrong?"

I try to come up with the perfect response. One that seems entirely out of my comprehension the longer those midnight eyes take me in. "My brother doesn't trust you."

"You got out of bed to tell me that?" He frowns and sits up, leaning back against the armrest. "It's not really a secret, sunshine."

"You already know?"

"Of course I do." He pauses to ponder me for a moment, his brows knit tight. "Did he tell you that, or did you work it out on your own?"

"Does it matter?"

Slowly, he stands and moves toward me, his height becoming so much larger than it ever has been before. All that bare skin. All that hard muscle. All that delicious ink.

"Yeah, it does. I don't think it's a smart move to tell a woman her safety has been placed in the hands of someone she can't trust."

I swallow over the dryness in my throat, not wanting to admit how right he is.

"But he did tell you." His eyes narrow. "Is that why you were upset after you got off the phone?"

I lick my lips, struggling to combat the sudden detox of moisture. My throat is dry, my tongue and mouth, too.

"You have nothing to worry about, Keira. Despite your brother's opinion, I would never hurt you."

A bark of derision leaves my mouth. It's forced. Another act. I need to pretend I'm highly cautious even though my intuition wants to wave green flags like it's Saint Paddy's day.

I *do* believe he would never hurt me.

I *do* trust he has my best interest at heart. How can I not after he shielded me against bullets with his own damn body?

"If you're scared of me, I can take you to someone else." His expression is pained as he speaks. "I'll drive you wherever you want to go." He bends down and retrieves his jacket from the floor. "Just tell me where we're headed."

He's truly ready to leave.

"I don't need to go anywhere," I admit.

He eyes me with trepidation. "Are you sure?"

I swallow, lick my lower lip, and fight to keep in control. "Why doesn't he trust you?"

"Because my loyalty has always been to Hunter first and foremost. It always will be. Cole doesn't appreciate the defiance."

No, my brother wouldn't. He expects fealty, a blood oath, and your firstborn... Or something along those lines.

"Is that all?" I can't tear my gaze away, too eager to decipher every change in him. "There has to be more to it than that."

"I'm sure there's a million reasons." He shrugs. "But while he's paying me, I don't give a fuck about a single one."

His sterility isn't appreciated. I guess I'm like Cole in that regard. I want loyalty. Devotion. I need more than callous disregard when it comes to my family. "I understand."

"I'm not after your understanding, Keira. I want your trust. After everything we've been through tonight, don't I deserve that?"

"Trust is difficult."

He gives a half-hearted smile. "I guess it takes more than putting my life on the line to make you happy." He throws my callousness at me with such softly spoken words.

I don't like the accusation. I don't appreciate how empty it makes me feel.

"You don't understand," I whisper.

"Try me."

I measure my breathing, not succumbing to the need to suck in deep lungsful of air. "Trust brings vulnerability. And I'm not allowed to be vulnerable."

"You're allowed to be whatever the hell you want. You're your own person. Don't ever forget that."

"No. I'm not. I can't be vulnerable or weak or scared."

He scoffs. "You *are* scared."

"No—"

"Yeah, you are." He cuts me off. "You're strong and stubborn and smart. But you're still fucking scared, and that's okay. You'd be stupid if you weren't."

I stare at him, drowning in the solemn sincerity in his expression. I want to believe his kindness. I'm dying to. "Cole is never scared."

"Cole is a psychopath. You're comparing apples to oranges."

I laugh despite the seriousness in his voice. "He's not psychotic. He's just..."

"Fucking crazy?" He approaches a step. "A narcissist?" The nearness increases. "Stop me if you want. I could go on for hours."

My smile lessens, the relief he's given me dying under the heavy thoughts of my brother. "You shouldn't joke about him like that. If he heard..."

"It isn't anything I wouldn't say to his face." He shrugs. "I work for him, and he has my loyalty. But that doesn't mean he gets my respect."

The brutal honesty surprises me. It also fills me with concern. "You disapprove of the way he does business?"

"It has nothing to do with business."

"Then what is it?"

He holds my gaze, his expression growing tight.

"Tell me." I inch closer, the sides of our feet brushing.

"That's a conversation for another day. You need to get some rest."

No. I'm finally getting somewhere. I can't stop now. "*Please.*"

His jaw ticks. His eyes harden. "He laid hands on you. I could never respect a man who does that."

I stare blankly, entirely overwhelmed by his vehement response.

There's not merely a lack of respect between my brother and this man. There's more. So much more. And if I can believe his fierce conviction, it has nothing to do with my family's criminal activities and everything to do with his concern for me.

Guilt mixes with my turbulent emotions.

I'm the reason Cole doesn't trust him.

I'm the one who has put a target on Decker's back.

He walks by me, severing the conversation as he stalks into the kitchen, the flick of the light stealing away the shadowed intimacy. "Do you want me to get you a drink? I found the liquor cupboard earlier."

I sigh and follow after him. "I don't want alcohol. Coffee, on the other hand..."

"That's not going to happen." He pulls open a cupboard above the counter and retrieves a scotch glass. "Caffeine is a bad idea when the aim is sleep."

"Well, what I need and what I'm capable of are two different things."

He moves to another cupboard, this one lined with bottles of all shapes and sizes—rum, tequila, gin.

He pulls out a vodka bottle, cracks the lid, and pours a shocking amount into the glass.

"I hope that's not for me." I remain on the other side of the counter.

"For relaxation purposes." He shuts the cupboard then turns to me, the bottle in one hand, the glass in the other.

"Are you going to have one with me?"

He gives a subtle shake of his head. "I can't."

"Because you're babysitting?"

"No, because I don't want you to take advantage of me."

I roll my eyes. "But you've poured enough to take down a wild beast."

He smirks, the expression hitting me hard as the glass is pushed toward me. "Well, sometimes you act like one."

I scowl, even though it's hard to fight a smile when he's looking at me like that, all self-assured with mussed hair and sleepy eyes.

"When have you ever seen me in beast mode?" I mutter.

"Have you already forgotten the first night we met?" He quirks a brow. "You were as wild as it gets. I didn't know if you were going to get out of your sister's house alive."

The memory steals the tweak from my lips. My actions haunt me. "I never thanked you for standing up for me."

"I didn't expect you to. Any self-respecting man would've done the same thing."

I don't answer. I can't.

The truth is, no matter how many times my family's employees have seen Cole and me fight, nobody has ever stepped in. Not once. Not even slightly. Not until Decker.

I raise the glass and throw back a dangerous amount of vodka. The liquid burns my throat and nose, making me cough. I expect him to laugh at me. I anticipate the superior smirk to have curved those gorgeous lips.

When I raise my gaze, his brows are pinched, his eyes filled with apology.

"I'm sorry," he murmurs. "I shouldn't have brought that up."

"Don't apologize." I rub my nose to fight the lingering tingle. "It's all in the past."

He grabs the bottle and rounds the counter, turning off the light before he leads the way to the sofa. "You've forgiven him?"

I follow, this time sipping the alcohol instead of trying to drown myself in it. "He's my brother," I hedge.

He eyes me as he places the vodka on the coffee table and slumps onto the sofa. The analysis is unnerving, his stare telling me he's well aware I didn't answer his question.

He pats the space beside him, offering me a seat so close and personal my skin already tingles. I hesitate, my gaze drifting to the recliner a few feet away, then returning to the tempting position fraught with danger.

"I won't bite." He winks. "I prefer to lick."

"There you go again with the wisecracks." I take a seat at the far end of the sofa and turn to him, curling my legs beneath my bottom. "You're uncomfortable being serious, aren't you?"

He ponders the question, his expression exaggerated. "Maybe."

"I guess you already know it's endearing in a really unsettling kind of way."

He chuckles. "I can't help being irresistible. It's been a problem since birth."

We sit for a while, the silence comfortable as the glow from the television flickers over his face like a kaleidoscope.

"Have you and Cole ever been close?" He stretches his arm over the head rest, his strong hand within reach.

"Define close." I don't like this subject. It's too personal. Entirely intrusive. "You've already seen us at our worst."

"He was worried you were going to do something stupid. I don't think he knew any other way to make you listen." He speaks without emotion, as if we're discussing the weather instead of a physical assault.

"You're defending him now?"

"Fuck no. What he did was unforgivable. I'm just really shitty when it comes to consoling women."

Warmth enters my chest, the happy tingle taking its time to reach my face and pull at my lips. "Thank you."

He frowns. "For what? The shitty attempt at comfort?"

"No. I'm not talking about the conversation. I mean everything—for shielding me in the restaurant, for handling my meltdown, for literally taking the shirt off your back."

He shrugs. "The shirt looks better on you anyway."

"It does, doesn't it?"

His eyes narrow on mine the slightest bit. Then slowly his gaze lowers, trekking my body, over the material of his shirt right to the edge of my exposed thighs curled at my side.

He has the strangest way of manipulating me. Of making me relaxed and ready to verbally spar, then stealing away the fun to replace it with palpable anticipation.

I don't just watch him taking me in, I feel it. The attraction shivers down my spine. The lust coils in my belly.

"Are you ready to go to bed yet?" he murmurs.

I stiffen, unsure of the meaning behind his question.

"Alone, Keira. I think we need to cut and run before this conversation takes us somewhere we'll regret."

I agree, but the thought of the dark bedroom on the other side of the house strips me of any warm and fuzzies.

"I don't want to go back down there." I turn to the television, hoping my diverted gaze will lessen the vulnerability of my admission. "I'd like to stay here with you. If that's okay."

I see him watching me through my peripheral vision. I can't escape it. His attention wraps around me, adding to the warmth ignited by the vodka.

"If you're staying, you should at least catch some zs." He pushes to his feet, grabs a cushion from the closest recliner, then sits back down. "Here." He pats the makeshift pillow on his lap. "Lie down."

"No, I'm good. Honest." I finish the last of the vodka in one gulp and place the glass on the coffee table.

"Please, Keira. At some point tomorrow I'll have to sleep, and I need to know you're going to be able to stay awake while

I'm out of it." He pats the cushion again. "Come on. Trust me."

It's not merely a case of dominating the exhausting T-word I can't seem to wrangle. There's more. So much more. And I can't share a single word of it with him.

"It's only for a few hours," he whispers. "You'll feel better once the sun comes up."

It's ridiculous how long I remain silent pretending contemplation when my mind is already made up.

"I'll just rest for a little while." I stretch out, slowly inching myself closer to press my head on the cushion.

He peers down at me, dark and intense. I can't look away. I don't want to. There are answers in those soulful eyes, and I need to hear them all.

"Sleep, sunshine."

"With you staring at me?" I purr.

He grabs a remote from the armrest and switches off the television, plunging the room into darkness. "That better?"

No, it's not. Not even close.

I can still see him. Can still feel his severity bearing down on me through the shadows, inching its way under my skin.

6

DECKER

I watch her for too damn long, attempting to get into her head. To figure her out.

Instead, I get caught up noticing the different stages of her sleep.

I see everything. Every twitch, every breath.

I become fascinated with her intricacies as the hours pass. The thick eyelashes that flutter, the ones in the middle longer than those on the outer edges. Her smooth skin, with the tiniest scar above her chin. The perfectly sculpted eyebrows. Her soft hair. The flawless braid.

She makes noises. The sweetest whimpers.

I find myself tensing, waiting for the next murmur of sound, not wanting the scrape of my own inhale to disrupt the experience.

This stupidity is commonly known as sleep deprivation.

She could be confused for someone weak and defenseless in this moment. She could... But she isn't.

I know better.

This woman is strong and smart. And so fucking beautiful it's hard not to become wrapped up in the thought of tasting her.

Fuck. I need to wake the hell up.

I've earned a modicum of her trust, and now I have to be careful how I treat it. I can't be reckless. I've gotta keep my mind on the task at hand, and I definitely have to ignore the way my shirt creeps up her thigh every time she moves.

I have to... And I'm fucking struggling.

Between the hours of five and six, I place bets on how much skin will be exposed. By the time the sun rises, I have the slightest glimpse of white lace at her hip, the sight of the skimpy material the sweetest torture against a sleep-starved man.

At eight, she starts to stir, her brow furrowing, nose scrunching.

I slide my hand from her hair and the other from her shoulder, placing one on the arm rest, the other at my side. Casual as fuck. Then I close my eyes and rest my head back, feigning unconsciousness as she shifts, wakes, then gently creeps off my lap.

I should let her walk away. She would need to decompress after greeting the day with a bird's-eye view of my crotch. But as soon as her warmth leaves me, my pulse rises and lust claws deep.

I catch her tiptoeing around the sofa, her hair a mess, her face pale.

"Did you sleep well?" I ask.

"Jesus, Decker," she gasps, her hand shooting to her throat. "Can you stop pretending you're asleep? That's the second time you've scared the crap out of me."

I grin. "Sorry."

"No, you're not." She finger combs her hair behind her ears, the long, wavy lengths fanning her shoulders. She looks different this morning, the gentleness of sleep still evident in her features.

She isn't a member of a crime-riddled family at the moment. She's a normal woman. A gorgeous woman. With my fucking shirt hanging from her thighs like a pinup model.

Her gaze scours the floor, her teeth digging into her lower lip. "You haven't seen a hair tie floating around, have you?" She waves a hand in a circular motion, indicating my crotch. "It would've fallen out while I slept."

It fell… Or someone pulled it out in an attempt to play with her hair.

"I haven't seen it." Not in a few hours, anyway. "Do you need to search?" I raise the cushion from my lap and hold my arms wide, ready for her to mount a full-scale search around my dick.

She throws her head back and laughs. "You're a troublemaker when you haven't slept, do you know that?"

She's right. I'm stirring trouble where trouble shouldn't be stirred. I can't help it. Those ocean eyes of hers are fucking with my mind, making me crazy.

I drop the cushion to the sofa and stand, the thin black tie falling out from somewhere between my legs.

"Here." I hand it over, our fingers brushing for brief seconds.

The touch is more than a scrape of skin against skin. The contact brings a jolt of awareness, her sultry mouth hypnotizing as her tongue snakes out to moisten her lower lip.

She swallows and takes the offering, her gaze holding mine for long, drawn-out seconds. The connection feels like a test. A game of chicken I have no plan to lose.

"You should leave it out," I murmur. "It looks nice."

She hesitates. Unmoving. For a second, I think she might humor me. Or maybe try to impress me. Then something shifts in her features.

Her chin rises, her eyes harden. She ties her hair back in quick, efficient movements and reclaims the control I can't seem to find. "It's too annoying to keep out."

I nod. Shrug. Act unfazed even though the slight change in her demeanor has woken me up to the reality of my thread-bare restraint.

She's not someone I can mess around with—physically or emotionally. She's not even someone I should be attracted to. There's a heap of can'ts, shouldn'ts, and what-the-fucks surrounding Keira, and it needs to stay that way.

"What are we going to do about breakfast?" She runs her hands down the material of the shirt, trying to straighten the wrinkles.

"I'm more focused on what you're going to do about clothes." Every time she moves, she gets closer and closer to showing off that lace thong.

"Why is that?" she teases, glancing down at herself. "Don't you think I look good in your shirt anymore?"

It's my turn to laugh. "Who's the troublemaker now?"

She chuckles, the flash of her easy smile making me question if she was adopted at birth. She's nothing like her brother. Nothing like her father or uncle, either.

"I actually think those few hours sleep made things worse. My head is pounding like I've got a hangover from hell." She rubs her temples. "Coffee and a deliriously unhealthy breakfast is the only thing likely to save my soul today."

"Okay." I rub my hands together. Getting out of here is a good distraction. "Let me take a quick shower to wake up, then we can hit the road."

I drive out of Westport and along the highway for roughly ten miles to the closest town. It's nothing special. Just a tiny little place with enough amenities to handle what we need.

Keira is still bare-legged, dressed in nothing but my shirt, while my chest is exposed beneath my suit jacket. Not the best attire when we want to lay low, which means clothing is higher on the agenda than food.

"I'm buying you a skirt and blouse, right?" I park in front of a women's clothing store and cut the engine.

"Yes, please. Anything with an elastic waistband will help, seeing as though I can't try it on."

"Well, you can. It's your decision to hide in the car."

She glowers. "I'm wearing a men's dress shirt and nothing else."

I slide from the car then lean down to meet her gaze. "And I look like a fucking gigolo with my abs on display."

Her eyes fill with mirth. "But they're such pretty abs."

It's not a compliment. There's too much humor in her

tone. It doesn't stop her words from packing a punch, though. The dreamy bat of her lashes is just another conniving taunt.

"I'll be back in a minute. Don't go anywhere." I scan the street, triple checking nobody is paying us attention. It's early on Saturday morning, and the only people around are oldies or mothers with young children. But we're still driving around the middle of nowhere in a Porsche, which means the occasional stare is unavoidable.

After a flirtatious fifteen minutes with the young blonde shop assistant, I leave the store, my hands full of shopping bags as I slide back into the sports car.

"That looks like a lot more than a skirt and blouse." Her eyes bug as I hand over the purchases.

"The woman in there had the gift of the gab. I ended up giving her your sizes, and in return she set out a heap of clothes. I wasn't going to stick around and coordinate ensembles, so I bought them all."

"And I see you earned her phone number in the process."

"You were watching me, baby doll?" I retrieve the business card the woman gave me and hand that over, too. "This is in case you have any problems with the sizes."

"Sure it is." She eyes me with derision, before opening the first bag to glance inside. "There has to be enough clothes here to last a week."

"Good." I start the engine and pull from the curb. "I'm not sure how long we're going to be hanging out together, so at least this gives you some options."

She leans down, toeing her feet into a white skirt, then dragging it up her legs to shimmy it over her ass.

It's an impressive show I pretend not to watch from the corner of my eye. "We passed a diner on the way in, is that good enough for breakfast?"

"You don't want to get a shirt first?"

Shit. My stomach rumbles in protest. "I'll have to leave the shopping spree until later. I'm too hungry."

"Thank God. I don't think I can last much longer without sustenance." She tugs the hem down her thighs, covering perfect skin before she moves her attention to the buttons of my dress shirt.

"Do you want me to pull into an alley to give you privacy?" I drag my gaze over the passing cars, willing the passengers not to pay her attention.

"It's not like you haven't seen it all before."

I may have seen it, enjoyed it, and committed it to memory, but that doesn't mean I'm comfortable with her sharing the goods with any Tom, Dick, or buck-tooth Bill in the vicinity.

"It's not me I'm worried about." The thought of someone else looking at her makes me edgy. Goddamn twitchy.

I tighten my fingers around the steering wheel and pull up to a set of traffic lights. My jaw locks while I glare at the approaching Chevy in my rear-view that stops in the lane beside us.

The male driver is young, with shaggy hair and a flannelette shirt. For a second, I think Keira is going to skip his attention. Then he lazily glances our way and does a double-take when he notices her gaping shirt as she works at unclasping the last of her buttons.

"You've got an audience." I inch forward to meet the asshole's gaze, shooting him a look so scathing a smart man would contemplate his mortality.

He doesn't take my expression for the warning it is. Instead, he grins like he's about to blow in his pants.

"Keira," I growl, "you might want to cover up until the light changes."

She ignores me. The peeping tom, too.

She doesn't care at all. Not about the perfect chest she has on display or the smooth stomach as she shimmies out of my shirt and reaches down to pull out a light pink blouse from one of the shopping bags.

My palms sweat. My pulse fucking pounds.

I don't know why I give a shit, but I do. The anger coursing through me is unwarranted and fucking toxic.

To make matters worse, she struggles to maneuver her arm into the sleeve, her cleavage gaping as she bends forward.

"Jesus Christ," I mutter.

The shaggy fucker is practically laughing at his good fortune while my skin crawls.

"I've got something else you can look at, asshole." I reach for my gun.

"Don't you dare," she warns, finally working one arm into the sleeve. "Just ignore him."

Ignore him?

Ignore him.

I can't fucking breathe through the need to kill him.

I check the lights. Still red. Then I glance around the intersection.

"For fuck's sake. What is taking so long?" Apart from Grandpa Joe driving his white van past at five miles an hour, nobody else is on the road. The universe is mocking me with this bullshit. "Fuck this."

I press my foot on the accelerator. *Hard*. The tires screech as we surge forward. At this point, a ticket is better than a murder charge.

"What the hell, Decker?" Keira scrambles to clutch her belt and the door handle for support.

"The guy beside us was practically jerking off at your strip tease," I snarl.

"And running a red light and potentially smashing my brother's car is worth stopping the five second thrill of some random stranger?"

"Fuck yes." I ease off the pedal and cut down a side-street, not willing to trust my waning restraint if Chevy Boy decides to follow. "Somehow I think your brother would approve of my actions."

"I think he'd be more likely to kill you for endangering the Porsche." She wiggles, repositioning herself in the seat as she fixes the first button, her gaze heating the side of my face. "And besides, it's *my* modesty to protect. Not his. I've got more concerning things to worry about at the moment."

"You could've figured that out before I pimp-walked through the clothing store on your behalf. Minutes ago, you were all shy and innocent, not wanting anyone to misinterpret your lack of clothing as a walk of shame. Now you've got it all hanging out, practically screaming 'have at it, boys.'"

"Are we really arguing about this?"

Yes, we fucking are, and no, it doesn't make sense. I'm acting like a jealous little bitch over Cole Torian's sister. "I'm here to protect you in whatever way necessary."

"And I appreciate that, officer, but you can cut the crap when it comes to anyone not wielding a gun."

I grind my teeth and focus on the road, wishing the asphalt would open up and swallow me whole. "It's the lack of sleep," I growl. "And I'm fucking hungry."

She snickers. "Don't worry. I get it."

No, she doesn't. She has no clue I'd love to whisk her away from this shit, like a badass Prince Charming. But I'm still not sure if she needs to be saved. Or wants to be, for that matter.

"You can pull back onto the main road. I'm done." She tugs at the front of her shirt and grins. "All censored for your approval."

"Not funny." I turn the car around and take the fastest route back to the diner.

"Come on." Her grin turns to a smirk. "You've gotta admit it's a little funny."

"Nope. Unless you want me waving my dick around in public to distract attention from you, let's agree to keep our clothes on."

She presses her lips tight, her chest vibrating with silent laughter. "Who says I'd be opposed to you taking your clothes off?"

Fuck. Me.

The last thing I need right now is more complication. Increased temptation. I still have the crystal-clear recollection of her in the shower last night.

Half-naked.

Wet.

Vulnerable.

"For the sake of your brother not killing me, I'm going to take that as a fucking cruel joke."

"Okay." Her laughter fades as she grabs a pair of black flip-flops from the bag and slips them on. "For the sake of my brother not killing you, I'll pretend I was joking."

Jesus.

I cling to the steering wheel while I drive to the diner, then park the car and reclaim my shirt. Seconds later I'm striding inside, her soft footfalls following behind me.

I don't face her until we reach the counter. Even then it's hard not to stake a claim on all the perfection that Chevy-driving asshole was trying to visually violate. "Can you order me whatever you're having, along with enough food to take home for the rest of the day?" I hand over my wallet. "I've gotta make some calls."

"Okay..." She frowns. "Sure."

"You're going to be fine on your own for five minutes, aren't you?"

"I think I can handle it." She stares up at the billboard menu. "But don't be too long. I might get bored and start stripping for tips."

I scowl, pissed off that the creative side of my brain can conjure up a visual faster than I can form a comeback.

I don't even bother replying. There's no point. The gray matter swirling around in my skull has the consistency of butter as I stalk from the building, her soft chuckle haunting my every step. I continue to the far end of the parking lot and pull out my cell, quickly switching the sim cards to make a private call I've been dreading.

"Hey, baby, I was wondering when you'd get in contact." Anissa's voice is sickeningly sweet.

"I've been busy." I glance back at the diner, too paranoid not to look over my shoulder.

"So I've heard. Where are you?"

"Doesn't matter. But I won't be back this afternoon. I can't catch up today."

There's a beat of tense silence. "This is the second time you've cancelled our plans."

"I'm sorry, it can't be helped." I'm not sorry and she knows it, but it's a part of the game we play. She acts sweet and innocent while I pretend to give a fuck.

"You're with someone." She drops the saccharine from her tone. "Who?"

"It doesn't matter."

"Bullshit," she snaps, revealing the bitch she hides beneath this pathetic act. "You know it does. Tell me."

"I've warned you before, Nissa. Don't hound me."

"And I've warned you. *Don't fuck with me.*"

I should've walked away from her months ago. I still should, if only I didn't need her, and she didn't need me, too. We've got a unique relationship based on threats and lies. Smoke and mirrors.

She isn't the drug I crave. But she's the dealer. The gatekeeper.

"Fine. It doesn't matter, anyway." She bottles her anger. "I know who you're with. It's not hard to figure out."

"Then I hope you also know you can trust me."

Her derisive laugh is barely audible over the passing traffic. "I doubt that, but I've got hope. And a backup plan if you fuck me over."

I close my eyes and pinch the bridge of my nose. Anissa is nothing if not entirely strategic. I've always been well aware of what she's capable of, and I got involved with her anyway. "I won't."

I can't.

Despite her poison, this woman is a necessity in my life.

"Good. Be smart, Decker. We're great together. The last thing you want to do is mess it up."

7

KEIRA

Breakfast arrives while Decker is still outside, on his second phone call.

I wait a few minutes, watching him, trying to decipher the meaning behind his rigid stance and straight shoulders. He hid his face from view for most of his conversations, playing with the device between calls, if the hustle in his arms was anything to go by. But even with his back to me, I can tell he's restless.

On edge.

A few clicks further along the agitated path he'd been on while I undressed in the car.

I slide to the side of the booth, preparing to go outside and rescue him from himself, when he pockets his cell and makes his way across the parking lot to come inside.

I watch his approach, noticing his anxiety dissipate the closer he gets.

He's comfortable around me.

I'm not sure if that's a good thing.

"I'm sorry I took so long," he says as he slides into the other side of the booth.

"That's okay." I push his opened wallet toward him, his license on display. "Sebastian Decker." I let his name curl around my tongue and play along with the life outlined in the identification, even though I'm well aware the men who surround me on a daily basis have fake IDs and equally fake personas. The thing is, I've never cared before. Not until now, when I itch to know Decker's truth. I crave it more than my own safety. "I never would've guessed you were a California baby."

"I wasn't. I only spent a few years there before I came to Portland." He ignores the wallet and grabs his cutlery to start attacking his meal. "Did you enjoy snooping?"

"I didn't snoop. You gave me your wallet to pay." I take a bite of toast and wait until he meets my gaze. "And I didn't think your identity was a secret."

"It's not." He pushes the wallet back toward me. "Have at it. I've got nothing to hide."

His transparency is comforting. I'm almost tempted to believe him.

"Was that Cole on the phone?"

He nods. "Yeah. I'm supposed to pass on the message that there's money in the office safe if you need it. Apparently, you should know where it is, along with the combination."

"Okay. Thank you." I didn't contemplate what goodies could be stashed in my father's office. But I should've. My head isn't screwed on, and it damn well needs to be. "Did you speak to Hunter, too?"

"No." He fills his mouth with a forkful of food, the momentary transparency suddenly clouded.

I can't fight the growing curiosity. "Who did you speak to on the second call?"

"A friend." He meets my gaze, the connection seeming forced. "I had to cancel some plans."

I'm guilty of overanalyzing, I know that, and now is no exception. I judge every aspect of his expression—the faux calm, the playful eye contact.

"You had to cancel plans with a friend from the other side of the parking lot?"

He forks more food, chews, and takes the time to contemplate his response. "It was a woman, Keira."

"Oh." My shock bubbles free. At least that explains why he didn't act on the lust I'd seen in his eyes last night. Of course he's got women clambering for a piece of him. The world wouldn't make sense if he didn't.

"Your girlfriend?" I hedge.

A slow smile spreads across his lips. A taunting grin. "A friend."

"A friend you sleep with." It's not a question. Intuition already has my mind made up.

"You're awfully inquisitive this morning, poppet."

I shrug, unwilling to deny the obvious. "We're spending a lot of time together. It's only natural we get to know each other, right?"

"If that's the case, let's talk about you for a while."

My pulse hikes at the diversion. I can't help the unease that strikes when people try to get to know me. But unease is better than jealousy. Especially when caused by someone who could be a wolf in sheep's clothing. "Okay. I can handle that."

The conversation eases into lighter territory as we eat. He asks me where I went to school—homeschooled. He attempts to guess my hobbies, my likes and dislikes.

Strangely enough, he isn't too far off the mark. He's noticed how I favor champagne over spirits, and my taste in music. He's paid me far more attention than I've paid him, and I thought I'd watched from the shadows quite well.

A lot of time passes while we talk, our plates being cleared long ago, when I finally realize the dark smudges under his eyes. He's practically the living dead, his lack of sleep becoming more obvious in his features.

"Come on, sugar tits." I slide from the booth and jerk my head toward the door. "Let's go."

"Sugar tits?" He snorts.

I grab our takeaway food from the table and lead the way outside into the morning sun. "You're always calling me stupid names. It's my turn now."

"I'd never call you sugar tits."

"How do you know you haven't already?"

"I'd remember." He unlocks the Porsche and stands at the hood, watching me as I walk to the passenger side.

"How?"

67

"Because I know, for a fact, I've never referenced your tits like that."

I snort out a laugh. "Because you're such a gentleman?"

"Fuck no." He stalks to the driver's door and stares at me over the roof of the car. "Because your tits are beyond description, and I'd never devalue them with an endearment like that."

My cheeks heat.

Seriously, I'm goddamn blushing at his weirdly flattering compliment. "Right..." I open my door, and he follows me as I slide inside. "I guess now is a good time to bring the conversation back to your girlfriend."

"I told you I don't have one, gummy bear." He starts the ignition and shoots me a glance. "But my imaginary girlfriend sounds like she'd be a point of contention if she existed."

I clear my throat. "I think we've gone too far down this garden path, don't you?"

He snickers. "Yeah, I guess we have."

He pulls from the parking lot and turns toward Westport.

"Aren't you going to get some new clothes first?"

"Fuck." His head flops forward in exhaustion before he focuses back on the road. "No. I can't. I'm seconds from crashing."

"I'll help. It won't take long."

"Seriously, I can't. I'm dead on my feet." He glances my way, his brows pinched as he takes me in. "Do you need to get something else before we head home?"

Yes, I do. I have to stop playing around in this fake, flirty dream-state and get my hands on a burner phone.

I need to determine my suspicions about last night's shooter, preferably before my brother does. But telling Sebastian will leave me open to scrutiny I'm not ready for.

"It's nothing that can't wait." The lie curdles in my belly.

I don't know how much time I have up my sleeve. It could be days. Hours. Any minute now, Cole could find out who's responsible, and I'm sure his reaction will only put our family in more danger.

"You sure?"

I nod despite my unease. I'll have to figure out another way. "Take us home, captain."

He shoots me a grin and drives back to the safe house.

Once we arrive, he ushers me inside through the garage entry, still playing the protector role as he carries my shopping bags inside.

"I'll only need a few hours. Wake me if you're worried about anything."

"I won't need to." I take my new clothes from him. "I'll be too busy sorting these out."

"Enjoy." He winks and strides toward the other end of the house, disappearing into one of the bedrooms.

For the next thirty minutes, I waste time taking tags off clothes, then trying them on. He bought me enough to fill a wardrobe. There are sun dresses, jeans, a cardigan, ballet flats, and that's without mentioning all the skimpy lace underwear.

He must have spent a fortune, and the debt doesn't sit well with me for numerous reasons.

For starters, he still confuses me. I can't pin him down, not his thoughts or his actions. He's too kind. Too protective. Too...

He's just too much for me to believe at the moment.

I walk into the laundry and check the cupboards for detergent, finding what I need stashed in an almost bare cupboard beside an unopened bottle of fabric softener. I shove my clothes into the washing machine, not really paying attention as I become distracted by dreamy thoughts that have no place in my life.

Sebastian isn't real.

He's another illusion.

A flawless actor.

But what if he wasn't?

I put the washing machine to work and can't help going in search of his resting place. The least I can do is wash his clothes. Well, that's the reason I give myself for tiptoeing down the hall in search of him.

I find him in the furthest room, in the same position he had on the sofa last night, his arm covering his face, his chest on display. I can't help wondering what lies beneath the cream

69

sheet draped over his hips. Boxers? Briefs? Full-frontal nudity?

I creep forward, becoming hypnotized by the allure of the tattoos etched across muscled skin. The woman on his bicep tracks my movements, her tear-streaked cheeks squeezing at my chest.

The designs speak of damage. Heartache and pain. Brutality and beauty.

I step closer, to the side of the bed, and listen to his breathing. Deep in. Heavy out. Rhythmic. Calm. Controlled.

Even in sleep, he's fascinating. Despite the rumors and speculation, contrary to the secrets I know he keeps and the danger of the fake, fake, fake, his intrigue still holds me captive.

I tilt my head, taking in every inch of visible flesh. There are no defensive marks on his body. No wounds or scars. His skin is innocent apart from the ink defining his emotional injuries. But is his soul equally pristine?

It kills me not knowing.

He grunts, and I hold my breath. Freeze.

I wait for him to wake, but thankfully he doesn't stir.

Slowly, I inch back, lifting his clothes from the floor—the suit pants, shirt, and socks. I leave his jacket where it is, unwilling to test my novice washing skills on something that should probably be dry cleaned. Then I make my way back to the laundry and place his clothes with mine.

It seems intimate—his socks tangling with my underwear and dresses. It also seems wrong. Like I've taken this a step too far. And no, it's not just about the mingled clothing.

I'm faltering.

Sometimes this friendly, flirty act hasn't been an act at all.

It's real. There's truth in this charade.

I close the lid on the washing machine harder than I should and promise myself to leave the bitter taste of romance behind.

I change my focus to something safer—scavenging through each room of the house. I find new toothbrushes and paste in the main bathroom, and put them to use immediately. There's toilet paper, soap, deodorant, and tissues. Blankets are in the hallway cupboard. Fresh sheets and additional pillows, too.

I eat half a sandwich for lunch, but it's not because I'm hungry. I'm delaying the inevitable stroll through my father's office, which I can't put off any longer.

I drag my feet down the hall, toward the memories that are far from fond, and stop in the entry to rest my shoulder against the frame.

This room is the only part of the house untouched by renovations. No doubt it was from my father's demands. He wouldn't have wanted anyone in his personal space. He never did.

Even though he hasn't been here for a long time, his presence lingers close, grazing my skin with its rough texture. He used to sit behind that large oak desk, his frown tight, his annoyance at being interrupted always evident.

His tightly guarded love and affection only dissipated once my mother died. It's as if she took it with her—all his softness, all the care. But then again, he was never truly caring to begin with.

I suck in a deep breath and walk inside, taking in the stocked bookshelves, running my fingers over the criminal biographies and psychology texts.

I ignore the threat looming ahead and keep my gaze trained on the furniture, letting the memories creep into my mind as I approach the desk.

Cole was the only child welcomed in here. When he was little, I'm told he would sit and play in the corner while my father worked. He was always a part of the family business, even before he could contemplate what all the conversations meant.

He didn't need to become desensitized to the brutality because he grew up on the severity. It was always his world.

In contrast, Layla and I were drip fed. We didn't understand a lot of it until later. Much, much later when we had no choice but to come to terms with reality and make it work in our favor.

I reach the desk and place my hands on the shiny wood,

needing the support before I raise my gaze to stare at the looming portrait of my mother.

My heart climbs into my throat as she peers down at me.

She's ethereal up there. Heavenly with her gentle smile and loving eyes. I'd do anything to get her back. Maybe then the family I was always sworn to honor wouldn't be riddled with lies and betrayal.

She could've kept us whole.

She could've protected me and my siblings.

"I miss you, Mom." I walk toward her, struggling to remain composed as I grab the heavy frame encasing her and take it off the wall. "I wish you were here."

I place her on the desk, her gaze tracking my every move as I turn and face the safe I've revealed. The dark gray metal looms before me, the keypad cold to the touch as I enter the family pin code.

The door releases, and I pull it wide to expose a stack of cash and a gun. But the item making my pulse pound is the phone laying almost camouflaged against the black velvet interior.

"Thank God."

I snatch at the device, sweet relief rushing through me as I turn it on and wait for the software to load. When the screen brightens, it shows a depleted battery with less than forty percent charge. But that's okay. I can make this work.

I pat my hand around the bottom of the safe, searching for a power cord that isn't there.

Damn it.

I'm determined to remain positive, even though forty percent won't get me far when I have to search to find the numbers I need. I keep scouring the office, checking my father's desk drawers and the empty filing cabinets. I even rush to the kitchen to scour there, too.

Nothing.

There's no way to charge the cell, which means my time is limited.

Shit.

I open an internet app and type in familiar businesses and

contact names. I work frantically, jotting down notes and people of interest until the battery life is dwindled by half. I'm about to connect my first call when a ringtone breaks the silence, the sound coming from the far end of the house— Sebastian's phone.

Fucking hell.

I stare at the device in my palm, wanting and needing to use it, but I'm not willing to get caught making the necessary calls. I can't risk being overheard.

With a huff of frustration, I turn off the cell and place it back in the safe. It will have to stay there until later. Then I tiptoe down the hall toward Sebastian's room, the sound of his sleep-roughened voice tickling the hair at the back of my neck as I approach.

"What's up, Hunt?"

I stop before I reach his opened door and plaster myself against the wall, listening to the one-sided conversation.

"I was good until you woke me," he growls. "I haven't had a lick of sleep."

There's a pause. A rustle of sheets.

"Have you found any leads?" He sighs. "There's gotta be something. Who owned the car?"

I tilt my head, needing to hear every roughly mumbled word.

"Well, if it was stolen, who did they steal it from?" He huffs. "I need to get my ass back home to help you guys look. I can't do dick here when I don't have a computer."

My heart clenches. He wants to leave?

"She's good. Taking everything in stride."

My pulse increases at the change in topic, and I guess it's also from the softness in his voice when he talks about me. I want to understand him. I need to. Even more so now that he's pushing to go home.

"No. I slept on the sofa, asshole. I didn't go anywhere near her rocket pocket."

I press my lips tight and struggle not to laugh.

"Torian doesn't need to worry," he continues. "I'll protect her. As long as there's air in my lungs, Keira will be safe."

My laughter fades. Evaporates. I stare at the wall opposite me, trying not to become overwhelmed by his adamant conviction.

He's vowed to protect me.

He's vowed, even if his own life ends in the process.

Why?

The conversation continues, turning into snide banter as I become lost in the darkened forest of my thoughts.

I can't remember ever hearing someone speak about me like Sebastian just did. Yes, my brother values my safety. He demands it. But my protection in the eyes of my family is more of a strategy.

If we all stay safe, we all stay strong.

Not even my father has spoken about protecting me the way Sebastian has—*As long as there's air in my lungs.*

My chest tightens.

Again, why? I don't know if I should be comforted or concerned.

There's another rustle of sheets and the squeak of the bed frame. I panic, unsure if he's about to catch me spying.

I push from the wall and enter the doorway with a forced smile, but my expression doesn't matter. He doesn't turn to me. He sits on the edge of the mattress, hunched over, his head in his free hand, his bare feet on the carpet.

"She's here now. Do I need to pass on any messages?"

He tilts his head, meeting my gaze. His demeanor doesn't change. He barely acknowledges my presence. He still looks weary. Entirely drained. The lines of exhaustion in his features beg to be touched. Gently softened with the glide of a finger.

My palms tingle. My pulse increases as I move closer.

"Fuck off, Hunt." He lowers his focus to the floor, his tone still holding the lingering gravel of sleep. "I told you, I'm treating her like a queen. Unlike you, I know how to look after a woman."

He doesn't shift as I approach. There's not even a ripple of muscle. And there are so many muscles—back, arms, stomach, and God, his legs.

I bite my lower lip and wonder what it would be like to sink my teeth into him instead.

"Tell him I look forward to speaking to him," he drawls. "Call me if anything changes."

He lowers the cell, presses a button, then throws the device to the pillows before lifting his chin to look at me.

"Hey," he murmurs.

"Hey."

I itch to touch him.

"How's Hunter?"

He huffs out a tired breath. "Annoying, as always. But he said I might be able to take you home tomorrow if things stay quiet."

"Okay." I keep my emotions in check. Every single one of them. "Is he any closer to finding out who was responsible?"

"No, not yet."

I nod, becoming endeared by the lazy softness of him. With the raise of a hand, I could run my fingers through his hair. I could feel the heat of his skin. He's there. Right there in front of me.

He frowns. "What's going on, sweetness?"

I shrug and pretend those endearments don't hit me hard between the thighs. "You still look tired."

"It'll take a few minutes for me to wake up."

I want to be the one to wake him. I want him to trust me enough to remain tired and lethargic, too. It's a strange feeling, and I'm not sure if it's due to strategy or emotion, but it's there nonetheless, the delicious thrill curling its way around my belly.

I reach out, unable to hold back any longer, and run my fingers through the dark strands of his hair. It's my first deliberate touch. The connection made due to something other than fear or reliance. I'm sending a clear message, one I see reciprocated in his expression as he holds my gaze.

"Keira..." My name is a warning that brings a delicious thrill.

"Mmm?" I scrape my nails over his scalp.

He groans, the deep sound vibrating from his chest.

"You're going to send me straight back to sleep if you keep doing that."

"Really?" I cock a brow. "That wasn't my intent."

His eyes narrow, and I hold my breath, waiting for him to call me out on my flirtation. Going down this road isn't a good idea. Not for either of us.

"What is your intent?" His gaze is sharp, reading me, trying to figure out what's going on in this messed up brain of mine.

"I don't know." I'm stuck between wants, needs, and responsibility. Morality, necessity, and danger. "But I should stop, shouldn't I?"

"Yeah." He leans his head into my touch. Not backing away. Not retreating.

I literally have him in the palm of my hand.

Power bleeds through me, coursing from the inside out. I tingle. Everywhere. My stomach flutters with the strength of a thousand butterflies. My skin burns.

"And what if I don't?" I ask. "What happens then?"

His nostrils flare, his hands tensing as they lay against the bed covers. "I think we're both well aware of what happens then, cupcake."

8

DECKER

Her nails against my skin... Her gentle, seductive words... Those eyes. *Fuck*. Those gorgeous innocent eyes.

All of it messes with my sleep-addled brain.

I'm hallucinating. Or worse, she's playing me, and I can't even decipher the deception.

"You were in here earlier." I hold her gaze, looking for a glimpse of betrayal. "Did you find what you were looking for?"

"Of course you were still awake." She chuckles, her nails still trekking a deliriously intense trail over my scalp. "I came in to get your clothes. I've already washed them. It shouldn't be long until they're dry."

I smother my surprise. "You didn't have to do that."

"I wanted to. It's the least I can do." She inches closer, her legs brushing my bent knees. "Not that I'm the best at laundry. But it's the thought that counts, right?"

I don't care about the clothes. I wouldn't give a shit if she shredded them to pieces. "Sure is."

With the way she's looking down at me, her appraisal delicate and pure, I'd settle for walking around half-naked until we have to go back to Portland.

"I also found the money Cole was talking about in the safe." Her nails rake deeper, the bite of pain an intoxicating thrill. "I can repay you for all the cash you've spent."

"I don't want your money."

"It's not my money. It's yours. I owe it to you."

"Fine," I mutter, no longer willing to be distracted from her touch. "We can sort it out later."

She smiles, slow and sweet. "You're still exhausted. Why don't you get some more sleep?"

Getting horizontal is the only thing on my mind, but sleep has nothing to do with it. I can feel her everywhere—in my blood, with each beat of my heart, in every twitch of my fingers.

I want her.

I fucking need her.

I stare into those eyes, trying to determine what's being hidden by her seduction. She entered my room for a reason, and I'm not delusional in thinking it was for sex. "What are you doing in here, Keira?"

Why is she touching me?

Tempting me.

Playing games.

She waits, taking her time to form the perfect answer. "I don't know."

"That's not like you," I keep my voice low. "You're not indecisive. You know exactly what you want. So, tell me. What are you hiding behind those ocean eyes?"

She sucks in a slow breath, her nails pausing at the back of my scalp. "I find it hard to read you. Usually, people aren't that difficult to understand. But with you I'm struggling."

My pulse rises, eager for her to continue the trail of those fingers. "Is that all this is? You're trying to read me?"

"No." She rakes her teeth over her lower lip. Sweet. Uncharacteristically virtuous. "It's more than that."

I'm struggling to read this situation myself. She's not usually like this. Close. Soft. Almost malleable. I'm seeing it more and more. First, in the shower last night, now here, in my room, while I'm half naked.

I'm tempted to grab her. To pull her close and drag her down to the mattress on top of me despite the stupidity. And there's so much fucking stupidity.

The temptation before me is enough to have me brushing

aside the threat of her brother. Fuck Torian. Fuck her entire family. As long as I can fuck her, right?

Wrong.

Focus, asshole.

There's too much at stake to literally blow this now. "You should get out of here, hot stuff. You don't want this."

"I told myself the same thing." Her nails working in circles. "I keep telling myself. But here I am. And I can't seem to find the will to leave."

Her fingers move behind my ears, the scrape igniting a shiver that rushes through my chest. She treks her touch to my neck, along my jaw, and stops at my chin to nudge her knuckles into my skin and tilt my face closer to hers.

She's unpredictable.

Undeniable.

"Do you want me to fuck you, Keira?" I murmur. "Because that's what's going to happen if you don't get out of here."

She swallows and shakes her head. "No, I don't want to be fucked." She leans in and glides the delicate pad of her fingers over my growing stubble. "I want to get to know you. The kind Sebastian. The protective guy I glimpsed the first night we met."

"There's nothing kind about me, honey."

"Just charm and sarcasm, right?"

"Right."

"I don't believe you." She smiles, but the humor doesn't reach her eyes. "In fact, I think that's another reason why Cole doesn't trust you. You're too sweet. Too nice. You don't fit in."

That may have been the case years ago.

It sure as shit ain't now, though.

Life circumstances have made me the perfect player in this crime-riddled family. I'm here because I fit like a fucking glove.

I grab the back of her thighs and yank her forward, trapping her between my legs. She gasps, those baby blues flashing as she grabs my shoulders to stabilize herself.

"If you're looking for nice, you've come to the wrong guy." I grab the front of her blouse and tug her close. "If you want sweet, I'm not that guy either."

There's no room for weakness in this world. Not around her family and definitely not in the bedroom. If she expects a limp dick, she's got another thing coming.

"I just want you," she whispers. "The real you."

I tug her blouse harder, forcing her lips to mine. She whimpers as our mouths collide, and I keep tug, tug, tugging her forward until she climbs onto the bed. Onto me. She straddles my hips, her skirt creeping higher up her perfect thighs.

There's no sweetness. Not one fucking thing kind about our kiss.

I part her lips with my tongue, demanding entrance she allows too easily. There's no fight in her, only surrender. The sweetest fucking surrender I eagerly devour as she nestles on top of my crotch.

We're chest to chest, not a breath of space between us, and still she's not close enough.

I want more.

I need everything.

I shove my hand into her hair and fist the long strands. I palm her ass, guiding her into a gentle rock against my pulsing cock.

She's perfect. She's always been perfect. And having her nestled against my shaft, her lips on mine, is the sweetest fucking victory I've ever tasted.

But we're not supposed to be together.

Never were. Never should be.

If only the lust coursing between us didn't feel like divine fucking intervention brought us here.

She places her hand on my chest, lightly pushing, breaking the kiss. "Why did you save me last night?" Her panted breaths brush against my skin.

"Why?" I find it hard to concentrate when her kiss-darkened lips are a constant distraction. "Because I didn't want you to get hurt."

"But why? Why risk your life to save mine? You barely know me."

"I know you, Keira. It feels like I've known you for a long time."

She shakes her head, our noses brushing. "No, you don't. I barely know myself."

I don't buy it.

I can't.

"Then maybe it's a gut feeling I have," I hedge. "I've been infatuated with you since the first night we met. That doesn't happen for no reason."

"I'm sure there are many reasons—the thrill of the chase... The desire for something you're not supposed to have... Lust..."

I incline my head. "It could be all the above. And the list wouldn't be complete without noting how devastated I would've been to see your perfect body marked by a bullet hole." I slide my hands down her back and over her tailbone. "I've pictured a lot of things going into this ass of yours, but a bullet ain't one of them."

Her lips quirk and she rolls her eyes. "Always with the humor."

"That wasn't humor. That's the God's honest truth."

She chuckles and brushes her lips over mine. "You're not putting anything in my ass, Sebastian Decker."

"Maybe not today or tomorrow. But if we go down this path, I most definitely will, my sexy goddess."

She pulls back, scrutinizing me with a mix of concern and exhilaration. There's innocence, too.

"You've never let anyone play there before?" I squeeze her ass. Hard.

She sucks in a breath and shakes her head. "No."

My pulse pounds harder. The desire to claim her becomes a living, breathing thing inside my chest, demanding action. "You have no idea how fucking hard that makes me. I'm—"

My cell rings, cutting off my words and stealing the lust-filled mania.

Keira glances toward the pillows, then back at me, wrapping her hands around my neck, her fingers playing with the hair at my nape. "Ignore it."

"Why? Who is it?"

She leans in, reclaiming my mouth, deliberately trying to distract me.

I groan and struggle to fight temptation. "It's Cole, isn't it?"

She keeps kissing me as the trill continues.

Goddamn it.

"I can't ignore him." I pull back and meet her gaze. Unwanted clarity sinks into my veins, smothering the lust.

"Go on, then." She climbs from my lap and moves to stand beside the bed.

"Have I told you how much I despise your brother?" I snatch my cell from the pillow.

"No, but it's been implied more than once." She chuckles, yet the humor doesn't reach her eyes.

We both know this call will mark the end of whatever this thing is between us. Torian's perfect timing has stolen the buzz and brought too much fucking clarity.

"Don't go anywhere." I reach for her hand, only to have her back away.

"I'm not." But she does. She keeps retreating, placing more and more space between us.

Fuck Torian.

Fuck him and his horrible fucking timing.

I connect the call and raise the cell to my ear. "What's up?" I don't look away from her. I keep reading her expression, trying to figure out if the change in her features is from disappointment or something more.

"Nothing," he grates. "I just called for an update. Where are you?"

"Still at the safe house. In bed. Trying to get some fucking sleep."

"Cry me a river. How's Keira?"

"Good." Clearly annoyed that I answered this phone call if her pinched brows are anything to go by, but good nonetheless. "Want to talk to her?"

"She's with you?" he snarls.

"She's not riding my dick, if that's what you're asking." I

keep holding her gaze, noting the narrowing of her eyes, the stiffening of her shoulders. "I was offering to go find her."

There's a pause, the seconds of silent contemplation ticking by.

"Torian, do you want me to get her or not?"

"Yes." His answer is a barely audible mutter. "But first I need to speak to you about the drive-by. Hunter seems to think you can help find the culprit."

"That depends on what you've already tried. I don't know the first thing about what's going on over there."

"Not a hell of a lot. We don't have any leads. I've got no idea who's targeting us, or why. Whoever is responsible is a coward who doesn't want to claim responsibility."

"It might not be cowardice. It could be strategic. Both incidents could even be a coincidence."

"First my uncle, now this. It's not a fucking coincidence."

No, it's not likely, but stranger things have happened. And when you have a list of enemies a mile long, it wouldn't be a stretch to get targeted by more than one at the same time. "What about the official investigation? Do you have access to that information?"

"Not currently."

His tone implies he can gain access, though. I assume all he'd have to do is grease a palm or two.

"If you think the same person is responsible," I continue, "there's more than likely going to be a point of conversion in those files. All I need to do is find it."

"What else would you need?"

"My laptop."

"Give me your home address, and I'll get someone to pick it up."

No. *Fuck no.* "I'll come and get it. I'll drive us back overnight—"

"Like hell you will. I don't want Keira in Portland yet."

"Then you need to get me a new computer because you sure as shit aren't going through my house."

He gives a derisive laugh. "Who says I haven't already?"

I say. I'd fucking know.

83

My home is a fortress, not necessarily impenetrable, but I get surveillance notifications whenever someone sets foot on the property. Even the neighbor's cat can't escape detection.

"Why don't you want me going through your house, Decker?" he taunts. "Have you got something to hide?"

"Apart from my granny panty fetish, not really. But you're a little too judgmental for my liking, so I think it's best to keep our relationship strictly professional."

"I'll get you a computer," Torian grates. "Is there anything else?"

"Let me think on it. I'll text you a list."

"Make it quick. I'll send Hunter out to see you tomorrow if nothing happens in the meantime."

"Yeah. Okay. Leave it with me."

"Have you found my sister yet?" he snips as if he anticipated her being at my side all along.

"Yeah. Hold on." I raise my attention and find her staring down at me. No, she's staring right through me, her eyes blank, lips parted, skin pale. "Keira?"

She blinks out of the trance and pastes on a smile. "Mmm?"

"Cole wants to speak to you." I cover the mouthpiece with my palm. "What's wrong?"

"Nothing." She approaches and holds out a hand for the device.

"You're not a good liar."

"I'm the best liar," she counters, grabbing the cell to raise it to her ear. "Cole?" She turns away from me, hiding her face from view.

She remains quiet for a while, taking short steps toward the door. She's trying to distance herself from me as she gets closer to her brother. I won't stand in her way. Not this time. In the future it might be a different story.

I push from the bed and stalk to the adjoining bathroom to rinse my face. The water doesn't help to clear my head, but it scrambles the words drifting from the next room for a few brief moments until I hear her muttered affirmations.

"Hmm... Okay... Yes... I understand."

I don't deliberately eavesdrop. Her answers are just there, the sound of her voice reaching my ears as if I was made to listen to nothing but her.

"I'm not sleeping with him," she murmurs.

I walked to the door, needing to see her, and cock my hip against the frame. She's sitting on the bed, her focus rising to meet mine.

"I don't like this," she says to him. "You're not involving me in decisions, and I need to know what's going on." She frowns, clenching her jaw. "Yes. I know. I'll speak to you soon."

She disconnects the call and cradles my phone in her hands.

I was right when I anticipated the moment between us ending. The lust I'd seen in her eyes is gone. There's no picking up where we left off.

"Your brother is an asshole," I grate.

She gives a half-hearted grin. "What did he do this time?"

"Every time you talk to him, your mood changes. I don't like the effect he has on you. I don't like the way he treats you."

She schools her expression, the emotion draining from her features to leave me staring at a blank slate. "You watch me too closely. Maybe you're seeing things that aren't even there."

"I'm seeing what's right in front of me, Keira. I'm seeing you."

She either doesn't like being seen or isn't used to being noticed. I'm not sure which.

"Do you want me to quit watching?" I push from the doorframe and pad into the room. "Would you prefer if I didn't see you at all?"

"I didn't say that."

There's still distance between us. More emotional than physical.

I want to get her back to the place we'd been before the phone call. To the hot and sweaty. To the imminent fucking.

I stop before her, our position switched from when she first entered the room. I stare down at her, reading a myriad of thoughts in those eyes. She still wants me, but not like she did before.

Cole has her questioning me. Again. And I fucking hate it.

"You regret kissing me," I mutter.

"I don't regret the kiss. I regret where we were when it happened."

"In the bedroom?" I know that's not the case, but my aim is to keep her talking. To keep elaborating.

"No." She shakes her head. "In a safe house. Surrounded by drama and obligation."

"Neither one of us were obligated to participate." I reach out, running the backs of my fingers down her cheek. "But I guess it's best if we forget how close we came to complicating things."

"Are you sure we haven't already?"

I stroke my knuckles over her smooth skin. Slow. Lazy. "It was just a kiss."

"Just a kiss?" Her brows rise. "It felt like more than that to me."

Good.

About fucking time.

"Either way, it's over." I drop my hand to my side.

She winces, and I leave her with the same sterility she's given me as I stalk to the head of the bed and reclaim my position on the mattress. I cross my legs at the ankles and put my hands behind my head, waiting for her to bite.

"Why?" she whispers.

It's always one inch forward, two yards back with her. I always have to be strategic.

She acts like a wild animal, tentatively taking the bites of nourishment I provide, then running for the hills when I try to get something in return.

All I want is her trust. That's it.

Nothing more. Nothing less.

For now, at least.

"Because if Cole found out, he'd think my interest in you was payback."

"Payback for what?" She turns to face me, cocking a bent knee onto the mattress.

She feeds on the crumbs I spread before her. She always

86

devours the insight into my life. She craves my secrets. It's the only trick I have up my sleeve to reel her back in when she flees.

"A fucking lifetime of debt I'm supposed to owe him."

"Money?" she accuses.

I laugh, the sound caustic to my own ears. "No, not money. Cole demands more of me than that."

She climbs onto the bed and sits with her legs tucked beneath her. "Like what?"

"You name it." I shrug. "The debt changes depending on his mood."

"Why? What did you do?"

"I didn't do a damn thing." I don't restrain my anger. "Sarah took something from him. Something she deserved. And Hunter and I refused to let her take the fall."

Her expression doesn't falter. She continues to stare at me.

"You already know the story," I muse. The knowledge is written all over her face.

"Sarah told me a few things. My sister did, too. The rest I pulled together on my own." She shrugs. "But I didn't know about the debt. I didn't realize you were here against your will."

"I'm not *here* working for your brother because I enjoy his generous hospitality. But I'm *here*, in Westport, because I'd do anything to keep you safe."

She nods, the movement slow, lazy, and entirely unconvincing.

"You don't believe me."

She releases a huff of derision. "Actually, I do." She crawls toward the head of the bed and lies down beside me. "That's the problem."

"One of many." I shoot her a smirk. "If Cole finds out I took advantage of you, he'll make the drive-by look like a confetti toss."

"From what I recall, I'm the one who came to you, remember?"

"I'm not going to forget any time soon." Not about her lips or the fucking brilliant way she kept grinding against me. My dick is on a hair trigger at the mere memory. "But do you really think it matters? He's not going to give a shit who jumped who first. Either way, he's going to want to see me six feet under."

"Yet you kissed me anyway." She inches toward me, nestling into my side. "I've always said you have a death wish."

I wrap an arm around her and pull her close. "And I've always said you're nothing but trouble."

She chuckles. "I think you might be right."

She places a hand on my stomach and her cheek against my chest. We lie there, silent and comfortable, as my eyes grow heavy and her breathing deepens. I'm seconds away from slumber. I'm sure she is, too.

"Sebastian?" she murmurs.

"Yeah?"

"Is it crazy that despite what you just said, I still want to kiss you again?"

I close my eyes and grin at the ceiling. "No, sugar. It's not crazy. It just makes things fucking complicated, that's all."

9

DECKER

I WAKE UP IN A DARK ROOM, THE FURNITURE BARELY recognizable through the shadows. It takes a few seconds to blink away the lethargy and remember where I am—with Keira, in the safe house, secluded from the rest of the world.

I groan and reach my hands above my head to stretch my tired muscles. I expect to hear a sleepy response from her in return.

Nothing comes.

She's no longer curled into me.

"Keira?" I reach across her side of the mattress. It's empty. Cold.

I groan again, this time in annoyance. I'm losing my edge. I should've woken when she climbed out of my arms. Instead, I didn't even stir when she fled the room.

I throw back the covers and slide from the bed, grabbing my phone from between the pillows before I stalk for the hall. The house is dead. Not a breath of life to fill the emptiness.

"Keira?" My voice fractures the silence, my bare feet slapping against tile.

I enter the living room and find no sign of her. Everything is in its place—the cushions on the sofa, the television remote, the chairs at the dining table.

"Keira?" I speak louder, the edge of panic creeping into my tone.

I walk to the garage where Torian's Porsche lies in wait. Then I stalk to the laundry, and the bedrooms along the hall, my pulse increasing as I yank open doors and slam them shut again.

I make my way through every square inch of the house, not wanting to believe she's gone even though it's crystal fucking clear.

She's not here.

She's not anywhere.

Panic squeezes at my ribs, the pain building.

"*Keira?*" I hold my breath waiting for a reply.

Nothing.

Not a fucking thing.

"*Fuck.*" I run back to the bedroom to retrieve my gun from the nightstand drawer and struggle not to lose my shit.

She's gone. But how? Where?

I wouldn't have slept through someone breaking in. If she'd been attacked, I would've heard it.

Adrenaline rushes through my veins. Fear curdles in my gut.

Every inch of me pulses with the need to fight, yet I don't even know my opponent. "*Keira.*"

I sprint for the back door, needing to search the yard, and find the deadbolt already unlocked.

Ice-cold dread fills my reality. I picture her broken body. Bloodied. Bruised. Dead. It's all I can see. I can even smell it— the tainted scent of death and decay.

No.

I stumble outside, my finger poised to dial Hunter's number, when I hear something. The faintest voice. I swing around, aiming my gun on a bright glow in the back corner of the yard. A white light. The illumination of a phone.

"Keira?"

Murmured words hit my ears. The soft utterance of "I've gotta go" turning my blood to lava.

I run toward her, my weapon still drawn, my eyes squinted through the dim moonlight. "What the hell are you doing out here?" My harsh tone purges the toxic panic from my system. "Are you alone?"

She jerks back, the cell clutched in her left hand. "Yes. *Christ*. Lower the goddamn gun."

My throat threatens to close. My limbs fucking shake. My head is a pounding mess of turbulence, and I still can't come to grips with her standing before me. Whole. Entirely unscathed. And glaring back at me like *I'm* the one in the wrong.

I thought I'd lost her. I thought I'd never see her again.

"Where did you get the fucking phone?" I lower the gun and take a menacing step forward, my hands trembling with the need to grab her to make sure she's real.

"Calm down." She drops her arms to her sides. "I found it in my father's office."

"Calm down? *Calm the fuck down*? Do you know how scared I was when I couldn't find you?" My heartrate lessens, but the anger lives on. I can't get rid of it. "I've been searching the fucking house. I've been yelling your fucking name."

"I sat out in the sun all afternoon. I wanted some fresh air. Then night fell, and it was just as beaut—"

"I don't want to hear it." I grind my teeth, holding in another harsh reply that's destined only to prolong the argument. I count out the seconds. Fight against the rage. Then give up and grab the crook of her arm. "Get inside."

"Excuse me?" She yanks away from my hold. "Do you know who the hell you're talking to?"

I bark out a venomous laugh. "Oh, I know, princess. I *fucking know*. It's not like a Torian ever lets anyone forget."

Her face falls and slowly she pulls herself together, squaring her shoulders, lifting her chin. "You're overreacting."

"Tell that to the prick who put forty-seven bullets in the ceiling of your family's restaurant. No one has a clue who ordered the attack. For all you know, someone could've put a tracker on your brother's car. They could be watching you right now."

She glances over her shoulder, my words sinking in as she scans the darkness.

"It's a little late for that, don't you think?" I clench my fists.

I grind my teeth. I do everything and anything to try to lessen my insanity. "It was a fucking stupid move, Keira. You should know better."

She shakes her head and stares at me in confusion. For long moments all I can hear are my panted exhales and her non-verbal judgement. It's loud. So fucking loud.

"Why are you being such an asshole?"

"I'm the asshole?" I point the barrel of the gun at my chest. "I'm the bad guy in this situation?" I throw my arms in the air and let them fall to my sides. "My apologies for caring. I'll try harder not to give a shit in the future."

I have two options—sling her over my shoulder and carry her stupid ass inside, or walk away and calm down in private.

Well, both aren't really options.

One is a desire, the other is a fucking necessity.

It takes all my effort to stalk toward the house and leave her standing on her own. But I'm not in a good enough place to walk inside without slamming the fucking door behind me.

Fuck this shit.

Fuck it.

I storm into the kitchen, slam my gun and phone onto the counter, and hunch over as I grip the cold marble in a white-knuckled grip.

I need to pull myself together. I'm overreacting. And I can't fucking deny the insanity isn't merely about Keira.

I've been here before.

I've drowned in fear.

I've suffocated under panic.

This is a warped kind of déjà vu I can't get away from quick enough. I struggle to fight the need to pummel my fist into something.

I'd fallen asleep beside her. I probably even had a smile on my face. Then I woke up in a nightmare I hadn't prepared for. I'd been on a fucking high. I'd been winning a battle I'd been losing for so damn long.

Then...this.

I shove from the counter and yank open the fridge to take out the lasagna we picked up from the diner. I remove the meal from the plastic container, reheat it, then drop my plate to clatter on the dining table as I take a seat and start feeding my face.

I ignore Keira. I pretend my focus isn't entirely on my peripheral vision which is stalking the darkness of the back yard as I fork food into my mouth. I don't even flinch as the sensor light illuminates the back deck.

She walks forward, coming to sit on a wooden lounge chair and wrapping herself in a blanket.

It's cold out there. I'd barely felt it when I stalked outside in my boxers, but her lithe body would be chilled all over. And now I feel fucking guilty because she's obviously keeping her distance from the asshole hiding out inside.

I fight the need to lecture her again. I ignore the rampant pulse demanding I go to her and purge all the bullshit clogging my veins.

I need to stay away. And I want to be close.

The opposing forces are pulling me apart.

It doesn't take long for her to come inside on her own, dragging the blanket behind her. Wordlessly, she demands all my attention even though I don't look at her. It's enough that I feel her through every beat of my pulse.

I anticipate every softly padded footstep as she approaches. I hear the delicate scrape of the blanket against the furniture as she draws near.

"I'm sorry I scared you." She stops beside me, within arm's reach.

I keep chewing, keep venting my frustration on the food I'm decimating between my teeth. It's not safe to talk. Not yet. There's still too much adrenaline eating up my marrow.

She drops the blanket to the floor and scoots onto the chair beside me, the smooth skin of her legs eating up my peripheral vision.

"When I came here with my family, I was never allowed outside," she speaks softly. "When I was little, we were given excuses—either the lawn had been sprayed with weed chemicals or a wild animal had been seen in the neighborhood. As we got older, the excuses stopped, but the rule of staying inside always remained. We were told it wasn't safe, no matter how many armed men guarded the property."

She sucks in a deep breath and lets it out slowly. "When I woke up this afternoon, the house felt different. For the first time since my mother died, this place didn't seem like a prison. And when I came into the living room and found it flowing with warmth and sunlight, I couldn't resist breaking my father's rules. I think I actually needed to break them to prove to myself I'm not living in his gilded cage anymore."

She's not helping to lower my pulse. I don't care what story she has or how many rules she wants to break.

I shove the last piece of lasagna in my mouth and push from the seat, dumping the dirty plate in the sink.

"You're going to ignore me now?"

I clutch the counter and bite back a snarl. "You accused me of being an asshole. I'm keeping my mouth shut to stop you from flinging the same insult again."

"You *were* being an asshole."

"And I'll continue to be if we keep talking about this bullshit. There's a fucking reason you weren't allowed outside, Keira."

"I know... Like I said, I'm sorry."

"You need to be more careful until we know who the enemy is." I turn to face her, one hand still clutching the kitchen counter. "Mistakes like that could get us both killed."

She winces, and the pained expression deals me another generous hand of guilt.

"I'm not trying to be an asshole," I grate. "I'm—"

"I don't have a problem with your honesty. It's how similar you sound to my father."

My muscles tense, every inch of me growing rigid. "I'll never be anything like him, or anyone else in your family, for that matter. The only thing we have in common is our need to keep you safe."

She nods, her eyes turning somber.

I want to go to her. To touch. To soothe. But that won't achieve a thing, not when my anger will turn to lust and we'll be fucking in the space of a heartbeat. "Who were you talking to on the phone?"

Her lips fall into a flat line, then seconds later she's beaming me a deceptive smile. "Friends. I wanted them to know I'm okay."

Anxiety and distraction—that's the story her features give. Lies and deceit. Fucking hell. For once, I wish I could believe her.

"Friends?" I approach, moving to stand beside her chair. "I bet they were happy to hear from you."

She nods. "Yeah, they were."

I hold out a hand. "Can I have a look at the phone?"

"Why?" Her brows knit tight. "It's almost out of battery."

"I won't take long." I keep my hand outstretched, waiting, scrutinizing.

She doesn't move, deliberately masking her expression, removing all sense of emotion to leave me staring at a blank slate. I have to remind myself she has every right not to trust me, but fuck, sometime soon I hope this tiresome game will end.

"Who were you really talking with?"

Her jaw tightens and she inches forward, about to slide from the chair.

"You weren't talking to friends, were you?" I growl.

More adrenaline floods my veins as I wonder what trouble is headed our way.

She's smarter than this.

I could've sworn she was.

She scowls. "You're being an asshole again."

"An asshole who fucking cares about you." I return her look of defiance. "You still don't get it. I'm here for you. No one but you. Why is it so hard to tell me the fucking truth?"

"Because trust doesn't come easily." She raises her voice. "I'm trying, Sebastian. I shared the story about my childhood, didn't I? I'm letting you in as fast as I can, but it takes time."

"We don't have time if you're using a traceable phone."

"It's not traceable." She scoots off the chair, her feet landing on the tile beside mine, bringing us chest to chest. "I may have done a few stupid things, but I'm not completely dense."

I keep my hands at my sides, instead of where they want to be—on her arms. I'm so fucking angry, but all I can see are those eyes. That mouth. The tongue that glides out to moisten her lower lip.

She tilts her face toward mine, the temptation getting closer.

"Did you tell anyone where we are?" I inch forward, her breath faintly brushing my skin.

"No."

My hips press into hers, my hardening cock pulsing between us. "Did you say anything that could risk your safety?"

She swallows and shakes her head. "No."

Damn it to hell. I've never been more caught up in a woman like this before. I've never been this intrigued. This enslaved.

I want her.

I need her.

I have to fucking have her.

"You should get out of here before I do something we both regret."

Her breath hitches, and those intense blue eyes flare. "Again, no."

10

DECKER

I STEAL HER MOUTH. HER BREATH. HER KISSES.

I force out my frustration with every swipe of my tongue. I let go of my anger through the tight grip of my fingers through her hair.

"Take off the blouse."

She obeys, her hands traveling down the buttons in a frantic rush. I shove the material off her shoulders, my mouth never leaving hers, and reach around her back to unclasp her bra. My palms scour her body, down her arms, along her waist, to the sides of her breasts.

I groan at the perfection and pull away to take in the sight.

"God, you drive me to madness." I slam my mouth back down on hers, my tongue delving deep.

She claws at my chest, her nails puncturing skin as I grab her waist and place her on the table. Her legs encircle my hips, her skirt rising to the apex of her thighs.

"I want you naked." I tug at her underwear, making her shuffle as I lower them over her ass.

I couldn't think before. I'd been delirious with rage. Now is no different, but the delirium is from lust. I still can't form a coherent thought. I'm lost in her. Mindless.

She grips the waistband of my boxers, shoving them down my thighs to pool on the floor. Our arms are everywhere. Touching. Tangling. Eager for more.

"There's no going back from this," I warn.

She nods, our noses brushing, lips touching.

"I mean it." I inch away to meet her gaze. "I won't be sated with a quick fuck. If this happens, you're mine and mine alone."

Her lips part on silent words.

"I won't share you, Keira. Not your heart or your mind." I reach a hand between us, sliding my fingers over her mound to her slit. She's wet. Slick and fucking dripping. "Not with anyone. I'll breathe nothing but you, and you'll know nothing but me in return. No other man will exist. Not to touch you. Or to rule over you. Not your uncle. Not your father. And certainly not your fucking brother."

I'm trying to scare her. Not a lot. Just enough to make her see what's at stake.

"Do you understand?" I growl. "When it comes to you, I'm not only after the physical. I'll demand more than you can imagine. More than you're probably willing to give."

This goes beyond sex. It's about claiming her. Bringing her to my side—to my team. Stealing her away from a callous brother and a monster of a father. She doesn't deserve the life they've given her. It's not right that she was born into the wrong family.

"Sebastian..." My name is a plea to stop.

"I want to save you, Keira." I grip her chin. "Please let me fucking save you."

Her lips press together as she blinks up at me with concern. She wants to pull away, and I can't let her. I won't.

"You don't need to live like this. You deserve better."

She shakes her head. "I don't."

"Bullshit."

"This is my world. I'm the same as my brother, Sebastian. I'm no different."

"You don't believe that." I stroke her cheek. Run my fingers along her jaw.

"I do." She brushes her lips over mine. "Maybe I'm worse."

"You're nothing like him." I run the pad of my thumb over

her clit, making her jolt. "You never could be. I wouldn't be here if you were."

I press harder on her sex, making her eyes roll.

"Oh, God." She gasps. "That feels incredible."

"I can make it feel even better if you say yes to me, baby." I slide my fingertips through her slit, teasing her entrance. "Tell me you want this."

She doesn't rush to answer. She takes a moment, prolonging the anticipation that burns a hole through my chest.

"Yes." She shudders. "I want you."

A growl rumbles beneath my sternum. The victory is invigorating to the point of hysteria. She wiggles as I stroke her, a soft hum vibrating from her throat.

"Protection?" I ask.

She shakes her head. "If you're safe, we don't need it."

"You sure?" I'm clean. I trust she's the same. "I won't ask twice."

She cocks a brow. "And I won't repeat myself."

I smirk and grab her ass, yanking her to the edge of the table. There's no space between us. We're chest to chest. Hip to hip.

I grip my cock, running the head back and forth through her slickness. She groans, palming my cheek as she molds our mouths together.

There's never been a better feeling. Not physically. Not emotionally. I'm caught up in her. Tangled beyond the ability to get out unscathed.

This will change everything.

I squeeze my eyes shut, denying the thoughts any room in my mind, and thrust into her. Hard.

She squeals. I'm not convinced it's a pleasure-filled sound. She turns rigid. Her hands gripping my shoulders like a lifeline.

"Keira?" Her pussy is suctioned around me, squeezing my dick within an inch of its life. She's so damn wet. So fucking tight. "Are you okay?"

"It's been a while. That's all." She murmurs in my ear as she clings to my shoulders. "Go slow."

This woman is all about the torture. A leisurely pace is going to be hell to maintain. I grind into her. Retreating. Advancing. The gentle rhythm is a killer against my control.

In slow increments, she relaxes—her claws, her legs, her shoulders. She begins to roll her hips with my motions, undulating against me, kissing my neck, my jaw, my cheek.

She whimpers as I move. Moans.

God, the sound is fucking intoxicating.

"If you keep making noises like that, slow isn't going to be a possibility for much longer."

She chuckles. "Maybe slow is no longer necessary."

She's teasing me. Tormenting.

I don't care. I can't get enough.

She's beautiful. So fucking gorgeous. "What are you doing to me?"

I rock into her. Faster. Harder.

She doesn't protest, but those whimpers continue.

The room fills with the slush of her dripping pussy milking me. The slap of flesh on flesh. She curls a hand around my neck and arches her back, those perfect tits thrusting in my direction.

I lean over, sucking a nipple into my mouth. I nibble. I grate. I lap and lap and fucking lap until she's jolting with pleasure.

"This is crazy." Her thighs tighten. Her cunt grips like a vice. "I want to come."

"Then do it, gorgeous." I leave a trail of kisses along her chest, all the way to her neck, right below her ear. "Let go."

She shakes her head in refusal, and I know it has nothing to do with a lack of want. It's more than that. She can't let down her guard. She won't. Not entirely.

"Trust me," I demand. Or maybe I'm begging. Pleading. "Trust me enough to enjoy this."

She whimpers, not stopping the rhythmic undulation.

I can barely see straight. "Tell me what you need."

"You," she pants. "Just you."

She throws her head back, leaning one hand on the table, all that smooth, flawless skin on display from neck to pussy.

A masterpiece.

A siren.

The perfect weapon that's now in my very own arsenal. "You're a fucking dream, Keira. You're perfect. You're mine."

"Sebastian," she whimpers. "*Sebastian*."

Her pussy contracts around my dick, her orgasm hitting with a feminine moan.

I match her rhythm, slamming home. My balls tighten. The base of my shaft, too. I'm done. It's all over.

I come, clinging to her, kissing her, my fingers gripping deep enough I'm probably leaving imperfections on her beautiful skin.

Nothing else in the world exists while I'm buried inside her. Not the past I'd kill to change. Or the temperamental present. And especially not the rocky future headed our way.

It's just us.

Me and her.

And I wish it could stay this way.

"I..." She sighs, her movements slowing. "I..."

"You?" I pull back, placing a kiss on her forehead as I retreat. "Can't finish a sentence because I rocked your fucking world?"

She grins and slumps forward, draping herself over me as she pants. "I don't know why I expected something other than cocky humor at a time like this."

I bury my face in her hair. "I'm always willing to give you all the cock-y you need."

She shoves me away, scoffing through her laughter. "I need to clean up."

I nod, but my hands refuse to give her up.

"Which means you're going to have to move so I can get to the bathroom." She beams up at me, her eyes dazzling, her face more mesmerizing than words can describe.

I keep nodding. "I will. Just not ready to let go of you yet."

The grin turns shy. Almost embarrassed.

Shit.

I'm done for.

She fucking owns me.

"You said it's been a while." I run my fingers through her hair, swiping the stray strands behind her ear as I give in to curiosity. "How long?"

Her cheeks darken with the cutest blush. "Long enough that I needed time to adjust."

Yeah, I got that part. I'd initially hurt her, and I feel like a fucking chump for doing it. But I'm still confused.

"What's with the abstinence?" It doesn't make sense. She's phenomenal. Fucking captivating. Men would fall to their knees to please her. "You don't like sex?"

She sobers, the glaze of lust blinking from her eyes. "It comes down to trust, Sebastian. Everything does." She places her palm on my chest, gently pushing. "Let me clean up."

I backtrack, allowing her to scoot from the table and hustle into the hall.

While she's gone, I pull on my boxers and knit my fingers behind the back of my head as reality jackhammers its way into my skull.

Tonight is a game changer.

This thing with Keira will affect my relationship with Hunter. With Torian. And I can't forget Anissa, too.

Everything will shift, and I can only hope it's for the best, because my life doesn't have room for any more wrong turns.

I go in search of the laundry to find my clothes, giving her a few minutes alone. I don't find anything in the washing machine, so I check the dryer, the warmth still radiating from the clothes as I pull out my dress shirt.

The material is clean, crisp, and scented like a florist as I shove my arm into the sleeve and proceed to get my hand stuck at the cuff.

"What the fuck?" I jab my arm harder, getting my fist through the restriction and deal with the same exact issue with the other arm.

She shrank my shirt.

My only fucking shirt.

The cuffs ride up my forearms, tight as sutures. And I can only clasp the bottom three buttons across my stomach.

"Perfect." I chuckle. "Fucking perfect."

Keira sure as shit wasn't joking about her lack of laundry skills.

I don't even bother grabbing my pants. They're a problem I'll have to deal with tomorrow. Instead, I scramble through the dryer and pull out something for her in the hopes the material will be just as tight and revealing.

I grab a see-through pair of panties and a silken slip of nightwear, then stalk my ass back down the hall.

When I don't find her in the living area, I divert my trek to the bathroom, and lean my shoulder against the door frame to find her facing the mirror, eyes blank, mouth lax.

She's off with the fairies, glancing into space.

"I'd stare too if I had a reflection like yours," I taunt.

Her lips quirk as she blinks to attention and turns to me. "Sure you would."

I hand over her clothes and watch as she slips them on too easily. Not a glimpse of fucking shrinkage in sight while she covers her tempting body. If anything, the black nightdress swims around her waist.

"What happened to your shirt?" She eyes me up and down.

"*You* happened." I raise my arms to show the new tight fit. "I can't even clasp the top buttons."

"You look..." She covers her mouth with a hand, but it doesn't hide the laughter in her eyes.

"Fucking ridiculous?" I ask.

She snickers. "Kinda."

"Hey. Not nice." I grab her, pulling her into me as I lean my ass against the vanity. "What are you still doing hiding in here, anyway?"

She drags her gaze from mine and plays with my collar. "Clearing my head."

"What are you thinking about this time?"

"Everything and nothing." Her fingers graze the front of

103

my shirt, her palms splaying across my pecs. "I want to trust you, Sebastian."

Wants to—meaning she currently doesn't.

I clench my jaw, fighting frustration.

"Despite what you might think, it's not easy for me to let people in. But I'm trying." She sucks in a deep breath and lets it out in a sigh. "I haven't had sex in years. *Many* years."

I'd make a joke if it wasn't for her somber tone. An influx of trepidation fills the room, putting me on edge. "There's nothing wrong with that."

"And I've only been with two men. Three including you."

I nod and struggle not to shudder under the uncomfortable prickle at the back of my neck. "I appreciate you telling me."

"That's not all." Her eyes meet mine, the ocean blue stormy and turbulent. "My first sexual experience wasn't consensual."

11

DECKER

My blood turns to fire, the burn settling into my bones. "You were..."

She nods. "It's okay. You don't need to say it."

There's no fragility in her voice. She's strong. Far stronger than I am at hearing the admission.

I shake my head, still unable to finish my sentence. I can't even say the fucking word. All I can do is pull her closer and cling tight.

"Sebastian, really, it's all right." She hugs me back, comforting me when it should be the other way around. "It happened a long time ago."

"When?"

"I was a child. Barely fourteen."

"*Fuck.*" The curse comes out in a rasp.

How did I miss this information when I've dug into every aspect of her life?

"Don't worry. I've come to terms with my mistakes. I refuse to let it affect me anymore."

"*Your* mistakes?" I inch her away, holding her at arm's length so I can meet her gaze. "How could you blame yourself for something like this? You were a fucking kid."

"I wasn't to blame, no. But I wasn't free from fault either. I should've been more careful." She shrugs. "I trusted someone I didn't truly know."

The same way I've been pressuring her to trust me.

Jesus. Fuck.

Guilt pummels me.

I've pushed. I've manipulated. I've instigated a million different tactics to get what I want, not knowing what I was truly asking for.

"That's why I'm telling you," she adds. "Not because I want you to pity me. Or because I need to justify my short list of lovers. I want you to know why it's difficult for me to open up."

"I understand." I'm an asshole. The biggest fucking asshole. "You don't have to say another word."

I've made her feel obliged to cut herself open and bleed her secrets, all because I demanded her trust.

"Do you want to take this out into the living room?" I slide along the vanity, inching toward the door as I grab her hand. "Have you eaten dinner? You must be hungry. Let me warm up the lasagna for you."

She grips my fingers, pulling me back. "Please don't get weird on me now. I'm not fragile."

"I'm not being weird." I attempt a smile. "And I sure as hell know you're tough as nails."

"Good." She closes in, sauntering by me in her silken nightdress. "Because I'd have to tie you to a bed and torture you for days if you started treating me like glass."

"Wait. That bed torture thing is an option?" I fake the joke, hoping it comes out lighthearted when my chest weighs more than a ton.

She chuckles. "Not a good one, no."

"To you, maybe." I follow her into the hall and pretend I'm not holding onto her emotional baggage tighter than she is. I can't quit picturing what she must have gone through as I reheat her meal.

I struggle to stop the brutal thoughts of a violated young girl as she eats.

My sadistic imagination runs wild with the carnage, stretching out the silence into long uncomfortable minutes.

"You're going to have to suck it up," she mutters around a bite of lasagna. "Stop thinking about it."

"I'm not."

"*Sure.*" She rolls her eyes. "I'm not the person you're picturing, Sebastian. I haven't been weakened by it. I'm stronger."

I smile despite my doubts.

But she *is* strong.

I *do* know that.

I just hate that some low-life piece of shit forced her to be that way. "I wasn't thinking—"

"And I like sex," she adds.

I give her a half-hearted smile and lean forward, stretching my arm across the table to brush her wrist. "I learned that firsthand, remember?"

Her lips quirk. "I remember."

I try to hold onto the companionable mood. I cling and fucking cling, but it drifts, being snatched away by more tumultuous thoughts.

She sighs. "What part of this is eating away at you?"

I don't want to ask. Well, I do, but even a dumb fuck like me knows it's inappropriate.

"Just ask, Sebastian."

"Okay." I pull my arm back and sit up straight. "You said you've come to terms with what happened. And that you enjoy sex, but you've only slept with one other guy..."

Her actions don't really gel with the story.

"There are reasons for my abstinence."

"Do most of them revolve around having a psychotic brother?"

She presses her lips tight, containing a laugh. "No, not a lot. The lack of talent swimming in my family's social circles is actually the biggest reason. Then there's the risk of sleeping with someone who is only trying to get close to Cole. Along with the whole drug thing, too."

"Drug thing?"

She gives a barely-there nod. "Despite my family's

association with narcotics, I don't approve of using, have never used myself, and I don't want to be with anyone who does."

"How do you know I don't fall into that category?"

She gives me a coy smile. "You're not the only one who's been paying attention."

I should be concerned. Instead, I'm turned on as all fuck. "You've been spying on me, sunshine?"

"I wouldn't call it that." She pushes from her chair and takes the dirty plate to the sink. "I've just noticed you. A lot."

I smirk.

"Don't turn all cocky on me again. I've been doing my due diligence, that's all."

I release an exaggerated sigh. "Don't treat you like glass. Don't get cocky. Don't shove my dick up your ass. Jeez, Keira, you're a bossy little thing."

Her cheeks darken, and those lips keep twitching in mirth. "I'm going to pretend you didn't say that." She walks around the kitchen and heads toward the sofa. "Come watch television with me for a while."

I oblige, even though the last thing I want to do is stare at anything other than her. The next few hours are spent on the corner of the sofa, her head on my lap, my hands in her hair, as a mindless sitcom plays on the screen.

This time I play with the delicate strands without remorse. I drag my fingers through the lengths and enjoy the calm. I could easily kid myself into believing I have a sweet and innocent woman resting against me. That we could have a normal life with a normal outlook for the future.

But none of that is true.

We're all guilty of a long list of crimes. And the reality of the situation is that I've just taken a giant leap closer to having a clip unloaded in my skull because I slept with Torian's sister.

Hopefully I'm lucky enough not to see the bullet coming.

"I know you're probably still wide awake after your fifteen-hour nap this afternoon," she sits up and turns to face me, "but I'm wrecked. I'm going to take a shower and crawl into bed. Where do you plan on sleeping?"

"On you." I grin. "Sorry, I meant in bed beside you."

"Sure you did." Her lips curve, but there's little flirtation, no excitement. The mood between us is different, her playful banter replaced with committed intent.

There's no backing out now.

We're a thing. Together. And yes, that's daunting as fuck.

"Let me tidy up out here, and I'll meet you in the bedroom soon." I kiss her temple, and we both push to our feet. "Enjoy the shower."

She pads away, leaving me to do a full interior check of the house. I test the windows and doors, making sure they're all secure before I start cleaning the dirty dishes in the sink.

What I should be doing is contacting Hunter, calling Anissa, even telling Torian about the cell Keira found to make sure it's untraceable. But I'm not ready to kill this buzz just yet.

External influences will only drag us apart. I need to establish myself in her life before that happens.

Once the kitchen is tidy, I turn off the television and the lights, take a quick detour to the main bathroom to brush my teeth, then make my way to the bedroom. The bedside lamp casts a dull glow over the master bed. The water echoes through the pipes in the adjoining bathroom.

I contemplate joining her, bathing her, salivating over the sight of her body covered in rivulets of water.

And I would, if only it didn't feel like I was pushing my luck.

I have to take this slow. Do things right. Make sure she's comfortable.

I pull back the bed covers and shuck my kiddie-sized shirt, letting it fall to the floor.

As the water turns off, I climb into bed and wait with my hands behind my head on the pillow until she walks back into the room.

"How was your shower?"

"Lonely." She gives me a pointed look before flicking off the lamp and crawling onto the other side of the mattress.

She nestles into me, allowing me to wrap my arm behind her neck as she huddles close, her warmth sinking under my skin. The smell of soap fills my lungs. The itch of temptation twitches through my fingers.

I haven't had beauty in my life for a long time. Only darkness. Hatred and punishment.

I've lived to work, and worked to live. Nothing else has mattered.

Until now.

Until Keira.

"Are you tired?" she asks.

"Not really. But it doesn't matter. I don't mind lying here with you."

She stretches her arm over my chest, her hand resting against my ribs. "What are we going to do tomorrow?"

I shrug. "Hunter will meet up with us at some point, and I need to get some clothes. If you're up to it, I think we should stock up on supplies so we don't have to leave the house again."

She nods. "Okay. That sounds good to me."

"Is there anything you want to do?"

She hugs me tighter. "I need to call Layla. But apart from that, I'm happy just to spend time with you. I want to get to know you better. I want to learn who you are."

No, she doesn't.

She only wants to get to know the playful Sebastian. The persona. If she knew the parts of me I keep hidden she wouldn't be nestled this close.

"Sebastian?"

"Mmm?"

"Thank you for everything today."

For someone entirely badass, she has a tendency of surprising me with her sweet as nectar routine. "Are you referring to me pulling a gun on you in the back yard? Or when I berated you in the car for stripping?"

She huffs out a barely audible chuckle. "I'm talking about you listening when I needed you to."

"You don't have to keep thanking me. You should know by now that I'd do anything for you."

"It's starting to sink in." She pauses, long enough to make me feel like a sappy chump. "I don't open up to many people.

It was nice to have someone to confide in. It's as though a weight has been lifted."

My pulse increases.

This, right here, is everything I've been waiting for since the first night I set her in my sights. I've wanted to carry her burdens. To be her confidant.

"You feel like home, Sebastian," she whispers. "I've never felt this way before."

I tug her closer. "It's the same for me."

Her fingers circle over my skin, forming an intricate pattern. "There's something else I want you to know." Her tone holds the same ominous ring from our earlier conversation. This time I refuse to let it spook me.

"You can tell me anything."

She moves her hand to my chest, her palm resting directly above my heart. "You know how my father hasn't shown his face around here in a long time?"

"Yeah." I know. I've been watching. Everyone has. The cops, the Feds, the DEA. "He's somewhere in the Greek Islands contemplating retirement, right?"

"No."

The sharp denial piques my interest.

I focus on my breathing, making sure it doesn't betray my rampant curiosity. News on Luther Torian is a goldmine. One that many people would kill to gain access to. Including me. But unlike the secret she divulged earlier, I'm probably not the best person to spill Luther gossip to.

If she isn't comfortable with the way I taunt Cole, there's a high probability she won't appreciate me hating on her father.

"He's gone, Sebastian."

"Gone?" I let the question hang. "What does that mean?"

"He's not coming back. He's dead."

I don't react. I don't fucking move.

She isn't making any sense. A man like Luther Torian doesn't simply die without the whole world noticing.

Her world. *Our* world.

"Sebastian?"

Shit. "I don't know what to say."

I can't give her my sympathies, because I don't have any. Not a single one. Not for a sick motherfucker like her father. The feelings currently slamming into me aren't anything she would want to hear about.

She sits up, the delicate skin of her shoulders glowing red from the bedside clock. I'm not sure what the hell is going on, but something isn't right. She shouldn't be blurting out this information. Not to me. Not to anyone.

Not unless I've finally wormed my way under her beautiful skin.

"I appreciate you telling me." I reach out, strumming my fingers over her nightdress. "But why? Try as I might, you know I'm horrible at the whole comfort thing. I don't have the first clue of what to do when it comes to other people's grief."

"I don't need your comfort. I suppose I'm finally realizing that every moment we've shared has revolved around you being my warrior. It started the first night we met and hasn't stopped since. When I need protection, you're always the provider. And right now, I need that protection more than ever." She glances over her shoulder, her shadowed eyes meeting mine. "My family is in a really bad position, and Cole continues to keep me in the dark with all his plans. I don't know who else to count on."

Victory rushes through my veins. It's fucking pathetic at a time like this, but extracting her from the clutches of her psychotic family has always been my aim. At least as far as she's concerned.

And here she is doing it all on her own.

She's breaking the tight leash her brother chained around her neck.

She's starting to take drastic actions to revolt.

Praise the fucking Lord.

"Tell me what to do, Sebastian."

I fight to focus on her instead of the celebratory dance running riot in my head. "It's okay." I tug her down, reclaiming her at my side. "I'm not going to let anything happen to you. I'll keep you safe."

"Do you really believe that? Everything is such a mess at

the moment."

"It will get better. I promise."

Problem is, it's going to get a whole lot worse before that rainbow beams down its pot of gold.

Once Luther's death is broadcasted to Torian's enemies, we're all in trouble—Hunter, Sarah, and every other son of a bitch who works for Cole.

There will be a fight for power. A struggle with anyone who wants to take over the multi-million-dollar drug trade in Oregon, along with the innumerable illegal contracts that bring a huge amount of money to the family.

We're all going to have a target on our backs.

A fucking bullseye.

"I don't want you to worry about it anymore, okay?" I raise my hand to her hair. "I'll figure something out. I always do."

She nods, nuzzling her nose against my ribs. "I appreciate you, Sebastian."

"I know." I also know she would quickly change her mind if she knew the extent of my gratitude over karma finally catching up with her old man.

I'd seriously dance a jig on that fucker's grave.

Luther Torian used to be a bastard of brutality. Even Hunter was scared of the son of a bitch who made Cole look like a saint.

And now he's gone. He slipped quietly into the afterlife while the rest of the world remains scared despite his lack of existence.

Well played, Torians. Well played.

I hold Keira close and battle the questions demanding to be answered. I need to know everything. Every fucking thing. When did it happen? How? Why? Who?

But I can't ask. Not yet. I need to wait until the dust settles. Drilling her for information will only make her uneasy.

So I'm forced to lie here in silence as her breathing descends into smooth, rhythmic inhales. Her head would be a heavy place right now, filled with death, destruction, and fear. Maybe it always has been. God knows how long she's had to bottle a lifetime worth of secrets.

And one day I'll have them all. It's only a matter of time and patience.

Patience—the one trait I've never had.

I roll away from her, needing distance to help lessen the hunger for answers. Only the space between us doesn't relieve my appetite. I throw back the covers, slide from bed, and grab my cell from the pocket of my shirt on the floor.

I don't know what to do.

Keeping this information bottled feels like I'm handling a nuclear bomb.

Hunter and Sarah are sitting ducks if I keep this news to myself. Anyone back in Portland is in the firing line. Including Layla and Stella. Doesn't Cole see that?

But I can't betray Keira. Not when she finally let me in. She gave me her body. Her secrets. Her trust.

Jesus Christ. I'm damned if I do and fucked sideways if I don't.

Decisions, decisions.

I clench my teeth hard enough for my jaw to ache and stalk for the back of the house. I have to do something. I can't stand here like a dumb fuck who's too chicken shit to make a decision.

I won't.

To hell with that.

I remove the cell case and retrieve the second sim hidden in the secret compartment. I shove out the back door, being hit with the cold night air as I start dialing.

I'm not going to tell anyone about Luther. Not yet. But I can take steps to make things right between me and Keira.

"Is everything okay?" Anissa says in greeting.

My pulse increases, building into a deep throb in my ears. I question what I'm about to say. What I'm about to do.

"Decker?"

"Yeah. I'm here." I wince and run a hand through my hair. "We're done, Niss. It's over."

"What? Why?" Her voice hardens. "What's going on?"

"I don't need you anymore. Don't contact me again."

12

DECKER

I'M STARING AT THE SUNRISE CREEPING OVER THE ceiling, hands behind my head, when Keira starts to stir beside me.

I didn't sleep, and it wasn't from lack of trying.

It took forever for me to come to terms with Luther's death. I didn't believe it. Didn't want to. Then things started to make perfect sense—the drive-by, Richard's assassination attempt, Cole's demand for Keira to be taken out of town.

Someone else already knows.

The power struggle has started.

Which is fucking great. I signed on for a lot of fucked up shit when I began working for this family, but helping them win a war isn't one of them.

Keira's long, labored breaths fade and she groans as she snuggles closer. "Good morning."

"Morning."

I need to convince her to leave. To walk the fuck away from this life. This family.

Her brother will be too busy keeping himself alive to track us down. At least to start off with. He'll have assholes from every direction attempting to kick him from his power pedestal. And by the time he does have the freedom to play hide-and-seek, we'll be long gone.

It will take months, if not years, to re-assert control, if he's even capable of holding onto it.

This is the perfect time to get out. To move on. To start over.

"How long have you been awake?" she murmurs. "You should've nudged me."

I couldn't have woken her even if I wanted to, probably not if my life depended on it. She'd been too peaceful. Too tempting with the covers below her waist, her cleavage gaping from her nightdress.

"I didn't sleep much. I guess I didn't need to after yesterday."

She sits and runs a hand through her hair. "You must be starving. Give me a few minutes to freshen up, then we can go out for breakfast."

"There's no rush. I still need to get ready and call Hunter to see when he's arriving."

I've been thinking about calling him ever since I figured out the truth. I should've gotten in contact hours ago. As soon as I heard the news of the century.

Instead, I lay here staring at the same spot on the ceiling, torturing myself at the thought of betraying Keira. It's too late now, though. My mind is made up. Telling Hunter isn't betrayal. It's taking the first step in an effort to keep her shielded from the violence about to rain down on us.

"I won't be long." She throws back the sheet and slides from the mattress, her seductive stride eating up the distance to the bathroom before she closes the door behind her.

I wait until the water turns on, then drag my ass from bed. Like last night, I walk into the back yard and connect the call in privacy.

"Now's not a great time," he greets.

"It's not great here either. But what I'm going to tell you can't wait."

"*Jesus*. Please tell me you didn't sleep with her."

"That's not why I'm calling."

"But you're not denying it either," he snarls. "*Fuck*, Deck. One day you're going to have to stop being the wild card and actually take responsibility. I swear to God, Torian will bend you over and fuck you so hard you're tasting dick for months."

"As delightful as that sounds, it's not why I called." I pinch the bridge of my nose and close my eyes. Maybe if I squeeze hard enough I'll have an aneurism and not have to deal with this shit. "Like I said, I've got news."

There's a pause, the briefest silent acknowledgement of the seriousness I'm about to share. "Go on, then," he grates. "Tell me."

"Keira and I got to talking last night, and she dropped a bomb I wasn't expecting. It's big, Hunt. Real big."

"Do you want me to play Twenty-Questions, or are you planning on spitting it the fuck out?"

I drop my arm to my side and stare across the open expanse of the yard. There's no life out here. No vibrancy. No feeling.

It could be considered beautiful with its sculpted statues and manicured gardens, but the property is devoid of warmth. Just like I've come to expect from anything the Torian name touches. Anything except the gorgeous woman waiting inside. "Luther is dead."

Silence.

Hunter doesn't respond.

Not in seconds. Not for long moments. Not even when I lower the cell to make sure the call is still connected. "Hunt?"

"I heard," he growls. "And Keira just gave you this information out of the blue?"

"Yeah. She's starting to trust me."

"Where are you?"

"Still at the safe house. We're about to head out for a bite to eat, but I'm not sure what the fuck I should do about this. You realize what it means, right? We're caught in the middle of a power struggle."

"Who have you told?"

"Nobody."

There's another pause. The silence of thick, punishing contemplation. "We can't discuss this over the phone. I'm coming to you. I'll call when I'm close."

"You're still bringing a laptop, right?"

"Yeah." There's a rustle in the background. A jangle of keys. "I picked one up yesterday."

"You didn't happen to buy a phone charger, too, did you? My cell is going to die if it doesn't get some juice soon."

"I'll bring one of my spares."

The line disconnects, leaving me with more punishing silence.

Remorse hits harder than I anticipate. And I'd expected that fucker to be punishing.

I don't know how I'm supposed to face Keira now. Do I tell her? Should I explain?

No, I can't.

She's the type to run first and ask questions later, which will only put her in more danger.

My betrayal has to remain a secret for now.

Hunter will keep his mouth shut. I don't doubt him in the slightest. And he *had* to be informed. I couldn't live with his blood on my hands. There's enough of that shit tainting my soul already.

The swish of an opening door hits my ears, and I turn to find Keira stepping onto the deck. The guilt increases with the soft smile she gives me. There's trust in those eyes, the gentle affection clawing me from the inside out.

Fuck.

She's a fucking sight, too. Her hair is braided over one shoulder. A white cardigan hangs loose on her shoulders, partially covering the top of her light blue sundress. The style is feminine. Laid back. Not a hint of filthy rich, drug-lord's daughter in sight.

"Are you ready to leave?" she asks.

"Let me take a quick shower." I head toward her, drowning in the need to drag her to some place far, far away from this bullshit. "Hunter is on his way. Hopefully he'll meet us in town while we're still eating breakfast. I don't want to hang around in public any longer than necessary."

"We can always bring the food back to the house. He could meet us here."

"No. He doesn't need to know the location of this place."

She frowns. "You'd keep that from him?"

"It's not my secret to tell." The words burn my throat. I'm pretending my white-knight armor is shining when it's tarnished as fuck.

Her eyes turn soft as she blinks back at me in unwarranted appreciation. "You're a good man, Sebastian."

Jesus.

I scoff. "Far from it, angel."

Maybe I was at one time. Back when life was simple and contracted killings were in the movies, not my weekly schedule.

"It's either jokes or deflected compliments," she muses, inching toward me to wrap her arms around my waist. "Is that a technique to hide the real you?"

I fight to keep my muscles relaxed. "Yeah. I guess." I kiss her forehead. "Deep down, I'm a sensitive guy who loves to write poetry and rescue injured wildlife."

She arches a brow.

"And knitting," I add. "I love knitting."

She nudges me in the ribs. "Great. More jokes."

I lean in and kiss her lips, tasting the mint from her toothpaste. "I'll never stop joking around when the end result is one of your smiles."

Her brow peaks higher. "Another joke?"

"No. That one was cheesy honesty." I grab her around the waist and carry her into the house, leading her to the sofa. "What's the obsession with getting in my head?"

"There's no obsession. Just curiosity."

I collapse onto the cushions and drag her down with me. I could get through a few more hours without food if it meant keeping her here. On top of me. Skin to skin. "Well, I'm curious about getting your clothes off."

She straddles my waist and runs her hands around my neck. "You know I'm starving, right?"

"I've got something that can sate your appetite."

Her lips tweak. "Your dick isn't going to stop my stomach from grumbling."

I lean into her, brushing the growing stubble along my jaw against her cheek. "Obviously, you haven't been introduced to oral."

She breaks out in a fit of laughter—eyes bright, cheeks high, skin flushed.

Pure beauty.

"I haven't been introduced, Sebastian." She draws out my name, that sultry mouth working around the syllables like a fucking wet dream. "But I know what it is."

I can picture her tongue grazing along my shaft, her saliva covering me from base to tip. I raise a hand and brush my thumb over her lower lip, tracing a path down her throat.

She will gag as she gets used to my size, her eyes will water. Her mouth, too.

I'll fucking love it.

"You're serious." She holds my gaze, all that bubbling humor vanishing as lust takes its place. "You want me to do this now?"

"No." I need to shower. Brush my teeth. Gain restraint. "I'll hold onto that fantasy for a little while longer."

I scoop her up and drop her onto the far side of the sofa, her back falling against the cushioned arm rest. "Take off your underwear."

"*What?*" She scrambles to sit up straight. "You just said—"

"I said I don't want *you* to do anything. I didn't say anything about me." I lift the bottom of her dress, taking in the sight of white lace panties. "Get them off."

"Sebastian..." Her eyes are frantic. A mix of anxious anticipation and nervous excitement.

"*Off*, Keira." Fuck it. I grab the waistband and tug them down myself. "I'm fucking starving."

I want her. The taste. The touch. The sound.

I'm dying to get between her legs.

I'm dying for the distraction, too.

She shimmies as I tug at the material, dragging them along her calves, over her ankles, to drop them to the floor.

"Spread your legs," I demand.

Her shoulders straighten. She grows rigid.

Shit. I need to go slow with her. Be fucking gentle.

I place my hands on her knees, exposing her slowly. "I'm going to taste you, Keira."

"I already got that part," she teases. "I just want to know what's taking so long."

I smirk, giving her a game-on look she won't forget in a while. I sink my face between those legs, wrapping my arms around her thighs to position her right where I need her.

She smells of soap, the fucking purity smothering the scent of arousal. But I'll make sure that doesn't last long.

I rake my teeth across her mound, grazing sensitive skin as I hold her gaze.

"I'm not going to break," she whispers.

"You wouldn't say that if you knew what I'm capable of."

My first lick is light. Gentle. I flick her clit and revel in the jolt of her hips. It's a prelude. The appetizer. I keep swiping the bundle of nerves. Back and forth. Slow and patient.

Her jolts continue, settling into a roll of hips to meet every brush of tongue, as she slides a hand through my hair. It's a request. A silent demand for more.

I don't need to be told twice.

I inch lower, my dick jolting as I part her folds and taste her arousal. There's nothing but sweet bliss. Pure euphoria.

She grips my hair, fucking wrenches it between tight fingers.

I lick harder, faster, delving deep.

She whimpers. Moans. The noise fills my ears and sinks into my soul.

I unwrap an arm from around her thigh and cup her ass, using my thumb to penetrate her. The sound of her pleasure increases. Everything does. The need. The rush.

I pulse, building a punishing rhythm as I suck on her clit. I crave her pleasure, if only to sate my guilt. I can't stand the thought of her hating me.

"Deeper," she demands, her thighs tightening around my head.

I close my eyes and fight against blowing in my pants like a fucking kid.

"Oh, God." Her back arches and that tight pussy gets even tighter as she milks my thumb with her orgasm.

Her juices cover my face, and those soft muffled moans continue to torment me in the sweetest possible way until her orgasm diminishes and she's left sated and lax.

I'm no longer going to question how the daughter of someone heinous can be so fucking perfect. She just is. That's all there is to it. I can't get her out of my head. I never could. And I'm not going to fight it anymore.

I retreat and wipe a hand over my mouth.

Her thighs are red from the graze of my stubble. Her pussy glistens, fucking beckoning me.

"Sebastian..." She stares at me, her breathing rushed, her eyes playful. "That was..."

"The start of an obsession," I finish for her. "A day won't go by without me wanting to repeat that."

She lowers her dress, covering her brilliance. "You'll have to teach me how to return the favor."

My dick jolts, the imminent orgasm still threatening to blow. "One day." When she's ready and I've got a lick of restraint to stop me from choking her with my dick. "I'm going to take a shower."

"Do you want me to join you?"

"Not today, jelly bean."

She winces, alerting me to the unintentional rejection.

I stand, my cock poking proud from beneath my boxers. "Babe, I'm so fucking turned on I'm seconds from blowing."

"And?"

"And it's not going to be pretty. If I had you right now, it would be hard and fast and rough. You don't want that. Not yet." I reach out, brushing my fingers over her flushed cheek. "I'll be back soon."

She nods. "Okay."

ONE JERK-OFF SHOWER SESSION LATER, I'M DRESSED IN MY kiddie shirt and driving out of the property gates.

Everything is different from yesterday—my relationship with Keira, my plans for the future, my perspective.

Even my concentration is shot to shit.

I turn from one street to the next, picturing the spread thighs of the woman beside me instead of focusing on traffic. She's all I see. All I feel.

It's a problem. A fucking great problem.

I can't remember ever being this attracted to a woman. This infatuated. It's exhilarating. And disturbing. I guess I should put a lid on it for a while.

I should...If only I knew how.

This thing between us is an avalanche. The freefall. The build of power. The upcoming carnage.

I let out a deep breath and flick a glance to the rear-view mirror. A white car follows us. One I hadn't noticed approaching. Great, I've driven miles without conscious thought of anything but the woman beside me.

I'm getting sloppy. Fucking careless.

I force my attention back on the road and pull myself out of auto-pilot. Today is going to be filled with tough decisions. This meeting with Hunt needs my full attention. I have to focus.

I check the rear-view again, this time finding the white car riding my ass. I narrow my gaze, my stomach hollowing as the vehicle becomes familiar. An even more familiar woman sits behind the wheel.

Fuck.

Anissa found me.

Even worse is the thought of how she did it. Did she hack my cell? Or was she always watching?

Keira touches my arm, and I jolt from the unexpected connection.

"Sebastian?" Her brows pinch in concern. "What's wrong?"

"Nothing." I bite back the growl in my voice and return my attention to the mirror. "Just concentrating on the road, that's all."

I flick my indicator, preparing to turn off the highway and

into the small town. My tail follows, inching the nose of her car closer to my bumper.

She wants to cause trouble. *Big* trouble. And I'm not sure I know how to stop her.

"Is someone following us?" Keira swivels in her seat to look out the back window. "Answer me."

I grind my molars. "Yeah. We've got a tail."

A tail we won't outrun. Not easily. Or without attracting attention. I'm going to have to talk to Anissa. She's not going to leave me alone until I face her.

"What do we do? Can we outrun them?"

"No. It's okay. I know who it is."

She keeps her focus out the back window. "It's a woman."

"Yes," I mutter the confirmation.

"Is she a friend of yours?"

"No."

"Then how did she know where to find us?" Anger creeps into her voice.

"I don't fucking know, which obviously isn't good. I have to pull over." I straddle my attention between the road in front and the bitch behind as I drive into the main street of town. "I need you to stay in the car. Don't get out. Don't even look through the back window. It's best if you remain out of sight, keep your belt on, and be ready for us to leave as soon as I get back."

"Am I in danger?"

Good question. "I don't fucking know." I hold her gaze for long seconds, then return my attention to the road. "I'm not going to let anything happen to you. Just follow my instructions and you'll be fine."

I indicate. Anissa copies.

I pull to the curb. She follows.

I cut the engine, unfasten my belt, and open the door as my pulse pounds in my ears. "Remember what I said. Don't move. I need you to lay low until I get back."

She nods. "I will."

I slide from my seat, but Keira reaches across the car interior and grabs my wrist.

124

"Wait," she pleads. "Please be careful." Her eyes implore me more than her words, the glassy blue depths hitting me in the feels.

I fake a grin. "You know my motto—it's better to be safe than stupid."

She winces. "Don't joke at a time like this. I'm worried about you."

It's not me she needs to worry about. "I've got this under control."

I pat her hand then climb from the car, all humor vanishing as I shut the door and turn to find Anissa leaning against the side of the white SUV.

I storm ahead, waiting until I reach her hood before I snarl, "What the fuck are you doing here?"

She smiles, the curve of lips sinister. "Hey, lover. How are you?"

I scan the sidewalk, not appreciating the audience. "Why are you here?"

She crosses her feet at the ankles, her arms over her chest. "Your call was out of character. I was hoping you woke up and realized you made a mistake."

"There's no mistake. I'm done. You need to back off."

Her smile doesn't falter. "That's not how this works." She pushes from the car and closes the space between us.

I'm tempted to back away. Only because I don't want her close enough to sink her nails in. But I refuse to retreat.

"You promised to stick by me," she purrs. "You can't leave now."

I don't mistake her statement for anything other than the threat it is.

"We had a mutually beneficial agreement." I measure my tone, refusing to lose my cool. "And your part of the deal is no longer relevant. So, like I said, we're done."

"We're not done until I say we are." She leans close, whispering in my ear. "I call the shots here."

I turn my head to face her, those venomous lips bare inches from mine. "Like hell you do."

"Oh, come on. Don't be like that. Where's that sweet

Decker I know? The one who always used to say my name with reverence."

My nostrils flare. "Quit playing games."

"I'm not." Her smile widens, a tiny dimple peeking out. "But make a woman happy and say my name one last time."

I glare. "Not gonna happen."

"Say it or I go over there and introduce myself to your travel companion."

Fucking bitch.

I want to hurt her. Strangle her. If I was Torian, she'd already be dead.

"Anissa," I grate.

She chuckles. "You've gotta say all of it, sweetie. My first name. My last. And don't forget the title."

My nostrils flare as I clench my fists. "You're fucking with the wrong person."

"Funny, I was thinking the same thing about you." Her smile tightens and her eyes blaze in fury. "Now address me properly."

My pulse pounds beneath tightening ribs as I utter the words that make my stomach turn. "Special Agent Anissa Fox."

Her flirty smile falls back into place. "Good boy. Now make sure you keep repeating my name in your head every time you think about backing out on our fucking agreement."

"There is no agreement," I snarl.

"Because you think Luther is dead, right? That's the only assumption I could make from your 'I don't need you anymore' comment."

I fight a fucking war inside myself, unsure whether to answer her or make more threats of my own. "It doesn't matter. I'm out."

"Oh, honey, it matters. You know it does." She inches closer, narrowing her gaze to scrutinize my expression. "Where did you get the information?"

I press my lips into a tight line, scowling out my refusal to answer.

"I thought you were smarter than that, Deck. I know very

few people who would cut ties before determining fact from fiction."

"As far as I'm concerned, the news is concrete."

She raises her brows. "Yet in the last five hours, not one of my sources could confirm a damn thing."

My palms sweat with the need to do something, *anything*, to shut her up.

"You wanted to take them down," she snips. "*You* came to me for help, remember?"

"And now I've got what I wanted. Richard is out. Luther is dead. The fairytale lives on. Just as soon as you get out of my fucking face."

She narrows her eyes. "They've messed with you, haven't they? She got in your head. She worked you over."

"No." I lean close, unable to control my breathing. I'm livid. Furious. "*I* worked *her* over. How else do you think I got the fucking information, you conniving bitch?"

"You think this is me being a bitch?" She snickers. "Sweetie, I'm only doing my job, and to be honest, I'm just getting started."

She pulls a cell from her jeans pocket and taps the screen, opening icons and folders. "If you bail on me and Luther isn't dead, I'll make sure not only you get named as an informant, but your best buddy, too."

She holds up the device, showing me a picture of Hunter beside a guy I don't recognize. She flicks through more images, displaying different locations with various people, all of them interacting with Hunt in some way.

"The men in these pictures are undercover agents," she explains. "I spent months setting up these scenarios, ensuring we had the necessary leverage to tie him to us. All it took was a bump to the shoulder, a dropped piece of paper or a wallet. Anything at all, really, to make the shot look like an exchange of information."

I stare at the collection, my heart pounding, my blood boiling. The images are damning. Cole won't waste a second contemplating their legitimacy.

"I'm sorry, Decker, but you're too valuable to simply walk

away. If you leave, I'll make sure your friend gets exposed as a traitor." She keeps flicking the screen, moving to similar pictures with Sarah. "His fiancée, too."

I see red, my vision narrowing into spiteful slits. "You're going to get innocent people killed."

"Innocent? Really? That's a stretch."

I react without thought, grabbing my gun from my waistband and stepping close as I ram it under her chin.

I shouldn't be surprised she doesn't respond in shock or fear. Instead, she keeps that smile in place like the fucking psychotic bitch I know her to be.

She's sweet to smell. Sweet to touch. And I know from experience, she's sweet to taste, too. But everything else about this woman is bitter. Tainted. Evil. She does a lot of wrong things for a person who is supposed to be on the right side of the law.

"Don't mess with me." I get in her face. "What you're doing is illegal. You can't fucking manipulate me."

"I already have." She maintains her grin. If anything, she appears empowered by my weapon.

It sickening.

"*Sebastian.*"

I wince at the sound of Keira's voice and the subsequent slam of the Porsche door.

"*Let her go.*"

"Yeah, Decker," Anissa taunts in a whisper. "Let me go."

I step away, shoving my gun into the back of my pants. "Get back in the car, Keira."

Her footsteps rush up behind me, stopping a few feet away. "What are you doing?"

"Get back in the fucking car," I growl and glance over my shoulder to give her a warning look.

Her eyes are wild with pain and confusion. She doesn't understand what's going on, and that's a good thing. I can talk myself out of an ignorant situation. What I can't do is manipulate her once she knows the truth.

"*The car,*" I snap. "*Get back in it.*"

Her lips part on silent words.

"Yeah, bitch," Anissa adds. "This is none of your fucking business."

Keira balks, clearly daunted by a woman who would reject help when being threatened by a gun. And for the first time, I'm thankful for the agent's input. She's maintaining my cover, if only a little.

Keira steps back, once, twice. She meets my eyes, but the confusion doesn't leave her gaze. She's panicked. Traumatized.

I raise my hands in surrender. "Give me a few minutes and I'll explain."

She retreats another step and another, not acknowledging me.

Fuck. I can't hold her hand through this while Anissa watches. I need to attack the closest threat before I can set things right.

I turn back to the witch and lower my arms to my side. "Leave."

There are more footfalls. The pace fast and frantic. The sound becomes distant. Keira is running. Fleeing. It takes every ounce of my strength not to sprint after her and show Anissa just how much the enemy means to me.

"You're sleeping with her?" she asks. "Isn't that kinda messed up given your situation?"

It is. It fucking is. But I also know Keira isn't the enemy.

It's her father.

Her uncle.

And maybe Cole, too.

I know she's innocent of their crimes.

"I don't need my morality questioned by someone like you." Besides, the situation is too fucking complicated to explain. It was never supposed to go this far.

I wanted to watch their family from the outside. From my safe position working surveillance for Hunter. But then Sarah came along.

It wasn't in the plan to get sucked into the inner circles. I didn't anticipate getting forced to work for them.

"Well, then, what's it going to be? Are you going to stick to our arrangement, or do I leak these photos of your buddies?"

129

Keira's retreating steps haunt me.

I can't stand it.

"If you haven't blown my cover, I'll keep helping you," I seethe. "But you need to give me some fucking space so I can keep working this angle with her."

"I'll do one better." She winks. "I'll do you a favor."

I frown as she straightens to full height and glances over my shoulder in the direction Keira fled. Her face crumples, turning into an emotional montage.

I can't resist my curiosity. I glance behind me to see Keira staring at us from the building at the corner of the street.

She looks devastated. Betrayed. It takes all my determination to turn back to Anissa, only to see her palm rushing toward my face to slap me hard across the cheek.

"*Motherfucker.*" I pull away from her. "What the fuck was that for?"

She backtracks, one tormented slide after another. "*You told me you loved me,*" she screams. "*You fucking cheating bastard.*"

"Jesus Christ," I mutter.

She's still playing the relationship angle, giving me an out that feels too fucking complicated for my current level of exhaustion.

"Thanks. This is very fucking helpful."

"*I hate you.*" She stumbles toward her car. "*You're dead to me.*"

"That's enough," I hiss. She's attracting too much attention.

She drops the act as she pulls her car door wide. "If I were you, I'd start chasing your girl before she has a chance to hide."

"Fuck you," I grate.

"Jealousy is better than the truth, Decker." She climbs into the vehicle and closes the door behind her, giving me one last wink as she starts the ignition.

13

KEIRA

I RUN ALONG THE SIDE OF THE BRICK BUILDING, HOPING I'll find an alley to lead me far from here.

I need to think.

Think. Think. Think.

What am I doing? What have I done?

Everything had been going so well, then that woman appeared and knocked me off my axis.

"*Keira*," he shouts, his heavy footfalls sounding in the distance. "Please stop."

I cringe.

Goddamn it. What have I gotten myself into? Cole is going to kill me.

"Keira..." He's closing in on me. Eating up the distance. "Let me explain."

"Don't." I slow my stride to a power walk and continue to the back of the building. I don't find the getaway I need. There's only a head-high wire fence with no gate.

There's no escaping this. No escaping him.

I plant my feet, and he halts beside me, his shadow looming.

"It's not what you think." His hand gently glides over the low of my back. "You need to hear me out."

"I *need to*?"

"Please, Keira." He pulls me into his chest. "She means nothing to me."

I turn toward him, my game face fully intact. "Do you think I care about some other woman? Christ, Decker, you're the one who demanded commitment. Not me."

He grows a foot taller, his shoulders straightening. "Then why did you run? Why are you pissed at me?"

My pulse grows frantic the longer he stares, the rapid pounding in my chest becoming painful as he holds my gaze.

"I'm livid because you made me believe my safety was at risk when what you were really doing was putting space between your booty calls."

I make this about his job. About the commitment he's made to my brother. I refuse to let it be about anything else.

"You made me think I was in danger, when there was no threat at all." I shove out of his hold, placing space between us.

His nostrils flare as he glances away, letting out a huff of frustration. "I didn't mean for that to happen."

"In front of me?" I seethe. "Or at all?"

"At all," he grates. "She's not a woman who can be ignored. If I didn't pull over and speak to her, she would've followed until I did. She would've made a bigger scene."

"Making a scene is the least of your worries. You need to remember why you're here and who you work for. My protection isn't something you can push aside whenever your girlfriend shows up."

"Your protection?" His eyes harden as he meets my gaze. "Are you really going to keep playing this like it's a work related problem? It's clear you're jealous, and you don't need to be."

I bite back a retort that would only prove his point. "We can make this about sex if you like, Decker, the *unprotected sex* we had after you led me to believe you weren't sleeping around."

"I'm not sleeping around. And stop calling me Decker. You know my fucking name."

I'm not here to do him any favors. I can't. I'm beyond

reasoning. "Is she the woman you cancelled plans with yesterday?"

"Yes," he growls. "But it doesn't change a thing—"

"Because she's only an old friend?"

"It's complicated."

"It always is." I start toward the street, needing to find another escape route.

"Come on, Keira. I understand why you're upset. Honestly, I am, too. But the last thing I want to do is hurt you." His footsteps follow. "*Please,* believe me when I say I'm sorry."

"Believing in someone is a luxury I can't afford." Case in point—our current situation.

He grabs my arm and turns me to face him, his eyes shining with sincerity. "I shouldn't have contacted her, okay? I don't want anything to do with her. Not anymore. But like I said, it's complicated."

"How complicated?" The question slips past my defenses without permission.

He doesn't respond, only holds my gaze, the clue to my answer flickering in his tight expression.

"Tell me," I demand, "before I find a phone and call Cole."

He sighs. "She isn't someone who can be denied. She always gets what she wants. One way or another."

I hate her already. Even more than I already did. "And what she wants is you?"

"Today, yes. Who knows what she'll want tomorrow." He shrugs. "But I'm not interested in her. I promise."

I should've scratched her eyes out instead of running to her aid. Only problem is, that's another point I can't ignore. "You were threatening her with a gun."

"Because she was threatening *you*. I'm not going to apologize for being possessive. I'll shut down anyone who contemplates putting you in harm's way. I've told you this a hundred times."

The words sink deep, the sincerity in his eyes sinking deeper. He's trying to weave me under his spell again.

He reaches out, stroking his thumb over my cheek. "I'll stop at nothing to keep you safe."

"And what if it's you I need to be kept safe from?"

His hand falls. "Is that how you feel?"

I don't know how to answer. Strategy or honesty. Truth or lies. "Getting involved with you was a mistake."

"Bullshit. You don't believe that."

I don't know what I believe anymore.

"Keira." He whispers my name, the syllables drowning in sorrow. "Deep down, you know this is real. What we've got isn't something that should be thrown away."

I scoff. "That's awfully poetic."

His fingers loosen around mine, his touch climbing my arm, moving along my shoulder, burning a frantic trail until he gently clasps the back of my neck. He demands my attention with the possessive hold. He commands my eyes to meet his without a single word.

I blink back at his fierce expression, my breathing growing ragged. I lick my lip. I shudder. All my responses are involuntary. When it comes to Sebastian, I guess they always are.

"It's not poetic. It's the fucking truth." His fingers stroke back and forth along my sensitive skin. "Neither one of us wanted this. But it happened. And I'm not going to let you convince me it doesn't mean anything to you. Because I know it does."

I clamp my lips tight.

I'm not going to confirm or deny.

"Keira. Please." His face is scrunched in pain. "I'm—"

His sentence is cut short by the melodic sound of his cell, the loud ring echoing through the alley.

"Shit." He lowers his hand from my neck to retrieve a phone from his pocket. "I need to answer this. It'll be Hunter."

I nod. "Go ahead."

He stares at me, the cell palmed in his hand. "Not until you tell me we're good."

The phone continues to ring, the annoying tone forever tattooed in my brain to remind me of the moment I made a decision that would either make me sink or swim.

"We're good," I whisper.

His features relax, the slightest smile tugging at his lips as he connects the call and raises it to his ear. "Hunt? Where are you?"

He wraps a hand around my waist, and I don't deny the touch. I've made my decision. I need to stick to it.

"How far away?" He backs me into the wall as he speaks, his hips pressing into mine. "Yeah. We're already here. After you take the turn off, you'll see the Porsche parked on the side of the road."

His heat sinks into me, the exposed skin of his chest tempting.

"I'll see you in a minute." He disconnects the call and places the cell into his pocket. "They're almost here."

"They?" Has my brother come to save me from making more poor decisions? Or would he pressure me to make more?

"Hunt and Sarah. We need to meet them at the car."

"Okay." I inch along the wall, only to have him stop me with a strong hand on my waist.

"Say it again," he begs. "Tell me I didn't fuck things up."

My stomach churns. There's no right answer when there's too much wrong in this situation.

"I'll get over it." I swallow and force myself to follow the path I've chosen. "We're good, Sebastian."

That smile returns a second before he steals a kiss. His lips are harsh and possessive. They claim me, taking me over, dragging me under. Then, just as quick, they're gone.

"You're killing me, you know that?" He grins. "I don't know what it is about you, but I swear you're slaying me one slow inch at a time."

Maybe I am.

Maybe he's doing the same to me.

I guess only time will tell.

"We better get going." I maneuver out from against him and lead the way. "Hunter doesn't seem like the type to appreciate waiting."

"Hunter's not the type to appreciate much of anything." He catches up to me, slinging an arm around my shoulders.

We walk to the car, and neither of us has words to fill the

135

uncomfortable void as we pause to lean side-by-side against the hood. It's my fault. I went from zero to sixty in a heartbeat with this man. I pulled all the stops. Then had to swerve off course when that woman showed up.

Which sparks to life an important question. "How did she find us?"

He stares at the road, not a single flicker marring his expression. "My guess? She put some tracking app on my phone."

I frown. "You let her mess around with your cell?"

He keeps ogling the same spot of asphalt near his feet. "I think she's used it once or twice to make a call. Who knows what she did during that time. I'll have to ditch it and buy a burner until we get back to Portland."

My brows knit tighter. He's too calm. He doesn't understand what all this means. "Sebastian..." I don't know how to broach the consequences.

He crosses his arms over his chest. "Let it go."

I can't. Tracking him means she'd have a wealth of information. Every job he's done for my family would be traceable. Any alibi we gave him could be exposed as a lie. And the safe house... *Shit.* She would know the exact location of where we're staying, now and when my family needs to hide in the future. "You don't understand what this means."

"I know exactly what it means, Keira." His voice is barely audible. "And I know what needs to be done, too. Let me handle it."

My heart squeezes. We're both talking about the same thing. About killing a woman because of her infatuation. Nausea swirls in my gut, the sensation multiplying the longer we stand in silence.

I can't drag my gaze away from him. I watch his profile as he raises his attention to the oncoming traffic, his disposition calm despite the death that's about to lay at his feet.

He fits into my family better than I thought. His puzzle piece slides in right beside mine. I don't know if it's a good thing, or bad. Should I appreciate his familiarity or be disappointed that he's so similar to Cole?

"They're here." He pushes from the hood and stands tall as a black Chevy Suburban pulls in behind us.

I join him, greeting Hunter and Sarah with a faux smile while they climb from the car.

"I'm glad you're safe," Sarah says in greeting. If those words came from any other person, I'd expect a hug to come with it, but she's not the type. She cares to the fullest and despises shows of affection in equal measure.

On the outside, she's a total badass. Entirely dark, from her black tank, skirt, and fuck-me boots. But on the inside, I know she isn't that tough.

Then there's Hunter, who approaches with the same scowl that's been tattooed on his face from the first moment we met.

"Thanks for the concern, sweetness," Sebastian drawls. "I knew you'd miss me."

She turns her attention to him, eyeing his clothes with derision. "What's with the shirt? Did you become a stripper and forget to tell me?"

"Sure did." He grins. "Want a lap dance?"

I bristle, all the hairs on the back of my neck rising in jealousy.

"Quit the shit," Hunter scolds. "And why the fuck are you dressed like that?"

"I'm setting a new—"

"It's my fault," I admit, already sick of the playful joker. Minutes ago Sebastian had been someone else. Someone brutal and honest. The guy beside me is different, and I have no clue which personality is the fake one. "I shrunk his shirt, and we haven't had a chance to buy him any new clothes."

Hunter juts his chin in acknowledgement, then focuses on Sebastian as if I no longer exist. "We need to go somewhere and talk."

Sebastian nods. "There's a diner further up the road. We can go there."

"The women can," Hunter clarifies. "You and I are going to find someplace private."

There's a pause of silence, the beat of contemplation slipping through us all.

They're going to leave me behind. Alone. Unprotected.

I'm not overly concerned. Nobody is likely to find me out here. Except Sebastian's formidable ex. And even if she did approach me, there's a thing or two I'd like to get off my chest as far as she's concerned.

"I'm not going anywhere without Keira." Sebastian's brows pull tight. "She stays with me."

"Sarah can take over for a while. We won't be gone long. We'll take a short drive. We don't need to go far."

"Sarah?" Sebastian scoffs.

"Yeah, me." She crosses her arms over her chest. "Please be dumb enough to tell me you don't think I'm capable."

"Well, okay, seeing as though you—"

"Seriously, shut the fuck up," Hunter snaps, his viciousness making me jolt. "We need to get moving."

"No." Sebastian loses the playful expression. "I said I'm not leaving her. We can have a private conversation wherever the hell you like, but I'm keeping her in my sights."

There's an emotional standoff. One fierce man staring down another.

"You're not thinking straight," Hunter snarls through clenched teeth. "We need to talk. *In private.*"

This is never going to end. Not without a fistfight. Or worse.

Sarah meets my gaze and raises a brow in question. I know what she's asking. And I guess I should've opened my mouth sooner, but the display of overbearing protection is hard to ignore. It penetrates the drama-filled thoughts from earlier and leaves me a little more susceptible to Sebastian's charm.

"I'll be fine." I incline my head in the direction of the diner and start striding out the distance. "I can take care of myself until you get back."

"Keira, wait." Sebastian jogs after me, rounds me up to walk backward in an effort to hold my gaze. "I don't want to leave you."

"I know. But Hunter isn't giving you a choice." I paste on a smile. "Go. Do whatever you need to do. I'll be waiting for you once you get back."

He stops and grabs my arms, his eyes filling with furious concern. "I don't—"

"It's not a big deal." I place a hand over his and squeeze. "The sooner you go, the sooner you come back."

"Are you sure?" He scrutinizes me.

"She's sure." Sarah approaches my side. "Hurry up and get out of here before my man bursts an artery." She grabs my wrist and tugs. "Come on, Kee. Let's have some girl bonding time."

She leads me away, my hand falling from Sebastian's arm as he stands tall in defiance.

"I'll be right back," he mutters.

"Take your time," Sarah calls out over her shoulder. "The two of us have a lot to discuss."

I feel him watching me as I leave. The warm tingle follows my every step. When I'm about to turn the corner, I glance over my shoulder, and there he is, still in the same spot, staring at me.

"You two hooked up, didn't you?" Sarah drops my arm. "I thought Hunter was joking when he mentioned it this morning."

"Excuse me?" My attention snaps to her. "Hunter said something?"

"He speculated that Decker couldn't keep his dick in his pants. But now it's obvious. That right there went above and beyond protection. He's hooked."

"No comment." I increase my pace. I'm not sure why.

I guess I'm trying to outrun the conversation. Or Sarah entirely. And she lets me. For the most part. She hangs back a little, allowing me to walk a few steps in front, until we reach the diner.

I push the door wide, letting her enter before me.

"There's no outrunning this conversation." She smirks as she passes. "I'll buy you a coffee so we can settle in and discuss you and Decker fucking."

She says it loud enough to draw attention. Loud enough to turn my cheeks to flame. Then struts those boots to the far wall to claim a booth.

I should leave. I seriously doubt anyone nearby is going to make me more uncomfortable then she is. Coffee be damned. Waterboarding would be more enjoyable than this.

It's no secret I don't talk sex with friends. For starters, I don't have a lot of people I can confide in, and second, I don't have a lot of sex.

Who the hell am I kidding? I have none of either.

Not until Sebastian, who seems to be trying to fulfil my needs on both.

"Are you waiting to be seated?" A waitress asks.

I cringe. "No, I'm waiting for hell to open up and swallow me whole."

She frowns.

"I'm fine," I mutter and drag my feet toward the booth.

Sarah still has the smug expression plastered on her pretty face. It brings me chills as I slide into the opposite seat.

"We're not discussing it." I place my hands on the table and look her straight in the eye. "Anything about Sebastian is off limits."

"Sebastian?" She purses her lips. "Is that his name?"

I ignore her and glance at the waitress approaching our table.

"What would you like to or—"

"A strong coffee, please. Very strong. And a bagel, too."

Sarah chuckles. "I'll have the same."

"Why don't you try decaf?" I taunt. Caffeine is the last thing this interrogator needs.

Her lips quirk in amusement as the waitress finishes writing up our order and leaves us alone.

"You're edgy. Why?" She scrutinizes me. "It's just sex, right?"

Yeah. There's nothing else going on. Not at all.

Not one damn thing.

"That's exactly right." I grab a salt shaker to keep my hands busy. "So drop it."

Her mouth continues to provoke me. "You like him." It comes out as an accusation. "I mean you *really* like him."

140

"The only thing I'd like at the moment is an end to this conversation."

"Why?" She relaxes back into her seat, her expression losing its humor. "What's the big deal?"

"That's exactly it, there *is* no big deal. We had sex. That's it. End of story."

"Wow." Her eyes widen. "Was he that bad?"

"*No.* He wasn't bad at all." I can't help defending him. "He was good."

"Good?" she rants. "That's not really a glowing reference."

"*Jesus.*" I throw my hands in the air. "He was mind-blowing. He rocked my world. I saw stars and unicorns, and maybe a baby llama, too. Is that better?"

She laughs. "Yeah. Better. Although the mention of farm animals is a little disturbing."

I hang my head. "You're killing me."

The laughter continues. It's uncharacteristic for her. She's not usually an overtly happy person. It must be her sadistic side coming out to play.

"So, tell me," she starts, "if you saw stars and frogs and fairies, why isn't this a big deal?"

I drag in a deep breath and hold it tight in my lungs, letting the burn distract me. "Because nothing can come of it."

"Why?"

I scoff. "Sebastian isn't the best poster boy for a healthy relationship."

"And you think Hunter and I are?"

"I..."

She has a point.

Her relationship with her fiancé seems flawless. They're perfect together. Happy. In sync. Committed. But my issues are far deeper than I let on.

"It's not that easy." Nothing about this situation is. It's messy and complicated. It's downright scary at times.

"I know." She nods. "There's your brother, who will wear Sebastian's skin like a coat. And the two of you being together will draw attention. You'll be his weakness and become a bigger target for anyone wanting to mess with the family. But he's obviously infatuated with you."

"I don't know what he is." That's the problem. He has secrets. Lots of them. And after this morning, it's clear he's hiding things that are dangerous.

"Then find out. Ask him. Or just sit back and see where this llama sex takes you."

I roll my eyes. "Do you twist Hunter's words as much as you twist mine?"

She ponders the question. "Yeah, I guess I do." She shrugs. "See, no relationship is perfect."

I smile through my contemplation. She's right. No relationship is perfect. But most aren't built entirely on lies, either.

14

DECKER

"GET IN THE PORSCHE," HUNTER DEMANDS AS HE STRIDES for the passenger door. "You're driving."

"Is that really necessary? Why the fuck can't we just stay here?"

He doesn't answer, just keeps pounding out the steps around the hood. He's more volatile than I anticipated, which isn't good.

I thought he'd be edgy from the news—an upcoming power struggle isn't something anyone wants to be involved in—but we can make a plan. We can get in front of this before it blows in our faces. "Do you have a destination in mind?"

"I'll give you directions."

I yank open my door, and we both slide inside.

"Head out of town." Hunter clasps his belt, and I start the ignition. "Toward Portland."

I nod and pull from the curb, the small town being left behind in the rear-view as we steamroll closer toward apprehension. "Are you going to start talking?"

"When we pull over. I don't trust this car isn't bugged."

I hold tight to the steering wheel and wonder if he's right. Not only could the authorities be listening, but it's a possibility Torian could've placed a recording device in his own car.

All those phone calls via Bluetooth, or any conversation

he's held behind the wheel could be kept and used to his advantage...along with all those I've had with Keira.

Shit.

"You need to start talking." I demand. "I know something's wr—"

"Here." He focuses out his window, tapping his finger against the glass. "Pull over."

"You sure?" He's pointing toward a dilapidated barn. The structure is barely holding its own, the wooden wall planks filled with dark, rotted cracks exposing the black inside. One gust of wind and the fucker is going to fall.

"Yes. Pull into the drive and park at the gate. We can walk the rest of the way."

"You want to go inside?"

He scowls at me. "What's with you questioning me this morning? You're getting on my nerves."

"Feeling's mutual." I pull into the dirt drive and cut the engine.

Being at each other's throats isn't a great way to face this storm. We have to be a team. Focused and reliable. I need to be on his good side if there's any hope he'll help me convince Keira to run from this mess.

"Get moving. I don't want to keep the girls waiting." Hunter is out and striding for the fence before I can release my belt.

He doesn't want to keep them waiting?

I didn't want to leave them in the first fucking place.

Something is seriously eating Hunter's ass right now and it's not an A-grade hooker.

I rush from the car, slamming the door behind me. "Hey." I jog to catch up. "What's going on?"

"You tell me." He opens the gate, holding it wide until I walk through. "This morning has been a fucking disaster."

"Because Luther went to meet his maker?" I continue along the drive, rocks and dirt crunching under my shoes.

"Among other things, but we'll get to the rest later." He lags half a step behind, his heavy frame taking up the corner of my eye. "First, I want to know what Keira told you."

144

"It's like I said on the phone—Her dad is counting worms, and they're keeping it quiet while they prepare for the approaching shit storm."

"I still don't understand why she would tell you when nobody else has been told. Not even me."

"Is that what this is about?" I huff out a chuckle. "You're pissed because your best buddy, Torian, didn't tell you first?"

"Like I'd give a fuck about that. I just want answers. I want to know why she would blab to you."

I glance over my shoulder and waggle my brows at his fierce expression. I wouldn't have guessed it possible, but his face becomes stonier. Those eyes harden to disapproving slits. His lips flatten into a straight line.

"So, you did fuck her," he grates.

"That's such a crass term for the magic we shared."

"It must've been some monumental fuck to have her spilling her family secrets."

I shrug. "What can I say? My moves bring out the trust in people."

"Torians don't trust," he snarls. "You know that." He slows his pace, falling further behind as we reach the barn. "Who else have you told?"

"Nobody." I grab the splintered door in both hands and have to lift to get it to budge. "I called you—"

A heavy weight slams into my back, buckling my knees and shoving me into the rotted wood.

"What the—" My gun is yanked from my pants as I right myself, the barrel jabbing into my ribs.

"Get inside," Hunt mutters. "*Move.*"

I freeze, the world stopping around me as I relive every move I've made in the last forty-eight hours in an attempt to pinpoint my failure. "Is that a gun in your pocket or are you—"

Pain explodes through the back of my skull, the impact coming from his knuckles or maybe the butt of the gun.

"Open the fucking door. We're not doing this out here."

"And what is this, exactly?" I murmur. "Because I'm fucking clueless."

Cold metal presses to the top of my spine. "Inside. *Now.*"

I scramble to figure out what's going on. What he knows. How I've failed. "You're being a dick, Hunt. Cut the shit and tell me what's got your panties in a twist."

"Don't try my patience, motherfucker."

Fuck.

I have no clue what's going on. No fucking idea what has turned my friend against me. I lift the door, adrenaline coursing through me.

My head throbs as I shove inside, dust billowing at my feet. I inch into the darkened interior, the nudges from Hunt prodding me forward.

Splinters of light pierce through the broken walls. Cobwebs blanket the beams along the ceiling. This place is empty, apart from the dread filling the space to capacity.

It's certainly not the nicest place to die.

I guess it's not the worst, either.

"Who do you work for?" He shoves me forward with a heavy hand between my shoulder blades.

I stumble, gaining enough space to turn and face him. "You're paranoid." I scowl at him. At my friend. My only fucking friend.

"And you're a fucking traitor." He aims the weapon at my chest, his arm strong, his resignation even stronger. I can see it in his eyes. He's capable of pulling the trigger. He's considering killing me.

"What have I told you about skipping your meds?" I raise my hands in surrender. "I don't know what's gotten into you today—"

"Who do you work for?" he demands. "Is it the fucking DEA?"

"I work for you. I've always worked for you."

His eyes flare. His jaw ticks.

He knows. He fucking knows.

How?

"Tell me what's going on." I step closer. "Whatever it is, you've got the wrong impression."

"Do I?" He raises a brow. "In the early hours of this morning, one of Torian's cop friends calls to tell him an

146

informant has started whispering about Luther's death. Not long after, you give me the same information."

Fucking Anissa.

That bitch exposed me.

"And you're blaming me for the leak?" I scoff and lower my hands. "Fuck, man, you said it yourself, I called after the cop. Who knows who found out before I did. Keira has probably told all her friends. And then there's Layla. Or even Cole. It's obviously not a well kept secret."

"It's not a secret, you piece of shit. It's a lie."

A lie?

A fucking lie.

I school my expression, facing the news head-on as hell rains down on me.

"He isn't dead, you dumb fuck." He lunges for me, one hand grabbing my throat while the other keeps me in place with the threat of a bullet. "From what I can piece together, it was a bullshit story to flush out a rat." He tightens his grip, restricting my breath. "Keira set you up. She tested you. She fucking played you."

I raise my chin, sinking into the pain taking over my throat, letting it sharpen my thoughts. "No." I don't believe it. I won't. "She must have told someone else. I didn't breathe a word to anyone but you."

He glares his fury, his stare more lethal than any weapon. "The game is over. Quit the fucking act."

Fuck.

I'm done.

Dead.

"Hunt..." I swallow to clear the rasp from my voice. I can't believe Keira betrayed me. I can't figure out when. I don't understand how. "Let me explain."

"*Fuck.*" He shoves me. "It's fucking true?" He retreats a step and another, the gun still trained on me. "*Jesus. Fuck.*"

Guilt takes over, the toxic agony rushing my veins, pounding into every limb, through all my organs.

"Let me tell you every—"

He rushes forward, grabbing me around the waist to haul

me to the ground. My head hits the dirt. All the air leaves my lungs. I grapple to get on top, but I can't bring myself to fight him. I fucking can't.

He straddles my waist, the gun still pointed, as he strikes with punishing blows. He punches my chest, my ribs, my stomach. Agony takes over my insides, the wounds more emotional than physical.

"Fight back, you dog."

I can't. I don't want to.

I deserve the punishment. I've earned the beating.

"Do you know what you've done?" He keeps his fist cocked, preparing to make another strike. "You've put my neck on the line. You've made me look like a fucking accomplice. But that's not the worst of it. You've done this to Sarah, and that's un-fucking-forgivable."

He punches my sternum, the crack of bone ringing in my ears. I don't do a thing to stop him. I won't deny him the retribution. Not for himself. And definitely not for his woman.

"I had no choice," I wheeze.

He lets out a derisive laugh. "Money or freedom? What did the DEA offer you?"

"It's not like that." I shake my head and grunt as he lands another blow. "Luther is involved in horrible shit you can't even imagine. He—"

"*Are you really going to make this about morality?*" he roars. "I'm paid to kill people. *You're* paid to help me."

"It's more than—"

He lands another blow, this one against my jaw, the smash of teeth and tongue filling my mouth with blood.

"*It's more than death?*" he bellows. "Fuck you, you traitorous little fuck. How am I going to explain this to Cole? How the fuck do I tell him you're the informant?"

Wait. What?

"He doesn't know?" I mumble through a mouth full of gore.

"Nobody fucking knows. He thinks it was another external attack to take down his family. He's pulling his hair out trying to find the culprit."

"But Keira..."

"Hasn't answered his calls. As far as I can tell, the dead-father strategy was something she thought of on her own."

"You're telling me you had no proof?" I huff out a chuckle and my ribs protest with a bite of pain. "You were working on a hunch?" My laughter becomes maniacal. Delirious. "I fucked myself over? All I had to do was keep my mouth shut."

He grabs me by the shoulders and slams my back down on the ground. "If it wasn't today, your dumb ass would've fucked up sooner or later." He climbs off me, coming to stand beside my hip. "Get on your feet."

"No." I remain one with the earth and spit the coppery taste from my mouth. "If you're in such a hurry to kill me, you can do it like a coward."

He grabs the front of my shirt, twisting the material in his fist. "I'm in no hurry. I'm happy to make this slow if you like."

"I'd prefer if you fucking listened." I prepare to play the only card I have—knowledge. "I've got years of research at my house. I've got thousands and thousands of files you're going to want to see. Let me show you what they're doing. Give me the chance to explain why I'm here."

"I don't give a shit. I'll *never* give a shit."

"Maybe not, but Sarah will. And she'll never forgive you once she finds out. Especially if my death is on your hands."

His jaw ticks.

"Come on, Luke. You don't want to kill me."

He stiffens at the sound of his real name, his fury surging.

"If you do this," I continue, "I promise you'll lose Sarah. She'll leave you as soon as she learns the truth."

His hold on my shirt tightens as he presses the barrel right between my eyes. "If it's so important, tell me."

I smirk, and my swollen lower lip protests over the movement. "You know that information is the only leverage I have."

"You're wrong." His voice softens. Slows. The defeated tone inciting fear. "You've got no leverage. You've got nothing but lies."

My friend disappears from sight, a cold-blooded killer

149

taking his place. The barrel presses harder against my skull and I see death swirling in his eyes. My death.

He's going to pull the trigger.

He's going to end my life.

"I'm sorry," I murmur.

His eyes glaze, the depth of his breaths increasing. He's preparing himself, finding the necessary calm to do the job.

"Hunt, believe me, I'm fuckin' sorry." For the past, the present, and now, the future.

I duck to the left and slam his wrist upward, breaking the lethal trajectory of his weapon. The gun fires, the blast ringing in my ears as the bullet shoots toward the ceiling.

He swings back toward me, and I latch onto his hand, shoving it in a high arc as I lean in and strike with a double elbow slash, the menacing blow hitting the right side of his jaw, then returning against his left. His head jerks with the motions. He stumbles.

I don't let go. I swing around into him, my back to his chest as I wrench his arm over my shoulder. His elbow hyperextends. He tries to choke me as I jerk him down, once, twice, threatening to break the joint before he gives in and drops the weapon.

I keep him hostage as I kick the gun away and watch it skitter through the dust. He pummels my face with his free hand. But it's not until he gouges at my eyes that I have to drop to my haunches and set him free.

I scramble away and turn to face him nursing his elbow, his feet spread wide, knees bent, preparing for battle even though shock is written all over his face.

He's never seen me fight. He probably thought this smartass, tech head had no moves. Truth is, my skills have always been capable of rivaling his own. I didn't storm into hell armed with nothing but a computer and a cocky attitude.

I knew I'd have to fight for my life one day.

Fight or die.

"What's wrong, Hunt?" I raise my brows, letting the adrenaline take over. "You didn't anticipate me kicking your ass?"

I studied him. I know he works best when he's calm and in control. I don't plan on letting him have either.

He smirks, the curve of lips predatory and feral. "You fight like a little bitch."

"Says the man who had to lower himself to eye gouging."

"Lower myself?" He laughs. "I've been wanting to ruin your pretty boy face for a while." He inches forward, beckoning me with his left hand. "Come on. Let's finish this."

"I don't want to finish it." I steady myself, hands raised, waiting for him to strike. "I want you to walk out of here and go find my research."

"You think I don't want that?" He comes closer, almost close enough to pounce. "If this was just me and you, things would be different. But I can't protect Sarah from Torian. Not every minute of every damn day. You put me in the middle of this. And I'll do whatever it takes to protect her."

"We can leave. All three of us. We'll start over somewhere new."

"You want me to run away with you?" He snickers. "That's fuckin' sweet. But I don't run with snitches." He rushes me, coming forward with right-left-right punches.

The first blow hits my nose, then I block the next two strikes and take a hard step right at his last swing. As he moves by me, I launch my fist into the side of his face, knocking him off balance.

"Motherfucker." He rushes me again with a sloppy, uncalculated assault that I defend with a sharp side kick to the shin.

He snarls, his eyes flaring with fury. "Kicking? Seriously? Where the fuck did you learn to fight?"

"Look, man. I told you, we don't need to do this." I raise my hands in surrender. "Walk away while you still can."

"Still can?" He snickers. "Jesus, you're one cocky prick."

And that's exactly what I need to be to put him off his game. I can already feel his frustration. I can see it in his impulsive moves.

He clenches his fists and holds them in front of his chest. "This is how real men fight. With their hands."

I shrug. "Seems like all it's doing is getting your butt whooped."

I counter his circling steps, watching his every move, reading his expression. I know he'll swing first. He lacks the patience to wait me out.

"How long did you study me before you figured out a way for us to work together?" He feigns relaxation his expression doesn't back up. He's tense, tight, almost panicked.

"You came to me for help, remember? You instigated this."

He flashes his teeth in a snarl, my verbal strike inflicting injury to his ego.

In reality, it took months to find a way into his life. Then many more to train to fit the role. Hunter's weakness has always been technology—computers, hacking, online surveillance.

With a million hours' study, I became a master. I built a name for myself so quickly in the Portland criminal circles that Hunter came running to me.

He lunges, swinging a powerful blow. I dodge the punch, grab his wrist, and swing out my leg, using his own momentum to knock him off balance.

He falls to his back, and I go down with him, bending his wrist while pinning his chest with my knee.

"I'm not doing this anymore," I growl.

He swings at me with his left hand and bucks, fighting like an animal. I slice at the blows and grab the attacking arm, pinning it with force.

"Go to my house. Find the information. Then pick a side."

The look he gives me is the most brutal offense. My bruises don't mean shit. That pain will eventually fade. But I'll never forget the loathing in his eyes. I won't lose the guilt of what I've done to him.

His lip curls. "Get fuc—"

I lunge forward, head butting him right above the eyes. The impact ricochets through my skull, temporarily blinding me. But it does the trick.

It's nighty-night for the big, bad Hunter.

15

DECKER

I GRAB HIS BELONGINGS—KEYS, WALLET, PHONE, GUN—you name it, I've got it. Then I run for the car, hightailing it back into town.

I pull over at the start of the main street and scan the shopfronts, looking for any reinforcements who may have arrived to protect Keira.

I could keep running. I *should* keep running.

It's not like I'm capable of taking down Luther from the inside anymore. But Hunter's right. I've dragged him and Sarah into this. Torian will kill them as soon as he finds out I'm the informant. He'll consider them accomplices. At the very least, he'll hold Hunter responsible.

And as trigger-happy as my friend was moments ago, I'm not going to let them take the fall for something I've done. I don't want him punished.

But Keira...

I clench my teeth, fighting back anger. She set me up. She manipulated me with her body, making me sink head deep into her game.

It's her fault we're all in this position, and she's the one who has to fix it.

I park the Porsche behind the diner and run back to Hunter's Chevy. The Suburban will attract less attention, and I guess I get a kick out of stealing Hunt's car.

I fill the tank with gas and wash up in the bathroom, cleaning away the blood and gore the best I can.

I get supplies. I make calls. I do everything and anything possible to set my next move into action before I park in front of the diner and spy on the traitorous woman inside.

Keira and Sarah are seated against the wall. Smiling. Laughing. The only sign of apprehension comes from the way Keira continues to glance at her watch—waiting for me? Or waiting for her brother to save her?

I climb from the car, my clothes covered in dirt, and jog up the sidewalk, meeting her gaze through the window.

Her smile is instantaneous. Immediate deception. There's no glimmer of fear or panic. Then a split second later the expression flickers, flittering away as she scrutinizes my swelling face.

I shove past the glass door and meet her near the counter.

"You're hurt." Her eyes are wide, her lips parted in shock.

I keep one hand at my back, near my gun, as I lead them toward the door. "We need to leave." I'm on edge, every muscle tense, waiting for her to end the charade.

"What happened?" She rushes to follow, bathing me in fake concern. Her acting skills are in full force, which is a great sign. It means she's still playing the game. "Who did this to you?"

"They know we're here. We need to hit the road."

"They?" Her voice fractures.

Sarah comes up behind her. "Where's Hunter?"

"He's tying up loose ends."

"Loose ends?" the little liar whispers.

I ignore her, pinning my stern focus on Sarah, wordlessly telling her that's all the information I can give. "He won't be long. Be ready to leave once he gets here."

She gives a tight nod. "Is he okay?"

"He faired better than I did." I continue to the door. "We've swapped cars. Hunt has the Porsche to try to take the heat off us as we run. I'll take the Suburban."

"Why don't we go back to Portland with them?" Keira's voice is frantic. "Aren't we better to stay in a group?"

"No." I can barely stand to look at her, can hardly glance her way without wanting to wrap my hands around her neck. "We need to get off the grid."

"But—"

"Trust me," I growl.

I gain the slightest solace betraying her, manipulating her, lying straight to her beautiful face. I gain even more when she nods, seeming to come to terms with the plan.

"Okay..." Her throat works over a heavy swallow. "I trust you."

Everything inside me revolts. My pulse. My heart. My stomach takes a dive, too. Even though I know she's acting, I still can't see it. Not the slightest flicker of a charade.

She's fucking brilliant in her deception.

Entirely flawless.

I squeeze her arm in a fake show of support, then turn back to Sarah.

"I'm sorry." I hate that she'll soon see me in the same light I see Keira. She's going to hate me. Despise me. "I don't want to leave you here like this." The depth of my apology runs far below the surface. She won't understand it now, but hopefully, once I'm gone and my actions become clear, she'll make sense of it.

"It's okay. Go. Keep Keira safe."

"I will. But I fucking hate this." I'm not like the snake at her side. I don't enjoy lying to people who trust me.

"You're getting soft, Deck. And making me uncomfortable at the same time." She frowns and jerks her chin toward the door. "Hurry up and get moving."

Fucking hell. I don't want to leave her. I'm struggling to walk away. Sarah has become a major part of my life. She's a gorgeous woman. A moral woman. Lethally so. It's a good thing I'm not going to be around when she finds out what I've done.

"Don't miss me too much." I paste on a grin and lean in to kiss her temple.

She rolls her eyes as I retreat, not allowing a second of softness. "Be careful. Guard her with your life."

"I'll do everything I can." I shove open the door. "When Hunt gets here, you need to remind him to go to my house. There's stuff I need him to pick up."

I don't look back as I escape onto the sidewalk, Keira following close behind. We jog to Hunter's car and climb in. I don't spare a second as I gun the engine and pull from the curb.

She doesn't talk as we speed down the highway, her hands fidgeting in her lap. She's giving me the same act she did when we fled Portland. An exact replica of the innocent actress.

I can't blame her, seeing as though the duplicity worked so well the first time. Obviously, it's a familiar role, a default, because beneath the fragility is a calculated bitch planning her next strike.

"Do you still have that phone?" I ask.

"Yes. But it's flat. There's no battery." She fumbles in her cardigan pocket and pulls out the device. "I need to buy a charger."

"No, you don't." I lower my window and grab the cell to throw it to the wind. I watch in my mirror as it bounces and shatters along the road behind us, the destruction a comforting sight.

"*Sebastian.*" She raises from her seat to stare out the back window. "Why did you do that?"

"I don't know how they tracked us. I'm not willing to take any chances."

"What about your cell? I need to call Cole. I want to know what's going on."

"Sorry, babe. I've already ditched mine. We need to get off the grid as soon as possible."

Those fingers increase their nervous wringing. Her leg begins to jitter. "Where are we going?"

Her panic is an aphrodisiac. I can't get enough. "As far away as possible. I've already filled the tank with gas. I have no plans to pull over until we've disappeared."

"Are you sure going home isn't a better option? If people are coming after us, I'd prefer to be moving toward my family. Not away."

I glance at her and give a grin filled with pure menace. "Aren't I good enough anymore?"

I want her to bite. I *need* her to. My blood rushes with adrenaline, waiting for the finish line. But now isn't the time to let her know I'm already aware of her lies. Not when I'm behind the wheel.

"It's not that..." Her leg jolts faster. "I'm just nervous about being out in the open."

"Don't worry." I reach over, sliding my hand behind her head to squeeze the back of her neck. It takes all my strength not to grip hard. To sink my fingers into muscle and inflict pain. "Hunter and I dealt with the issue. Moving forward, I'll be more cautious. I promise nobody will find us."

Not a fucking soul.

Not until I'm ready.

My palm itches, needing to feel her pulse quicken beneath my touch. I hunger to cause more fear. Instigate more panic. Instead, she leans into my hand and briefly closes her eyes, pretending to gain comfort from the connection.

Conniving little bitch.

She's brilliant in her betrayal. Mesmerizing.

I keep my hand in place, lazily tracing silent threats into her skin while she pretends to enjoy the affection.

It's a romantic picture from the outside. A curious state of normal I would've liked to explore if this wasn't the fucking Twilight Zone.

But it is.

All of this is fake—the vulnerability, the friendship, the beauty.

"Are you okay?" she whispers, breaking the stable silence.

Out of all the questions she could've asked, this one fills me with the most anger. She should be curious about the imaginary men following us. Or how I plan to keep her safe. Or when she's going to see her family again.

Instead, she pretends to care about me. *Me*. The man she's slowly leading to execution.

"I'm tough." I shoot her a wink and place both hands back

on the wheel. "It takes a hell of a lot more to get me six feet under."

"Your face is pretty beat up. You're bruised everywhere—your jaw, your cheek, your bottom lip."

I keep smiling through her nauseating charade of pity. Keep pretending, just like she does. There's a beat of silence, an awkward, fractured beat that thickens the air between us.

"Sebastian, I need to tell you something."

My lungs tighten, my ribs restricting my breathing. "I'm all ears."

The quiet returns, the moments passing with building anticipation.

I glance her way, seeing her brow furrowed as her teeth dig into her lower lip. "What is it?"

She sucks in a breath and lets it out slowly. "I lied to you."

"Oh, yeah?" My hands tighten around the steering wheel.

She nods. "This morning...When I said I didn't care about you being with that woman."

For fuck's sake. This shit is already getting old.

"I do care, Sebastian. The jealousy is eating me up."

I focus on the road, my knuckles turning white with my harsh grip.

Not only is she saying my name in that sickly sincere tone, she's playing the endearing card on top of the stacked deck of deceit.

Fuck her.

Fuck those soft eyes that seem to blink with genuine honesty. And the tempting lips making her lies easy to believe. She was born to fool me.

"I told you, she means nothing."

"I know." Her voice fractures. "And I believe you. I guess I just wanted you to know I wasn't unaffected by her. She made me realize how much I've enjoyed this time with you, despite the reasons behind being stuck together."

I grin. At her. At the lies. At the fucking absurdity of this entire situation. "I've enjoyed it, too."

I'll enjoy it even more once she knows the truth.

I turn my focus her way, needing to shoot her a smug

glance she will hopefully look back on later. But I regret the glimpse immediately.

She's staring at me, her body turned my way, her cheek pressed against the head rest. That gorgeous mouth of hers is kicked at one side, her eyes gentle.

I don't understand how she can be so undeniably beautiful and entirely monstrous at the same time. The body of a goddess with the strategic mind of the devil.

"You should get some rest." I press my foot harder on the accelerator. "It's going to be another long day."

"I couldn't sleep even if I wanted to. I've got too many questions."

I bet she does.

The more answers she has, the better she can control me.

"Now isn't the time. My head is killing me." Not a lie. My brain is seriously fucking with my vision. My bottom lip is swollen and throbbing. And my ribs protest with every inhale.

"I understand. But I need to know, Sebastian. Once you've had time to decompress and think things through, I want you to tell me everything that happened while you were gone. It's important."

I nod. "We can talk tonight." We'll talk about everything. Every fucking thing she's been hiding from me. "For now, just let me concentrate on getting us somewhere safe."

HOURS GO BY WITH NOTHING BUT THE SOUND OF ASPHALT beneath the tires and the crinkle of junk food wrappers as we decimate the stash of snacks I purchased at the gas station.

The further I drive, the less I see. There hasn't been a house in miles, or a street sign, for that matter, which means I'm headed in the right direction. The eerie desolation is familiar.

"I think I'm going to have to ask you to pull over again." Keira stretches her arms above her head. "My bladder is beginning to protest."

"We're almost there. Can you wait ten minutes? Maybe twenty?"

She sits up straight. "There's a town nearby? I haven't seen any sign of life for half an hour."

"There's a house up ahead. That's where we're staying."

She leans closer to her window, scanning the scenery. "You had a destination in mind all along? I thought you were aimlessly driving."

"I don't usually do anything aimlessly. And if memory serves, the house should come into view once we get over this hill."

As predicted, my brother's home appears as a small speck toward the horizon. It's all alone. A solitary building in the middle of nowhere. A hermit's dream. A kidnapped victim's nightmare.

Twenty minutes later, I turn onto the long dirt drive, a trail of dust billowing in our wake as we approach the place I chose to have our showdown.

There's no sign of life. No cars. No crops. No cattle. Not a glimmer of help in sight. Just a house and more than enough room for a scream to die on the wind.

She inches forward in her seat. "How do you know about this place?"

"From an online rental site. I've stayed here once before." I drive into the house yard, the smaller block fenced off from the mass of vacant land. A pebbled path leads to the front door, but I steer onto the grass and park by the side of the garage to hide the car from the road.

"It looks nice." She unfastens her belt and opens her door. "What are we going to do about food? And both of us are back to having no clothes."

"Don't worry. The host told me the fridge would be stocked. And I'm not seeing the lack of clothing as a bad thing." I wink at her and slide from the car, my bruised muscles aching in protest.

I'm not looking forward to checking my injuries, but my heart pounds in anticipation as the seconds tick down to the moment when I get to tell Keira she's far from safe with me.

I can't fucking wait to wipe that saccharine smile from her

face. For those eyes to blink at me in fear instead of sweet manipulation.

"Is the front door unlocked?" She starts walking for the house, probably trying to reiterate the story about needing to use the bathroom, when I'd bet my life she wants to hunt for a phone.

"The key should be under the mat."

She increases her pace, disappearing inside while I open the trunk and take inventory. There's a laptop case, a new phone, and a gray duffle bag—Hunter's trusty tool kit.

I leave the computer and phone, not wanting Keira to know she has a way of communicating with the outside world, and lug the bag.

I don't see her again for ten minutes. I hear the flush of the toilet as I enter the kitchen and dump my supplies on the counter. Then her footfalls trek through the rooms, the pace frantic.

"Did the rental listing mention a landline?" she calls out. "I can't find one anywhere."

I smirk as I pull two beers from the fridge. "There's no landline. Or internet. We're on our own little island out here."

I crack a can of beer open and take a gulp as she comes to stand in the doorway.

"I need to call Cole. He'll be worried."

"Don't stress. Hunter would've told him the plan."

"What plan?" She pads forward, her feet devoid of socks. "You still haven't told me anything."

"I will. First—drink." I hold a beer out in her direction. "We've got all the time in the world to talk."

She takes the can from me, her brow furrowed. "Why do I get the feeling you're trying to avoid the conversation?"

I laugh, and the rushed movement of my chest produces a stab of pain through my ribs.

"Sebastian?" Her frown deepens and she steps closer, her concerned gaze flicking between my eyes. "Those bruises on your face aren't the extent of your injuries, are they?"

The sharp stab turns into one motherfucker of a throb, her charade weighing down on me. I'd once thought she was a phenomenal woman. I guess I still do, just not in the admirable ways I'd once assumed.

"It's okay."

She steps closer, stopping toe to toe. "No, it's not." She grips the bottom of my shirt and tries to lift, only to have the tight material restrict around my stomach. Then she sets her sights on my buttons, frantically undoing them to stare at my chest.

"*Jesus.*" She clasps a hand over her mouth and steps back. "What did they do to you?"

I don't avert my gaze from hers. My injuries aren't going anywhere. But her affection soon will—the meticulous act.

"You need a doctor," she demands.

"I've already told you, you can't get rid of me that easily. I'll be fine." I take a deep pull of alcohol and lean back against the counter.

She peers up at me, her eyes pleading. "Sebastian, please. Let me drive you to a hospital."

I hear the truth through the lies—*Let me drive you to civilization where I can find a phone.*

"We're not going anywhere."

"I'm worried about you." Her hands raise to my face, her palms cupping my cheeks and the heavy stubble beneath. "And you're scaring me. What happens if there's internal bleeding? What do I do if you pass out?"

Resentment burns through my veins. I despise her bullshit concern. I fucking loathe it. I can't even answer her without blowing what little hold I have on fury.

"Talk to me." She leans in, her hips pressed against mine.

Her expression is sickening. The position of her thigh between my legs is a blatant strategy.

I hate it.

I hate this.

And, God, I wish I hated her.

But my dick hasn't read the memo. I grow hard, my erection rubbing against her. Despite everything—mainly self-preservation and common fucking sense—my base desires run rampant.

I want to fuck her.

Fuck her over.

I lean close, my mouth a breath away from hers. "I'm not interested in talking."

Her eyes widen. Her tongue snakes out to slowly moisten her lips. "You're hurt..."

"I'm hungry," I growl, my tone letting her know my appetite has nothing to do with food.

"Sebastian..."

I wait for her to continue. To confess. To fucking open her mouth and tell me what a lying, traitorous snake she is in an attempt to stop this moving any further.

The words never come.

She eyes me, those baby blues intense as she slowly leans in, approaching me like I'm a wild animal she shouldn't want to touch. But she does touch. She brushes her mouth over mine, the connection soft and devastating. Everything inside me wages war. Control struggles with lust. Anger fights with desire. Sense battles with complete and utter lunacy.

She pulls me under her spell. Slaughtering me. Reclaiming me as her fucking puppet.

She's had me hooked since we first met.

All this time I've been her pawn.

I smash my mouth against hers, parting her lips with my tongue to delve deep. I punish her with my kiss, detesting her with every swipe of connection.

She's slow to react. I think she might pull away.

Then her hands find my chest, and she moans. Mewls. The needy sounds only increase my livid rage.

She pushes my jacket from my shoulders and rips at the buttons of my shirt. Her touch journeys over my injuries, gentle, caring. The delicate nature is a reminder to keep my head. To stay in control because she's always on top of her game.

"I can't wait to fuck you." I speak into her mouth.

Her arms circle my back, those fingers searching until she finds my gun and begins to pull it from my waistband.

"*Don't.*" I snatch the weapon from her grip.

She stares at me, wide-eyed. "I only wanted to get it out of the way."

Like hell.

Does she really expect me to believe that?

Fuck.

Was she going to shoot me?

"Let me take care of it." I push the weapon along the counter, out of reach, then walk us to the other side of the kitchen, pressing her into the drawers.

"I wouldn't have fired it by accident," she murmurs. "I know my way around a gun."

"I don't doubt it. But after this morning, it's best if your fingerprints stay far away."

She recoils, her lips parting for a brief moment before she slowly nods. "I will. I promise."

I slam my mouth back on hers with punishing force as I wrench at my belt and lower my zipper. She's all over my dick in seconds, stroking, squeezing, working the length through her angel soft skin.

We're all hands and lips and tongues. Lust and deception and lies. It's a storm of manipulation. A tsunami of wrong.

Flashbacks of the last few days pummel me. Stabbing me. Punishing unlike any other assault.

We'd had a connection. An attraction. I believed she was going to be mine.

"Turn around." I can't stand the fucking sight of her. I grab her shoulders, spin her, and bend her to my will. "Let me show my innocent little baby a thing or two."

Those lies cut the deepest. All that bullshit about being sexually assaulted. There's a reason I never found that information when I dug into her life. Everything she told me was fabricated. I'm starting to believe the whole fucking shooting was staged to bring us together so she could work her deceitful magic.

She's splayed over the counter in seconds, her dress lifted above her ass, her thong shoved to her ankles.

I squeeze her thighs, making her squeal before I delve

164

higher, skimming her traitorous pussy with my fingertips. She's wet, dripping at the thought of undermining me.

Again.

I position my cock at her entrance and slam home. The jolt jars my ribs, the pain physical as well as emotional. I stand frozen, battling self-loathing while she grinds against me.

This isn't a virtuous woman. I'd gobbled up that bullshit like a seafood buffet.

Nothing was real.

Not a damn thing.

She lied about everything, and the thought of her misleading me about contraception makes my blood turn cold. How do I know she's not trying to get pregnant in another elaborate scheme to set me up?

Jesus. The last thing I want is a child spawned from this monster. The thought of my genes matched with those of a family bathed in sins and destruction... *Fuck.*

I slam into her. Over and over.

I loathe her, yet I can't leave her alone.

I want to punish her, but I'm only torturing myself.

My dick quits. It taps out, unable to function through the mud in my head. And here I was thinking this situation couldn't get any worse.

I slow my movements, only to have her glance over her shoulder to meet my gaze with lust-filled confusion, then even worse, pity.

"Sebastian?"

I step back, my limp cock falling free of her bear trap. My self-respect falling even further.

"Fuck." I yank at my pants, zip, belt up, and prepare for battle.

"Sebastian..."

I can't play these games anymore. It's clear she's far better at pretending than I am. She's got no heart. No fucking soul.

She turns, reaching out to grab my arm. "It's okay."

"Is it?" Her touch seeps under my skin, poisoning my veins. "Do you really think this is okay? From my point of view it couldn't be worse."

"You need to rest. We shouldn't be doing this while you're hurt."

"My dick isn't playing Sleeping Beauty because of my injuries," I snarl. "Disgust is the only reason I can't keep it hard long enough to finish."

She jerks back as if I've slapped her. "Disgust? Over what?"

"*You.*" I hold her gaze, letting the fear in her eyes strengthen me. "Drop the act, peaches. I know you set me up."

16

DECKER

She stiffens, her body instantly rigid, her face draining of color.

I allow her time to process. Give her the sweet, delicious seconds for my words to sink in. "Want me to give you a few minutes to strategize your way out of this one?"

She remains silent for a minute. Then two. Finally, resignation blinks into her eyes, and she begins righting her clothes. Her movements are violent, a frantic storm of yanked underwear and loose hair.

I lean against the fridge, pretending I'm calm and in control when my pulse is erratic. "How long have you known I'm the informant?"

She doesn't answer. She keeps those lips pressed tight as she straightens her dress and flips her hair out from beneath the collar of her cardigan. She's striving for anger when I can clearly see panic in her features.

"How long, Keira?"

She stalks away, and I stop her with a tight grip around her wrist, yanking her back to my side. She glares at me, her eyes filled with fury.

"*How long?*" I growl.

"Two minutes." She snatches her arm away. "You're the last person I thought capable of snitching."

I chuckle under my breath. "That's a nice story, but I don't believe you. You've known for a while. You used that sweet pussy of yours to distract me from the truth."

She winces.

"Don't worry. If I whored myself out for my family, I'd be embarrassed to admit it, too."

Her arm snaps up, flying toward my face.

I grab her wrist before she can slap me and entwine our fingers with force. "I've suffered enough injuries because of you today."

"I can't believe it was you this whole time." She pulls away, claiming disgust when she had no problem fucking me a few minutes prior. "You're the one who's been betraying my family?"

"Pretending you weren't setting me up is a waste of time."

Her gaze meets mine, vicious and stony. "I didn't know."

I clench my teeth, my patience lost. I walk into her, pushing her backward to cage her against the counter, my face a breath from hers. "Stop lying to me."

Her eyes blaze with emotion—fear, anger, heartbreak. The kaleidoscope changes so quickly I'm not sure which one she expects me to believe.

She leans back, placing an inch of space between us. "Sebastian, I didn't..." She shakes her head, her face draining of color.

"How long?" I snap.

"Get off me." She pushes at my chest, digging her fingers into ribs I'm sure are fractured.

I grunt through the pain, stumbling back, and she rushes out from beneath me. I clench my teeth and clutch the counter, trying to figure out the motives behind her continued denial.

"I'm going to grow tired of this pretty fucking quickly. I already know you lied about your father. There's no point pretending."

She maneuvers around the dining table, using it as a shield. A fucking pathetic one at best.

"That table won't save you," I drawl. "There's no phone out here. No communication devices. Not another soul for miles. Nobody even knows you're here. So I suggest you stop fighting the inevitable."

"You need to let me go." She grips the back of one of the wooden chairs. "Cole will track you down if you hurt me. He won't give up."

I laugh. "He'll have to beat Hunter to it."

"He knows?" Her brows skyrocket. "That's why he took you away to talk this morning." Slowly, her face slackens. "He never came back. What did you do to him?"

"Far less than he did to me, that's for sure." I point to my face, my ribs, and take solace in the fact she's doesn't assume Hunter is my accomplice. Yes, it might be another ploy, but I'll take whatever solace I can get at this stage.

"Is he safe?" she demands.

"He's safer than you are. Now sit down."

A rapid exhale rushes from her lips and her gaze shoots around the room—to the door leading outside, the entrance to the hall, the pictures on the wall, then finally the duffle on the counter. "What are you going to do? Kill me?"

"Let's take it one step at a time. First, I want answers. How long have you known?" I repeat. "What did I do that tipped you off?"

She shakes her head in denial.

"You're going to tell me everything, Keira. Either by choice or by force."

She becomes more frantic with the assessment of her surroundings. She takes in the chairs around her, the knives in the distant cutting block, the empty fruit bowl in the center of the table. She wants to hurt me, and I'm a sick motherfucker for the buzz of anticipation shooting through my limbs.

"Before you consider running, please understand that your position will get a lot worse once I catch you. I don't want to make use of my handy bag of goodies."

Her gaze flicks to the gray duffle again. "What's in there?"

"Hunter's tools." I grin. "Let your imagination run wild with the possibilities."

"*Stop it*," she snaps. "I know you won't hurt me."

"Either sit down or I'll come grab you and tie you in place.

It's your choice. And God knows I'm itching for a reason to manhandle you." I snatch at the duffle, sliding it toward me. I yank open the zipper and pull out the cable ties, electrical tape, rope, and pliers, placing them on display along the counter. "This is the last time I ask—how long have you known?"

"I've told you," she pleads. "I didn't know."

"Then why tell me the bullshit story about your father?"

"To prove your loyalty. I thought it would be an easy way to convince Cole you're on our side. I told you a huge secret—"

"A huge fucking lie," I clarify.

"Yes." She nods. "I told you a huge lie to convince him we could trust you. I thought you were different."

"Oh, believe me, I thought you were different, too, precious. But your story doesn't make sense. You would never risk a rumor like that getting out."

"Exactly. I didn't have any doubts of your loyalty."

"Bullshit." I snatch the cable ties off the counter and stalk around the table toward her. "Do you want me to tell you what I think happened?"

She pulls out a chair, slowing my chase.

"You and Cole organized the shooting, making sure I was by your side when the bullets strategically hit the ceiling to ensure nobody got hurt. Your brother then demanded I protect you, and you led us out of town to a place where you could attempt to seduce answers out of me. Am I close?"

She keeps retreating, her position always opposite to mine.

"The breakdown in the shower was bullshit," I accuse. "Sleeping on the sofa with me was a strategy to win me over. You fucked me in an attempt to get under my skin. And that sob story about being raped was a load of fucking crap."

"No." She shakes her head, reiterating her lies.

"You and Cole planned the entire thing to confirm your suspicions, and voila, here they are." I lunge, climbing onto a chair, then the table to dash along the wood.

She screams, the sound reverberating off the walls as she sprints for the hall.

I jump to the ground, catching her from behind in two

steps. I cage her arms to her sides, her ass bucking against me as I place my mouth near her ear. "Chasing you feels as good as I thought it would."

She struggles, killing my chest with the wild-beast routine while I drag her to the closest chair and force her to take a seat. I straddle her, pinning her in place as I loop one tie around her wrist and the wooden slat of the backrest, making the plastic strip cling tight. Then I do the same with her other arm, keeping her strapped to the chair.

"You son of a bitch." She kicks, bucks, and yanks at her arms.

I move off her, glancing down to admire my handiwork. "There. That's better." I tower above her to watch the show. "Throw a tantrum, by all means, but you ain't going anywhere until I have what I want."

She shouts in frustration, her chest rising and falling with heavy breaths. "*Fuck you.*"

I quirk a brow. "Been there, done that. I don't plan on being a repeat offender."

"I swear to God, Decker, Cole will make sure your body is never found."

I shrug. "I know. That's the beauty of this—I have nothing left to lose. My fate is already set. But I can make sure I take a few souls with me on my trip to hell."

Her rampant breathing increases.

"You're not the naive innocent you pretend to be." I slide onto the table in front of her and place my feet on her seat, either side of her thighs. The slightest cage to add to her restriction.

She holds my stare. "I've told you, and I'll keep telling you —I had no idea you were a lying piece of shit. The story about my father was a test. I thought you'd keep your mouth shut."

I lean forward, my elbows on my knees as I bring our faces close. I watch her for long moments, staring into those eyes, reading her expression. "Such a pretty little liar," I murmur. "I always knew you were the best weapon in your brother's arsenal."

"If you're right, then why isn't he here?" She cocks a brow

in defiance. "If this was all an elaborate scheme to set you up, why am I strapped to a chair while you hold me hostage?"

She fractures my thought process. But only momentarily. "Because you didn't tell him about the lie. You deviated from the plan. Then your phone ran out of battery, and now you're stuck trying to clean up the mess."

"Even so, if I organized something with my brother, he would've had men watching us the entire time. You never would've been able to drag me out here. They would've been all over you. You know that."

I sit up straight, trying to sort the truth from the deception. What aren't I seeing? What have I missed?

"There was no plan, Sebastian. I didn't know you were the informant. I didn't even suspect you."

I run a hand over my mouth, thinking, thinking, thinking. She's manipulating me again. She's working a new strategy, and I've got no fucking clue what it is. But I have no intention of succumbing.

"Let's switch topics for a moment." I cock my head to the side, studying her. "Tell me, do you know what your uncle was doing the night he got splattered over the front of that SUV?"

Her eyes flare with awareness. With knowledge.

"You *do* know," I taunt. "I can see it on your face."

"He was at a whorehouse. So what?"

"Is that what you call it? A whorehouse?" I laugh, the sound bitter. Her ability to fuck me while deceiving me makes far more sense now. "You know, I watched you for a long time. I seriously thought I knew it all, and I'm ashamed to admit I was wrong."

I gently grab her chin, flaunting my control. "I know better now. You're just like your uncle, aren't you? You've got the same filthy perversions as the generation before you. You've been in on it the whole time."

Her skin turns ashen beneath my touch.

I'm getting closer to the truth. I can see it. Feel it.

"Answer me." My tone is a menacing threat.

"I don't know what you're talking about. My uncle was at a

brothel the night he got run down. If you've heard a different story, it's news to me."

I stroke my fingers along her jaw, over her bottom lip. The more I stare, the more I notice.

Her eyes are the deepest blue, the outer edges melting into green. And those lips, those dark tempting lips, are ten times more beautiful as they tremble.

"Sebastian..."

I slide my hand to her throat, my fingertips grazing her carotid, her heavy swallow pressing into my palm. "Mmm?"

"Tell me what you think my uncle was doing."

I let a lazy smirk take over. "I don't *think*, Keira. I *know*."

"Then tell me," she whispers.

"Okay. I'll play along." I'm enjoying this part of the game. The revenge. The torture. It's the justice I've been craving for years. "Your uncle was breaking in sex slaves."

"No." I push to my feet, only to be dragged back down by the ties binding my arms to the seat. "You're lying."

"Is that guilt I see in your eyes?" He clucks his tongue. "Silly me. I'd convinced myself you knew nothing about the human trafficking."

"What you see in my eyes is disgust. *For you.*" I've hated my uncle for years. Despised him. But I won't believe he's capable of this. I refuse. "You're digging for evidence. And it's not going to work. You won't turn me against my family. Especially not with far-fetched stories."

"You want proof?" He remains on the table, the sides of his feet pressing tight against my thighs. "Should I show you the names of the girls in this state who've gone missing over the last few years and how the Torian name can be linked to more than a third of them?"

My heart stops. "*All. Lies.*"

"I can tell you exactly how it happens. I know every move that's made." He leans closer. "Your uncle claims to be a bigshot movie producer, or the owner of a modeling agency, or whatever else his victim needs to reach their dreams. He fawns over his targets, making them feel special as he promises them the world. He takes them to fancy restaurants, buys them expensive clothes, then clinches the deal with an overseas trip which is supposed to mark the start of their career. That's when your daddy takes over."

My father?

My stomach revolts, twisting and turning.

My dad started a modeling agency years ago. It was a hobby, a 'bit of fun on the side,' he'd told me. I'd even designed his website with images he'd contracted from an overseas photographer. "I don't believe you."

He shrugs. "It's a little late to claim that when I'm already convinced you're involved."

"No." I shake my head. "You're wrong. About all of us."

"The case is closed on your dad and uncle, pumpkin. There's no question about it."

"Then why haven't they been arrested?" I raise a brow, trying to convince myself of their innocence.

He frowns at me as if I'm stupid. "Maybe because dear ol' dad has been hiding out in another country. And Uncle Dick is practically a part of the produce section."

"No, no, no." I keep shaking my head. "Why are you doing this? Is it for money? Is that what the authorities are giving you?"

"I didn't snitch for greed. I did it for me. For the pleasure of your demise. There's no game show prize waiting for me at the end of this. Only the thrill of seeing you all rot in prison like you deserve."

My heart clenches, the erratic beats painful. I don't understand. I don't want to.

"Come on, Keira. It's bad enough that you say you're not involved, but to pretend you didn't know, or your family is incapable, is an insult." He gives me a condescending smile. "It's not like you guys have ever been on the right side of the law."

"If I knew, I would never let that happen. Me, of all people, would never *ever*, let that happen."

"You, of all people?" His words drip with condescension.

"Yes. *Me, of all people.*"

"Oh." He rolls his eyes. "Because of your traumatic sexual past, right?"

My eyes blaze in fury. I hadn't lied about my history despite his theory of this being a game.

I'd wanted to tell him more. So much more. All my secrets had been his to own. But I'd needed to test him first. I had no choice in sharing the story about my father's death. It was the quickest way to see if he was loyal. Honest. I knew a revelation as monumental as the mighty Luther Torian's passing would either be spread in an instant, or held tight because of our connection.

I didn't want to delay my feelings for him.

I didn't want to draw out the trial.

I had to prove I was right about Sebastian, and I didn't care how that happened as long as it happened quickly.

But it turns out Cole had been right all along.

My brother's suspicions were on point, and now I can only assume the damage caused if Sebastian has circulated the lie.

I blink through the anger burning in my eyes, and a heated trail slides down my cheek. He watches the path of the lone tear, seeming mesmerized, until I swipe it away with my shoulder.

"That's fucking brilliant," he whispers in awe. "You're a seductress and the most flawless actress all rolled into one."

"Stop it." I scream and tug at my bindings.

"Are you crying because you think it will fool me? Or is it because you know you're going to get locked up for a very, very long time?" He leans close, getting in my face. "Don't worry. You're one of the pretty ones. I'm sure you'll make a good little bitch."

I hold his gaze, ignoring the blur in my vision as I force myself not to blink. "I had no clue." I lean forward, showing him I'm not scared. I'm not daunted. "I only lied to you about my father because I was falling for you. *Because I cared about you.* You're the one who betrayed me."

I don't recognize him anymore. I don't even recognize my own voice.

My vision continues to blur, but it's not just from building tears. It's from the manic hysteria I'm trying to hold in. My heart beats wildly. My chest is so heavy I can barely breathe.

I become lost down a rabbit hole of mental anguish. My demons haunt me. My history crucifies me.

I hyperventilate, my throat punishingly tight. My face is on fire. My heart, my lungs, my everything pounds and squeezes hard enough to kill me. I can't think past the horror. I can't see through the images my mind conjures of all those tortured women.

"Keira." He scowls, his face growing shadowed, the edges of my vision darkening. "*Keira.*" He shakes me, pushing back a small part of the overwhelming tide of emotion. "Cut the crap. I'm not falling for your shit."

My throat clogs with revulsion. "How many—" I croak. "How many women?"

"Who knows. It's a lucrative business. Your father knows how to cover his tracks." His expression hardens. "It could be hundreds. Maybe thousands."

Bile rushes into my mouth, and I swallow to bite back the need to purge. I know what it's like to be physically manipulated, for my body to be used. I know, and it fills me with blinding...everything. Sorrow. Fury. Fear.

"They always make sure those women leave the country of their own free will. Happy and fucking eager to please. And they actually follow through with the photo shoots. But not until after they've lived it up with booze, sex, and drugs. Lots of pictures are taken of that, too. And always uploaded to social media. That's how the corrupt cops in foreign countries can tell the families back home that the women went off the rails due to addiction or poor decisions."

I suck in lungfuls of breath, trying to push through the pummeling nausea. "I'm going to be sick."

He scoffs. "Do you think I care?"

His sterility makes my anguish ten times worse. I'm not the person he thinks I am. I'm not that type of monster.

I try to stand again, only to fall back in place under the restricting ties. Heat consumes my throat and mouth. I crane my neck to the side and tilt my face away. I lean as far as my bindings allow and retch the toxic sludge in heaving waves.

"Jesus Christ." Sebastian shoves from the table.

I continue to vomit the contents of my stomach. Tears follow, streaking my cheeks, staining my soul. I don't stop until my belly is empty. Then I wipe my mouth on my shoulder and hang my head as I sob.

"Quit it," he growls.

"I didn't know." My lips tremble as I turn my face toward him. "I swear."

He glares at me. There's a wealth of hatred in those eyes, but maybe there's the slightest bit of doubt, too.

He wants to believe me. I know he does.

"Please, Sebastian. You have to trust me. I never—"

He slams a palm down on the table. "Trust you? Are you kidding? I can barely bring myself to look at you."

"You lied to me, too," I say in a rush. "But I'm not the enemy here."

"You're not the victim either," he snarls through gritted teeth.

He pushes away from the table and storms to the kitchen. He stands there for a moment, clutching the counter, silent and still.

I want to say something, anything to break him out of this anger, only the words form in disjointed sentences. I can't think straight, not with the nuclear explosion of reality devastating my mind and the heartache taking over my chest.

"You know me." I swallow to ease the taste of bile. "I know you." I heave out a breath. I frown through the overwhelming confusion. If only I could focus so everything would make sense. "Sebastian, please explain all this to me. I don't under—"

"Shut up."

I balk at his continued vehemence. "I don't know the real you, do I?" The realization comes with an icy cold chill.

The harsh reality I thought I'd been living in wasn't reality at all. *That* existence was the fairytale. *That life,* full of deception and betrayal, was nothing in comparison to the truth.

He yanks open the duffle, his movements filled with livid rage as he pulls out a utility knife.

Oh, God.

He swings back around, lifting the blade while he walks toward me.

"No." I shake my head. "Please, Sebastian, don't do this. I promise I can prove I'm not involved. Just give me a chance."

"How?"

How? Jesus. I don't know. "Let me call Cole. Let me call Layla. Or my father."

"What the fuck is a phone call going to do?" He keeps approaching, not stopping until he's in my face. His livid rage steals away the gentle man I thought I knew.

He grabs my upper arm, drawing it high, making my wrist ache as it pulls against the plastic binding.

He's going to stab me.

Kill me.

I thought at a time like this I'd fight like hell. All I want to do is get on my knees and beg. Not only for my life. I want to plead for forgiveness for not recognizing my family's sins. I need to pray for absolution.

I should've known.

I should've paid more attention.

"I don't know how to make you believe me. Tell me what to do. Tell me how to make this right."

He lowers the blade to my wrist as horror fills my veins. I can't watch the metal penetrate. I refuse to witness the start of my own death. So I stare at him instead. I focus on his dark eyes, the deep pull of his brows, those tight lips that still seem entirely beautiful despite the tight line they're now clamped in.

He's going to slice my wrists. I'm going to bleed out.

"You're not this man, Sebastian. I know you're not. And you should know I don't deserve this. I shouldn't be punished for the crimes of someone else."

He narrows his gaze on me, his lip curled in a snarl. "The only thing I know is that I'm fucking sick of you playing the victim."

He starts wiggling the blade, and I hold my breath, waiting for the pain to breach my panic.

"All those women your family stole *are the victims*." The knife stops moving, and my arm falls free. "My *fucking sister* is the victim."

I hear static after those defining words—*my fucking sister*.

I don't pay attention as he releases my other arm. I don't feel fear or hysteria or disgust. I'm hollow. Empty.

That's why he's doing this? His sister is the reason he became a traitor to the most dangerous family in the state?

I stare up at him, a million questions waiting on immovable lips. I can't speak. I barely breathe.

He flings my other arm away and turns, heading back to the kitchen. He snatches the duffle, his gun, and his can of beer before stalking to the back door.

"Don't bother running," he snarls. "If I have to chase you again, I won't be as kind when I catch you." He grabs the door handle and pulls it wide. "Clean up your fucking mess."

18

DECKER

I SIT ON THE BACK DECK, THE BEER CAN NOW WARM IN MY hand after hours spent staring at the setting sun. I can't go back inside, and it's not only because my brother's house is now filled with the smell of vomit.

I can't stand to look at her. I can't keep questioning the facts just because of her pleading blue-eyed gaze. So I'll continue to hide out here, drowning in doubt.

I'm not worried she'll run. I'm too fucking drained to give a shit. But even if she does, we're miles from civilization. More than a day's trek to salvation if she has hopes of escaping.

All the external doors are locked except for the one a few feet to my right. She's caged. Unless she decides to climb through a window, which I have no doubt she will. In that case, I'll hear her and have another chance for retribution once I chase her down.

I think that's the only thought keeping me upright—the possibility of sprinting after her, scaring her, punishing her.

There's no sound out here. Not even the whimsical chirp of a bird. There's only the breeze rustling through the dried grass and the heavy beat of my pulse echoing in my ears.

I never should've told her about my sister. I hate her having insight into that part of my life. But those words had burst free, demanding to be heard. After all this time, I wanted someone to know the truth.

My life changed the moment I realized Penny had been taken.

Now there's no hiding the darkness shadowing me, or the crimes I've committed to get here.

I'm not the man I once was. That happy-go-lucky fucker is gone. The naive sack of shit who lived a simple life is dead and buried. And I guess the guy I became soon will be too, but that shit won't be a metaphor.

My days are numbered. The finish line to failure is fast advancing, and I have no clue how to stop its approach.

I raise my beer and take a long pull. I don't know where to go from here. I'm not sure there's a way out, or if I'd even take it if there is. I've spent years seeking answers. Striving for revenge. I no longer know how to live any other way.

Footsteps approach from inside, and I lower my drink to listen. Her figure cuts through the yellow light beaming through the glass panes of the door. Her presence tickles the back of my fucking neck.

Don't come out here.

Don't you fucking dare.

The door opens and she slowly steps outside, walking to the railing to look out over the vast expanse of vacant land as she clings to the cuffs of her cardigan.

She remains quiet, her silence eating up the night until it feels like I've been staring at her for hours.

"How long?" she whispers.

I take another mouthful of beer and drag my gaze from her slender body. I hate the attraction that lingers when I look at her. I fucking loathe it after everything she's done.

She turns to face me, her face blotchy with the remnants of crocodile tears.

I won't be fooled. Not again.

"How long have you been trying to take down my family?"

"Why?" I glare. "What cunning plan have you concocted to use against me?"

"I want to help."

"*Help?*" I scoff. "Go back inside. You're wasting your breath talking to me."

182

She lowers her gaze, playing a meek, apologetic role that doesn't suit her. Not anymore.

"Then why tell me? Why am I here?"

I can't answer that. I honestly don't know.

Originally, I feared for Hunter and Sarah's safety. At least that's what I told myself, even though I know better than anyone that those two can look after themselves.

I guess I'd wanted to prove Hunter wrong.

I knew he believed Keira had set me up. But, Jesus, I'd hoped like hell he'd been smoking crack, too.

The whole drive here I hated on her, despising every fucking breath, while also wishing she'd do or say something to prove Hunt wrong. That somehow he'd been mistaken. That I hadn't been fooled into falling for her.

"I didn't tell you anything you didn't already know." I take another chug of beer to drown my pity party.

She leans back against the railing, her hands resting behind her ass. Calm. Subdued. "What do you plan on doing with me?"

"Whatever I like," I grate. "And the more you annoy me, the worse the options get. So leave me the fuck alone."

Her chin hitches. "You won't kill me, Sebastian. I know you won't. You've said it yourself, you're not like my brother, and I know that wasn't a lie."

"Do you?" I'm not entirely sure she's right. If given the chance, I'd kill her father. I'd kill her uncle as well. And despite her claims of Cole's innocence regarding women trafficking, I'm pretty sure I could fuck him up without feeling an ounce of guilt, too.

I could massacre her entire family and dance a fucking jig in their blood. I wouldn't care how I had to do it. With my bare hands. Up close or from a distance. With a knife or a bullet or a fucking frying pan.

I'm at the point where I'd pay good money to look deep into the eyes of those motherfuckers while I revel in their pleas for mercy.

"Are you seriously that confident I wouldn't bury you out here if I had proof of your involvement?"

"But you don't," she murmurs. "And you never will, because I'm not involved. Neither are Layla or Cole, and I'd bet my life on it."

I raise my brows. "You might regret that wager one day."

"I won't. I don't have the slightest doubt."

"Give it time. Earlier you were certain your uncle and father weren't involved either."

She lowers her attention to the wooden slats of the porch. "That's different. Layla is too kindhearted to even imagine doing something like this. And Cole..."

"And Cole what?" I sneer. "Is he kindhearted, too? Have you forgotten he tried to strangle you the first night we met?"

Her gaze darts to mine, her mouth parting on a confession that doesn't breach her lips.

"Go on, say it," I taunt. "Weave me another bedtime story."

She sighs, her shoulders slumping with the deep exhale. "Cole never tried to strangle me."

"Oh, yeah? Then what would you call it?"

"A ritual. An act." She keeps clinging to the cuffs of her cardigan, pulling on them like a lifeline. "Whenever someone new comes to work for my family, Cole and I put on a show to pretend we have a temperamental relationship—a weak spot that could be manipulated. It's an easy way to flush out those trying to tear us apart. But the truth is the opposite."

I frown, reliving that night in my mind. She'd been scared. Cole had been in a rage.

It was all for show.

Fuckers.

"He tells me everything, Sebastian. He has since our mother died. I know how you came to work for us. I know about the hits my brother has ordered and why. I know where our money comes from and how it's laundered. I know everything."

I throw back my beer and take a long pull, emptying the can. "So, you act like a docile puppet when you're really a coldhearted bitch. No surprise there."

Her jaw tenses. "That's not entirely true. I'm not a good

184

person, I've never claimed to be, but I'm not guilty of what you're accusing me of. I need you to stop judging me through your anger and listen for a minute."

"I don't need to do shit." I crush the can in my fist. "Are you forgetting this is personal for me? *I know* what your family does. Quit trying to talk your way out of the facts."

"I'm not. You say you have all the proof you need on my father and uncle. And I believe you." She winces. "But you need to let me plead my case for me and my siblings. Let me prove Cole isn't involved. I think if you understand he's not capable of this, you'll realize Layla and I are innocent, too."

I throw the can toward the door and scowl at her, impatient.

"*Please.*" She chews on her lower lip. There's no seduction in the expression. Only feigned desperation. Pretend fear. "I was six when I was first sexually assaulted by someone I trusted."

"Jesus Christ." The diversion back to this conversation is enough to make my tired head spin. "I swear to God, Keira, I'll lose my shit if I have to listen to more of your lies."

Her throat works over a heavy swallow but she holds my gaze, determined. "I didn't know what was happening at first. My parents were in the kitchen. Cole was on the floor watching television right in front of me, while I sat side-by-side on the sofa with an attacker I'd grown to admire."

"Stop it," I mutter. "You're wasting your breath."

"He started complementing me," she continues as if I didn't speak. "Whispering right in my ear about how I was such a pretty little girl as his index finger ran in circles on my thigh, just below the hem of my skirt."

She's doing it again, trying to delude me with her sob stories.

It won't work.

I can't let it.

I clench my hands into fists, hating how her lies hypnotize me even though I know the truth.

"I can still remember how it felt." She lowers her attention to her feet. "The lone finger that changed to a full splayed

185

palm which worked its way beneath my clothes. When he reached the crotch of my underwear he smiled and chuckled an apology, pretending the intimate touch had been an accident."

I run a hand over my face and clench my teeth to maintain control. How the fuck does she do it? How can she spin her web of fiction like it's the truth?

"He did it in plain sight. Mere feet from Cole. I could hear my parents talking clearly in the next room. It made me think he mustn't be doing anything wrong if he wasn't trying to hide it."

"Nice story," I mutter. "You done yet?"

She lifts her gaze to mine, but the annoyance I anticipate isn't in her expression. Her forehead is etched in pain. Her eyes are glassy and filled with exhaustion.

I despise her beauty. I hate her duplicity. Most of all, I loathe the way she makes me want to believe her.

"He did it often, Sebastian. And I was too young to understand the severity of his actions. Whenever he came around, he'd hug me tighter than anyone else. He'd pay me more attention than Layla or Cole."

Her gaze trails off, disappearing in memory. "We'd always play chasies, and when he caught me it was usually with a splayed hand across my chest or my ass. I guess I always knew he was doing something wrong, but he was kind to me. He made me feel beautiful and bought me expensive gifts. As a little girl, I guess my greed for shiny new toys outweighed the discomfort."

"Just like your dad buys for the women he sells to the highest bidder."

She cringes. "Yeah. I guess you're right. And I was brainwashed in the same way. But then the casual touches turned into something more. His appetite increased the older I got, and I didn't know how to make—"

"*Keira*," I warn, needing her to stop before I give in. "You're not going to fool me with this. I'm never going to believe you."

I spin my own lies in the hopes she'll quit this vicious cycle. My hands itch to comfort her.

Her—a cunning, heartless bitch.

She shrugs, her face filled with resignation. "When I was twelve, my dad threw a party at our house. All the adults were drinking and talking loud. I could hear them from my room upstairs because us kids had been forbidden to join the fun." Her chin trembles. "That night he came into my room and laid beside me. I could smell the alcohol on his breath as he touched himself...right there...on my bed...while I pretended to sleep."

"*Stop*," my voice fractures.

Her eyes glaze with unshed tears. "No. Not until you believe me."

I scoff. "Don't hold your breath."

She wraps one arm around her middle, hugging herself. "Like I told you, I was fourteen when he raped me. I could never lie about that. Cole is the one who saved me by storming into my room and dragging a grown man off me. My brother never left my side. He stayed with me while I cried, his own tears mingling with mine as everyone continued to party downstairs."

"Yet there's no police report," I accuse. "I've dug deep enough into your life I've practically given you an enema. And not once have I found evidence of this."

"I couldn't report it."

"Of course not," I snap. "God forbid you ever have one piece of proof to backup your bullshit."

Her eyes harden, her spite finally coming out to play. "I couldn't report it because—"

"Shut it, Keira." I shove to my feet, ready to go inside just so I can get away from her.

"I couldn't report it—"

"I said *shut the fuck up*." I descend upon her in five fierce steps to grasp her upper arm.

Her hand raises in defense, or at least I think it does, until I catch the glint of silver as it sails toward my neck. The blade pierces my skin, the bite of pain barely felt over my rising fury.

Fuck. Me.

She's done it again.

She's fucking played me.

Jesus. Fucking. Christ.

I deserve to have my throat slashed. If I get out of this, I swear to God I'll do it myself for being so fucking stupid.

"How fast can you move, Sebastian?" she hisses. "Can you disarm me before I slice through your carotid? Because like you've mentioned before, there's nobody here to save you. There's no phone. No devices. No people. You'll bleed out before I reach the main road."

Her gaze flickers between my eyes, frantic even though I estimate she's got more than a fifty-fifty chance of doing exactly what she's threatened.

"Slice deep," I snarl, "because if the cut isn't fatal, what I inflict on you will be."

She shakes her head. "I'm not doing this to hurt you. I'm doing it to earn your trust."

She sucks in a deep breath and retreats, the kitchen knife clattering to the floor as she raises her hands in surrender.

My heart beats in an erratic pulse, waiting for the punchline to her joke.

"I couldn't report the rape because my attacker would never have gone to prison, no matter what I said." She articulates the words slowly. Succinctly. "Just like you said, criminal charges don't stick to men like my uncle."

My muscles pull taut, every inch of my skin crawling. "Richard?"

"Yes." She inclines her head. "Richard."

She steps toward the back door and reaches for the knob. "I didn't lie to you about the rape, and I wasn't playing games when I broke down the night of the shooting. The only reason I told you my father died is because I wanted nothing more than to trust you. I had to prove to myself you were the guy I thought you were, especially when I was falling for you."

Jesus. She's working me like a pro. "And now you know I'm not that guy."

"Now I know you're a better person than the man I fell

for." Her gaze pleads with me. "But you still don't believe me, do you?"

I clench my jaw. Unable to open my mouth.

I can't let her know she's reclaimed the upper hand.

I won't give her the satisfaction of knowing I'm hooked.

"Okay. I get it." She doesn't break our gaze, just keeps staring, keeps wordlessly pleading. "And I guess it won't make a difference if I tell you I'm responsible for putting Richard in hospital."

It takes all my strength not to jump at the information. She's feeding me exactly what I want to hear, but I can't let myself believe her.

Fuck me, I just can't.

She pauses briefly, waiting for a reply I refuse to give. Then she pulls the door wide and disappears inside, leaving me alone to deal with my increased self-loathing.

19

KEIRA

The house smells like the discarded contents of my stomach as I drag my feet inside.

I don't know what else to do other than reclaim the cleaning products from beneath the kitchen sink and start scrubbing the floor again. I crawl on hands and knees, polishing the tile when what I really need to do is scramble out of this torturous limbo.

I don't want to believe my father is capable of such destruction. I don't want to, yet, deep down, I already know the truth.

He's a monster. Not merely a criminal, but the devil himself.

In contrast, Sebastian has made himself into a vengeful angel. A hopeful savior.

Righteous.

Honorable.

Perfect.

And I betrayed him.

I scrub the floor harder, cleaning the tile like I want to cleanse my soul. My arms burn from the tension. My fingers ache with my tight grip.

Sebastian's right. I'm guilty. Even if I didn't participate. Even though I didn't have a clue. These atrocities were done by my family. My own flesh. There's no way I can free myself from blame.

I sit back on my haunches, unsure how to right all the wrongs. I can't fathom the pain I've caused with my ignorance.

I should've known.

Should've fucking known.

I push to my feet and pack away the chemicals. Then I make myself a coffee and sit down at the dining table while I wait for the masked scent of bile to die a slow death.

I sip from my mug, the liquid tasteless as I try to figure out my future when I have no control over the outcome. I'm still Sebastian's prisoner, and I don't think he has any plan to change the dynamic anytime soon. I also don't have the will to run. Or the desire.

What I want is for him to believe me. To finally trust me despite what I'm guilty of. But he doesn't come back inside to face me. Not even once my coffee has turned cold and the forced solitude makes me hollow. He leaves me to battle my demons on my own, and I can't help thinking about those that plague him.

He pretended to be Hunter's friend. His accomplice.

He faked his way into my heart. My body.

I guess I would've done the same.

If Layla had been one of the women taken... If Stella...

My lungs clench through torturous inhales. I can't fall down that mine-filled rabbit hole. All I can concentrate on is knowing I would've deceived or destroyed anyone who stood in my way of revenge.

But that doesn't make me feel any better for being the one Sebastian wants to punish. I don't like being his enemy. I want to go back to the place where he gave me kindness and protection.

His lust and adoration.

The fake fairytale.

I sigh and push from the table to pour the remaining dregs of coffee down the sink. The pungent scent of bile follows me with each step, smothering my nostrils and taunting my gag reflex.

This house needs fresh air. *Lots* of fresh air.

I walk from the kitchen and into the hall, finding the first bedroom with its queen size bed and lone bedside table. I increase my pace across the room, thankful for the distraction as I unlock the window and push the glass panel high.

The night breeze rushes through the gauze, filling my lungs with relief. I suck in a deep breath, only to have it rush back out at the sound of a slamming door.

I swing around, on alert as heavy footfalls thunder through the house.

"*Keira,*" Sebastian bellows.

I hesitate. I've waited over an hour for him to come inside and face me. To see me. The real me.

But the fury in his voice is a crystal clear indication he isn't ready to see anything other than his cemented misconceptions.

"*Keira.*"

I remain still, tracing the sound of his pounding footsteps from the dining area to the hall. I can't stand to speak to him like this. Not with raised voices and more drugging adrenaline.

My chest squeezes as he skitters to a stop in the doorway, his eyes blazing, his chest heaving.

He glances from me, to the open window, then back again. Judging. Convicting. "Trying to escape?"

I slump my shoulders while he continues to cast me as the enemy, his narrowed gaze too vicious for me to hold. "I'm trying to get rid of the smell." I turn my focus to the floor and drag my feet toward him, stopping before the doorway where he blocks my path. "Please move."

I ask for the one thing I don't want—space.

What I need is his proximity. I need him to face me. To face *this.* And, God, more than anything, I need him to believe me.

But he steps to the side, breaking with me with his cold dismissal.

I can't stand his continued hatred. His loathing. I'm not the person he thinks I am and I have to fight from the pull to slap some sense into him.

Bitter resentment coils in my blood making my limbs throb

192

as I squeeze by him and stalk further down the hall, to the next bedroom. I repeat my actions, making a beeline for the window and gripping the pane to thrust it high.

"Quit it." His menacing steps follow. "Leave them closed."

For the briefest second, I contemplate obeying him. It's only a blip in time. A breath of acquiescence before my spine grows rigid and I take hold of my anger.

I inch away from the window, leaving it open, then make toward him at his barricaded position at the door.

This time he doesn't move out of my way. He blocks my escape, his chest broad, his shoulders wide. "I said leave it closed."

"And I say we need fresh air." I hold his dark stare. "Or are you too scared you won't catch me if I run?"

He takes a predatory step in my direction, those chocolate eyes punishing through menacing slits.

My pulse spikes. A breath hitches through my lips. I backtrack, my pulse pounding in my throat as I retreat from his animosity. The toxicity of his malice coils around me, making my heart fracture.

"I'm not scared of anything," he grates.

I believe him.

He's not filled with fear. The emotion overtaking him is in stark contrast.

There's so much revulsion. A wealth of disgust and hostility. But up this close, there's more. Pain ebbs off him. I can see it now. There are fissures of misery in those eyes. Tiny glimmers of agony and torment.

Despite trying to hide it, his suffering matches my own.

It's like an awakening.

Slowly, I come to understand how the sarcasm and humor has hidden the tortured man beneath. He's pretended to be the joker, when his reality is shadowed by anguish.

"I have no reason to run." I take another retreating step toward the window.

His jaw ticks as he stalks closer. "If you knew how I felt, you would."

"Then tell me." My words fracture through parched lips.

"Explain why I should be scared, because I'm not. You would never hurt me. Not physically, despite how you're trying to emotionally tear me apart."

He stops, his shoulders stiffening as if my admission has inflicted a bone-deep wound. "You've got a short memory. It wasn't long ago you thought I was going to kill you with a utility knife."

"That wasn't you. You were mindless. I never—"

"It was me," he snaps. "The real me."

"So who is the man I spent the last forty-eight hours with? Who's the guy I've known for months?"

He releases a derisive scoff. "You mean the schmuck who eagerly lapped up your attention? That guy doesn't exist."

He's lying. I refuse to believe otherwise.

I know fake people. I've been surrounded by them all my life. And the man from the safe house wasn't one of those. He was caring and kind, despite his deceptions.

"You liked me," I accuse.

He'd wanted me. That part hadn't been an act. He'd slept with me without revulsion or disgust. It wasn't until we came here—until he knew I'd lied—that he couldn't stomach touching me.

He'd thought I was innocent until I'd given Cole what he wanted by testing the man who risked his life to protect me.

"It wasn't an act for you either, was it?" I scan his eyes, searching for threads of the truth in those dark depths. "You felt the same way I did."

He doesn't move. Doesn't even blink.

Hope sparks inside me, the sweet, delicious optimism working its way through my veins until he releases a sigh of exhaustion.

"I'm fucking tired, Keira. We're going to have to postpone this delusional conversation until tomorrow."

"Why? Sleep won't change our situation. The truth will still be here no matter how tired you are."

"Sleep will bring patience, which is something I don't have with you at the moment."

I can live without his patience. What I can't endure is

another minute without his honesty. "I'll make this easier for you. Just tell me why you slept with me in Westport. Was it because you wanted to, or because you thought it would get you closer to the truth?"

He stares at me. Stares right through me. There's no warmth. No kindness. No Sebastian. There's only sorrow and detachment. He's a shell of the man I once knew.

"Close the window," he mutters.

"No. Not until you answer me."

"Close the fucking window, Keira."

He's trying to scare me with his vicious tone, but there's no fear left. There's only determination and the strongest sense of perseverance.

"You were attracted to me," I demand. "You *wanted me.*"

His nostrils flare. "All in the past, honey."

My insides react. Squeezing. Tingling. "What changed? Do you hate me now because I told one lie? Because I tried to protect myself with the same dedication you protected me with?"

He falls quiet, those tired eyes lazily blinking back at me with sterility.

"Answer me," I plead. "Tell me how I'm the bad person when I betrayed you once, yet you made me fall for someone who doesn't exist."

"Can you hear yourself? Are you really begging for me? You're practically on your knees for a fucking informant." His nose scrunches in disgust. "If only Daddy could see you now."

Rage shoots to the forefront. "Don't throw him in my face." I take a menacing step forward. "Don't hold me accountable for my father's actions. *I* didn't do this. *I* didn't hurt you. *I* didn't take your sister."

He winces. "No, you did something worse. You made me crave the daughter of my sister's murderer."

His admission slices through me, piercing skin, muscle, and bone. I've been waiting for this truth. It's what I wanted. I just never anticipated it would tear me apart like this. "And I fell for a man who's trying to put my father in prison. I fell for the guy who deceived my family for months, if not years. I fell for you, despite your intentions." I swallow over the ache in my throat. "And I don't regret it, Sebastian."

His hands clench at his sides.

He's going to yell at me again. He's poised to lash out.

My heart pounds in tumultuous arrhythmia, anticipating the onslaught. Every second lasts an eternity waiting for him to berate me.

But he doesn't.

His expression doesn't change. He's still harsh and unforgiving, as he retreats from his predatory stance to slump back onto the mattress and runs a hand through his hair. "Tell me about your uncle. How did he end up in the hospital?"

My chest continues its accelerated pulse. His question isn't a white flag, but it's something. The door he slammed closed on us has inched open just a little. "I paid someone."

He raises a brow in disbelief. "Why now? Why not all those years ago?"

"When I was fourteen? I wasn't capable of plotting murder back then."

"I mean when you became an adult. Why didn't you do something as soon as you were capable? When you turned twenty, or twenty-one, or any other year since. Why now and not earlier?"

"I guess I didn't want to awaken old ghosts." I return to the window and lean against the sill. "After he hurt me, he stopped coming around. I don't know if he thought I'd tell my father or if Cole would. But he kept his distance and concentrated on business instead of family. Which gave me the space I needed to move on."

"Until?"

I force down the emotions trying to bubble to the surface. I breathe in the calm I need to continue this conversation. "Until Stella turned six."

"Stella?" His eyes flash with rage. "He didn't—"

"No." I shake my head. "He's never touched her. I made sure of it. He may have groomed me at an early age, but I educated her even earlier, making sure she never spent time alone with him.

That didn't stop him from thinking about it, though. I watched the way he interacted with her. How he'd make her laugh. How they'd hug. I knew what was going on in that sick mind of his."

I pause, waiting for an acceptance of my truth, praying and pleading silently for him to believe me.

"Keep going." His expression doesn't soften. He doesn't give a hint of sympathy or solidarity. "Tell me everything."

I have to be thankful for the slightest glimmer of curiosity. For the baby steps. "I knew it was only a matter of time. So I took the law into my own hands and paid for someone to take him out."

"You paid for them to kill him, and they fucked up?"

"No." I cringe. "I'm the one who fucked up. I found someone willing to do the job and paid half the arranged price up front..."

"Then?"

"Then I chickened out." I swallow over the admission.

"You changed your mind?"

"No. I still wanted him dead. But I hadn't thought about the danger I'd put everyone in. With my father spending longer and longer out of the country, I realized I couldn't risk weakening our defenses."

"I don't get it. How does making him a vegetable help the situation?"

"It doesn't. I tried to break the contract, or at least put it on hold. But apparently there's no take-backsys when it comes to arranging a hit."

One side of his mouth kicks in a half-hearted smirk.

That's all he gives me. A slight change in expression. A casual tweak of lips.

The tepid simplicity is blindingly beautiful.

His slight hint of friendship turns my insides to flame, and I'm weak-kneed for him all over again. "In hindsight, I guess I should've asked Hunter to do it."

"Why didn't you?"

"Because I knew he wouldn't do the job without permission from Cole. And my brother still has no clue I'm responsible." I stare at him, waiting for him to realize the secret I've just laid at his feet.

Nobody knows why Richard was run down.

Nobody is aware I tried to have someone in my own family slaughtered.

Nobody but the murderer I hired and now the man seated before me. The same man who could crush my heart that sits firmly in his calloused hands.

Sebastian could give this information to my siblings. The authorities. The media. I've handed him my skeletons. I've given him my whole fucking closet.

"Why couldn't you get Cole to arrange the hit in the first place?" he asks. "You said he was there for you."

"Because family doesn't kill family."

"Is that one of your father's rules?" He crosses his arms over his chest, his lips flattening into a tight line. "Your uncle raped you, Keira. The punishment fits the crime."

There he is, the protective man I know.

I may not have an understanding of who Sebastian really is, but the way he feels for me was never a lie.

"It doesn't matter." I shrug. "You never turn your back on family. You can punish them, but death is reserved for enemies, not uncles."

"Enemies like me." His eyes sparkle with mischief. His death wish lingers again. He lets out a derisive chuckle and lowers his gaze. "So, this hitman refused to let you back out of the contract, then fucked up the hit anyway?"

"No. I'm certain the change in plan was deliberate."

"Why?" He straightens, inching closer to the edge of the bed.

"He figured out who I am. Now he's trying to extort me for more than double the price and demanding I make the drop in person. I don't know what to do. I'm smart enough to realize he's going to keep extorting me no matter how much I pay, but I don't know how to make it stop. And it's not merely intimidating phone calls anymore." I bite my lip, not wanting to tell him everything, and dying to spill my guts at the same time. "He's escalated to physical threats."

His chin hitches, his eyes glazing as he becomes lost in thought, the wild contemplation written all over his face.

"The drive-by..." He scowls. "You said you were responsible. You told me you were to blame."

I don't move, don't breathe while he realizes even more of my truth.

"*Fuck.*" He pushes to his feet. "You've known who it was all along—"

"No." I push from the window sill. "I'm not entirely certain. I still haven't confirmed it. I tried making some calls last night, but I didn't get any answers. I don't have his phone number. All the information is stored in my cell, which is back in Portland."

"Who is he?"

I swallow over the dryness overwhelming my throat.

"Keira?" He approaches, closing in on me. "Who did you pay?"

"I don't know. I found him on the dark web. I thought he was a nobody from out of town."

"A nobody that had the balls to shoot up one of your family's restaurants?" He gets closer. He's there. Right there. His hips brushing mine. "Give me his name."

I work my lips together, buying time, hating the disappointment bearing down on me before I admit, "I don't know."

"Jesus." Concern seeps into his eyes.

Concern for me?

"I thought I'd done everything right. I made contact. I arranged the hit. I even drove to Salem and placed the first half of the money in a locker before he knew where I was making the drop so he wouldn't be able to stake out the scene. It all went smoothly. I'd made threats, telling him I had my team watching him to ensure he didn't take off with the cash without fulfilling his part of the agreement."

"What happened when you changed your mind?"

I heave out a breath, fighting the tingle in my fingers demanding I reach out and touch him. "I contacted him online. I told him not to go ahead with the hit, but he refused to discuss the situation unless it was in person."

"You didn't, did you?"

"No." I shake my head. "I convinced him to call me on a burner number. But the verbal communication took away my power. I became flustered, and slowly, he chipped away at my anonymity. Before long, I was sure he'd figured out who I was."

"Fuck." He turns away, massaging his forehead. "That's when he realized extorting you was a far bigger cash cow than killing your uncle."

"Yes."

"This is an impressive mess you've gotten yourself into." He keeps his back to me, those strong shoulders calling for my hands.

"I know." I need his help. I want it. Crave it. "I owe him money, and Torians always pay their debts. But I can't approach him on my own." I take cautious steps toward him. I don't stop until his body is within reach. "I don't know how to fix this."

"Some shit can't be fixed."

I'm not deluded into thinking his response is aimed squarely at the hitman issue. He's referring to this mess as a whole. He's talking about us.

I place my hands on his waist, needing to reclaim our connection. "Please..."

He stiffens, every muscle rippling under my touch while I fight for words.

"Will you come with me?" My lungs seize under the agonizing request. My ears burn waiting for his response. "Can you tell me what to do to fix this?"

"You want my help?" He swings around, incredulous. All those fissures of torment and pain disappear under a renewed show of fury. "How the fuck do you expect me to fix anything now that you've put a target on my back?"

My hands fall to my sides, my fingers trembling with both adrenaline and anguish as I withdraw.

"Don't confuse my curiosity for concern, Keira." He looks me up and down, judging me again and finding me unworthy.

"You've ratted me out, and it's only a matter of time before your actions put me six feet under."

I retreat at the verbal punch and watch in silence as he stalks for the door.

"Close the fucking window," he snaps. "It's time you got some rest."

"Sebast—"

"You've got five minutes to take a shower before I come back and restrain you to the bed."

20

DECKER

I snatch a t-shirt from my brother's wardrobe, then trudge to the bathroom and throw it inside the steam-filled room while Keira showers.

She doesn't protest the intrusion. Or acknowledge the clothes I've given her to wear. She doesn't even make a sound apart from the slight shift in the shower's spray before I slam the door shut.

The damn woman has me tied in knots.

This whole situation is a cluster fuck of epic proportions.

The worst part is the demanding urge to help her. It's the biggest bitch slap my intuition has ever handed me, and I don't know how to bury the impulse.

While I wait for her to finish her shower, I retrieve Hunter's handy duffle of goodies and dump it on the floor in the room where she will sleep.

A few minutes later, she returns to the room, my brother's shirt billowing at her thighs, her hair damp and hanging around her shoulders.

She entices me like no other. She always has.

The woman embroiled in more crime than a small country. The daughter of my sister's murderer. The sister to the man who will soon kill me.

She's my weakness, my downfall, and still I can't ignore the temptation of her.

"What are you doing?" she asks as I weave a cable tie through the one already looped around a wooden slat in the designer bed head.

"I'm creating shackles."

She sighs. "You don't have to do this. I'm not going anywhere."

"I know." I pull back the covers and pat the mattress. "Get in."

She glares at me, but that's the extent of her protest. She climbs on the bed and remains quiet as I secure a cable tie around her wrist, then another at her ankle.

She can't complain. I've set up the restrains in the middle of the bed. She has the ability to rest on her stomach or her back. She's not spread starfish like I could've demanded. If anything, I've been highly accommodating.

"Where are you sleeping?"

"Wherever the fuck I want." I cover her with the quilt, cutting off the sight of her laying like a BDSM pinup model. The only problem is, instead of her body slaying me with temptation, her eyes implore me with wounded emotion.

She wordlessly begs for my trust. She tears me apart with those big baby blues.

"I don't want to hear from you until sunup." I need to erect a big fucking wall between us. It's the only way I'll stay sane.

I start for the hall, flicking off the light and closing the bedroom door as I pass.

She doesn't wail on me like I expect. Not a single word leaves her lips as I pause outside the room, waiting for a theatrical reaction to make me feel like less of a prick.

I'm still waiting for a dramatic response as I shower. And again, when I pull on a clean pair of boxers from the drawers in the main bedroom.

She continues to surprise me as I climb into my brother's bed and listen to the eerie silence. I didn't expect her to take her punishment quietly. I also didn't anticipate feeling like such a sack of shit at having her tied like a prisoner in the next room. But there's no other choice.

She would run if left to free-range the house. Or worse, she would attempt to punish me for all the fun-filled choices I've made, and only end up getting hurt in the process.

It's safer to have her restrained.

Smarter.

I keep telling myself that while I fade in and out of guilt-ridden consciousness.

I wake with every subtle squeak of her mattress as the hours pass. I picture her tossing and turning. It isn't until three in the morning that those squeaks become something more.

There's rustling, grating, and the continued snarl of something hard running over tough plastic. Then the slightest footsteps and the lightest squeak of a door hinge.

I'm not surprised she freed herself. To be honest, I would've been disappointed if she hadn't made an effort to escape. What I'm not looking forward to is the retaliation. The revenge.

Yesterday, I would've eaten that shit up like prime rib. Now, I can't stop the dull ache under my sternum. The thought of continuously fighting with her makes my stomach turn.

I retrieve my gun from under my pillow and hold it frozen at my side. I keep my breathing heavy, feigning sleep, as her slim silhouette enters the doorway.

She creeps into the room, one slow step after another. I can't see her face in the darkness, but I feel her stare. She's scrutinizing my breathing, waiting for a sign to show her I'm prepared to fend off her attack.

I continue to inhale deep and exhale slow as she approaches the foot of the bed. I have no clue what I'm going to do when she reaches my side. I'll have to fend off a weapon; that much is clear. She didn't yank or tug her way out of those cable ties. There's a blade on her somewhere.

What I don't understand is why she didn't finish the job earlier when she held my jugular hostage. Did my refusal to help her with the hitman situation make her change her mind?

She doesn't continue toward my side of the mattress like I expect. Instead, she heads in the opposite direction, making my breathing falter for a second while I try to figure out why she's moving to the left of the bed.

Slowly, she raises the covers, and I scowl through the darkness as I battle confusion.

Is she going to try to suffocate me? Really?

Of all the ways to attempt homicide, this is a shitty one. I'm so goddamn disappointed in her poor excuse for a murder plot that I gently glide my grip away from the gun to free both my hands. This way I'll have the ability to shake some fucking sense into her.

Then the bed dips, and her weight nestles onto the mattress.

I hold my breath, my ears attuned to her movements, my muscles tense and poised for her strike.

But she doesn't.

Slowly, silently, she inches under the covers as if preparing for a secret slumber party.

I keep waiting for the violence to start. I stare into the shadows and bite my tongue to stop myself from asking what the hell she's doing, even though the answer is clear. She's snuggling into the bed, her back toward me, her head on the pillow.

The question is—why?

Once she's settled, she doesn't move, not one fucking inch. She just lays there. Less than a foot away.

I don't get it.

What's her plan? What's the strategy?

I remain on alert, waiting a lifetime for her to pounce.

Thirty minutes pass, and she still hasn't budged. The only thing that changes is her breathing, the inhales deep, the exhales languid.

I don't know what's more fucked up—her freeing herself of the cable ties and escaping her room, only to crawl in bed beside the man who's keeping her captive, or me for being the sick son of a bitch who relaxes under the wash of relief at having her close.

I'm one dumb fuck for ignoring the inner voice telling me she's playing me. That everything she's said and done has been one shovelful of bullshit after another. And this right here is merely another steaming load.

But it's hard. It's really fucking hard, when all I want to do is believe her.

No matter what I do, I can't convince myself she's the enemy. I struggle to see anything heinous and vindictive about her. Instead, I've battled with the obsession that comes with wanting her.

And maybe it's the lack of sleep or the emotional exhaustion, but I'm too fucking tired to fight it anymore. I'm too battered and bruised, and not from Hunter's beating. It's the months spent searching for revenge I no longer think is achievable.

I want her—the Keira I had before she stabbed me in the back.

I crave the woman who needed my protection. The one I would've taken a bullet for.

I keep staring at her shadowed form, the minutes ticking while the world stands still. Nothing changes. Not the relaxation in her body. Not the deathly silence. Nothing but my restraint.

I'm drawn to her.

My palms sweat with the need to feel her soft skin.

I can't fight the stupidity anymore. What's the point in struggling, anyway? I've got nothing left to lose. I no longer care what happens. Not about anything other than touching her. My hands have to be on her. If that gives her the opportunity to effortlessly slit my throat, then so be it.

She can kill me.

She can bathe in my blood and increase the destruction her family has rained on mine because there's nothing I can do to stop the pummeling thoughts that tell me she's innocent. That *I'm the one* who's treated her like hell and not the other way around.

I grab my gun, sliding it back under the far side of my pillow, and gently inch my way toward her. I listen for a change in her breathing. I continue to be attuned to her movements.

She doesn't flinch.

I creep closer and closer, her heat seeping into me right before skin touches skin. That's when everything stops. The gentle ebb and flow of sound ceases. She snaps rigid. I do, too.

But I don't retreat. I can't.

I nestle against her. Spooning. Her arms and thighs are bare against mine. The only thing between us is a thin cotton shirt and silken boxers as I weave my hand around her waist and drag her back into me.

She doesn't fight me. She doesn't succumb either.

Her body remains tight, while I rest my head on her pillow and place a kiss to the back of her neck.

That's all it is. A brief brush of lips against her skin, but it's everything.

The show of affection is my acquiescence. My capitulation to the devil.

She sucks in a shuddering breath, and one by one those muscles loosen. I hold her. Cling to her. I don't look forward to ever having to let her go.

"Sebastian..."

I shake my head. "Don't."

I can't face her questions. Her lies. I just need this. *Her*. For a little longer, until clarity sets in and I hate myself for succumbing all over again.

"Go to sleep." I close my eyes, squeezing them tight. "We can keep fighting in the morning."

The bullshit isn't going anywhere. No matter how much I want her—need her—it doesn't change our situation. We're enemies, and that shit will never be resolved.

I wake up to her shifting in my arms. It's only a faint movement, but I'm instantly alert, my eyes flashing open to the sunlight seeping through the edge of the curtains.

It's late. If the brightness of the room is any indication, it's close to midday.

I raise on one elbow, my swollen face and battered chest

not appreciating the shift as I stare down at the woman in my arms. She's still resting, her eyes closed, her body soft.

I no longer fight to understand the cloying feelings threatening to overwhelm me. Instead, I savor the calm. I teach myself to enjoy the temporary peace. Because it sure as fuck won't last.

"You're awake?" she murmurs.

"Yeah." I inch away from her, not wanting to crowd her now that the bitter light of day has arrived.

"Don't go. Lay with me a little longer."

She doesn't open her eyes. She lets those words do the pleading for her. And that's all it takes—her words, her tone, the delicate sweep of those sultry lips. I wish for nothing more than to go back to the safe house where neither one of us had a clue we were deceiving each other.

I miss that ignorance.

"There's no point putting off the inevitable." I keep backing away.

"Let me pretend for a few more minutes," she begs. "I'm not ready for this to end."

She slays me. And I'm the stupid chump who can't fucking deny her. I can't deny myself either.

I let out a frustrated breath and sink back onto the mattress, reclaiming my position behind her with my arm draped around her stomach.

We're both insane.

We lie so much we can't face the truth.

"Thank you," she whispers.

I hate those words. I despise how they make me feel like more of a man for providing her with what she needs. There's nothing more unhealthy than the two of us together.

"Quit thanking me," I mutter. "We're not doing ourselves any favors by pretending."

"This isn't me pretending, Sebastian. This is me hoping you'll come to your senses and find the strength to trust me." Her hand finds mine, entwining our fingers. It's all romantic and shit. A dreamy existence in a waking nightmare.

"You said it yourself, trust doesn't come easily."

She nods. "And yet I found the will to trust you."

No, she didn't. She doesn't trust me at all.

"I know what you're thinking," she utters. "And you're wrong. I *do* trust you. I trusted you enough to risk starting a rumor that would endanger everyone I love. I hope, in time, you'll be able to look beyond your anger to see what really happened."

There is no anger. Not anymore.

All that's left is pathetic weakness and punishing betrayal —for both of us.

"Please tell me about your sister." There's a delicate edge to her tone. A fragility that rips me apart. Like she's been contemplating how to ask for hours.

My defenses shoot up. All those barriers I've honed through a dark sense of humor and a morbid death wish come out in full force.

Telling her more about Penny isn't something I should do. Yet it's everything I crave at the same time.

"What do you want to know?" I become her slave, brushing my lips over her shoulder, the scent of her clean skin filling my lungs.

"Everything." She squeezes my hand. "How old is she? What is she like? When was she taken?"

I focus on the freckles along her arm, determined not to close my eyes and face the sister who will stare back at me.

"She was..." Too young. Too sweet. Too vulnerable. "Smart."

I place a kiss on her neck and swallow over the ache in my throat. It shouldn't be this hard to talk about Penny. The last thing I want is for the world to forget her. "She always had her head buried in a book. But what she had in brains she lacked in life experience. She didn't spend a lot of time in the real world."

Keira doesn't respond. She listens, never losing grip of my fingers.

"She didn't wear make-up or dress in trendy clothes. She didn't need to. She was pretty without all the glitz. Hell, from what I remember, she didn't even pay the opposite sex much attention. Yet those high school boys were always testing my patience."

"You were a protective older brother?"

"The worst." I let out a breath of solemn laughter. "I remember this one guy who kept coming over because he wanted to hang out with her. Every time I'd tell him to get lost, but he wouldn't listen. So I slashed his bike tires and told him I'd do the same to his throat if he ever stepped foot on our property again."

She glances at me over her shoulder. "You didn't."

"I did. I didn't feel an ounce of guilt either. I knew what he was after even though she had no clue."

"I'm guessing you've never shied away from a fight." She turns toward me, those bright eyes taking in the war wounds that must be littered all over my face.

"I got into a few. But nothing that wasn't fueled by teenage hormones." I give a half-hearted smirk that quickly fades. "After I finished school, I packed up and moved out of town, just like my older brother had done a few years before. We weren't there to look out for her anymore. She had nobody to keep the assholes at bay."

"You speak about her in past tense." She pauses, the silence punishing.

"Yeah. I guess it's easier that way." My chest tightens with the coward's admission.

"Do you have any proof she's no longer alive?"

I swallow over the bile edging its way up my throat. "The Greek authorities like to think so. Her DNA at a shallow, burned out grave is enough to satisfy their investigation. But all they found was a tooth and some hair. Nothing substantial."

"So there's hope?"

"Hope?" My voice fractures. "No. I could never hope she was living through hell every day. I prefer to believe she's at peace. But until I have concrete evidence, the thought of her suffering will haunt me."

Her face crumples. "You blame yourself."

"Yes. I should've listened when she told me about the modeling contract. She'd never mentioned stepping foot in front of a camera before. Not once. It came from so far left field that I didn't ask the questions I should've. I got caught up in her excitement about traveling the world. All it would've taken was an internet search on your father's bullshit company."

"Then hold him accountable." Her voice hardens. "Don't blame yourself. It isn't healthy."

"If you haven't noticed, none of this shit is healthy. My life is as fucked as they come. And yours isn't any better."

She winces and lowers her gaze to my chest. "If I could get my hands on a phone, I could sort this out. I'll call Cole…"

I glare. "Is that what this is all about?" The bed? The proximity? The subtle manipulation? "You're not getting your hands on a fucking phone."

I shuffle backward toward the edge of the mattress, curing my stupidity. She's screwed me all over again and every goddamn time I'm surprised.

"Please don't." She grabs my arm. "I'm sorry. I shouldn't have asked for a phone. I wasn't trying to betray you or escape. I just want to keep talking. I want us to get back to the way things were."

"Back to when we were lying through our teeth? Why? What good can come from that?" I wait for a response to stop me from leaving. I honestly want her to say something to make me stay in this fantasy world. But what can possibly be said to change this situation?

There's no righting all our wrongs.

There are too fucking many.

"I want to help you." She implores me with sad eyes, her teeth nibbling into her lower lip. "Together we can make this right."

I chuckle and shove from the mattress. "Nothing can make this right. The best I can hope for is a lifelong prison sentence for your father. That's the end game. You can't unrape all those women. Nobody can reverse the pain that's already been inflicted."

She sits up, bundling the covers in her lap. "That's what I mean. I can help you get him arrested."

I wish it were that easy. In fact, I'm pretty fucking pissed it isn't. "You can't help me. My cover is already blown. But you can work with the Feds—"

She shakes her head. "I won't work with the authorities. I'll work with you. We can do this together. You can't give up now."

"I'm not giving up," I grate, hating the accusation. Fighting for my sister is all I have... *Had...* The battle is out of my hands now.

"Then what do you call it?" she asks.

I clench my teeth and ball my fists. "I call it self-fucking-preservation."

She scrambles from the bed. "My father needs to be stopped. You can't walk away now."

"Do you think I want to walk?" Fury spreads through me like wildfire. "I've got no fucking choice but to run." I can't stop my voice from rising. "You ratted me out. Hunter knows I'm the informant. And by now Cole and Sarah would too. I can't get inside information anymore. I'm useless. Everything I've worked for is gone."

Her face pales.

"The rest of my life will be spent hiding from your brother, Keira, and that's only if Hunt doesn't get to me first."

Her throat works over a heavy swallow. "I'll speak to my brother."

"Words won't change the level of my betrayal. Your brother is going to fucking kill me the first chance he gets."

"I have more power than you think. Have faith in me."

I wish I could. Seriously, I do. But my fate is set. I either hide or die.

"I'm going to take a shower." I stalk for the bathroom, needing to lock myself away from her deluded beliefs. I can't be the one to make her feel better about this, no matter how much I want to.

"Sebastian, wait."

She rushes after me, almost making the distance before I close the door on her.

"Please." She pleads through the barrier between us. "I'll figure something out. Let me talk to Cole."

I smother a derisive laugh. She'll *talk* to him—a guy with unfathomable determination when it comes to slaying his enemies. I bet that conversation goes down like a cheerleader at an after party.

I strip and climb into the shower, not bothering to wait for the water to warm before I sink under the harsh chill.

"Please, Sebastian."

Christ. This woman doesn't let up.

I step under the spray and raise my swollen face to the water. The pain blocks out her pleas as I rest one hand against the tile to keep myself upright.

Talking to Cole won't change a thing. No matter what she says to try to convince him I'm innocent, he won't spare a second thought when it comes to ending my life. I've known that all along. I set out for revenge knowing I'd have little chance to make it out alive. The likelihood of getting caught was always high.

At least I have a head start to escape.

Once I freshen up, I'll pack a few of my brother's things and flee. I can cross multiple state borders before dark. And I'll keep crossing them, changing cars and IDs along the way—

A foreign noise breaks me from my plans, and I lean my head toward the glass shower screen to listen.

The door jangles. She's trying to pick the fucking lock.

I huff out a defeated breath as she breaks in. I've gotta give it to her, she's persistent as shit.

She approaches me, the sight of her taking up my peripheral vision.

"I can fix this." Her determination bears down on me from the other side of the glass. My dick isn't immune. Her tenacity is sexy as hell, no matter how hard I battle to ignore it.

I slink back under the water, keeping my head bowed, my hand against the tile.

"Sebastian..." She opens the screen. "Let me talk to Cole. I can work this out. I'll bet my life on it."

I don't respond. Well, apart from my cock that continues to thicken.

"*Sebastian*," she snaps. "Listen to me." She steps inside the shower, sliding along the wall in front of me, her shoulder grazing my splayed hand.

"What the hell are you doing?" I growl.

"You should know that I hate when you ignore me."

"Yeah, I do. But this isn't a place you want to be right now."

She sighs. "Yes, it is. We need to work this out."

"Not right now, we don't." I straighten, backing away from her. "Get out of here."

"Not until you listen to me. Cole will—"

"*No. You* listen to *me*." I narrow my stare. "Comprehending this conversation would be problematic at the best of times. But when I'm hard as a fucking rock, there's absolutely no chance. So I suggest you get out of my face."

The slightest frown knits her brows, then understanding dawns in those naive eyes. She swallows, hard, and her tongue dashes out to lick her lower lip. "I'm not leaving."

"Don't do this to me," I beg.

I don't want to fuck her again. I can't. The thought of leaving her behind is hard enough without giving in to the addiction one more time.

"I'll fix this," she whispers.

I press my forehead to hers and close my eyes. "You can't. If I stay, I'm dead."

"I'll protect you."

I let out a breath of laughter. "Yeah? And how are you going to do that?"

Her hand weaves around my neck, her nails scraping my scalp. "I'll do whatever necessary. Just like you did for me." She leans in, her nose brushing mine, the splash of warm water trickling down our faces. "I've fallen for you, Sebastian. I can't let you go."

"That's the adrenaline talking. It's the fear." It's probably a case of Stockholm Syndrome, too.

"No, it's not. I've felt this way since before the shooting."

She digs those nails deeper, demanding my attention. "I'm never scared when I'm with you. I feel safe. I'm home." Her lips brush my jaw. My cheek. "I need this to work. I don't care what it takes."

What it takes could be her life. I refuse to be responsible for that.

I pull back, opening my eyes as I cup her face in both hands. "Listen. Hunter is going to come after me. And if he went through my house like I wanted him to, he's going to find this place real fucking soon."

"How? We're in the middle of nowhere."

"We're in the middle of my brother's house," I confess. "I called in a few favors and asked him to disappear for a few days."

Her eyes flare, the panic evident before being smothered with more of her determination. "Then we run. Together. We get out of here. We hide."

"You don't want to leave your family, beautiful. You couldn't live without Layla or Stella. And you told me last night how close you are to Cole."

"It will only be temporary." She brushes her mouth over mine, slaughtering me with the sexual plea. "We can figure out—"

"This isn't a negotiation." I wish I could find a way to make this work, but the truth is, her optimism has no place here. Hunter will never forgive me, and Torian will take pleasure in putting a price on my head.

It's over.

"I'm leaving here, Keira, and you're not coming with me."

21

KEIRA

I shove at his chest. "Why are you so goddamn stubborn?"

Those dark eyes turn pained. "I've already lost someone I care about. I have no plans of letting that happen again."

My stomach revolts in both anguish and anger. "That's not good enough." I get in his face, the shower's spray dousing my shirt, making the material cling to my skin. "I've lost someone, too. I know how it feels. It's the reason I won't let you go."

He gives a sad smile. "Keira..."

"*Don't*," I scold. "For once, just listen."

He sucks in a breath and straightens, placing space between us. "Fine. I'm listening."

My heart thumps in my ears. I don't know what to say to make him stay. There's only hope and want and so much need spurring me to fill the silence. "Once Cole finds out about our father, he will disown him. He knows what I went through with Richard. He would never associate our name with that type of—"

"That's not the point, buttercup. The issue here is that I'm an informant. I gave the Feds enough probable cause to wiretap your uncle's phone. It's only a matter of time before they take you all down, and I fucking helped."

"You're not the first, and you won't be the last. People have been feeding the Feds information since before I was born. It's nothing new. They rarely find anything that sticks. And when they do, we've got men on their payroll to help us out. I'm not worried."

"Can you hear yourself?" He cringes. "I fucking betrayed your family."

"You did what was necessary to fight for your sister."

"Cole won't see it that way. *You* shouldn't even see it that way."

I give him a sad smile, pouring my heartfelt affection into the expression. "What I see is someone who should be admired for their strength. You're fearless, Sebastian. You did what was right for you and yours without worrying about the consequences."

He closes his eyes briefly, his brows pinched. "You're being delusional, princess." He pins me with a placating expression, his lips pulled into a sad smile.

"No, I'm not. If the authorities had anything on us, they would've used it by now. There's nothing they can do."

"They've already told me exactly what they're going to do. If I run out on them before they can make an arrest, those assholes are going to make Sarah and Hunt look like rats." His eyes narrow as he leans close. "And look at me, already running."

He appears entirely tortured. But I still have to ask. "Are they? Rats, I mean. Are they involved?"

"*No.*" His response is vehement. "Why do you think Hunt tried to kill me yesterday? Nobody fucking knew except the agent I've been working with. And she's going to set up Hunt and Sarah as soon as she finds out I've high-tailed it. She probably already has."

My belly does that tumbling, squeezing thing again. "If only one agent knows, then maybe that's the answer. We take her out. Problem solved."

He winces. "You need to stop fighting. This shit can't be fixed."

I won't.

I can't.

"I'm not ready to let you go."

He gives me a sad smile. "I wish there was an alternative."

I inch closer, my soaked chest leaning into his, the hard length of his cock pushing into my abdomen. His jaw ticks as he backtracks, moving to the far wall of the enclosed space.

I don't allow for any distance between us as I follow.

"You want me." I reach a hand between us and grab his length. The hiss of his breath is sweet victory. "You can't deny it."

"You're right, I can't." His eyes soften. "But fucking you isn't going to make me change my mind about risking your life. I won't be seduced into hurting you."

"Hurting me?" I falter. I almost break.

This isn't about my safety. It's about his. When it comes to my family I can look after myself.

"Yes, hurting you," he repeats. "Hunter and Cole will come after me, guns blazing. It's too dangerous for you to be anywhere near me. I should already be gone."

I want to shove some sense into him. But the sight of his bruised and battered body keeps me in check. "No."

"Yes," he growls. "I need to get as far away from you as possible."

I crumple, my insides turning to dust with his continued protection. "I'm begging you." My fragility is clear in the fracturing of my tone. My throat burns. My eyes, too. "Don't run. I don't want this to end."

He grabs the wet material of my shirt, scrunching it in tight fists. "Give it a day or two. Once you're back home with your family, this will be nothing but a bad memory."

"Like hell it will." I snuggle into him, my mouth an inch from his before dawning hits me hard in the ribs. "Is that what I'll be to you? A bad memory?"

His face pinches, his hands still clinging to my shirt. "I've wanted to save you since the first moment I laid eyes on you. I could've run that night and not worried about Cole wasting the time or effort to hunt me down. But in the back of my mind, I thought if I couldn't save Penny, the least I could do is save you."

"You *have* saved me."

He reaches a hand between us, the pad of his thumb brushing my bottom lip. "It wasn't real, remember? That defining moment for me was nothing but a lie for you. I'm not who you think I am, and you're not who I thought you were, either. You'll realize that once you've had time to think."

"I don't need time. Or space. Or whatever else you want to suggest next." I clutch his wrist, keeping his hand at my mouth. "My mind is clear. My decision is made. We may have fabricated stories that brought us together, but we're here for a reason."

"Yeah, because I tried to take on the biggest crime family in the state and failed."

"No. You're *here*." I tap my chest. My heart. "You're in here for a reason."

He cups my cheek, and those eyes fill with pity. "Keira—"

"Don't." I squeeze his wrist. "Don't you dare tell me you're still leaving."

He sighs and tugs against my hold to lower his arm to his side. "Then I don't know what you expect me to say."

"Don't say anything. Just be with me." I pull the sodden shirt over my head to bare my body to him. "Help me make this work."

His chin hitches. His eyes flare.

"I need you, Sebastian." I drag the waistband of my underwear down my thighs, letting them fall to the floor. "I know you need me, too."

He's contemplating surrender. I can taste the sweet victory on my tongue. I can see the effect temptation has on him.

"Manipulation runs deep in those veins, doesn't it, baby cakes?"

I guess I should be insulted.

I'm not.

I know it's his last ditch effort to reject me. I'm wearing him down. Convincing him of what we both need. "I can be manipulative. But that isn't what this is. What you're feeling is a connection you know you can't deny. There's a reason this seems right despite all the reasons it should be wrong."

"That's the thing—" He reaches around me and shuts off the water with harsh twists of his wrists. "This doesn't seem right at all. The way I feel for you—the way I've *always* felt for you—is a fucking disgrace to my family."

He grabs me around the waist and carries me, soaked and dripping, to the bed where he lays me down. The sheets grow damp beneath me, and my skin prickles with a harsh chill. But the worst part is the way he backs away, retreating as if he's finally found the strength to cut ties.

"I'm going to grab a bite to eat, pack some things, then get out of here. You won't be alone for long. Hunter will find you soon."

He starts for the door, and I panic.

I don't know what to do. I'm out of ideas to make him stay. "Sebastian."

He pauses, and I do something so out of character my whole body trembles as he glances over his shoulder.

I slide a hand over my waist, down my stomach to the apex of my thighs. With my heart hammering in my chest, I part my legs to him.

I'm no stranger to my own touch, but I've never considered myself a temptress. The desire to instigate sex has never been a driving force for me. Not until now, when I have no other tricks up my sleeve.

He stares, his lip slowly curling into a snarl.

I don't know if the expression is from disgusted fury or despised temptation. I don't know anything anymore... anything but want.

"Stop it," he growls.

I shake my head. "I can't."

I slide a finger along my pussy and close my eyes, moaning a little with the penetration. My pleasure is drowned under possible humiliation, but I pretend I'm swimming in lust. I work my finger in circles and cup my breast. I do all the sexy things I've seen and read about despite feeling fake the entire time.

"Keira, *stop*."

I don't listen. I continue my display, keeping my eyes squeezed shut to ward off the nerves.

"*Fuck*," he grates.

There's torment in his voice. So much anger and aggression aimed in my direction.

I'm not scared by it. He won't hurt me. I'm more concerned I'm hurting him for pushing an agenda he won't admit he wants to be a part of.

Blood rushes in my ears as I play with my clit, rubbing my thumb back and forth. I can't hear anything over my heartbeat. The loud throb echoes through me, increasing the anxiety.

I'm tempted to take a peek to see if he's watching. Maybe he already left the room. He could've walked away.

My heart pangs.

"You're killing me, shortie." His hands latch onto my ankles and drag me along the bed.

I squeal, opening my eyes to his anguished stare.

"Why are you doing this to me?" he murmurs. "Why do you keep playing games?"

I lean up on bent elbows. "There's no more games. I promise."

A myriad of emotions wash over his features— determination, uncertainty, and a glimmer of hope. They all mix together, showing me the kind soul buried behind the bruised and battered exterior.

"There's no more lies, either," I admit. "All I want is you."

I adore him. I won't even bother denying it. How can I when he challenged my father—the most powerful man I know? Sebastian stormed the castle. He made himself into a warrior and protected me every step of the way.

My dad couldn't even safeguard his wife from all the dangers he created. And he sure as hell didn't protect me from his own brother.

From birth, I've been sheltered, not shielded, and Sebastian is a breath of the freshest, purest air against that harsh reality.

He's strength and commitment and discipline.

Honor, morality, and pride.

He's far greater than someone with my track record deserves. But I guess I'm a slave to my bloodline, because despite knowing I'm undeserving, I'm not willing to give him up.

"I'm yours," I whisper. "Whether you want me or not."

His jaw ticks. "I fucking want you, Keira. I can't stop."

I sit up and drape my legs over the edge of the mattress, coming up close and personal with his bare waist. I hold his gaze as droplets trek his body, dripping from his hair to his chest, all the way down to the erection within reach.

He's a masterpiece. All that muscle. All that ink.

And now, knitting them together is all the pink and purple flesh caused from my lies.

My heart trembles beneath tightening ribs as I lean forward and place a kiss on his stomach. He peers down at me, his intensity bathing me, warming me. He fucking invigorates the hell out of me as I inch lower, dragging my lips on a slow trail until I'm nestled right next to the head of his cock.

I pause and watch him swallow deep. He has so much power over me, but right now, I can see that influence shift. I'm in control. He's at my mercy.

I tilt my head toward his sex.

He's thick and bulky. An entirely new discovery for me.

I've never done this before, and I know exactly why. I wasn't supposed to. This moment was made for Sebastian.

I lean closer, poking out my tongue to trail it along his shaft. I lick the water droplets. I taste the salty tease of him seeping from the head of his cock.

"*Jesus*," he hisses.

My tension eases, his curse uplifting in its ferocity. He fists my hair in his hands, the strands pulling tight.

I shudder, becoming a slave to his brutality. My pussy throbs. I have to squeeze my thighs tight to stem the ache. But then he steps away, and I'm petrified he's found the will to leave.

"Move back on the bed, sweetheart."

I nod, overwhelmed with relief as I comply.

He slides over me, gentle and slow, his heavy weight pressing me into the mattress. His mouth finds mine. His tongue delves deep. He kisses me like he's taking his last breath. He cups my face and grips my waist as if I'll skitter away in the wind.

He's everywhere. His hands. His mouth. His affection.

I'm royalty under his touch.

I rake my fingers into his hair and hold tight. "Promise me you won't leave."

He ignores me, nudging his hips into mine, the head of his cock parting my folds.

His stare holds all the promise I need. I see the commitment in his eyes. The pure, undeniable want for me, just like I want him.

I raise my ass off the bed, making him sink deeper. The pleasure is instantaneous. Every inch of me tingles, from my toes to my nipples, my fingers to my face.

I moan. I don't bother holding it in.

I'm not going to shy away from how he makes me feel.

I want everything he has to give, and I refuse to take it on a temporary basis. This can't stop. He can't walk away.

His hips begin to roll, the slow undulation sinking through me. We're made for each other. There's no denying how right this feels. He increases his pace, the kisses growing in intensity, the hands roaming my body seeming addicted to learning my curves.

My back arches off the bed. My hips rise to meet him.

We move in perfect harmony. Two people. One act.

Pure fate.

He's fucked me hard before, with strength and dominance. We've groaned and clawed as we sought our pleasure. That's the way I'd always thought sex would be. Rough. Hard. Punishing.

I never imagined it like this. Not with him. Not with anyone.

I never realized how soul crushing the connection could be. How one man would have the power to shatter me to my core and build me back up, piece by piece, with the heated, sweaty movements of his body.

I'm transfixed.

Enslaved.

He increases his pace, sliding into me and retreating in smooth synchronicity as he peers down at me.

I've never felt this beautiful. Entirely worshiped.

I'm overwhelmed with emotion as he whispers compliments I never would've imagined would be spoken about me. He speaks of my beauty. He murmurs his adoration.

You're gorgeous. You're perfect. You're mine.

Those words are everything.

I kiss him—his cheek, his jaw, his chin. He grazes his teeth across my neck and licks a delicate trail along my shoulder.

He tastes. Savors.

I wrap my legs around his waist, allowing him the deepest penetration. But it's also because I need to hold him. I have to cling tight. I refuse to let go.

He slides a hand between me and the mattress, cupping my ass.

Our movements increase, every thrust becoming harder, the pleasure growing more potent. I shake with the intensity, my body screaming for more.

His mouth devours my skin, the scrape of teeth and lap of tongue making me mindless.

"Sebastian..." I don't know what else to say. His name on my lips is all there is.

I'm not me anymore. I'm not singular in heart or body or soul. Everything I know has been entwined with this man. We're one. Never to be broken apart.

"I don't want this to end." I grip tighter to him and squeeze my thighs with his thrusts.

The thrill is intense. His affection becomes overwhelming.

"I wish I had the stamina to make this last all day, but you're too fucking perfect, Keira. You always have been."

I shudder, my limbs and nerves tingling until the vibrations culminate in my pussy and I fall over the edge.

I break apart, my neck arching with the euphoria as moans

escape my throat. I close my eyes, clinging to this moment, savoring the bliss while Sebastian's thrusts of release match the contraction of my pussy.

Flawless. Monumental. Intense.

I'm at the highest of highs, bathed in his tenderness and swimming in endorphins when everything begins to incrementally slow.

Our movements lessen. His kisses disappear. The pleasure dims while our panted breaths fade.

The warmth I'd been blanketed in seconds earlier becomes chilled as I open my eyes to the tortured man staring back at me.

"You're everything, Keira." His words sound like a goodbye. A whispered farewell.

"Good. Then don't leave."

He winces and buries his head against my neck. He falls quiet, not even his labored inhales heard over the pounding in my ears.

I don't release my hold. I continue to cling tight, convincing myself he's going to stay right up until his body turns rigid atop mine.

His emotional withdrawal is a living, breathing thing. I feel it escaping from between us, then in a rapid burst of movement he slides off me and shoves to his feet as if I've burned him.

"Sebastian..." I wait for his rejection, for the words that will call an end to all of this and shatter me into a million pieces. I don't know how else to fight this. I've begged. I've pleaded. I've used my body like a weapon.

"Do you hear that?" He cocks his head toward the window.

My pulse spikes. "Hear what?" I remain still, trying to hear the elusive sound. "What is it?"

"Someone's here." He lunges for the pillows and pulls out his gun. "You need to hide."

I scamper from the bed and spin in an anxiety-riddled circle, not sure if I should be looking for clothes or a weapon.

"Get in the bathroom and lock the door." He stalks to the

dresser and yanks out a pair of boxers, dragging them up his legs one-handed. "Don't come out until you know it's safe."

"I'm not leaving you on your own."

"Don't argue with me." He strides for the door. "You'll only get in my way."

22

DECKER

I RUSH DOWN THE HALL, MENTALLY PREPARING FOR battle, and peek out the glass panels of the front door.

"Who is it?" Keira's whisper travels from somewhere close.

"Peanut," I grate, "for once in your life will you listen to me and go hide."

"No." She tiptoes toward me, pulling a fresh shirt over her head as she approaches in a pair of baggy shorts that hang from her slim hips. "I need to know what's going on."

I sigh and return my focus outside. "There's a car coming up the drive."

It's a vehicle I don't recognize, but I can already identify the stocky build of the man behind the wheel.

"Who is it?"

"Hunter." He's the only person who could've figured out where I am, and he's too ego-driven to have given the information to Torian. My best buddy will want to be the victor in this situation.

She creeps up behind me, wrapping her arms around my waist. "What will he do?"

That list is too fucking long to contemplate. "Who knows."

He won't kill me in front of Keira. At least I hope not. I need to start praying that he's willing to take me back to Portland for Cole to deal with. That way, I'll have a chance to escape on route.

227

"Sebastian..." She clings closer, her warmth touching every part of me. "I'm scared."

"You've got nothing to worry about. He's here to take you home. It's me he's after."

"That's why I'm scared," she murmurs.

I want to believe her. God, how I want to believe her, but there's still the slightest twinge of doubt gnawing its way through my chest. "It'll be okay. Stay inside. Hide at the back of the house."

I grip the knob and turn, only to be stopped when she places her hand on mine.

"I'm not leaving you." She squeezes in front of me, her back to the door, her chest brushing against mine. "I know you doubt me. I can hear it in your voice. But I'm here, Sebastian. I'm right where I want to be."

"In the line of fire?"

"If that's what it comes down to, then yes." She spins, yanks open the door, and slides outside.

I wait for her to flee. To escape. To run to the man who pummeled my body to a pulp mere hours ago.

She doesn't.

She flicks her gaze between the black Mercedes and the house, making sure she positions herself between us both.

"Jesus Christ." She's suicidal. I follow her outside, and she continues to keep me as her shadow, mimicking each of my steps to ensure I stay behind her. "Get out of my way, tiger."

"No. I'm not going to let them hurt you."

The car inches into the yard and circles to the front of the house. It's then I notice Hunt isn't alone. His trusty sidekick, Sarah, is in the passenger seat, her face impassive as they pull to a stop.

"Move." I'm trying like hell to be patient, but having her in front of me feels beyond wrong. I want her at *my* back. I'm the one who needs to protect her.

She grabs my left hand and wraps it around her stomach, her touch comforting and soft. Then she yanks at my right, raising the gun to aim it toward her face.

"*Fucking hell.*" I pull away. "I'm not playing you as my hostage."

"*Please.*" She turns to me, her eyes pleading. "He's going to kill you."

"I can take care of myself. All you're doing is making this worse by distracting me." I drag her behind me, ignoring her scrambling, scratching protests as I shield her with my body. "Or maybe that's the plan." I inflict the emotional blow in the hopes of diverting her attention.

It works.

She stops protesting, her pain at my accusation taking over her features as she blinks those baby blues my way. "You'll never trust me again, will you?"

"How 'bout I trust that you're going to stay behind me and keep quiet while I handle this?"

She presses her lips tight.

I don't wait for another response. I swing around to face our visitors as they climb from the car, both of them scowling at me, no guns drawn.

Sarah is the first to step away from the vehicle, which is surprising. I never would've imagined Hunt would let her breathe without permission in a situation like this, let alone allow her to walk toward me.

They know I'm armed. The weapon may be rested at my side, but despite my laidback stance, they both have to realize I'll fire shots to lay cover for an escape. And yet she approaches, her stride determined, her pinched expression increasing, while he stays at the driver's side door.

"What do we do?" Keira's question is barely audible as I stand my ground.

I don't move. Don't even flinch.

Sarah holds my gaze as she reaches the steps, and I start to wonder if she's the decoy to distract me from Hunter's kill shot.

"We went through your shit," she says in greeting.

"I figured as much. You wouldn't have found me otherwise." I clear my throat, trying to ignore the build of adrenaline. "Is my place still standing?"

She shrugs. "It's definitely not in the same state as when we arrived."

I'd probably give a shit if I had any possibility of returning home. But at the moment, I'm not convinced they'll let me make it through the day.

The thing that hurts, though, is what they would've done to all my research. All those years of searching. All those faces of innocent women. All those pictures of a sister I'll never see again.

She takes the first step, still scowling, but those harsh eyes are different. They're glazed. Glistening. Her nose scrunches as she takes another step, and another, coming to stand a foot away.

Regret hangs heavy in her expression, making me anxious as all fuck. Hunter knows I'd never hurt her. I couldn't. Maybe that's the beauty of their plan. He's letting her take me down effortlessly.

"You should've told me," she snarls. "I would've helped."

I stare at her. At the emotion building in her features, the trembling lips, the liquid building in her eyes. I feel heavy—my chest, my limbs, my soul. Everything weighs me down under her anger.

I frown. "I don't understand."

"If I would've known what they were capable of, I would've stood by you, helping every step of the way." She sniffs, her chin hitching slightly. "I would've found a way to kill everyone involved. Every single one of them, Decker."

Keira sucks in a breath, and from my peripheral vision I see her stiffen. Sarah is talking about Keira's family. Her father. Her uncle. Possibly her brother. No matter what they're capable of, those words would be hard to hear when spoken from someone you considered a friend.

"Why are you here?" I ask.

"I want to show my support."

I—singular. There's no 'we' or 'us' or mention of Hunter.

"You're not here to kick my ass for being the informant?"

The anger slowly fades into a sly grin. "Actually, I'm

strangely proud of your deceptive ways. I never would've thought you were smart enough to pull this off."

"Obviously, I'm not. Look where we are."

"You had me fooled."

I'm not convinced. This has to be an act. A scheme. But God knows why they're dragging out the end game. Hunt doesn't usually like to fuck with his prey. "Thanks?"

She steps forward. "Don't mention it. Now, give me a hug, you manipulative prick. I can't believe what you've been going through without me knowing."

She casts her arms wide, and I brace for an attack.

Sarah doesn't hug.

Ever.

This woman is the spokesperson for emotional detachment, so it's more than likely she's going to stab a knife into my back. And yet, I oddly crave the connection like a motherfucker.

I've allowed very few people into my life since Penny was taken. Three, to be exact. And those trio of souls are all staring at me, each of them capable of taking me down.

"Sebastian," Keira warns.

"It's okay." I spread my arms, willing to sink or swim, as I drag Sarah into me.

I hug her, waiting for the betrayal, expecting the sharp bite of a blade. It doesn't come. She rests into me, clinging tight as I glance at Hunter over her shoulder, his glare mutated to an epic level.

"I'm going to take a wild stab in the dark and assume your fiancé doesn't have the urge to hug this out like you do."

"Don't worry about him. He's still recovering from your scuffle yesterday. He can't ditch his migraine." She retreats, her hands falling to her sides. "But he hasn't breathed a word of this to Cole. That in itself is a huge sign of support despite his unwillingness to voice it."

Support? I'm still not buying it.

There has to be a catch. A hidden motive.

"There wasn't a scuffle yesterday, Sarah. That fucking ogre tried to kill me."

231

She rolls her eyes. "It sounds like you've both exaggerated your side of the story." She turns her attention to Keira, her expression transforming to a snarl as her arms cross over her chest. "Did you know about the trafficking?"

I glance at Keira, getting caught up in the shock spread across her features. She's traumatized by the harsh accusation. I have to admit, I am, too.

Sarah is usually the devoted feminist, slaying the dragons that enslave other women. But right here, right now, the only thing she looks eager to slay is an undeserving woman.

"No, she didn't," I answer.

"I didn't ask you. I want to hear it from her." Sarah levels her tone without quitting the glare. "Did you know they were selling sex slaves? Were you involved?"

Keira raises her chin in defiance and opens her mouth, only to snap it shut again. I can't tell if she's about to lash out or cry. I don't want to see either.

"I said she didn't know. And if I can believe her, you can, too." I walk for the front door, despising every second my back is turned to the homicidal fucker in the yard. "Let's go inside. This is going to be a long conversation that doesn't need to happen out here."

I pull the door wide and stare at Sarah, waiting for her to comply.

She takes her sweet-ass time, not hiding her animosity for Keira when she finally strides toward me and kicks off her shoes to leave them by the door. "It will take a lot more than your word to convince me she didn't know. Especially when she's the one who set you up."

I don't bite. I can't afford to.

This outcome is far better than the bullet to the brain I expected. But the sight of Keira's emotional struggle is far more punishing.

Those ocean eyes hold me captive, the pained depths ripping me apart.

"It's okay," I mouth.

She scoffs and turns her attention to the front yard. I follow her gaze, yet again finding the ire of one grumpy motherfucker bearing down on me like I encouraged a football team to live stream a group orgy with his mom.

"He doesn't look happy," she whispers.

"He's angry at me. Not you. He'd do anything for you and yours. You know that."

"That used to be the case." She starts toward me. "Who knows how he feels now."

She continues into the house on silent footfalls while I wait outside to see what the eye-gouger will do. Apparently, standing there scowling is all he's capable of because he doesn't budge an inch.

"Hey, asshole," I call out. "Are you coming inside?"

His lip curls. "What was that? I can't hear you over how stupid you are, you dumb fuck."

I guess that's as close as I'm going to get to a temporary cease fire.

I walk inside, locking the door behind me so I'm aware of when Hunt makes his next move. He won't stay outside for long. He's stubborn, but he's also impatient. He'll want to take action sooner rather than later, and although Sarah claims to be on my side, I'm not letting my guard down.

I make my way into the kitchen and find her at the sink, filling a glass with water from the tap. "Where's Keira?"

She shrugs. "Don't know. But it's best if she keeps her distance for now."

"Lay off her. She's gone through enough."

"Why do you believe her?" She shuts off the water and gulps from her glass. "She's the one who set you up."

"I've got my reasons." And I'm too fucking loath to admit all of them revolve around intuition and attraction instead of evidence. "I've spent enough time with her to believe she's innocent."

"Forgive me if I'm not as easily convinced."

"Isn't she supposed to be your friend?"

Her eyes harden. "I've been fucked over by people far closer to me than her."

I know that. I wish I didn't, but I'm well aware of the horrors she's endured.

"Decker, we only found your information ten hours ago. I've spent every minute since reading through those pages. Even on the car ride here. I'm still coming to terms with all of this."

"And so is she. You need to hear her out."

She raises a brow. "Or maybe you need to stop letting your dick make decisions."

I clench my teeth to stop a sharp reply. I breathe. I force calm. "If she's guilty, then what about Hunter? You have to hold him accountable, too. He's close as fuck to Torian."

She narrows her gaze for a spite-filled moment, then turns away, focusing out the kitchen window.

"You know I'm right," I say into the growing silence.

"Have I said Hunter is innocent?" she snaps. "This conversation is about *her*. Not him."

I straighten with the dawning realization.

Now I understand why Hunt didn't come up the drive with a barrel pointed at my head—she didn't let him.

They're fighting.

She's taken my side when he clearly hasn't. And like the lovesick fool he is for this woman, he doesn't want to upset her by slitting my throat in front of her. Great. All he's waiting for is privacy.

"Come on, Sarah. You can't believe he's in on this."

"You said it yourself, he's close to Torian. How could he be clueless?" She grips the counter, her shoulders slumping. "He always knows everything."

"He had no clue about me." I approach, moving to stand a few feet away. "He's capable of some pretty heavy shit. But for as long as I've worked with him, he's never done anything to anyone who wasn't deserving."

"I know." She hangs her head. "I just..."

"What? You don't trust him anymore?"

She glances over her shoulder, meeting my gaze. "I've been working with them, Decker. I've been helping a family who should be burning in hell."

"Not the entire family, Sare. They're not all responsible."

She shoves from the counter in frustration. "How do you know?"

"A gut feeling."

She gives me a look of incredulity. "Like I mentioned before, I think the body part you're referring to is a little further south."

"Maybe." I shrug. "I'll admit Keira has gotten under my skin. But there's more to it than that. She's battling her own demons. And if you can't trust her, you need to trust me until she proves herself to you."

"Trust you? The informant?" She laughs. "The guy who has made a life out of lying?"

"You would've done the same."

She nods. "Yeah. I would've... And I'm sorry about your sister."

I stare out the window, unable to stand her pity.

"Our baggage kinda looks the same, doesn't it?" She cocks her hip against the counter and crosses her arms over her chest. "I understand you a lot more than I did days ago."

"Are you falling for me, sweet cheeks?" I send her a smirk that she shoots down in flames.

"Don't pull that cocky, jokester bullshit on me, Decker. I know what it's like. And I'm here if you ever need to talk."

"You mean for now," I chuckle, "in the short space of time before Hunt kills me."

She winces. "He'll calm down. Eventually."

"I doubt it. I stabbed him in the back. I know him well enough to realize there's no way back from being his enemy."

"Obviously, you don't know him at all. Because being the informant isn't the reason he wants to gut you like a fish." She grabs her glass and takes another sip. "You're not even close to understanding him, Deck."

"Okay. I'll bite." I walk to the fridge and grab myself an apple from the crisper. "What am I missing here?"

"He's pissed off because you kept him in the dark. You pretended to be his friend and made him look like a fool."

"I don't think we're talking about the same guy. This is Hunter. The son of a bitch who gives no fucks about anyone or anything, except his pride and his fealty to the all-mighty Torian."

"That's a little harsh."

"Tell that to the eyeballs he tried to gouge yesterday."

She presses her lips tight, but her humor seeps through in the curving edges of her mouth. "How many people do you think he has in his life?"

"I don't know. He knows everyone."

"Yes, he knows everyone. That's his job. But he doesn't *have* anyone. Not apart from you and me. We're all he's got. And in one surprise revelation, you halved his support network." Her face turns somber. "Despite the weird testosterone-fueled, we-have-to-act-like-schoolyard-thugs thing you two have going on, he fucking adores you."

"Adores?" I drawl. "That sounds delightfully charming."

She glowers and points a finger at her chest. "My words. Not his."

I grin, because drilling down to the seriousness of this conversation isn't something I'm comfortable with. "You should've seen how much he adored me yesterday when he had a barrel between my eyes. That shit was affectionate as hell. I really felt the love."

"You mean when he warned you about being uncovered, then let you get away?"

"Oh, no, Sare bear." He came prepared to kill me. He was on a mission to seek revenge for his almighty leader. He chose money over friendship. "Despite what he might have told you, he didn't *let me* get away at all. I had to beat the fuck out of his ogre ass. And that shit ain't easy."

She raises a brow, her condescending look making me feel like I'm simple. "He *let you* get away, Decker. I'm pretty sure, deep down, you know that more than I do."

23

KEIRA

I HIDE OUT IN THE MAIN BEDROOM, SLUMPED ON THE mattress. I'm not in here because I'm intimidated by Sarah.

It's the opposite.

I'm fearful of what I'll do to her if she turns her accusatory face my way again.

Days ago, she was my friend. Now she dares to glare at me with disgust, as if I instigated my father's entire operation.

Her goddamn righteousness boils my blood.

She's no angel. I'm well aware of the things she does. How she works side-by-side with Hunter as a loan shark, or an enforcer, or whatever else my brother requires.

And yet I'm the heinous one? Go figure.

A *tap*, *tap*, *tap* sounds to my right. I panic at the intrusion and glance at the window, finding Hunter's menacing face staring back at me from outside.

I don't move. For a moment, I'm too scared to even think.

Although Sarah is being a bitch, Hunter is a cold-blooded killer, and right now I'd prefer her hatred to his possible intent.

"Open the fucking window," he mutters.

I remain cemented in place, not willing to sign my own death certificate.

His glare turns lethal. "Now. We need to talk."

The rap sheet of crimes he's committed for my family pokes at me from the back of my mind. The assault. The murder. He's killed people for far less than what my father has done. For all I know, he's turned his back on us and claimed Sarah's high moral code.

"Keira." His tone softens despite the harsh expression, his voice barely heard through the glass barrier between us. "We don't have much time."

I swallow over and over, trying to bottle my fear as my palms begin to sweat.

My brother trusts this man with his life. I should be able to trust him to hold a non-violent conversation. Shouldn't I?

I inch to my feet and take cautious steps across the room. My hands tremble as I reach for the window.

He stares me down. Stares so emotionless and heartlessly that I'm sure I'm making a huge mistake. Yet I refuse to let fear rule me as I flick the lock.

There's no pause for contemplation. In seconds, he has the screen unhitched, the pane raised, and is preparing to climb in.

"You couldn't use the front door?"

"I'm not ready to speak to that asshole yet." He winces as he hauls himself into the room, alluding to more injuries than the stark bruising across the bridge of his nose and under his eyes.

I retreat as he stands, his bulky frame dwarfing me. I aim my path toward the door, backtracking closer and closer to escape while I wait for him to attempt to crush my bones to make his bread.

"I fucking hate this," he murmurs.

"I didn't know." My admission is blurted like a frightened little bitch.

He jerks his head in a barely-there acknowledgement. He doesn't believe me. Or doesn't care.

"When did you figure out Decker was a snitch?"

"I didn't know about that either." I take another backward step and collide with the side of the bed frame, the corner of the thick wood stabbing into my thigh. "Shit."

Hunter's brows pinch, his face changing into a mask of incredulity. "Sit down before you hurt yourself." The words are a command. Almost a threat.

I shake my head. "I'm fine."

"Sit," he grates. "Your apprehension is making me fucking uncomfortable."

"Uncomfortable?" I've known this man a long time. I even thought I'd grown to trust him despite my aversion to the weakness. And over all the years watching him, I've never seen him uncomfortable.

In a rage, yes.

Menacingly cocky, definitely.

But never uncomfortable.

"Maybe angry is a better word," he snarls. "You're acting like I'm a threat, and it's seriously pissing me off. You should know better."

"I should know better?" I work the statement around in my head, denying its vehemence. "I've just found out my father is the devil. That the man who raised me is my worst nightmare. I've known nothing my entire life, Hunter, so forgive me if I question your motives."

He winces, the silent seconds ticking by before he murmurs, "Sorry."

The apology hits deep.

He doesn't have to repeat his command to sit because my legs collapse beneath me and I slump to the bed in a heap of emotional baggage.

"Tell me about Decker." He remains in place, the pinch of his brows tight. "How did you find out?"

"He blew his own cover once we got here. He just blurted it out."

"Did he hurt you?"

"No." My response comes instantly. But it's a lie. I'm beyond hurt by Sebastian. He didn't show one sign of relief when he found out Cole is still in the dark. He found out he hadn't been outed as the informant and not once did he celebrate us having more time together.

He's resigned to leaving.

Nothing I do will change his mind.

"You're lying." His eyes narrow. "What did he do to you?"

"Nothing." I shake my head and lower my gaze, my cheeks turning to flame.

"Bullshit," he snaps. "Tell me what he did."

I keep my mouth shut, too embarrassed to admit the truth.

"I'm going to fucking kill him." He starts for the door.

"*No.* Wait." I shove to my feet and rush to block his path with a shaking body and a splayed hand. "I promise he didn't hurt me."

"Then what are you hiding?"

My fingers are insignificant against the muscles of his chest, the rampant beat of his heart like a hammer beneath my palm.

"I'm not hiding anything." I cringe when his gaze intensifies. "What you see is shame. I fell for him. I fell really hard, Hunter. And the more minutes that pass, the further I fall. I can't seem to stop."

His lip curls. I'm not sure whether it's in frustration or incredulity.

"I think we both know he's never been one of us," I admit. "He's always been an outsider. The good, while we're the bad. And there's nothing I can do to change that."

"He's no saint. Don't go making him into something he's not."

"He is to me." I drop back to the mattress. "I've never wanted to change who I am more than I do right now."

"Yeah?" He sobers and comes to sit beside me. "I get it. I feel the same way about Sarah."

"Maybe you should listen to your own advice," I mutter. "She's no saint either."

"She's still far better than I deserve."

I disagree. I've always known she was perfectly matched for this man. Now her callousness makes it even more apparent. What that woman needs is a dose of her own medicine.

The worst part is that she's currently out there, alone with Sebastian, probably turning him against me.

"What did she say to you on the porch?" he asks.

240

I bark out a derisive laugh. "Not much. She just told me, in a not-so-subtle way, that she thinks I'm involved."

"Ignore her. She's lashing out. That's all. She's made herself into this badass defender of the weak and innocent. So having this happen right under her nose makes her feel like a failure."

"She's not the only one who feels that way."

"I know." He shoves a hand through his hair, his frustration so palpable I can feel it throb inside my chest. "This whole situation is fucked up."

"Uh huh." I lean into him, needing to ease his burden and rest my shoulder against his. "Never in a million years would I have thought my father was capable of this."

"What about Cole?" He wraps his arm around me and pulls me into his side. "Do you think he's involved?"

My stomach twists in knots, inspiring a mass production of bile. "I've sworn black and blue he has nothing to do with this... But if you're unsure, then maybe I should be, too."

Hunter knows my brother. He's one of the very few people who does. If he's in doubt, then I'm not sure I should be confident of Cole's innocence.

"No. Ignore me. I'm questioning everything at the moment."

"Me, too."

"Especially Decker." He shoots me a glance, then focuses toward the vacant corner of the room. "I can't get over that lying little fuck."

"He's not enjoying this either. He doesn't feel good about what he's done, despite how moral it is."

"There's no place for morality around here. That's not how things work."

"And maybe that should change. This never would've happened otherwise." I stare at my fingers clenched in my lap. "I need to fix it."

There's no other choice. I don't think I can move forward with these atrocities hanging over my head.

"You need to think long and hard before you contemplate getting involved."

"No, I don't. My thoughts on this won't change." Maybe if I'd reported my uncle for his crimes when I was little, or taken it into my own hands long ago, this never would've happened. I could've stopped it all before it even started. "I won't be a spectator in this life anymore. I don't care if I die trying. I *will* make my father pay."

He turns to me, his brows pulled tight, his eyes narrowed.

I hold my breath, waiting for him to tell me I'm an ignorant, whimsical fool. Instead, he slowly nods.

"It won't be easy."

"I know."

He pushes from the mattress and holds out a hand. "We're going to need a fucking brilliant plan."

"And Sebastian needs to be involved." I grasp his offering and push to my feet, waiting for his refusal. "Is that going to be a problem?"

"Yes." His grip tightens around my fingers. His jaw ticks, too. A multitude of frustration flows off of him, making my heart tighten. "But I'll do anything for Sarah. And right now, you both have the same goal in mind."

"Will you promise not to hurt him?"

"Nope." He doesn't release my hand as he leads me to the door.

"Hunter, please. This is serious."

"As serious as a grown man kicking me in the shin?"

I frown. "Excuse me?"

"Forget it." He drags me out into the hall. "I promise to behave. For now. Is that good enough?"

I roll my eyes. "Do I have a choice?"

"Not at all."

A derisive scoff leaves my lips. "Then I guess I'll have to deal. Just as long as you realize I'll take a bullet for that man if necessary."

He winces, and I'm not sure if it's in confusion or distaste. "Let's hope it doesn't come down to that."

He guides me along the hall, the murmur of conversation drifting from the kitchen. I can hear them talking. About me. The whispers don't stop until we reach the entry to the dining room to find them sitting opposite each other at the large wooden table, the space between them scattered with snacks.

I meet Sebastian's gaze, his expression growing pained when he lowers his focus to my grip on Hunter's hand.

"We need to talk." I squeeze the fingers entwined with mine then let go.

"It looks like you two have already been doing that." Sarah scowls. "Should we be thankful you've decided to include us?"

"Cut them a break." Sebastian drags out the chair beside him and raises a brow, wordlessly offering me the seat. "The big guy was too scared to knock on the front door. We don't want to frighten him away from a conversation."

"Funny." Hunter wanders forward and rests against the wall behind Sarah, relaxed, yet the readiness of battle is evident in the clench of his fists. "I guess I was trembling in my boots at the thought of you landing another kick to my shin, you fucking pussy."

I watch the exchange, unsure whether it's friendly fire, or something more sinister. They both appear tolerant and calm despite the underlying tension.

"Are we even capable of discussing this in a civil manner?" I make toward the offered chair and sit, my oversized shirt billowing over my thighs.

"This is civil." Sebastian grabs a granola bar from the center of the table and pushes it toward me. "You need to eat."

I grab the offering, my fingers deliberately sliding over his in a show of thanks before he moves his hand away.

"Start talking." Sarah doesn't quit scowling. "What have you two been scheming behind our backs?"

I raise an unimpressed brow as I break open the food wrapper and take a bite. "There wasn't any scheming. All we discussed is how I need to make this right. I can't let my father get away with what he's done."

"*You?*" Sarah drawls. "You mean *us*, right? What could you possibly do on your own? Well, apart from slapping your daddy on the wrist and telling him he's been a naughty boy. But given his proclivities, I'm sure he'd enjoy the hell out of that."

My throat clogs with a spike of fury. My pulse thumps. Everywhere. In my ears. My head. Behind my eyes. I clench my teeth and take a deep breath before I do something that will delay any possibility of fatherly vengeance. "Someone needs to shut her up before I do it myself."

She laughs. "I'd like to see you try."

"*Sarah*," Sebastian warns. "Either leash your bitchiness or I'll kick your ass out."

"Her bitchiness?" It's my turn for derision. "Is that what we're calling her personality these days?"

"Both of you, put a sock in it." Hunter's voice is a mere grumble of authority. "We don't have time to fuck around. At the moment, Cole thinks you two are hiding because you had the fuckers from the drive-by tailing you. But that bullshit story won't hold for long."

"I agree. I need to tell him what's going on." Bottling this news isn't healthy. Being separated from my family isn't helping either. "He needs to know the truth."

"About your father?" Sarah asks.

I glare through a sharp nod.

"And where, exactly, will you tell him you got the information? How are you going to explain the knowledge without exposing Decker?"

My skin turns clammy. My brother finding out the identity of the informant isn't my biggest issue. What I don't want to face is the reality of Sebastian leaving me.

But that *is* the reality.

He's no longer going to be a part of my life. He's walking away. He already made his choice clear. "Sebastian isn't sticking around. He's—"

"Like hell I'm not," he growls. "I'm not going anywhere if you're putting yourself in danger."

My heart stops, the missing beats consuming me.

Is that all I had to do to keep him close? Risk my safety?

I bottle a laugh in my tightening chest. I should've known.

"I'll look after her." Hunter crosses his arms over his chest. "You need to cut and run. As soon as Torian finds out, you're dead. Or worse."

"Who says he needs to find out anything?" Sarah counters. "We have to keep this to ourselves for now. How do we even know he's not involved?"

"*We know*," Hunter and I say in unison.

"Fine." She huffs. "You have unwavering faith in his innocence. But you need to realize Torian is going to want to take over as soon as he finds out. When that happens, we won't have a say in the outcome. And he sure as hell won't let his sister be involved."

The truth in her words is a betraying punishment.

I don't want her to be right. Yet she is.

"I agree," Sebastian murmurs. "You've said it yourself, Keira, there's different rules when it comes to dealing with family. If he learns the truth, it's only going to make this situation more complicated. And your father will never be punished accordingly."

He's right, too.

The severe frown pulling at Hunter's brow says he agrees.

"Okay." I nod. "So I won't tell him." Despite the guilt already eating away at my stomach.

"Are you capable of keeping something this big from him?" Sarah asks.

I glare at her. "I'm not a child. I've kept things from him before."

She holds up her hands in surrender. "I wasn't being a bitch this time. I was only asking if it's something you think you're capable of. I know you two are close, even though you lead people to believe otherwise."

The thinly veiled apology means nothing to me. Not when all her knives still linger in my back.

"She's capable." Sebastian grabs my hand in my lap, our fingers twining beneath the table. "You've got no idea what she's kept from her brother."

I plotted the murder of my uncle and kept it to myself. Planning the demise of my father should be no different.

It should.

Only it already feels a million times worse.

"Keeping Cole out of this is obviously ideal, but how the

fuck do we get Luther back in the country without him?" Hunter pushes from the wall and begins to pace. "No, Keira, but your old man hasn't given a shit about you for years. He's not going to drop everything and come running just because you ask him to."

I steel myself against the brutal truth—my father doesn't care. He never did. Not when I was a child. Not when I was a vulnerable teen. And definitely not now. "I know a way."

I know possibly the one and only driving force to get my father back in the country.

"Which is?" Sarah asks.

"I'll finish what I started weeks ago."

Sebastian's hand falls limp in my lap. He knows what I'm about to say, and there's no comforting hold to reassure me I'm making the right decision.

"I'm going to kill my uncle." I forge through the judgmental silence. "My father will return for the funeral. There's no way he'd miss it, despite the authorities breathing down his neck."

The quiet continues, the thickness expanding as all eyes turn to me.

"Finish what you started?" Hunter asks. "You're the one who ran down Richard?"

This time Sebastian doesn't answer the hard question for me. He straightens, his hand retreating.

"That's a story for another day." I swallow over the scratch in my throat. "Right now, we need to focus on the future, not the past."

Nobody fills the silence. The tension thickens, their judgment weighing down on me.

"You're not going anywhere near Richard," Sebastian mutters. "I'll take care of him."

No, he won't. But that's a conversation for later, too.

"What's this all about?" Sarah scrutinizes me. "Is there something else we need to know?"

"Only that I'm well aware of what my father and uncle are capable of. I'm not going to be lenient on either of them."

Her chin slowly rises, her lips parting as understanding begins to flicker to the surface.

I don't want her to delve into my past. I don't want her to even contemplate what I've been through. "We need to stop moving in circles and make a goddamn plan." I release a huff of frustration. "All any of you have done so far is poke at everything I say."

There's more silence. More judgment, too.

"What's the end game here, Keira?" Sebastian reclaims my hand, the touch gentle. "Are you talking about putting Luther in prison or..." He looks at me, our eyes meeting across an emotional battlefield.

There's a wealth of connection between us. A hidden conversation where he relays his protection and strength while I struggle not to confess my fear.

"No," I whisper. "Prison isn't an option. My father has the means to buy the best lawyers. Hell, he could grease the palms of an entire jury. Or pay a team to help him escape whatever cell they put him in." The overbearing weight of my father's power presses down on me. "He has men everywhere. There's nobody who can withstand his threats or influence."

"Which means?" Hunter asks.

I shuffle my ass back in my seat and sit at my full height. I raise my chin, straighten my shoulders, and become the warrior woman I've always considered myself to be. I think of my past. I contemplate Stella's future. I picture all those helpless, fractured women. Then I resign myself to the only outcome possible. "Death is the solution. For both of them."

Relief shadows my statement, but the underlying pain lingers.

He's my dad, and I'm planning his murder.

He was my mother's one and only love, and I vow to send him to his grave.

"First, I'll take care of my uncle." I clear my throat to dislodge the emotion roughening my words. "Then when my father returns for the funeral, we end this."

"I said I'd deal with Richard," Sebastian reaffirms. "Don't

even think about going near him. I'm not letting you get caught up in that again."

"Caught up in what?" Sarah asks.

"I *want* to do this," I demand. "I *need* to be the one who ends his life. I won't fail this time."

"You won't get a chance." He pushes from the table and stalks for the fridge, grabbing four cans of beer before returning to place them among the snacks.

He's still trying to protect me, that much is clear, but I won't let him this time. Not when it comes to Richard. "I'm capable, Sebastian."

"Really?" The question is an accusation. "There's a reason you didn't go ahead with the hit in the first place. Killing someone isn't a crime you want on your conscience."

"Excuse me." I shove from my chair. "That wasn't the reason, and you know it. I told you I didn't follow through because I didn't want to make my family vulnerable."

"Hold up." Sarah flattens her hands on the table. "So, you did run Richard down?"

Sebastian's jaw ticks, his nostrils flaring. He's beautiful. An exquisite show of masculine dominance. "Do you think you'll be helping your family's situation when your dad and Richard are dead and you're in prison? You don't want to spend the rest of your life behind bars."

"And you do?" I quip.

He doesn't snap at my ridicule. Instead, he cracks a can of beer and takes a long pull. "We're not arguing over this."

"You're right." I shove my chair back into place and stalk around the table. "We're not."

"Why don't we take a break?" Sarah glances between us. Back and forth. Over and over. "We can discuss this later."

"There's no need. Richard is mine to deal with." I continue toward the back door. "I'll never forgive anyone who gets in my way."

I pull the porch door wide, escape outside, then slam the wood shut behind me. The bang reverberates through my bones, shaking my soul. The vibration spurs me to move faster, to skitter down the steps and stride toward the end of the yard.

I have to get out of here.

To go home.

More than anything, I want to speak to my siblings. I need to hear a familiar voice. A calming, strengthening voice that won't have me questioning my every breath.

I keep pounding out the distance, not stopping when I reach the waist-high fence. I climb over the metal and keep walking along the dirt car track leading around the paddock, the pebbles and stones tormenting my feet.

It doesn't take long for my anger to dissipate and for regret to take its place.

I get it. Sebastian wants to protect me. He *always* wants to protect me. It's what endeared me to him in the first place. I can't grow to hate it now. I just need to make him understand.

I have to do this.

And yes, maybe he's right. Maybe I wasn't strong enough before, and I couldn't handle a hit marring my conscience. But things have changed.

I want Richard's death on my hands.

I need to be strong enough to make him pay, not only for his recent transgressions, but those he made against me in the past.

I don't stop until I'm half a mile from the house, the early afternoon sun beating down on me as an all-consuming hollowness creeps inside my chest. I haven't felt alone since before the shooting. It's been days with Sebastian within reach and readily accessible to keep me stable.

I need to learn to function without him.

Just because he's staying by my side for now doesn't mean he can for long. Cole will learn the truth eventually. The time will come when the man I adore is wrenched from my heart.

A scuffle of noise sounds behind me, inspiring hope.

It's him. I know it is. He's here to apologize. To make things right. And I want nothing more than to run to him and claim the warmth.

I turn, my eyes gentle in anticipation for the remorse I expect to see. But he's not the person behind me. I'm bitterly disappointed at the sight of Sarah a few feet away, her feet bare, the bottom of her jeans covered in red dirt as she navigates the stones in the path toward me.

"What are you doing out here?" I mutter.

Her ankle rolls, and she rights herself with a curse. "Do you mind if I join you?"

"Do I have a choice?"

"Yes, you do. I can leave you alone if you like. But I think you'd prefer to watch me suffer through an uncomfortable apology."

Jesus Christ. Sebastian told her. The pity is right there, written all over her face.

"I don't want an apology." I start toward her, retracing my steps toward the house.

I don't want anything from her. Not now. Not anymore.

"Then tell me what to do to make this better." She pauses in place and waits until I reach her side. "How do I fix this?"

"You don't. This is as good as it gets." I stride by her, and she hustles to follow.

"Despite me being a total dick, we're friends, Keira. I can make it up to you."

"That's where you're wrong. We're not friends. We never were. We couldn't have been if you were so eager to burn me at the stake."

She cringes. "I deserve that."

She deserves more. Much more.

"I'm sorry." Her words are pained. "I can't imagine what you've been through. I didn't realize. I honestly had no clue. And I hate myself for it."

"Sebastian had no right to tell you." I keep stalking away, the distance between me and the house seeming to grow further and further with each breath.

"He didn't say a word. I'm working on assumptions at this point and hoping my imagination is on overdrive."

"Your original assumptions about me were entirely off base. Why would this be any different?"

"Will you tell me?"

I try not to fracture from the regret in her voice.

She doesn't deserve my sympathy.

Goddamn it, she doesn't deserve anything from me. "I'll pass."

I lengthen my stride, increasing the pace of my escape. She doesn't try to keep up. I hear her fall back, the scuffle of rocks drifting behind as I approach the house yard.

I don't stop until my hand is on the fence.

"*Fuck*." Her curse splits the air.

I pause and glance over my shoulder, finding her looking at something shiny poking from the bottom of her foot.

"Motherfucker." She pulls out a sharp spike of glass and throws it into the long grass beside the trail.

I bite back a reply. I shouldn't care if she's hurt. I swear I don't despite the pang beneath my ribs that demands I help.

She limps forward. One step. Two.

Damn it.

"Are you okay?" I mutter.

"Yeah. I'd call this karma."

"I guess." I shrug. "If Karma turned into a lenient little bitch."

She shoots me a grin.

It's too easy. After what she put me through, the slide back into friendship needs to be harder.

I turn away in rejection and raise my leg to climb over the fence.

"Keira, wait."

I sigh, my shoulders slumping as I reluctantly face her hobbling toward me.

"I fucked up. Big time." Her usual expression of pride-filled strength becomes a softened plea for understanding. "But I'm begging you, is there any way I can make this up to you?"

I can't hold her focus. Not when she's efficiently wearing me down with the sincerity in her expression. I lower my gaze, over the wrinkles in her shirt, then further to the rectangular bulge in her jeans pocket.

I stop. Stare.

Maybe there is something she can do.

"Is that a cell?" I look her in the eye. "Let me call Cole."

She blinks, once, twice, her lips parting on silent words.

"That's how you make this up to me, Sarah. You give me that cell in your pocket and leave me alone to call my brother."

"Decker doesn't want you contacting him yet."

"I'm well aware of what Decker wants."

She glances toward the house, her forehead wrinkled from an internal battle I can practically hear. "They're going to kill me."

"That's a small price to pay."

She sighs and presses her lips tight as she bridges the space between us in a few limped steps and hands over the device. "I hope you know what you're doing."

I don't. Not at all. "I'll figure it out." I grab the cell and continue to hold her stare. "You can go inside now."

She doesn't budge. For a few brief seconds she holds my gaze, wordlessly pleading with me to change my mind.

"Go."

She huffs out a breath and throws her leg over the fence.

I wait for her to walk across the lawn, up the stairs to the porch, then into the house. Then my fingers are frantically flying over the cell screen, dialing one of the very few numbers I've committed to memory.

Cole answers on the first ring, his panicked voice loud and clear. "Where is she? Have you found her?"

I smile. I almost sob. "Are you referring to me, brother?"

"Jesus. I've been fucking worried. What happened? Are you safe?"

I close my eyes, fighting the burn.

I want to tell him everything. All the secrets. All the lies. All the deception our father has intricately woven into our lives.

"I'm—"

A loud crack of noise draws my attention to the back of the house. Sebastian stands there, the door wildly swinging back toward him as he stares at me, wide-eyed, shoulders tense.

I swallow at the defeat I see in his features.

I'm betraying him again. I'm hurting him.

"Everything is okay, Cole."

Sebastian descends the stairs in one leap and storms toward me, his stride menacing.

"Where are you?" Cole asks. "Why the fuck haven't you called?"

My heart lodges in my throat as Sebastian uses one hand to bound over the fence, coming to an overbearing stop right in front of me.

"I'm safe," I say into the phone. "Decker is looking after me."

His chin hitches in defiance as he stands tall, the pain of my deception evident in his eyes.

"We didn't mean to worry you," I continue. "But we had to get off the grid. We had a tail."

"Who?"

"I don't know. We lost them outside Newport."

"Where are you now?"

"I don't know that either. And I think it's best if I don't say anything more over the phone."

Sebastian's chest rises and falls with harsh breaths as he remains ramrod straight. I want to reach out and touch him. I have to ease the heartache. But what I'm going to say to Cole is far more important.

"You're upset," my brother growls. "I can hear it in your voice."

"It's just good to speak to you. And I miss home. I can't wait to see Layla and Stella."

"It's more than that, Keira. Tell me what's going on."

My hand trembles as I lower the phone to press the speaker button. Sebastian needs to hear this.

"You're right." I clear my throat. "Something *is* going on."

Dark eyes turned panicked as they stare down at me. Concern is written into every inch of him—his posture, his expression. I have to ignore it all and forge forward.

"I need to tell you something."

Sebastian makes a grab for the phone.

I dodge, holding up a hand as I mouth a plea for him to wait. "*Please.*"

He bares his teeth, his nostrils flaring while he fights against trusting me.

"Cole..." I turn away, facing the sun. "I..." The words stick in my throat. Clogging. Choking.

I'm about to change everything. I'm going to flip this script on its ass, and I'm not going to know if it's the right decision until it's already too late.

I fill my lungs to capacity, the tortured breath stabbing through my lungs, bearing down on my stomach. "I love him."

Silence reigns. Nobody utters a sound at my admission.

"I know you're angry," I murmur. "And that you don't trust him. But *I* do."

"Keira—"

"I'm not finished. We've been through a lot in the past few days. I've gone to hell and back, and he's been beside me the entire time."

"That's what he's paid for," he scolds. "I told him to protect you with his life."

"And he has. Without fail."

"We can discuss this when you get back—"

"We're discussing it now." I add steel to my tone. "We've slept together, Cole. We had unprotected sex, which means there's a possibility I'm pregnant. I could be carrying his child."

I hear Sebastian's sharp inhale. Cole's vicious curse is far louder.

I battle with panic, the overwhelming force threatening to take me down.

"Tell me where you are," he demands. "I'm coming to get you."

"No, you're not. I'm staying here for now. I'll come home soon. But until I do, I need you to realize this is what I want. *He's* what I want. I won't put up with any asshole behavior once we get back."

"I swear to God, Keira. Tell me where you are."

"I'm safe," I repeat. "That's all you need to know."

254

24

DECKER

She doesn't wait for a reply before disconnecting the call. She doesn't wait for me to pick my jaw up off the ground either.

She stands there, her arm falling to her side, the cell hanging limp in her hand as her back continues to face me.

"Was any of that true?" My question is barely audible.

"I'm not pregnant."

The gentle utter of her admission has no effect on me. My mind is rabid. My face seeps with sweat.

"I have a hormone implant," she admits. "I lied to Cole to buy us some time." She turns to face me, an apology written in her features. "This way, even if he does learn the truth, he'll pause long enough to contemplate the repercussions of his actions."

He'll pause.

She's not pregnant.

"You lied to your brother for me?" She's delusional if she thinks the deception will change Torian's actions, but still, she lied. For me. "Why?"

"You know why."

No, I'm pretty sure I'm clueless. Whenever I think I've got an edge on this woman, she pulls the rug out from beneath me.

"It's only temporary." She wraps her arms around her stomach, hugging herself in a show of such brutal vulnerability

I have to fight the need to drag her against me. "Once you leave, I can tell him there's no baby."

I nod, strangely wishing the fake story she concocted had a possibility of reality. But like she said, that lie of hers will only buy a pause in time. It won't stop Cole from gunning me down in the long run.

"What about the rest of the conversation, Tinkerbell? What else did you lie about?"

"Are you asking if I love you?"

Yeah. I am. I just can't find the fucking balls to open my mouth and say it.

She nibbles her lower lip, her brows pulling tighter by the second as she glances away. "I think I've loved you since you stuck up for me months ago. I don't think anyone could be exposed to your level of protection and care without falling hard, Sebastian."

Her words cut to my core, her admission slashing deep enough to scar. "So it's the badassery that won you over, not my sparkling personality?" I paste on a grin, hoping to suck the deep and crazy out of the conversation.

"You're no badass," she whispers. "You're the opposite—A good Samaritan with a frightening death wish, and really inappropriate timing with your smartass comments."

My grin lessens.

I can feel her fear. I can almost taste it.

"I don't have a death wish." I step forward, my feet falling hard against the dirt as she backs herself against the fence, keeping distance between us that I refuse to allow. "Not anymore." I continue to advance, not stopping until my hips cage hers in place. "I just know what I want and don't plan to stop until I get it."

"Which is retribution, right?" Her eyes turn pained. "That's all you're focused on."

"My hopes for retribution are delayed for now."

"Because I exposed you?"

"No. Because I'm focusing on something more important." I glide a hand into her hair, holding her possessively, never losing sight of those gorgeous eyes as I bring us chest to chest.

"Right now, all I want is to make sure you're safe. That's all that matters to me."

"Why? You've made it clear you don't feel the same way I do."

"Jesus, Keira." I close in on her with my free hand, dragging my thumb over the softness of her lower lip. "Who says I don't feel the same?"

Her face crumples, her baby blues tortured. "You do. In your actions and your plans."

"You know this has been a fucked up mess from the start, but how can you not see that I'd kill for you? Despite knowing what your father has been doing, I put my life on the line for you. And I'll continue to do the same, because there is no way in hell I'll let you anywhere near Richard."

"This isn't about him. I'm talking about you not being excited to hear your secret is safe. Hunter didn't tell Cole. And neither did I. But you never celebrated having more time with me. You don't care."

"I fucking care." I bring us face to face. Almost nose to nose. "But I've also gotta keep it real clear in my mind that leaving is the only conclusion here. A few extra days with you is huge, but we don't get a happily ever after. No matter how badly I want to give that to you."

"You're acting as if you're already gone."

"No, I'm not. I'm just trying to keep a level head. Your safety is the most important thing here. I can't lose sight of that."

"I'm scared you're losing sight of me entirely."

I wince.

Truth is, I wish I could lose sight of her. If that was a possibility I'd already be long gone. I would've taken my beating from Hunter yesterday and headed for the hills. My inability to let go of Keira is the only reason I'm still here. "I'll never do that. Not even once I'm gone."

"I'm going to do everything in my power to change things so you don't leave," she whispers against my lips. "I'll keep lying to Cole. I'll make that agent who's blackmailing you disappear. I'll do whatever it takes, Sebastian."

"Shh." I claim her mouth, brushing my lips over hers as she slays my fucking heart. "Let me handle it. I'll work something out."

She whimpers, her tongue sweeping mine.

I wish I wasn't lying. I wish I had faith. But this hole I've dug is too deep. You don't rat on the most powerful crime family in the state and live to tell the tale.

I'm a dead man walking. I can already feel the darkness of damnation.

"Promise me," she pleads. "Don't let this be another deception."

Fuck. She knows me too well. Her insight creeps into the furthest reaches of my mind. She's a part of me, stealing my secrets and reading my soul.

I kiss her deeper. Harder. With all my fucking heart and determination.

"Sebastian..." Her hand finds my chest, the pressure growing as she tries to push me away. "Please."

The doomsday clock sounds another tick. I don't want to betray her again. Not over this.

"*Please,*" she repeats. "I need to believe this can work."

"It can." I lean harder into her, grinding against her pelvis. "We'll figure it out."

Lies. All lies. But I'd promise her the world if it meant I'd get to continue hearing those needy little moans that vibrate against my mouth.

I'd do it all.

I'd do everything.

I fall into her. I burn. Every inch of me is attuned to every move she makes.

We're one.

It's intrinsic.

Fate.

At least for now.

I drown in her until I can no longer breathe. Long enough for me to pretend I'm someone else. Somewhere else. There's no approaching detonation. I don't have to walk away. I'm not going to break her heart. It's just us. A happy couple, without a care in the fucking world.

"I want to drive back to Portland tonight," she murmurs against my lips. "I don't want to wait any longer."

I turn numb. All the pleasure evaporates, leaving me cold and bitter.

"Okay..." I pull away, meeting the determination staring back at me. "But just so you know, I haven't changed my mind about Richard. You need to let me and Hunt handle it."

The hand on my chest grows talons, her nails digging into skin. "Don't fight me on this."

"I'm not fighting you, slick. I'm keeping you safe."

Her chin hitches, a wealth of strength building in her features. "No."

That's all she says. One word. A single, adamant denial.

She slides to the side, leaving me with a look filled with more force than reason.

She doesn't understand what she's asking. There's no fucking clue behind those gorgeous blue eyes as she leaps the fence and sashays her sexy ass toward the house while I'm stuck dealing with a hard dick and a hollow chest.

I watch her climb the stairs and turn toward the porch railing, Sarah coming outside to meet her. The two of them murmur together, their heads close, their camaraderie a fucking uncomfortable sight.

The last thing Keira needs is a master manipulator at her side. They could take down hell if they teamed up. And I sure as shit don't want that happening on my watch.

I leap the fence and stride to the house. They stop chatting as I approach, the cease of their Secret Squirrel conversation raising the hair on the back of my neck.

"We haven't finished talking, Keira."

She doesn't look at me. Doesn't even budge an inch to acknowledge my comment.

"I made sandwiches," Sarah offers. "Go inside and start eating without us. We'll join you soon."

I don't tear my gaze from Keira, but she doesn't glance my

way. She deliberately refuses, too busy holding the railing in a white-knuckle grip as she glares into the distance.

"Soon," I repeat in warning. "We don't have time to fuck around."

Sarah rolls her eyes. "We'll be there when we're ready."

It's a subtle fuck you, and I have no choice but to listen.

Instead of planting my feet like my ego demands, I act like a scolded puppy and slink inside to watch them from the other side of the glass-paneled door.

"Are they coming in?" Hunt mutters from his seat at the table.

I close my eyes for the briefest second, begging the holy heavens for strength while I'm stuck inside with this unforgiving motherfucker who could end our ceasefire at any moment. "Not until they've annoyed me enough to cause a hemorrhoid."

"Is Keira okay?"

I shrug. "Your guess is as good as mine."

"She looked fine a few minutes ago when you were groping her against the fence. What did you do to fuck it up?"

I clench my teeth and swing around to swipe my beer off the table, throwing back gulps like I'm dying of dehydration. Hunt's trying to make me snap, and I refuse. I'm not going to bite. Not until the alcohol numbs the bruises I already have to make way for the new ones he wants to give me.

I empty the can and retrieve another from the fridge. I waste time tidying up the mess Sarah made while creating the pile of sandwiches on the table. I fuck around, trying to play it cool while Sarah taunts me through the glass, frowning at me as she speaks.

I can't hear what she's saying, but I can tell it's filled with annoyance aimed in my direction. Revenge Barbie is getting in Keira's head, filling her with confidence and misconceptions about slaying dragons and taking over the world.

"Hunt, you better get control of your girl." I grip the counter and mentally count out my frustration. "She's starting to piss me off."

He scoffs. "Bite me. You two were best buddies when we arrived. Don't come crying to me now."

I'm still gripping the counter ten minutes later when Sarah walks inside, leaving Keira on the porch.

"What's going on?" Hunt pushes to his feet. "How is she?"

Sarah grabs one of the empty plates stacked on the table and begins grabbing sandwiches from the platter. "She's annoyed, which is entirely understandable when someone keeps treating her like a child."

I see red. My focus fucking glazes with anger. "Those are your words, not hers. She knows I'm not treating her like a fucking kid. Stop filling her head with bullshit."

"Then stop telling her what she can and can't do." She places down the plate piled with food and walks into the kitchen, bypassing my rage-filled position by the counter to open the cutlery drawer. "You'll never win this fight if you treat her like she's fragile."

I slam my palm down on the counter. "Goddamn it, she's not like you." My shoulders convulse with my labored breathing. "Killing someone will fuck with her head for the rest of her life."

"It's not your choice to make."

"It's not yours either. You've got no right to weigh in on this."

"I haven't done a damn thing. All I'm doing is listening to her vent." She retrieves a knife and slams the drawer shut.

"What the hell is that for?"

She scowls. "To cut my sandwiches. Is that okay, your highness?"

"Just as long as you're not using it to stab her in the back again."

Her lip curls as she stomps to the table. "I never stabbed her in the back, *Decker*. I said a few things I shouldn't have, but I've apologized, and she's been decent enough to forgive me. So I'm going to stay out there and chat things out while she's willing."

She holds the knife in a tight grip and picks up her filled plate. "Can I have the car keys?" She turns her focus to her fiancé. "I'm going to see if any of the clothes I packed will fit her. She can't keep wearing that oversized shirt and shorts."

"Yeah." He pulls a fob from his pocket and lobs it toward her. "If she doesn't find anything suitable, I can go for a drive."

"Thanks, babe." She turns on her heel and heads for the door, shooting me one last taunting glare before she walks outside and leads Keira from the porch.

I miss the sight of my blue-eyed goddess as soon as she's out of view.

I don't know how to fix this shit. Not the issue of her wanting to walk through hell unnecessarily. Or the gauntlet I'm going to face once her brother has my dick in a vise.

There are no easy options. No fucking path of least resistance.

There's only struggle and torment.

"Did Richard put hands on her?" Hunt murmurs.

I don't deny the mental images assailing me. I let the picture of Richard's hands on Keira take over in the hopes it will increase my understanding of her need to face him on her own.

But it doesn't.

No matter what I think, what I do, I can't stand the thought of her anywhere near him.

"Yeah." I stalk to the table and snatch a sandwich from the pile.

"How did they keep it a secret? I should've noticed."

"You weren't around back then."

"Back when?" His eyes narrow.

"When she was fourteen." I take a bite of bread and chew as I watch the avalanche of reality bear down on him.

His jaw sets. His shoulders straighten. "Fourteen?" He raises his voice. "Fucking fourteen?" He shoves back from the table, his chair clattering to the floor. "I don't fucking blame her for running him down."

"She didn't. She paid someone to do it."

He begins to pace, stalking back and forth. "Who?"

"The same asshole who shot up the restaurant."

He stops and swings around to meet my gaze, his face a

mask of confusion. "She paid someone to shoot up my engagement party?"

"No. She paid someone to take out Richard, then backed out of the contract. Now the motherfucker is blackmailing her."

"Who?" he repeats. "How do I find this fucker?"

"I don't know yet. But I'll figure it out. Hopefully before Torian gets his hands around my neck." I hold his gaze, my eyes pleading. "If I don't get the chance, I need you to promise to take care of him for me."

"I'm not doing shit for you." He continues pacing. "But I'll do it for her."

"Semantics, asshole." I take another snap of sandwich, not tasting the food as I swallow.

"No, not semantics. You don't deserve a damn thing from me, you self-righteous prick."

Self-righteous?

Self-fucking-righteous?

I return to the regular broadcast of biting my tongue, my anxiety building the longer Keira remains out of view. I slump into a seat and fill my gut despite the lack of hunger.

I don't want to eat at a time like this. I doubt I'll ever regain my appetite, but fuel is a necessary commodity. Or it will be once we sort out a plan.

"What did she tell Torian?" Hunt makes a dramatic show of flinging out a chair and sinking onto it. "I assume it wasn't anything dramatic, seeing as though you ran out there and punished her by shoving your tongue down her throat."

"You fixate on my love life way too much," I taunt. "Not gettin' enough at home, big guy?"

"I get plenty," he snarls. "At least I did until you fucked up my schedule."

"A well deserved punishment for trying to gouge my eyes out, if you ask me."

"You threw the rule book out the window when you started the five-year-old shin kicking."

"Yeah? What rules are there when it comes to my sister getting raped and tortured?"

He sobers, the bitterness fading from his expression. He lowers his focus to the table, remaining quiet through the thickening discomfort.

"Keira told Torian she's pregnant," I say to break the silence.

"What?" His head snaps up. "Are you serious?"

"Unfortunately." I slide my plate to the center of the table. "She thinks it will stop him from blowing my brains out."

"Is it true?"

"No." I push from my seat and go to the kitchen. "At least that's what she says."

"You can't blame me for asking. You're not known for doing the smartest shit."

"Thanks." I pull open the fridge and ignore the fresh insult. "Want a beer?"

"Yeah."

I walk back to the table and slide a can toward him. "We need to figure out this plan before Keira gets carried away with ideas of her own vigilante justice. We can give her something basic to do. Surveillance or some shit. Something to keep her busy and feel like she's played a pivotal role."

Hunt stares at me with an annoying level of patronizing judgement.

"What?"

He shrugs. "Nothin'."

"No, it's definitely something. You're looking at me as if you know more than I do."

"I know determined women, that's all."

"You know *one* determined, psychotic woman. Keira's nothing like Sarah."

"Maybe not." He takes a large gulp of beer. "But if Richard laid hands on her, shouldn't she have the right to fuck him up on her own terms?"

"You weren't with her after the shooting. You don't know how something like this would stick with her. She'll be eaten alive with remorse, regardless of how he deserves to rot in hell."

"Or she could be eaten alive with regret if she doesn't do it herself."

No. I don't believe that would happen.

She's got a big heart. She's not capable of murder. Not with her own hands.

"Look," Hunt grates. "I agree with you. I don't think she should be anywhere near him when he takes his last breath. But I want you to think about what she's missing out on before you take the option away from her."

"I've thought about it. I don't need to fixate on it anymore."

He shrugs. "Okay, then we make sure she knows it's not a possibility."

"We?" I raise a brow. "Are Hunt and Deck back together again, kickin' it like old times?"

He glares. "Don't push your luck, motherfucker."

I chuckle but take the warning like it's a death threat.

I don't push. Not at all.

I work my ass off to keep a level conversation sprinkled with sarcastic insults and blatant contempt. Just like the good ol' days.

We mutter murderous ideas at each other while we finish the sandwiches. We work out a plan for Richard, and Luther, and also that fucker who's blackmailing her. We'll knock them off one by one. Strategically. Quietly. Without a single lead weaving its way back to us.

"Keira wants to drive back tonight." I finish off another beer and throw the can across the kitchen, scoring a three-pointer in the sink. "I'm going to give her the rest of the afternoon to cool off and talk to her about the plan in the car. Even if we leave soon, we won't arrive until late. Hopefully, she'll be too tired to argue."

"Good luck with that."

I glance toward the porch, no longer able to ignore my need to lay eyes on her. "They've been out there for a long time."

"That's because neither one of them wants to be near us."

I push from my chair and walk to the back door, not seeing a soul in sight. "They're still out front."

Sarah's plate rests on the railing, a half-eaten sandwich sitting in the sun. It's quiet. Everything is detached, devoid and bare. But funnily enough, not Hunter.

Despite his thick layers of hatred, I'm grateful for his willingness to talk. It's more than I deserve. But it doesn't stop me wanting more.

His understanding would go a long way right about now.

The briefest flicker of empathy is all I ask.

"Do you plan on finishing me off after all this is done?" I keep my focus outside, not willing to betray my feelings on the subject.

"I haven't decided."

I nod, appreciating the honesty.

"Do you think you've got the balls to kick my ass again?" he asks.

"Apparently, I didn't kick your ass. I've been told you let me win."

He huffs out a derisive laugh. "You won, asshole. I was too surprised to know what to do."

My skin prickles, my senses unfamiliar with his thinly veiled compliment. "Surprised at the betrayal? Or—"

"You being an informant is beyond surprising. That shit falls into a category above and beyond. But I had a few hours to come to terms with it before we got to that barn. What threw me off was your ability to pack a punch. I guess I don't know shit when it comes to you."

Maybe there's a glimpse of truth in what Sarah told me earlier. I guess Hunt could be a hard man filled with gooey softness after all.

"I did it for my sister."

"I know," he grates, as if deliberately trying to harden up the conversation.

"And I wouldn't change a thing. Apart from getting my ass exposed."

"You're not exposed. Not entirely. We could still find a way to get her back."

"No. It's too late." I wince through the tightening in my throat. "I found out a few weeks ago that she's gone. It was

Murphy's fucking Law that Torian finally brings me into the fold, then days later I get news that they've found her DNA in a shallow grave."

That dreaded, uncomfortable silence creeps back in and makes itself at home for long seconds.

"That's tough." Hunt's words are measured. Gentle. "I'm sorry."

I frown, battling the feels like they're waging war against me. "Yeah, well, the good news is that I'm not going to have to grieve for long. You're going to take care of that shit by putting me six feet under."

"I'm not going to kill you, asshole. It's just bullshit that you didn't tell me in the first place."

"That was never an option and you know it. You're loyal to Torian. You would've gunned me down long ago."

"I was fucking loyal to you, too, you piece of shit," he seethes. "More fucking loyal than you were to me."

"And how would I have broached that conversation, *Hunt*?" I swing away from the door and glare at him. "There's no rulebook for this shit."

"We've worked together a long time. There was a lot of opportunity for you to open your fucking mouth and sing to me instead of chirping like a fucking canary to the Feds."

My lip curls as I hold in a snarl.

The judgmental prick has no idea how I've battled keeping my secrets from him. He doesn't know what I've been through.

There are a thousand possibilities that could've, should've, and would've happened with each decision I made. I had to come to terms with my actions. I can't go back and change any of them.

"What's done is done." I walk toward the table and shove my chair into place. "And I'm sick of wasting more time waiting on the girls to finish their make-up session. I'm going to go drag them back in here."

He remains in place as I leave the room and stride down the hall to the door. I scope the front yard through the glass, finding a pile of discarded clothes resting at the top of the stairs.

But I can't see them.

They're not on the porch or in the yard.

"Hunt."

Apprehension skitters down my spine. I press my head to the glass, trying to see further to the left and then the right.

That's when I notice the abnormality.

Something is missing.

Something fucking important.

"*Hunt.*" I yank the door wide and step outside.

His footsteps thump down the hall. "What?"

"Notice something absent in this pretty little picture?"

He glances around, taking in the open expanse of vacant land before his gaze settles right in the middle of the drive. "Fuck."

"Yeah. Fuck."

They've taken the car.

I barge past him to stalk down the hall. "You might want to get on the phone to that woman of yours and tell her to stop whatever the hell she thinks she's doing."

I enter my brother's room, heading straight for the wardrobe to pull out a pair of jeans and a clean shirt.

"Call her, Hunt," I yell, my words vibrating off the walls. "Get her on the fucking phone."

Once I'm dressed, I jog from the bedroom and find him in the kitchen, his cell in hand.

"She's not answering." He shoves the device in his pocket, only to have it beep with a message.

"What does it say?" I inch closer and lift my chin, trying to read the screen.

His jaw clenches. His nostrils flare.

He raises the cell to show me the text—*We thought you two needed some bonding time. We will see you back in Portland.*

"Get your shit," he growls. "We can catch them. They can't have gone far."

"Help me lock up." I rush into the kitchen and pull a plastic garbage bag from beneath the sink, filling it with snacks to last us the upcoming hours on the road.

Hunt disappears down the hall, the slam of a window pane echoing in the distance.

Minutes later, I meet him at the front door, and he shadows me as I jog around the side of the house to his car that I stole yesterday.

"*Fuck.*" Hunt stops dead in his tracks and shoves a hand through his hair. "Fucking Sarah."

I search for the trigger that set him off, my chest pounding, my limbs shaking as I find a kitchen knife protruding from the front passenger side tire. "Something gives me the distinct impression that they don't give a shit about us bonding."

"Ya think?" he drawls.

"They're going back to make a move on Richard." I break out in a cold sweat.

Keira's going to commit murder, without taking the time to create a proper plan. Without me there to help.

Jesus.

Hunter meets my gaze. "And without a spare fucking tire, we're never going to catch them in time."

25

KEIRA

THE HOURS SPENT ON THE ROAD, STRATEGIZING THE murder of one of my family, were some of the longest I've endured.

It's not like I haven't thought about Richard's death before. I've pictured it. I've even paid a man to complete the task. But I've never discussed every intricate detail that would lead to his last breath.

Sarah spoke each word with emotional detachment. She didn't appear fazed by the brutality. It was business. Nothing more. So I mimicked her demeanor, shoving all my fear and panic deep down inside.

I want this.

I need it.

His demise has to rest on my shoulders. I don't want Sebastian to be responsible. Or Hunter. Or even Sarah.

This needs to be all me.

I'm just nervous as hell at pulling the metaphorical trigger.

What if I freeze? Or get caught?

What happens if I can't think on my feet and I make a crucial mistake?

I suck in a shuddering breath, resting my hip against the cold metal of the car as I turn my attention to the hospital looming in front of me. The dominating building is bathed in shadow, the outside lights only illuminating the lower levels and leaving the dark rectangular windows to peer down at me.

"Are you sure you want to do this?" Sarah asks. Again. For the seventy-fifth time.

I've heard the question so many times it rings in my ears. "I'm sure."

"And you don't want me going in there with you?"

I wipe a hand over the arm of the leather jacket I borrowed, making sure the capped syringes are still firmly taped to my wrist. "No. It's better if I do this on my own. Less suspicion that way."

"We can only hope." She steps closer, grabbing the fringe of the long black wig to give it a jiggle. "At least you don't look recognizable."

The different hair, the colored contacts, the fake lashes, along with the full mask of plastered make-up that accentuates my cheekbones and slims down my face, have all worked together to transform me into someone else.

Someone who will hopefully slip into the ICU without drawing attention.

"Will you call Sebastian and let him know what's going on?" My heart clenches at the thought of him racing here to stop me. He needs to know he'll never make it in time. He can't. If he does, the whole plan could blow up in my face.

She nods. "He's going to be pissed."

"I know." God, how I know. The guilt over the anger and disappointment he would be harboring claws at me, digging deep into my soul. "But he gave me no choice."

This was my decision to make. Not his.

I'll own my actions.

The consequences, too.

"Just remember to keep your cool." Sarah continues to run her fingers through the long strands of the wig. "If something goes wrong, don't panic. Most people get caught making rash decisions."

I could laugh at the absurdity. Every decision I've made in the last three days has been rash.

Every. Single. One.

I don't know how to think differently anymore. The adrenaline-filled snap decisions have become my new norm.

"And I know you don't want to think about this..." She gives me a sad smile. "But if you get up there and can't follow through, it's not the end of the world. I'm not going anywhere. I'll stay right here in the parking lot, so you can come back and ask for help at any time."

She's wrong.

I can't back out twice. I don't want to prove Sebastian right. It's not an option. I failed a lot of women for not reporting my uncle when I was a child. And I've failed them every day since.

I won't do it a moment longer.

"You've helped enough already." I inch to the side, moving out of reach. "And we both came to the conclusion that this is an easy plan. In and out, remember? Undetected and unnoticed."

"I never said easy, Keira." Her brow furrows, the concern written all over her face. "Please tell me you're not jumping into this without being emotionally prepared. I need to know you're ready."

"I'm ready," I lie. "I've been ready for years."

I'm not ready. I never will be. But there's no way in hell I'll let fear keep me from giving Richard what he deserves.

"Okay." She reaches into the car, grabs the large bouquet of flowers lying in wait, and maneuvers them out the window to hand them to me. "I'll be waiting."

"Thanks." I grab the overbearing arrangement, holding it high in the crook of my elbow and take a steadying breath to keep the nerves at bay.

Taking the first step feels like the hardest part. I have to consciously think about putting one foot in front of the other. Heel, toe. Heel, toe. I keep my head strategically low, making the blooms and colored cellophane wrap shield my face from any hidden surveillance cameras. The long hair shrouding my cheeks helps, too.

It's my heart that causes the problems. The heavy beat

pulses in my throat as I stride through the sliding doors and straight into the nearest elevator.

The confined space suffocates me. I cling to the flowers like a lifeline, breathing nothing but the floral scent tattooing my nostrils.

I'll never be able to enjoy the smell again. Not without remembering this moment.

By the time I reach the ICU, I'm a sweating, shaking mess. The only thing saving me is a lifetime acting out a fake persona. I know how to exude confidence when I don't have it. I'm no stranger to playing a role.

I stroll down that hall, relaxed and laid back. My fear and overwhelming hysteria hidden. I blend, letting the bouquet shield me as I pass the nurses' station.

The closer I get to Richard's room, the more my chest aches with heavy beats. I've only been to see him once. The sight of him battered and lifeless could only keep me captive for a few minutes before I strode from this hall, and this hospital, for what I hoped would be forever.

I prayed I would never have to see him again. That divine intervention would fix this mess. Somehow. Some way.

I pinned my savior on the great unknown, and look how that turned out.

I know better now.

Nobody else can fix this.

It's me. All me.

"Excuse me, ma'am."

The voice calls from behind me, back toward the nurses' station.

I ignore it, hoping like hell the woman is speaking to someone else. I only have one more room to pass until I'm at my destination. Five more feet. A few pained breaths.

"Ma'am?"

My pulse becomes a deafening throb in my ears as rushed steps approach, freezing me in place. I don't know what to do. I can't fathom what to say. Have I been caught already? Did Sebastian make a call and warn staff about the crazy woman about to commit murder?

273

"I apologize for disturbing you." Her voice is closer now, almost right behind me, raising the hair on the back of my neck. "But flowers aren't allowed in the ICU."

All the air leaves my lungs in a barely audible heave. Relief washes through me, then just as fast as the relaxation arrived, it flees.

No flowers means no shield.

No shield means my face will be harder to hide.

Don't panic. I hear Sarah's voice in my mind. *Most people get caught making rash decisions.*

"I'm sorry. I didn't realize." I keep my gaze low and my back toward the nurse. "What should I do with them?"

"I can take them, if you like. We sometimes place them in other wards. I know it does little for your loved one, but it saves them from being wasted and helps to comfort other patients."

I nod and pivot toward her on the pads of my feet. I don't meet her gaze, I keep those flowers in line with my face as I hand them over. "Thank you."

I turn away and take the final steps to my uncle's room, my heart rampantly beating, while she wrestles with the bouquet.

"Are you here to see Mr. Torian?" she asks, killing me slowly.

I pause in the doorway, the darkness of the room within reach. "Yes."

There's a pause, another torturous, agonizing heartbeat.

"I'm sorry to bother you again, but we've been asked by family to take note of visitors. Only immediate relatives and pre-determined friends are allowed to visit."

The stipulation stinks of my brother. I should've known Cole would've transformed the hospital ward into a secure location.

I should've fucking known. But I didn't even think about his possible security measures.

My chest hollows.

Richard's room is here. *Right here.* And she's not going to let me step foot inside.

"Please," I whisper. "I haven't been able to see him since the accident. I promise I won't stay long."

"What's your name? You might already be on the list."

I close my eyes and send out a silent prayer. Yes, a fucking prayer...to God... to help me kill someone. The ridiculousness hits me like a violent slap across the face. "I'm not on the list. His family doesn't know about me."

My chest restricts. My limbs grow heavy. My heart thunders.

Every part of my body protests, *demanding* I flee. It takes all my strength to remain in place.

"Are you a friend? A work colleague?"

If I say I'm a colleague and she knows what my uncle does for a living, I'll never be allowed to step foot inside that room. And being a friend, who isn't close enough to make the list, seems like a long shot, too.

I need another strategy. Something to pull at her heart strings and worm my way into her trust.

I sniff and pull a handkerchief from my pocket as I delve into the haunted recesses of my mind. I retrieve memories that make my eyes burn. I pull forward images of my mother. I force myself to remember the funeral—the coffin, the flowers, the sobs from family and friends. I bathe myself in devastation and let the pain resurface, all in an effort to sell my story.

Then I glance over my shoulder and meet her gaze through drenched eyes. "I'm his mistress."

She stares at me with trepidation, her lips parting in shock. She shifts the flowers from one arm to the next, cradling them like a child in her silent contemplation.

She's older than I am. I guess in her mid-forties. Much closer to my uncle's age than I am, and I hope like hell she doesn't notice through my heavy make-up.

"Please." I blow my nose and force myself to relive the grief of years gone by. I cling tight to the horror, squeezing every inch of torment from those memories until a single tear treks down my cheek. "I only want a few minutes with him. Just in case..."

She winces, reaffirming that his situation is still dire.

"*Please.*"

She nods, retreating a step, then two. "Okay." She

275

continues walking backward toward the nurses' station. "But don't take too long."

Gratitude overwhelms me, suffocating me with its giddy tidal wave.

"Thank you." I dab at the moisture on my cheeks and pretend it takes all my strength to drag my feet forward to face a heartbreaking goodbye. I keep my focus straight ahead, away from the bed. Then I turn and close the door behind me, shoving the handkerchief in my pocket as the darkness of the room inches its way into my marrow.

I cling to the handle for long heartbeats and give myself a mental pep talk.

I'm *not* going to fail despite the attention I've drawn.

I'm *not* going to get caught even though I can feel the noose tightening around my neck, cutting off my air.

I'm *not*. I'm *not*. I'm *not*.

I switch my mindset, moving from relief to anger. To pain.

I relive Richard's lingering stare. His compliments. The unwanted touches. I remember that night and all the things he took from me. I shove every ounce of weakness deep down to the pit of my stomach and become my father's daughter.

The criminal.

A murderer.

I become emboldened. Strong. Un-fucking-beatable. Then I turn and face my demons.

Richard lies lifeless, innumerable tubes and IVs piercing his skin and delving under the covers of the clean, crisp bed. The right side of his face is bandaged, the white stark against the fading blue and purple bruising visible on his left.

His chest rises and falls. Slow and steady.

My feet move of their own accord, bringing me closer to Satan, until I'm stopped at the foot of the bed. I peer down at him and smile at how our positions have changed.

For a long time, he was the one with horror in his belly and violence in his soul, while I lay meek and vulnerable, unable to defend myself.

I gain the briefest insight into his sick perversion as I stand there. I acknowledge the rush of power. The tingle of adrenaline. I breathe in the approaching victory and square my shoulders against the unwanted niggle of building sins.

"Hello, Uncle." My lips kick as I curl every syllable around my tongue.

The more I stare, the more invigorated I become. My breathing quickens. My nerves tingle.

"It's been a long time since we last spoke." I lean over and swipe at the wrinkles in the bedding near his feet. "I've learned a lot about you since your accident."

I watch for the slightest flicker in his features. I'd give anything to know he can hear me. To have just one sign of acknowledgement.

But I get nothing. Not even a twitch.

I sigh and glance around the room, taking in the monitoring equipment, the cards on the bedside table, the Bible.

I roll my eyes.

Whoever thought religion could save this man had delusions beyond my comprehension. Nothing can save him. Not in this life or the next.

I walk around the bed and take a seat on the chair at his side.

Death coats my skin, tickling the back of my neck. I've never felt this way before. It's a strange mix of exhilaration and trepidation.

Good and evil.

Right and wrong.

I have two options. Only two. And both revolve around the syringes taped to my wrist beneath my jacket.

The potassium chloride overdose will mimic a heart attack and end his life. There will be no injuries to investigate or sign of foul play. The only thing left behind will be an elevated level of potassium in his bloodstream—the same elevation that would be present with a legitimate heart attack.

The first option is to inject into the IV line. The results will be fast, and I'll have mere seconds before the magic begins and the monitors alert nursing staff.

The alternative is to inject into the IV bag and walk away

without hearing any bells and whistles. I'd have time to escape the ward before his heart started to react.

I'd also be unsure whether I succeeded or failed. And that success is something I crave.

"I want it to be quick," I whisper. "Not because you don't deserve to suffer. It's because I want to be here when you die."

But the price of fulfilment could come at the cost of a prison sentence. And I'm not willing to let him affect my future like he has my past.

I stand and grab a pair of disposable gloves from the box on the wall. I quickly cover both hands, then unfasten the syringes from my wrists, placing one in my pocket for easy access.

My heart pounds in my throat. My tongue swells. My fingers tremble.

It's not fear.

No, that weakness is long gone.

What I feel is euphoria. A strange sense of ecstasy.

I grab the IV bag, twist the syringe onto the attachment, and hold my breath as I depress the plunger. I'm hyperaware of everything—sound, movement, thoughts—as the two liquids blend.

At any moment, the nurse could return.

I could walk from this room and be greeted by a security team.

Oh, God, what if this is a setup?

What if? What it? What if?

I gasp for air and shake away the paranoia, not willing to be taken down by my own mind as I shove the used syringe into my pocket and pull out the next.

I repeat my actions, this time pushing the plunger harder. Faster.

Once the last drop of lethal injection is administered, I stagger backward, fighting my building conscience as I shove all the evidence into my pockets.

"See you in hell, Richard." I don't recognize my own voice. It's foreign to my throbbing ears. "I hope you suffer for your sins."

I rush for the door, gripping the handle with a hand covered by my jacket sleeve. I wipe away my earlier prints in a frenzy of rabid movements and then escape the room.

There's no relief at the sight of the empty hall, only pure, delirious focus to measure my steps. I shake uncontrollably. My arms, legs, and hands quavering.

I want to run. To sprint.

My instincts beg me to flee. But I hold my pace, keeping my head low as I pull out my handkerchief and cover the lower half of my face while I pass the nurses station.

I'm almost hyperventilating when I reach the elevator. My breaths are short and shallow. Everything moves in slow motion.

Each heartbeat feels like an eternity waiting for the elevator doors to open. And when they do, my relief is so overwhelming I gasp out a breathy laugh.

It's too good to be true.

The rush of success floods my veins, the sensation ten times more exhilarating than adrenaline alone.

I escape into the confined space, no longer feeling suffocated, and smile at the graying man who enters behind me.

I'm no longer a victim.

Richard can't torment me anymore.

He can't hurt anyone else, either.

That part of my life is over, and all I want to do is rush into Sebastian's arms and start on something new.

I press the button for the ground floor, still smiling, still basking in success. Then something shatters the celebration. Something hard and unyielding that presses gently into the low of my back.

"It's a gun," the man murmurs. "Scream and you're dead."

26

DECKER

"Who, in their right mind, doesn't have a spare fucking tire?" I don't know how many times I've repeated the rhetorical question over the unending hours on the road. "It's fucking ridiculous."

Hunt had used the space where the tire should be and filled it with tactical shit—guns, ammo, knives. There was even equipment to make a fuel bomb.

"Who the hell has fertilizer on standby, yet no fucking spare tire?"

"You seriously need to shut the fuck up before I slam on the brakes and hope your thousand-year-old seatbelt fails."

The thousand-year-old seatbelt, and my brother's thousand-year-old Jeep, have seriously slowed the time it should've taken to get back to Portland. We found the beat-up pile of metal in his garage, the keys in the ignition, because even my brother is begging for someone to take this piece of crap off his hands. "Slamming on the brakes won't do shit when you're driving like a nanna."

"I've got my foot to the fucking floor," he grates. "It's the car that's lagging."

Frustration gave way to insanity three hundred miles ago, back when I gave up on trying to speak to Keira.

Sarah ignored all my attempts to get in contact. Every fucking one.

The only information we've had came half an hour ago.

One fucking phone call to cement my fears by telling us, "She's finishing this. I'll call again when it's over."

That's all she said. Two rushed sentences before Hunt snatched the phone away and took over the conversation.

"Head toward the parking lot." I scan the area surrounding the hospital. "They haven't been back in contact, so they've gotta still be here."

"They should be gone by now. It doesn't take this long."

He's right, but until we get confirmation, I'm going to assume they haven't finished the job. I'm also going to assume everything that could go wrong *did* go wrong. That panic isn't going to wear off until Keira is safe and sound in my arms.

They've rushed into this.

It's too soon.

"There." Hunt points toward the back of the half empty parking lot. "That's the car."

My stomach plummets as I turn my gaze in the direction of his finger. Sure enough, he's right. *Fuck.* What the hell could be taking so long?

"Sarah said she was waiting out here." Hunt's hands squeak as he white-knuckles the steering wheel. "Where the fuck is she?"

I lean forward as we pull into a parking space two cars away, glancing through the neighboring vehicle to find the Mercedes empty. "I've got a really shitty feeling about this."

"Well, that's a bonus." He cuts the engine and unclasps his belt. "And all that scientific research tried to tell me psychopaths don't have feelings."

"Funny." I scowl. "Are you really cracking jokes right now?"

"I can't help it." He attempts to mimic my voice, his face entirely deadpan. "I'm a funny guy."

"Fucking hilarious." I shove from the car, slamming the door behind me, before stalking to the Mercedes. I check the back seat as I pass. There's nothing in there. Not a scrap of paper or a piece of rubbish.

"Stop freaking out." Hunt comes up behind me, his gait casual. "They might have changed their plan and fled on foot."

I inch forward, checking out the front. It's clean, too. Nothing on the seats or along the dash. Nothing but the car keys dangling from the ignition.

"Jesus, Hunt." My stomach takes a nosedive. "I don't think their change of plan was deliberate."

He gets up close and peers over my shoulder.

He doesn't say a word. He doesn't have to. The sudden surge of panic ebbs off him.

I rush around the car, looking for a hint to tell me what the hell went down. "Something went wrong."

Something when terribly fucking wrong. But what?

Hunt pulls out his phone and starts dialing. Seconds later he's dialing again. Then again.

"Fuck." He massages his forehead. "Why the hell won't she answer her fucking phone?"

"Maybe because they've been caught." I pinch the bridge of my nose and ignore the bite of pain that comes from my growing headache. "Your woman pushed Keira into something she wasn't ready for, and now she's going to spend the rest of her life in prison."

"Sarah isn't stupid."

"Really?" I drop my hand to my side. "Her engagement to you says otherwise."

His eyes harden.

"You two never should've gotten involved." I focus on the sliding doors of the hospital. I will the glass panels to open and for Keira to walk out. I beg for her to appear before me. I fucking pray. "I'm going in there."

"Not yet, you won't." Hunt rests against the Mercedes. "You'll only draw attention. We need to wait a little longer."

"That's easy for you to say when Sarah's not the one committing murder."

"We're waiting," he repeats. "Suck it up and deal."

Oh, I suck it up, all right. I bottle that shit like it's gold, letting the panic and hysteria build into an uncontrollable force. Each second that ticks by feels like an hour as I pace behind the car. Any minute now, I'm certain I'll hear a police siren. Or a gunshot. Or Keira screaming for help.

The phantom sounds ring in my ears.

I scrutinize every person who approaches and leaves the hospital. I commit their clothing to memory in case I need the information later. At this point, everyone is the enemy. They all stand between me and the woman I need to protect.

"Is that..." Hunt pushes from the car, his gaze tracking the Porsche pulling into the other side of the parking lot.

"Oh, shit."

It's Torian.

I start walking, my pace increasing with every step as two men climb from the sports car. The fear and panic I had moments before is nothing in comparison to the sheer terror I feel now. "If he finds her..."

Christ, I have no idea what he'll do.

"Torian." I break into a jog. *"Hey, Torian."*

Hunter curses behind me, his footsteps following. "What the fuck are you doing?"

"He can't find out she's here." I keep running, keep bridging the distance, not giving a shit about the consequences. *"Torian."*

I catch his attention a few yards from the sliding doors. He stops and turns my way, not showing a hint of surprise at my appearance. What stares back at me is his usual mask of calm indifference.

I slow my pace and relax into a casual stride, inclining my head in greeting. "Hey, Mr. Boss Man." I switch my attention to the dark scowl of the tank at his side. "Luca. I haven't seen you in a while, buddy."

Luca Hart—Layla's brother-in-law. He's reckless and equally callous. He's also an ex-SEAL, and definitely not my buddy. The muscled-up fighting machine is the only guy I've met who's left the armed forces without a shred of national pride intact.

The guy hates everyone.

Especially me.

"What are you doing here?" Torian asks.

I point to my face, then lift my shirt to show my bruises as Hunter stops beside me. "I needed to get the rig checked. I think I've got a few fractured ribs."

"And you?" He turns his scrutiny to my accomplice.

"Decker needed me to hold his hand."

Torian raises a brow and nods. Slowly. There's no rush for answers, hint of panic, or twitch of hatred. Even after his conversation with Keira this afternoon, he's civil, and it's scary as fuck. "Where's my sister?"

"Don't worry, she's with Sarah."

It's the only answer that came to mind. But it's the wrong one. I don't realize my mistake until Hunter clears his throat in a subtle reprimand.

If Cole finds out what Keira is up to, Sarah will be accountable.

"Have you forgotten the instructions I gave you at the restaurant? You're responsible for her safety?" Torian smiles, wearing the expression like a threat.

"She's safe." Hunt claps me on the back. Hard. "Sarah has the situation under control."

"So he knocks her up and leaves her to fend for herself?" Luca crosses his arms over his chest and backs away an inch, scoping our surroundings like we're being watched. "He's not what I'd call father material."

I press my lips tight, half smirking, half scowling at the fucker who's throwing me under the bus. "Cool your horses about the daddy stuff. Although it's clear I'm an over-achiever, even I don't believe my swimmers are that efficient."

Luca snickers. "You're dead. You know that, right?"

"Seriously, don't go laying the blame on me." I raise my hands in surrender. "That woman is a fucking force of nature. I'd have to be blind, deaf, and dumb to turn down her advances."

"You amaze me." Torian speaks slowly. Softly. "I can't believe you'd be careless enough to use your distasteful sense of humor to disrespect my sister. You really do have a death wish, don't you?"

Beneath the calm façade, he's pissed.

If the tick under his eye is any indication, he's fucking furious.

"Look, Torian, I'm just trying to cut through the awkwardness here." I let my arms fall to my sides. "In all honesty, I care for Keira. I'd do anything for her."

He looks me up and down, his smile strong. "We'll see."

Hunter remains ramrod, his statue status letting me know he's tense as fuck. It's also a great indicator that my conversation skills are lacking.

"What are you doing here at this hour, anyway?" Hunt asks, diverting the conversation without subtlety. "Isn't it late to be making a visit?"

"Keeping a close eye on Richard. You two should come with us." He starts for the doors. "I'm sure he'd appreciate the extra company."

"Maybe some other time." Hunter steps back. "We need to get the girls."

"I'm not asking."

Shit. We don't have time for this.

I shoot a frantic glance at Hunt, and a whole heap of what-the-fuck-do-we-do silently passes between us. Keira could be running for her life while we stand here chatting. She could already be in custody.

"Hurry up." Luca jerks his chin. "Get moving."

The trill of a cell has Torian pausing inside the entrance, the sound increasing as he pulls the device from his jacket pocket and connects the call. "Yes?"

I face Hunter, my eyes wide in silent communication. *"What do we do?"* I mouth.

His shoulder hitches in the slightest shrug. *"What the fuck can we do?"*

I rub a hand over my jaw, hoping to inspire a spark of brilliance that doesn't come.

Hunt creeps closer. "He doesn't know anything at the moment. If we don't follow, he'll get suspicious."

"No." I shake my head. "He knows something—"

"He knows you're banging his sister. That's all."

There's more to it. There has to be.

285

"Thanks for the update." Torian's murmured words reclaim my attention. "I've already arrived. I'll see you in a minute."

He's meeting someone.

Is it Keira? Sarah?

I pivot back toward him, gaining no clues from his blank expression. "Is everything okay?"

"That's a good question." He places the cell in his suit jacket and heads toward the elevators.

My pulse pounds harder the further he walks. I'm not naive enough to think we've been dismissed. He expects us to tag along, like fucking puppies, or he'll blow a damn fuse.

Hunt obviously knows it, too, because he starts to follow. "We're leaving the first chance we get."

"Yeah," I mutter through clenched teeth. "First chance."

The elevator doors open on our approach, and all four of us enter. It isn't until the steel doors close that the confined space begins to resemble a tomb.

"That was the hospital on the phone." Torian presses the button for the ICU and levels his eyes on me. "Richard passed."

The news flash hits like a heavyweight champion, the impact bringing more fear, but also pride. Keira didn't fail. She accomplished what she set out to do, despite the stupidity.

So where the hell is she?

"What the fuck happened?" Luca asks.

"They suspect a heart attack." Torian's eyes don't lose their intensity as he waits for me to break. "But I'm sure I'll find out more information soon."

"Shit." I wince. "I'm sorry for your loss."

"Same here." Hunt shoves his hands in his pockets, all casual in his feigned surprise. "Do you want us to head out of here and start contacting the family?"

"Yeah, good idea." I nod. "We can get the process started."

"There's actually something more important you can do here." Torian turns to the elevator panel and presses the STOP button, the moving tomb jolting to a halt. "You can both cut the bullshit and tell me who killed Richard."

286

There's no emotion in his statement. No malice or anger. No heartbreak or grief. His voice doesn't even raise an octave, his words held inside this tiny space for no one else to hear.

"You said they suspected a heart attack." Hunter scrutinizes him. The act flawless. Believable. "Why do you think it's murder?"

"Because I received a call from hospital staff less than half an hour ago telling me Richard's mistress was paying him a visit."

A mistress? That was Keira's cover, a fucking mistress?

Jesus Christ, sweetheart. Why the hell did you do this without me?

"I have no clue who she is." I shrug. "I didn't know he had a mistress."

"Don't play dumb." Torian's eyes narrow. "The fact that you're here means you're involved. And I'll find out why later. For now, I just want to know who followed through with your manipulation."

"We didn't manipulate a fucking thing," Hunter growls. "Watch who you're accusing, because that shit can't be taken back."

There's no reply. No reaction. Apart from the few inches Torian grows as he contemplates his options.

Hunt has been his right-hand man for years. His enforcer.

Burning that bridge with unfounded allegations is a huge deal.

But it's also a huge fucking gamble pretending they're unfounded.

"Why don't we take a breather?" I raise my brows and look each man in the eye with a calm I don't feel. "It's been an eventful week. Let's not make it a stupid one."

"Says the man who slept with Keira," Luca mutters.

Hunter clears his throat, the sound vaguely close to a chuckle.

"I'm sorry, man." I meet the Navy asshole's gaze with fake sincerity. "Did I fuck your mother in a past life? Or are you threatened by me for another reason?"

"You're no threat," he sneers. "You're a fucking

287

embarrassment. You never should've been entrusted with Keira's safety."

The throat clearing happens again. This time there's no linger of laughter. It's a warning to stand down.

A fucking warning to me.

I clench my jaw and bare my teeth through the jealousy. He's jonesing for Keira. And apparently, I'm supposed to let that fly. "Thanks for the constructive criticism. I'll take it on board."

"Enough." Torian glares at me, the ferocity finally deserving of a gold star. "We'll discuss this later." He slams his fist against the STOP button, making the carriage jolt back into movement. "Until then, neither one of you steps foot out of my sight."

Great.

Fucking perfect.

We ascend surrounded in tension, all four of us a breath away from reaching for a weapon. The atmosphere doesn't change when the doors open. One by one, we pile out, Torian in the lead, Luca in the back, as we walk toward the start of the silent ICU.

The lights are dim, the late hours marked with desolate halls and gentle footfalls.

A lone woman stands from behind the nurses' station as we approach and hustles to greet us in the middle of the corridor.

"Mr. Torian?" She gives a sad smile. "My name is Carly. I spoke to you earlier."

All four of us come to stand shoulder to shoulder, forming a makeshift wall before her.

"Thanks for your call." He reaches out a hand for her to shake. "I appreciate you keeping me informed."

"There's no need to thank me. I just wish I hadn't had to make contact under these circumstances."

Torian inclines his head and releases her hand. "It can't be helped. My uncle has been fighting for a long time."

"Yes." Her brows pinch, and for a heartbeat she pauses. There's no mistaking her apprehension. "That's something I need to discuss with you." She glances along the barrier of muscle surrounding her and swallows. "Maybe in private."

"Privacy isn't necessary." He indicates the three of us with a wave of his hand. "These men know better than to betray my trust."

I cringe through yet another warning.

He's nothing if not repetitive.

"My concern is the woman who was with your uncle prior to his death." The nurse wrings her hands in front of her. "Like I mentioned on the phone, she wasn't on your approved visitor list, and the timing of his passing is oddly coincidental. Normally, the death of a man in Richard's position wouldn't require a coroner's investigation, but I think it's best—"

"No." Torian shakes his head. "She had every right to see him."

"But the timing... And she admitted she wasn't known to your family. Aren't you—"

"Her presence wasn't a surprise." He gives a sad smile. "She may have thought she wasn't known, but I endeavor to make sure there are no secrets or surprises when it comes to those I care about."

It's another warning.

Another threat.

"Not even the nursing staff have escaped my scrutiny," he continues. "I know about all the employees on this ward, Carly. I'm aware of their shifts, their address, down to the details of who they live with."

She stiffens.

It's a smart move. She should definitely be on edge.

"From memory, you've got a young daughter in prep-school, isn't that right?"

"Yes. That's right." She frowns. "But, Mr. Torian, what I'm trying to articulate is that I wouldn't be doing my job properly if I didn't push for an autopsy. I think it's necessary."

"No." Torian slams down her request. "My uncle is finally at rest. I refuse to allow his peace to be disturbed."

"I understand, but—"

"He said, 'no,'" Hunter grates. "Take the hint or the consequences."

Her mouth gapes, her fear-filled gaze snapping to Hunt.

"Carly," Torian diffuses the situation by reaching for her hand, "I'd appreciate if you worked with me to ensure the wishes of my family are met. We don't need to waste hospital resources here. My uncle fought for weeks, but now he's gone." There's another placating smile. "Now I need you to do whatever necessary to ensure there's no delay in laying him to rest."

She inches back, moving out of reach. "I don't think..."

"I'm no longer asking." He doesn't change his tone. That placating smile remains in place. "There won't be an autopsy. Or any further investigation. Do you understand?"

She glances over her shoulder, searching for help that's nowhere in sight.

I almost feel sorry for her. If only Keira's innocence didn't hang in the balance.

"Your continued care for Richard will be compensated," I offer, ready and willing to pay out of my own pocket. "This situation doesn't need to get complicated."

"Yes," Hunter adds. "Take the money and keep your daughter safe."

She exhales a shuddering breath, the depth of his threat delving deep.

"Are we clear, Carly?" Torian asks.

She nods, slow at first, then more definitive. "I understand."

"Good." He turns and stalks for the elevators.

There's no farewell to the deceased uncle. No grief or emotional turmoil.

Luca and Hunt follow, while I hang back with the woman frozen in place.

"You don't want to fuck with him." I grab her arm and give a supportive squeeze. "Do what he asks, and you and your daughter will be fine."

She jerks back, her lips trembling, her eyes full of tears. "Get your hand off me."

I comply, letting my arm fall. "Just stick to the script."

I leave her to battle her demons and follow the guys down the hall then into the open elevator.

We don't talk as the doors close. The tension does enough of that for us.

But once we're trapped inside, Luca points a menacing finger in Hunter's face. "You should've kept your mouth shut. You scared her."

"That's the fucking point. And also my job, asshole."

"Not for much longer."

Hunter shoots a glance to Torian for confirmation. "Are you kidding me? You want this guy at your side over me?"

"You haven't been at my side," Torian scolds. "You've been missing for two days."

"For good reason. I don't need to give you a play-by-play of my movements. But you should know I'm doing my job regardless."

The elevator doors open at the lobby, and Torian walks out without reacting, continuing outside to the path leading toward the parking lot.

"Don't fucking walk away from me." Hunter stalks after him. "I put my life on the line for you every goddamn day."

I jog to keep up and fall into step at his side. "Let him go. We've gotta get out of here."

"What's the hurry?" Luca asks from behind us. "Have you got someplace more important to be?"

"Yeah," I mutter. "You're mom's house. She's waiting for her daily dose of D."

"Keep talking, deadshit, it's gonna get you killed."

I grind my teeth through the distance to Torian, who waits at the start of the parking lot.

"I've got places to be." I bypass him and head toward the Jeep. "I'll check in later."

"I told you before, you're not leaving my sight."

I swing around, walking backward away from him. "You also told me to protect Keira. And I can't do that while I'm here holding your hand."

"Protect her from what?" He gives me a checkmate stare. "You said she was safe with Sarah."

My steps falter. "She is. But I'm not going to leave her for longer than necessary."

"Do you even know where she is? Could you take me to her?"

I can't answer. Not with the truth that will expose her secrets, or lies that will easily be uncovered.

"Was it Keira or Sarah?" He doesn't elaborate. He doesn't need to. I already understand the question.

"I don't know what you're talking about."

He smiles, the curve of lips more threatening than a scowl could ever be. "This is your last chance. Keira or Sarah?"

I keep my mouth shut, determined not to be disloyal to her.

"It was Keira," Hunt mutters. "She took him down."

My brain explodes.

He betrayed her.

He betrayed me.

What the fuck?

Torian's mouth pulls tight. His nostrils flare. I watch every flicker in his expression as he begins to realize his sister is a murderer. "You convinced her to take action against her own family." He continues to stare at me. "Why?"

Hunter's cell tone breaks the conversation, and he jams his hand into his pocket like a madman.

"Leave it," Torian demands. "I don't want any interruptions."

"I need to answer this."

"How much do you need it?" Torian faces him. "Do you need it more than your next breath?"

Hunt bares his teeth, his shoulders tense as he pulls his hand from his pocket and lets it rest at his side.

Luca hangs on the periphery, slowly inching his way toward me, his arm behind his back and in close contact to his weapon.

"Start from the beginning." Torian approaches, cocking his head to the side, attempting to read me as the *trill, trill, trill*

292

continues and finally dies. "Tell me exactly what you thought to achieve by brainwashing her."

"That's not how this went down." Hunter follows, all three of them approaching me like a death squad. "She did this on her own."

"I disagree. She's not the violent type."

I smother a laugh. The knife she had at my throat proves otherwise, but I'm not going to argue.

"You're after power," he accuses. "And you probably think me and Layla are the only ones left to deal with."

"You'll have to get through me first," Luca snarls at me. "And my brother, too."

"You're fucking paranoid." I drop the insult like a bomb. "Why the hell would I want to take over? I can't handle the level of psycho you've already forced onto me. Why the fuck would I want more?"

"My restaurant was targeted, my sister was discovered while in hiding. Now this." He throws an arm wide, indicating the hospital. "It's no coincidence you've been there every step of the way."

"*Your sister* has been there every step of the way." Hunter increases his pace and steps in front of him, blocking his path as the ringtone reignites. "I don't know the story like Deck does, but she's the common-fucking-denominator here. Not him. Or me."

I glare at the back of Hunter's head. I glare so fucking hard through the anger.

I know he's outing her because she's the least likely to be punished. But it still feels like he's being a bigger snitch than I've ever been.

"What story?" Torian shoves by him. "Tell me."

I keep my trap closed. I don't even open it when Luca settles behind me and the butt of his gun sails toward the back of my head.

My vision blackens with the blunt impact. My knees give out.

I stumble to the asphalt, falling at Torian's feet while

293

ringing resounds in my ears. This time it isn't the cell phone, the trill noise having disappeared again.

He peers down at me and grips a fistful of my hair. "What has she done?"

I chuckle. "I don't know what you're talking about."

Hunt curses. It's the prelude to Torian's fist finding my jaw.

My head swings with the impact. The pain clouds my thoughts. Then the fucking phone releases its siren call again.

"He needs to answer that." I spit blood from my mouth. "It's probably Keira. You can get all the answers you need right from the source."

He has to answer the fucking phone.

I need to know she's okay.

The constant appeal for connection makes my stomach twist. You don't call three times in a row to inform someone you're safe. You call three times when your life is on the line and you need a shitload of help.

"I don't want the story from her," he drawls, releasing my hair. "I want it from you."

"*Answer the fucking phone,*" I roar.

The ringtone vanishes, and I slump into the silence.

"Eventually, I'll call her," he taunts. "But I want to hear your version first. That way I can see which puzzle pieces match."

I chuckle and hang my head, no longer capable of looking the son of a bitch in the eye. "Why? Do you think she's going to lie to you? Don't you trust your own flesh and blood?"

"If she can lie about being pregnant, I'm sure she can lie about anything."

Jesus Christ. If he's known this entire time, why didn't he greet me with the accusation? Why wasn't a gun placed to my temple the second we stepped within reach?

This asshole's poise and tactics are beyond my fucking comprehension.

"Come on, Decker, don't you recall what I told the nurse? I take a vested interest in knowing everything, which includes my sister's health. I know she's taken measures to ensure she can't conceive." He steps closer, the toes of his polished black shoes taking up my vision. "I'll ask one more time—what's the story Hunter is alluding to?"

I promised I'd protect her.

If that means I need to keep her safe from her brother, then so be it.

At the moment, he thinks she finished a job someone else started. He doesn't know her involvement in the hit and run. He has no clue what caused the restaurant drive-by.

For now, her secrets are safe, and I won't change that.

"Why don't I tell you my story instead?" I raise my chin and meet his gaze. "I think you'd be more interested in my secrets."

"Decker," Hunter warns, "stop messing around."

Torian glances between us as the cell trills again.

"Fucking hell, Decker." Hunter raises his voice over the sound. "Keira's responsible for the hit and run. She paid a guy to do the job. He's the same guy who shot up the restaurant. And he's the same reason lover boy here is panicked about her safety. She's being blackmailed."

Torian scrutinizes me, trying to find the truth through the shock. "Is that true?"

"Call. Her." I enunciate the words slowly.

This time Hunt's phone isn't the one to break the silence. Torian's ringtone rings gently from inside his jacket.

"Answer it." I move to stand, only to be shoved back down by Luca. *Answer your fucking phone.*

He doesn't budge. He holds my stare, asserting his authority despite the danger to his sister.

"She's in trouble," I beg. "I know she's in fucking trouble. Just answer the phone. I'll tell you everything after you speak to her."

He reaches into his suit jacket and pulls out the device, glimpsing the screen for a second before he connects the call. "Sarah?"

Sarah?

I focus on Hunt, his concern just as visible as mine is overbearing.

"Who is this?" Torian's voice turns stony. "What do you want?"

I push to my feet and swing out a heavy elbow when Luca tries to stop me. "Either shoot me, or stop riding my fucking ass," I snarl. "I don't have the patience for your shit."

"What do you want?" Torian repeats. "Touch her again and I'll—"

Again.

My heart lurches at the word.

Touch her—*again.*

Someone has hurt her. *Is* hurting her.

"Where is she?" I reach for the phone only to have Hunt grab my wrist.

"Back off," he warns. "Let him talk."

Torian turns his back to us and takes steps in the opposite direction. "Where, Drake? Tell me where she is."

Drake? There's no second guessing who this unknown asshole might be. He's the guy responsible for the blackmail. The hard look in Hunt's eye says he thinks the same thing.

"Give me the phone." I stalk after Torian. "Let me speak to him."

"Airport Way? Which warehouse?"

"Torian, give me the phone." I make another attempt for the cell, and this time nobody stops me. Not even Torian. I snatch the device from him and plaster it to my ear. "Drake? *Keira?*"

The line is dead.

"I need to go," Torian says to Luca. "Take them back to the restaurant. Keep them there until I arrive." Then he runs toward his Porsche.

He *runs.*

This is the same man who barely breaks out in a brisk walk when he's under fire. And now he's winning a two-hundred-yard dash.

I start after him, only to have a heavy weight barrel into my chest.

Luca knocks me back with a splayed arm, then aims his

gun at me from the subtle position at his hip. "You heard him. You're coming with me."

"Like hell I am. I'm going after Keira."

There's a slam of a car door, the roar of an engine, then the heavy squeal of tires as Torian reverses from the parking space.

"Let me go." I get in his face, the seconds ticking by like hours.

"It's too late." Hunt grabs my arm and yanks me backward. "He's already gone. We need to take the Jeep."

"You're not going anywhere but the restaurant." Luca plants his feet. "Where's your car?"

"Didn't you hear the phone conversation?" Hunt snaps. "Torian's walking into a hostage negotiation on his own."

"You're not kidding me with this macho bullshit." He jerks the gun again. "You've got no intention of helping him, and every intention to run."

"Whoever has Keira has my woman, too. I ain't running from shit. I never do. You're the one who's being a traitor by letting Torian drive out of here, on his own, unprotected, and without a fucking plan."

Luca's expression flickers, the tight pinch of his features growing more adamant. "I can't let you go. He doesn't want you out of my sight, so that's where you'll stay."

"Then come with us," I snap.

He scowls. "You expect me to help you?"

"I expect you to do what's right for the fucking family."

He squares his chin, the waver in his expression now resembling indecision as he faces Hunt and flicks his gun in my direction. "I don't like him, let alone trust him."

Hunt shrugs. "Nobody does. It doesn't mean you pussy out of this."

"Are you kidding me?" I seethe. "We're stuck here because GI Joe has trust issues?"

He bares his teeth at me, but his weapon lowers an inch. Then another.

I don't hang around for him to holster the weapon like a Girl Scout. I run, not pausing to take a breath as I sprint toward the Jeep.

27

KEIRA

Rope burns sear my wrists. The corners of my mouth ache from the material gag. But that pain is nothing in comparison to the heavy throb in my stomach from where I was punched.

I'd willingly followed that man through the hospital. I'd had no other choice. Either I walked with him or I screamed for help, which would either end with a bullet in my skull or a police investigation that would retrace my steps to a murdered uncle.

He told me he had Sarah. That he'd seen us both in the parking lot and would be rewarded beyond measure when he took me back to Drake.

I didn't need to ask for clarity.

I was smart enough to figure out Drake was my hitman.

As soon as we were alone in a desolate hospital hall, I spoke in a rush, offering my captor bribes in exchange for my freedom. I promised large sums of money. Anonymity. Immunity. When those didn't work, I vowed retribution and scathing retaliation as he dragged me out a staff exit and led me through a soulless parking lot.

I pledged to give him a death full of so much pain and suffering that my threats must have started to sink in.

That's when he threw the punch.

He yanked me to face him and landed a blow to my stomach strong enough to cause bile to rush into my mouth.

My life went downhill from there.

He hauled me to a waiting car, the man in the backseat cradling Sarah's limp body, her face bruised, her cheek scratched. She'd put up a fight. She battled for her freedom.

All I'd done was crumple under one hit.

The realization threw me into fight mode. I kicked. I thrashed. I screamed my fucking lungs out. And then I woke here, in an empty warehouse, my arms bound to a chair as five unfamiliar faces stare down at me plus my gray-haired captor.

"Your brother will be here soon." A smirking man saunters closer to lower my gag. He's young. Around his mid-thirties. His blond hair spiked. His eyes light.

He's almost handsome. Almost beautiful.

If only I didn't recognize his voice.

"Drake." I force the name through my swollen throat. "Why are you doing this? I was going to get you the money. I still can."

The smirk increases. "Don't worry your pretty little head about it. It's all under control." He crouches before me and places a large hand high on my thigh. "And I actually prefer the theatrics. I've dreamed about this moment for weeks."

I clamp my teeth together as his palm slides back and forth. "If you don't remove your hand, my brother will make sure you have nightmares about this moment for years."

He chuckles, his fingers digging through my jeans and into skin. "You've got a sassy mouth. Be careful or I'll fill it with something you might not like."

A shudder ricochets through me, hitting every nerve. It's not a threat. This man is making a promise. But it's more than that, too.

He's dripping with confidence. Entirely fearless.

He plans to get something more than mere money from this exchange.

"You're not so tough after all, are you?" He pushes to his feet. "Don't worry, this will be over before you know it."

He returns to his posse a few feet away, and I frantically rush to scan my surroundings.

The warehouse is bigger than a small house, the large expanse entirely empty. Fluorescent bulbs dangle from the roof, six of them, to match the six windows along the left wall, the glass missing in places and stained with dirt, cobwebs, and grime in others. But no illumination shines from outside. There are no traffic lights or street lamps. Just darkness and the eerie feel of desolation.

We're not close to the city.

We're away from witnesses.

Far from help.

And it's cold in here, too. Hollow. Or maybe that's just me.

I glance over my left shoulder and find the same expanse of emptiness. All except for the pair of feminine feet right behind me. I suck in a breath and swing my head to look over the other shoulder.

Sarah lies limp on the cement floor, her body curled in a loose fetal position, her arms and legs snuggled in front of her. She doesn't move. I can barely make out the rise and fall of her chest. But it's there, the slightest increments letting me know she's still alive.

I remain still, trying not to show my attachment to this woman, while my insides wage war.

She shouldn't be here. This has nothing to do with her.

It's all me. All my fault.

The beep of a cell echoes through the open space, the touch of external life giving me the slightest hope. I drag my attention back to Drake, who now holds a cell in his hand.

"Ben said he's here. And alone." He jerks his head toward the door twenty yards away. "Liam, go out and help bring him in."

Him—my brother.

But he wouldn't have come on his own, would he?

"Kyle, you stay with the girls. The rest of you, follow me." Drake leads them across the warehouse.

"*Wait.*" The plea escapes my lips without thought. I don't know what to do, what to say. The only thing I can think of is distracting them while I buy Cole time to think through the poor decision to arrive alone. "Let me go, and I'll get you the money. I'll double what I owe."

"It's time for you to be quiet. Bottle that fear deep down inside and let it out once Torian gets in here." He winks at me. "Your tears will make this perfect."

"No, please. You need to listen."

He walks away.

"Drake, I'll get you the money."

He doesn't stop. He's not interested in me.

He only wants my brother.

My pulse kicks up a notch as Drake reaches his team at the door, a lone man slipping outside.

"Please," I murmur to the guard standing a few feet away. "It's Kyle, isn't it?"

He crosses his arms over his chest and pretends he didn't hear me.

"You need to untie my hands. Once Cole gets here, he's going to place a price on the head of everyone here. You could be the savior. Wouldn't you prefer to work for us instead?"

"Shut your mouth."

"I'm serious." I wiggle, trying to loosen my arms from the rope. "You're going to get hurt. Or worse."

I've never seen the inner workings of a hostage negotiation with my brother. I haven't heard him speak about one before, but I anticipate this interaction won't be civil. He's going to be furious—at these men *and* me.

"I said *shut up*."

"You're making a mistake..."

Kyle starts toward me, his menacing steps a fair indication he isn't interested in my caution. The hard slap across the face clinches my assumption.

My head swings with the blow, my cheek blazing.

I blink back tears, determined not to let this asshole see me cry, even though dams build in my eyes. The show of emotion isn't from weakness. It's from pain. From fury. Rage spreads through my veins like wildfire.

I snicker out a maniacal laugh. "You'll regret that."

301

His arm lashes out, aiming for my neck. I tense, every muscle rigid as I wait for another blow.

Instead, he chuckles and grabs the gag to yank it back in place. "Keep quiet or I'll glue your lips shut."

I yank at my bindings. I squirm. I throw a hissy fit, my actions hopefully disguising my attempt to jolt my chair closer and closer toward Sarah.

He doesn't notice the inches I gain as he moves back to stand with his arms crossed over his chest, his sight fixated on the men at the door. He doesn't even notice I spend the next few minutes staring down at my friend lying directly at my side.

She's so pale. Entirely fragile.

Hunter is going to kill me... That's if she gets out of here safely. If not, I'm sure he'll think of a punishment much worse than death. And I'll deserve that, too.

I'd begged her to bring me back to Portland and added a dash of emotional blackmail. Then I'd increased my argument with a feminist protest.

She hadn't been able to ignore my pleas to let me slay my own demons. Despite her obvious reluctance, she concocted the plan to steal Hunter's car and beat the men back to Richard.

Now she lies lifeless at my feet, the bruising on her face swelling as it darkens.

I wordlessly beg her to wake up. To blink. To show a sign that she's still okay.

I wiggle a little more, nudging my chair leg against her knee as a deafening pop echoes through our metal cage. The gunshot makes the world stop. I don't move, don't breathe. But the shock isn't enough for me to miss the jolt of Sarah's hands.

She heard it.

She's awake beneath those closed eyes.

As men shout orders, arm themselves, and fill the warehouse with panic, I continue to watch her, waiting for another sign that doesn't come.

"Sarah," I mumble into the gag. "Please, Sarah."

She doesn't blink or flinch. There's no sign of life for long seconds. Then her pinkie finger taps against the concrete, twice, in quick succession.

That's it. That's all the acknowledgement she gives me, and it's all I need.

I suck in a deep breath and sit up straight, trying not to let fear take over. I try so damn hard to picture my brother making the shot instead of taking it. Then the sound rings out again and again, the night being blasted with gunfire.

Kyle pulls out his gun and rushes to crouch behind my chair, while the men in the distance form a wall a few feet back from the door, acting as warriors to protect Drake, who remains behind them.

"I'm coming in," Cole yells from outside.

Sweet exhilaration fills my belly, growing and expanding. It takes all my restraint not to scream out in relief when the door swings wide and he storms inside, an unfamiliar man held hostage at his chest.

"The dead guy in the parking lot is the price you pay for messing with my family," he seethes. "How many more do you want to lose?"

He's okay. He's safe.

Not even a wrinkle or stain mars his tailored suit.

But he's still alone. There's no sign of Sebastian. No Hunter.

The men retreat as he approaches, their weapons at the ready, while the barrel of a gun slides across my temple from the coward at my back.

"Don't move," Kyle whispers in my ear. "You know I'll shoot."

I do as he says, not daring to move a muscle.

"She owes me money." Drake walks backward, leading the way toward me.

"*Then you come to me.*" Cole's voice roars through the empty space. "You never approach her. You never lay a hand *on my fucking family.*"

My eyes burn as I watch.

He isn't fearful. Not even when outnumbered six to one.

There's a wealth of determination ebbing from him. An undeniable lack of doubt.

But there's no doubt in Drake either. He turns his back to Cole and strides toward me with an open grin. "Your sister was a means to an end, my friend."

"I'm not your friend." Cole drags his hostage closer, the three goons following with him. "I will, however, be your executioner."

Drake laughs, the sound a strategic taunt as he swings around and pulls a gun from the back of his pants. I don't have a chance to scream. I barely feel myself blink as he fires, shooting Cole's prisoner in the stomach.

There's blood, so much blood, as the man wails and slumps to the ground.

What's worse is the look on my brother's face.

The confidence and sheer determination he had moments before is gone. I glimpse his shock, then the terror, before he hides the weakness under a mask of indifference.

Oh, God.

We're not going to make it out of here. We're all going to die. Just like the man on the floor who's coughing the life from his lungs.

"Don't look, Keira," Cole demands. "Close your fucking eyes."

No. I can't.

I've done this.

I started the chain reaction that will lead to our deaths.

"What are you going to do now, Torian?" Drake keeps his weapon raised, the barrel now pointing in Cole's direction. "You've got no hostage, and I've got a man with a gun to your sister's head."

Cole raises a brow. "Am I supposed to be impressed?"

"No, you're supposed to be scared. And you're also supposed to drop your weapon."

Cole complies, the gun falling to his feet. "You're going to have to try harder because all you're doing is digging yourself into a hole you won't get out of. No amount of owed money justifies your actions. You're all going to die for this."

"This stopped being about money a long time ago."

"You plan on taking over with these four, plus the guy hiding behind my sister?" Cole smirks and indicates the human wall protecting Drake with a wave of his hand. "My men are loyal. Whether I'm dead or alive, they won't stop until you're gunned down."

"Loyal? For starters, you came here alone. That doesn't scream loyalty to me." Drake moves to my side, and Kyle takes the hint to step away. "Not even your own flesh and blood is devoted to your family. Didn't Keira tell you about our agreement?"

Cole doesn't respond. He stands tall, unaffected by the taunts.

"I still don't have your attention?" Drake muses. "You're right, I'll have to try harder."

His fingers tangle in my hair, gentle at first, then he yanks at the strands, forcing my head back and a shriek from my throat. "Once you're dead, I'm going to hurt her. We're *all* going to hurt her."

My neck screams in protest, the pain taking over my shoulders. It's nothing in comparison to my regret.

"And everything you do to Keira will be reciprocated tenfold. If not by me, then by my father."

"I'll deal with that if it happens." Drake releases my hair and jerks his chin at one of his thugs. "Kill him."

My heart stops. I can't breathe.

I stare at Cole, wide-eyed and frantic, as I wordlessly beg for him to tell me what to do.

"Close your eyes, Kee."

No. I shake my head over and over as my heart kicks back into action, beating so wildly it pounds in my throat.

"*Please*," I plead into the gag. "*Please. Please. Please.*"

"Close your eyes." His words are gentle. Peaceful. "Don't remember me like this."

The man stops a foot away and aims for my brother's head.

This can't be happening. It can't.

How could one stupid decision cause me to be responsible for his death?

"Keira, *don't look*." This time it's a demand. An order. "Shut your eyes."

I keep shaking my head. *No. No. No.* But I listen.

For one last time, I promise to obey.

Tears blaze down my cheeks as I sob into the gag, my eyes squeezed shut, my chin tucked into my chest.

Then the gunshot sounds, and I scream and scream and scream.

28

DECKER

"Nice shot."

I ignore Hunt's compliment as I continue to stare at Keira through the broken window at the far end of the warehouse.

My heart hasn't stopped racing since Luca parked the Jeep at the far end of the road. I'd jumped out of the car before the engine stopped and ran from warehouse to warehouse searching for the Porsche.

I'd been the first to see the dead guy in the parking lot. The first to reach the side of the building and determine I had seconds to save Cole's life.

I hadn't thought, hadn't planned, hadn't strategized.

I aimed the barrel of my gun through the broken window, pulled the trigger, and watched Keira as the man fell to the floor with half his skull missing.

Her eyes remain clamped shut, her screams muffled through the gag.

"Why doesn't he talk to her?" I grate. "Why doesn't he open his fucking mouth and tell her he's still alive?"

She doesn't realize her brother stands before her while one of her captors lies dead at her feet.

"I don't know." Hunter keeps his gun trained on our enemy, the men taking cover behind the ringleader, who grabs Cole around the neck and uses him as a shield. "It's probably because he thinks the next bullet has his name on it."

"It will if we don't come up with a plan," Luca mutters. "I'm not sure about you guys, but I don't have a lot of experience with hostage negotiations. How the fuck do we get all three of them out alive?"

Pop, pop, pops slash around us, the return fire pinging against the side of the warehouse.

I drop to the ground, the dirt and pebbles scratching my cheek as I face Hunt. "What are you thinking?"

"I'm thinking this son of a bitch isn't smart. He's in an empty warehouse, without any cover, with nobody keeping watch. He's got no idea what he's doing, or who he's up against, but he obviously thinks he's invincible."

"That's a dangerous combination."

He winces. "My thoughts exactly. He'll kill them without considering the consequences."

"I need to make a call." I keep my voice low, out of Luca's range. "We won't get them out on our own."

He frowns at me, his brows tightening as understanding dawns. "No. You're not making any fucking calls. We do this on our own."

"We've got no other—"

"*No.* You're not letting that cat out of the bag, do you hear me? Keep your fucking mouth shut."

It isn't a warning about being a snitch. It's a caution not to blow my cover. Despite his woman being in there, this grumpy fucker is trying to protect me.

"Hunt, they're dead if I don't."

He glares. "And you're dead if you do. Don't be a pussy and give up yet. We've still got choices."

Like hell we do. I can't see one fucking option that's going to get Keira out of there alive. Hunt's gotta know his reputation isn't going to have Drake waving a white flag. This shit is serious. One rogue bullet and Keira is dead.

"Wipe the judgmental look off your face." He shoves to his feet as the last of the bullets sound. "I've got more invested in this than your twenty-four-hour fling."

I follow, wanting to knuckle dust him for the harsh comment.

It's been more than twenty-four hours with Keira.

I've spent months consumed with thoughts of her. I've waited a lifetime to have her close. Deceit or not, I'd do anything to keep her safe.

"Don't criticize our relationship." I fall in beside his position against the wall. "You don't know shit about us."

He shoots me a look of incredulity. "Focus, asshole."

I clench my jaw and peer inside. Keira has raised her head to face the scene before her, her eyes wide as her gaze searches her surroundings for answers.

Pride fills my lungs. Through all this, she's still got hope, which is more than I can muster at this point.

"I'm here, precious. I'm not going anywhere."

Hunt scowls at me. "Are you for real right now?"

"Stop worrying about me and get a fucking grip. You're the one who excels at this tactical shit. So be fucking tactical."

"Would you two shut up?" Luca hisses as he stalks toward the side of the building. "If you haven't noticed, we're about to have company. You might want to prepare."

He's right. A man is running through the warehouse, heading for the door.

I crouch and aim my gun along the wall toward the door, where Luca is acting like wallpaper. "He needs to get out of the way."

"No, don't shoot," Hunt whispers. "Let him take care of it. The less Drake knows about us out here, the better."

"Are you sure?" I creep closer, only to have Hunt place a warning hand on my shoulder.

"Just watch."

I do as he requests, sticking to my haunches as the door opens an inch.

The barrel of a gun peeks out, and a warning shot lashes into the distance.

Luca doesn't move. He remains in the shadows, propped against the warehouse until the guy creeps forward into the darkness.

The gunman's vision must take too long to adjust from the fluorescents. He stands there, doe-eyed, batting his lashes into the night. The second the door closes behind him he's grabbed by the wrist and flipped onto his back.

Luca follows him down in a knee slide that stops near the guy's shoulders, the move seeming like a practiced dance routine. The subsequent glide of hands over the enemy's face and the break of his neck is done with such smooth efficiency it almost looks artistic.

"Holy shit." I stare in shock. "He's got skills."

"Aren't you glad you didn't try to kick his ass earlier?"

"Yeah." I nod. "Really fucking glad." I shove to my feet and stalk the warehouse interior again. "What now?"

"Now we wing it." He aims his gun inside. "The warehouse is surrounded," he yells. "Put your weapons down and you'll live to see another day."

I watch Keira, watch her so damn intently as her face brightens.

The guy in front laughs, his arm wrapping tighter around Torian's neck while the two men behind him crouch for cover.

"That's gotta be Drake." I jerk my head in the guy's direction. "I'd bet my life he's the one blackmailing Keira."

"This has gone beyond blackmail. It's an assassination. He's making a power play."

"Is that you Hunter?" Drake calls. "You're late."

"And you're sloppy," he shouts back. "There's no way you're getting out of this alive."

"Even when I've got your girl?" Drake backtracks, dragging Torian toward Sarah lying lifeless on the floor. "From my perspective, I'm the only one walking out of here a happy man."

"Who is this fucker?" Hunter rubs his knuckles over his mouth. "And why does he know more about me than I do about him?"

"Probably because you've got a fucking huge reputation." My pulse pounds at my temples. Having that psychotic asshole in close proximity to both Sarah and Keira doesn't sit well with me. I can barely breathe through the panic. "What are we doing? We can't just stand here. He's going to do something."

"I want you inside, Hunt. *Now.*"

Drake shoves his boot into Sarah's ribs, but her limp body doesn't jolt from the impact. It stiffens. Spins. She launches from the cement, lashing out with a kick that has him stumbling to right himself with Torian's weight.

She swings out, jabbing at his throat, punching at his fist, only to be knocked out with a hard whack to the back of her head from the coward who had been hiding behind Keira.

Her legs buckle beneath her, her delicate frame crumpling to the floor.

"Son of a bitch." Hunter takes off, running for the door.

"*Wait.*" I sprint after him. "You can't rush in there."

I grab his arm only to be shoved away.

"Fuck off, Decker. You won't stop me." He barrels forward, approaching Luca, who spreads his feet and braces for impact.

"He's right." The Navy ninja blocks the path. "You know more about this shit than I do. You need to stay out here and call the shots. If you go in there, you're dead."

"I don't care. Get out of my way."

Hunt isn't thinking. He's reacting on fear, not tact.

Fuck. Fuck. Fuck.

"Let me go instead." I maneuver around them both. My life isn't a loss. Not when I'm dead already. "I've got a plan."

"What plan?" Luca defends against another one of Hunter's attempts to barge past, whacking him in the throat. "You better not fuck this up."

Hunt jackknifes, coughing and spluttering.

"I don't have time to lay a blueprint." I continue for the door and grip the handle. "You're going to have to trust me."

I pause, not waiting for permission, but still waiting for something. Anything.

I don't know what the fuck I'm doing here. All I need is a thumbs up from Hunt to tell me I'm making the right decision. All I get is a deadly stare as he continues to cough up a lung.

"Go." Luca juts his chin at me. "I'll watch your back the best I can."

The assurance doesn't sound promising, but me and Navy boat have come a long way from his threats to murder me. All I can do is have faith as I yank the door wide and brace for the unknown.

"I'm unarmed." I slide my gun along the cement floor. "I just want to talk."

I raise my hands in the air, my pulse pounding behind my eyes while I take the first step into the light.

Adrenaline is rich in my veins, heightening my senses and clearing my mind. Problem is, I lied. I don't have a plan. All I've got is the death wish I've clung to for too damn long, and the necessity to save Keira.

Her sobs ring in my ears, her heartache increasing with every inch I approach.

I don't look at her. I can't.

Those eyes will kill me. They'll kill us all.

"Who the fuck are you?" Drake faces me, his tight neck-hold keeping Torian pointed toward the windows. "I said I wanted Hunter."

"I'm more valuable than Hunt. I'm the guy who can help you make the right decisions to get you the position of power you want."

He snickers. "You think I need your help?"

"Yes. I do." I keep my hands at shoulder height and continue my slow pace forward. "You're not going to get your happily ever after if you kill Torian."

"And why is that?"

"I'll show you." Slowly, I lower my hands as two of his goons place me in their sights. "I don't have a weapon. I'm reaching to get my cell." I slide my fingers into my pocket and retrieve the device. "If you kill anyone else, Hunter won't let you out of here alive. But if you listen to me, and nobody else gets hurt, I'll tell you how you can get exactly what you want."

"Put it away." He repositions his choke hold, making Torian stumble backward. "You can go take a seat next to the rag doll on the floor."

"Wait." I dial a number, connect the call, and show them the screen. "This is a friend of mine."

"Hang up the phone," Drake snarls. "Turn it off."

"Why don't you take it instead?" I approach another step,

leaving a desolate yard of space between us as I reach the device toward him. "Here. All you need to do is listen."

Take the cell. Just inch forward and take the fucking cell.

"I'm losing patience," he seethes. "Either take a seat or a bullet. Your choice."

I raise my free hand in surrender. "Please. You're making a mistake. Killing Torian is going to piss off a lot of people."

"You're pissing off a lot of people." He swings his gun in my direction and pulls the trigger, the projectile skimming past my thigh. "That was a warning. The next one won't be."

"Okay. Let me do it for you." I press the speaker button and pray to hear something other than a dial tone. But I don't hear anything. Not even static. "Are you there?"

Silence reigns, the seconds ticking by while failure shadows every beat of my pulse.

"Decker?" Anissa's dubious voice breaks the quiet. "Where are you?"

A rush of breath leaves my lungs and the slightest glimmer of relief takes its place. "I need you to tell me your name. I need you to say it like you made me recite it yesterday."

Drake needs to know who she is without me prompting her. He has to believe she's telling the truth.

"Decker," she warns. "What's going on?"

"Put down the phone. Drop it. *Now.*"

"Anissa, please," I beg. "Just say it."

"Drop the fucking phone or someone dies."

Another heavy breath escapes, this one full of defeat.

If only Drake would take a step forward and move into the line of fire. If only I hadn't fucked things up with Anissa and she trusted me enough to tell me what everyone needed to hear.

If only.

If. Fucking. Only.

I look past Drake and the cowards behind him, and finally meet Keira's gaze. Those ocean blues are glassy as they plead back at me. She's begging for help, and for once I can't save her. I can't do a fucking thing to protect her this time.

I'm sorry.

313

She can't hear my thoughts, but I pray she understands my anguish over failing her. I don't know what else to do. This is going to end in a shootout, and the odds aren't in our favor.

"Okay." I crouch, placing the cell on the cement before I straighten to my full height. Death lingers close. I can feel it. The icy chill of nothingness nips at my fingers, preparing me for the worst.

Drake returns his aim to Torian, his focus still on me. "I don't know what your game is—"

"Decker, are you still there?" The strong, feminine voice rises from the ground. "I'm here. It's Special Agent Anissa Fox of the Federal Bureau of Investigation."

"*Shut it off*," Drake roars. "Someone shut it off."

"*Decker?*" she shouts. "Decker, answer me."

A gray-haired man runs forward, his gun aimed on me. He sweeps the cell off the ground, one hand madly working on the buttons when a single pop rings out. I feel the bullet skitter past my shoulder, the impact, throwing old man silver backward, instantly penetrating skin, then bone, then brain. He falls to the floor, the crack of skull the last thing I hear before *pop, pop, pops* slice around me.

I run. I fucking sprint while gunshots whistle from outside.

I rush toward the men crouching to take aim, bypassing the threat of their weapons as I leap for Keira.

I take her to the ground, both of us sliding into Sarah while five more shots ring out. I cover them both the best I can, straddling body parts and chair legs. It's a fucking mess as I cradle Keira's head in my hands and feel the soft hum of her sobs.

The heavy slap of a lifeless body falls behind me.

I don't know if it's Torian. I don't dare to look. The outcome is a double-edged sword when the only possibility of being with Keira is dependent on the death of her brother.

There's another shot, another clap of death hitting the cement.

Then silence.

I can't move. All I hear is ringing in my ears. All I feel is her life vibrating against my chest.

"They're down," Luca yells. "Hurry up and get out of there."

Thumping footfalls approach as I lean on one elbow and remove Keira's gag. "It's okay. It's over."

Her lips tremble, the tears still streaking her cheeks.

"It's okay. I promise." I wipe away the moisture and slam my mouth against hers, needing the split second of connection. "You're safe, buttercup. You're fucking safe."

She sobs into my mouth, her nose nuzzling mine as more tears flow.

"I've got your phone." Hunt's boots enter my line of sight and he crouches down next to Sarah. "You need to get moving."

He strokes her hair, trying to wake her, and gets a soft moan for his efforts.

She's okay. For now.

"He's right." I inch back and don't deny the euphoric twist to my stomach when Keira's eyes peer up at me with relief.

She's so fucking beautiful. Even here. Now. Surrounded by a mass of chaos.

Then her expression falters. Fractures. Her baby blues turn frantic, her skin immediately pale.

"No." She shakes her head. "*Cole, no.*"

I hear the click of a cocked gun a second before the barrel presses into the back of my skull.

"*Cole, please.*" She thrashes despite her bindings, her face a picture of grief and horror.

"It's okay." I climb off her, retreating slowly, and turn to face Torian.

This was always going to be the conclusion. If not here, then somewhere else. Somewhere soon.

"You're the snitch," he accuses.

I thought I'd be scared in the moments before my death. I anticipated hysteria. Panic. Maybe even regret. I feel none of that.

Nothing but calm now Keira is safe.

"Yeah." I hold his stare. "I'm your snitch."

"No. No. No," she wails. "Cole, stop, let me explain."

He doesn't acknowledge her pleas. I'm not sure he hears them through his anger. "For how long?"

"Back off." Hunter steps toward us, Sarah cradled in his arms. "You don't want to do this. Not here. Not now."

"Like hell I don't. I've been searching for this son of a bitch for too damn long."

"You've been searching, but it's not him." Hunter starts for the door. "He's not the fucking informant. He's covering for me. But I ain't talking shit in here. We need to leave."

"Bullshit." Torian's lip curls. "I know it's him. I've always known."

There's a wealth of conviction in his tone. An undeniable belief. It's the waver in his hand that catches me off guard and the slightest hint of uncertainty with his scrutinizing look.

He's not entirely convinced.

"You're a smart man," I mutter. "Too bad you didn't stop me a long time ago."

Hunt's not going to take the fall for me. Not even temporarily.

After everything that's happened this week, I'm too fucking tired of hiding in plain sight.

"*No.* They're both lying," Keira wails. "It was me. I worked with the Feds. It was all me, Cole. That's why you thought it was Sebastian, but could never find proof. It's because you never suspected me. You never would've imagined I'd be the one to betray you."

Torian's scrutiny increases, and his weapon lowers a click.

"Think about it." She wiggles in her toppled chair. "I killed Richard. I put us in this situation with Drake. I've lied to you about everything. It was all me."

"Keira, don't," I whisper.

The warehouse door swings open to slam against the metal wall, and Luca storms in. "Did you think I was joking?" He runs toward us. "We need to leave. I can hear sirens." He places a hand on Torian's extended arm and meets my gaze. "Everything else can wait."

A silent message passes between us. One that doesn't hold a threat of violence.

For once this Navy fucker isn't throwing me under the bus.

He might actually be trying to save me.

My fucking hero.

"What's it going to be, Torian?" I ask.

He doesn't move.

Dead bodies are scattered around us, Keira is bound to a chair that's toppled to the floor, and cops are approaching, yet he doesn't budge an inch.

"Cole. *Please*," she pleads. "You need to listen to me."

He steps closer, nuzzling the gun into my chest. "Don't even think about running." The metal presses harder, my life hanging in the balance of a hair-trigger. "I'll distract the cops. You make sure you get her out of here."

29

KEIRA

I jog beside Sebastian, twisting my wrist to bring back circulation. There's no one else in sight. No cars. No people. No life out here.

"I don't think the sirens are headed in our direction." I pant. "They're not coming for us."

"It doesn't matter." He encourages me to keep moving with a gentle hand at the curve of my back. "We don't want to hang around."

"What about the bodies? There's evidence."

"Your brother will make the necessary calls. He knows what he's doing."

I push my legs harder to keep up and glance over my shoulder to see Hunter running with Sarah in his arms. She winces with every jolt, her face pinched in pain.

My guilt becomes overwhelming. It's hard to breathe through the torment.

But it's what I deserve.

Everything that happened in the warehouse was my fault.

I put everyone's life at risk. My stupidity could've killed my brother, the man I love, and three more people I care about.

Sebastian presses harder on my back. "Keep running."

I nod and follow him around a bank of bushes to an old Jeep hidden in the darkness.

"Ride shotgun. Let Hunt lay Sarah down in the back."

He doesn't wait for me to comply. He climbs into the driver's seat, starting the ignition while I slide in the other side.

The engine splutters into action, jolting my bones over and over.

"She's a piece of work, isn't she?" Sebastian shoves the car into gear and inches us out of the shadows. "We had to drive this deathtrap back from my brother's house."

I grimace, letting the shame sauté my insides as we approach Hunter and wait for him to climb inside.

I attempt to think of ways to make up for my actions while we drive through streets bathed in moonlight. My mind becomes overwhelmed trying to fix something that seems shattered into a million pieces. Everything is a mess.

"Any requests on where we should go?" Sebastian keeps his gaze on the road, his knuckles white against the steering wheel despite his calm demeanor. "I need to know where I'm driving."

"Out of town." The words rasp from my sore throat. "You need to get as far away from Cole as possible."

The last time we had this discussion, I was fighting for him to stay. Now I want nothing more than to get out of here. To flee Portland. Escape my family. At least for a little while.

"Sarah needs medical attention." The glow of Hunter's cell beams from the back seat. "I've already texted my guy to meet us at Keira's house. It's the closest option."

"Then we have to pull over." I wiggle forward in my seat, speaking directly to Sebastian. "Hunter can take the car while we move on foot."

His fingers clench and re-clench against the wheel in his ongoing silence.

"Sebastian?"

"Put your seatbelt on." He shoots me a look of warning. "I'm not running anywhere."

"Cole isn't going to—"

"I don't want to hear it, Keira. Just let it go. I'll be fine."

Fine.

Why does nobody use that word for its intended purpose anymore?

"I don't think that means what you think it means." I repeat the phrase he spoke to me a lifetime ago. Back before the craziness. Prior to my love.

His mouth kicks at the side. It's slow. Subtle. The emotion hits me right in the chest, giving me the slightest hope for redemption.

"Please." I keep pleading. I guess I'll have to for a long time to make any sort of dint in the forgiveness I need to earn.

"We're not running." This time his statement is grated, demanding an end to the conversation.

I slink back in my seat and lean my head against the window, breathing slow through the building regret.

I'm going to lose him.

After everything we've been through, despite all the good he's done for me, this is going to end. And right now, it feels like it will kill me in the process.

Hunter's voice murmuring from the back seat doesn't help. He speaks to Sarah in hushed tones, promising to look after her, complimenting her bravery, and pleading for her forgiveness.

She whimpers through his admissions, her pain filling the car to capacity.

The intimacy is hauntingly beautiful as Sebastian veers around one corner, then another, his sterility promising something entirely different.

He doesn't want me anymore. I've burned that bridge.

And rightly so.

But I'm not ready to give up. There's still fight left in me despite the weary exhaustion.

By the time we reach my house, there's an older man waiting on my doorstep. He doesn't fit the wealthy neighborhood demographic with his loose sweatpants and dark hoodie. The only thing that suits his reputation is the doctor's bag hanging at his side, which looks entirely mismatched against his clothing.

"Have you got your keys?" Hunt opens his door and slides Sarah toward him along the back seat.

"No. I don't have anything." Not keys, a phone, or any self-respect. "Just break a window. Break them all. I don't care. All you need is the code for the alarm which is five-seven-two-nine."

He doesn't wait for more instructions. He hauls Sarah into his arms, kicks the door shut, and carries her around the front of the car to speak to the shifty doctor.

"We need to leave," I whisper. "Cole won't be far away."

Sebastian breaks my heart by cutting the engine. "I'm not running. I'm done hiding, too."

I hang my head, fighting frustration. "You wouldn't be on your own. I'd be with you. We can go together."

"You're not going anywhere. Your place is in Portland, with your family."

"If you haven't noticed, I've betrayed my entire bloodline. My place isn't here at all. It's with you." I glance his way and find him focused out the windshield. He can't even look at me anymore. "*Please*. You need to trust me."

He lets out a derisive laugh, and all I can do is squeeze my eyes shut against the pain.

"Trust isn't the issue," he murmurs. "I've always trusted you. Even when I shouldn't."

There's a jingle of keys, the opening of a door, then his slide out of the car.

I don't move, not apart from my jolt of shock when the door slams.

We need to leave. We *have* to.

There's no other option.

Cole will already be tracking us down. His temper will be in full force. Hysteria will make all his decisions for him.

My door swings wide, and a gentle hand glides over my thigh.

"They opened the house for us. Let's talk inside."

I open my eyes and stare down at the fingers splayed against my jeans. I remember all the times he's touched me—physically *and* emotionally. A wealth of craziness has been shared between us, but I've become even more rich in appreciation.

This man has become my world.

He's my everything.

Maybe Cole will understand.

"Keira, sweetheart, come on. You don't want to stay out here." He's crouched beside me, his gaze solemn. "I need to get you cleaned up."

"I don't get why you're fighting me on this. Yesterday, you were ready to run."

"We'll talk about it inside." He stands and holds out a hand.

I frown at his offering and ponder all the things that come with it—the resignation and surrender.

It means goodbye.

I swallow hard and place my fingers against his, dreading every step as he leads me into the house. He drops his hold when we reach the living room, focusing his attention on Sarah laid out along my sofa.

"Is she going to be okay?" he asks.

The doctor cradles her head in both hands, using his thumbs to press against her skull. "It's hard to tell without scans."

"No." Sarah winces. "No hospital. I'm not going back there."

"She's going to be okay." Hunt sits down on the arm rest, right near her head. "I'll make sure of it."

Sebastian nods. "Yell out if you need anything." He turns to me. "Is there some place private we can talk?"

I keep my gaze on Sarah, taking in every wince and hiss of pain.

"Keira? It's this way to your bedroom, right?"

He points a hand toward the hall, and I ignore my curiosity at how he knows the intimate details of my house. Nothing surprises me anymore.

"Yeah."

He leads the way down to the last room on the left, indicating for me to enter first before he closes the door behind us.

I drag my feet to the end of the bed, not willing to face him anymore. I don't know how to look at him and remain strong at the same time.

"How are you holding up?" he murmurs. "Has shock set in?"

"Is that a trick question?" Maybe I was wrong, maybe I can still be surprised, because he's not making any sense to me. "You know I'm frantic, Sebastian. And yes, I'm shocked as hell that you're keeping us here when Cole is on his way."

He reverts back to the silent treatment.

"Why won't you run?" I turn to face him, not holding back the frustration in my voice. "Are you waiting for an apology? Is that it? Because I'm sorry. I'm so goddamn sorry I didn't listen to you. What I did was selfish and stupid, but I didn't see that at the time. All I wanted was to be able to fight my own battles."

He focuses his attention on the bed, his gaze wandering over the beaded quilt and the mass of decorative pillows. "That's not what this is about."

"Then what is it?" I start toward him. "Tell me, and I'll do whatever needs to be done."

He closes his eyes for long seconds, then huffs out a sigh. "I don't want you to do anything, precious."

I stop before him and lean toward his line of vision until he meets my eyes. "What are you going to do when he gets here?"

"Nothing."

Nothing.

The word shudders through me, bringing an icy chill.

"I can't stop him, Keira. We both know that." He bridges the space between us and weaves his hands around my waist. His touch is everything—gentle, smooth, affectionate. "I just want to stay here while I can. No running. No hiding. No panic."

"He's going to—"

"It doesn't matter. It's out of our control."

"No, it's not." I slam my palm against his chest. "You're giving up, when we could be running. It wouldn't be forever. Only until he has the patience to listen to the full story. We can stay away until he forgives you."

"Forgives me? Really?" He snickers through a mocking smile. "You're not very good at this, pumpkin."

I shove at him. "This isn't a joke."

He's laughing at me. Laughing when so much hangs in the balance of every second that ticks by.

"Why won't you listen?" I grab his shirt, entangling my fingers in the material to tug, tug, tug some sense into him.

His humor fades, and those eyes turn somber. "Because if my minutes are numbered, I want to spend every second standing here with you... I'd just prefer it without the fighting."

"No." I shake my head and thump my fist against his chest. "*Please*."

He pulls me close, his arms a vise around me as he presses his lips to my temple. "Just enjoy what we've got."

"I'll die without you," I whisper.

"And I'll die for you. It's always been that way." He rocks me back and forth, moving us in a silent dance of farewell. "I love you. Never forget that, okay?"

I cling to him. To the words. To the warmth.

"I won't let go." My breathing begins to fracture, each breath getting shorter, sharper, until I'm hyperventilating. "I can't."

Tears fall, staining his shirt as I lean into his chest. I hold him with everything I have, and everything I'll ever be.

He found me. He saved me. He made me whole.

There's no going back from that.

A thunderous knock at the front door tears a gasp from my throat, and those arms clamp tighter.

"Shh. It's okay." He speaks into my hair. "Don't let go."

No.

No, no, no.

My limbs shake. I struggle to breathe.

I don't want this. I can't live through it.

My door handle turns, the wood inching wide to bring Hunter into view. "Do you want me to let him in?"

Sebastian nods. "Yeah."

"No." I vehemently shake my head. "Not yet."

Hunter winces, ignoring my protest as he disappears down the hall.

"Please, God, no." I yank at Sebastian's shirt. "It's not too late to get out of here."

"Don't worry." He steps back and takes hold of my wrists, his grip gentle. "Nothing is going to happen here. He'll take me for a ride. That's when I'll find a way out. *Then* I'll run. Okay?"

He's lying. I can tell this time.

I see the dishonesty in his eyes.

It's in the grief-stricken smile.

"You can't deceive me again. You know once you get in that car there's no coming back."

And I'll never learn the truth. Cole will never tell me what really happened.

"Hey." He leans close and nuzzles his nose against mine. "Do you know what I'm more certain of?"

I shake my head. I don't want to hear it. Nothing else matters.

"That you mean the world to me," he murmurs against my lips. "You're everything, Keira."

I squeeze my eyes closed, the heated trail along my cheeks growing wider.

My knees threaten to buckle, and all I do is hold the heartache tight inside my chest.

"Hey. Come on, sugar. It'll be okay." He brushes my cheeks, resolute.

I can't fathom his level of acceptance. I never will.

"It's time." He gives me a sad smile, never breaking our gaze. "We've got company."

I shoot a frantic glance to the door and find Cole standing there, his face a mask of harsh lines and barely contained rage.

"Get out of my house," I demand. "I don't want you here."

"Is that any way to greet your brother?" The question is a threat, his words intricately laced with more than disappointment.

"I won't let you hurt him."

"I'm unarmed, aren't I?"

"You are?" I scrutinize him. Up and down.

"Yes. Thanks to Hunt." He flicks open the sides of his jacket, then does an unenthusiastic turn with his hands out in front of him. "See. No gun."

I glance back at Sebastian in confusion.

He gives me an unconvincing smile, his eyes speaking of distrust. He's waiting for the other shoe to drop, and I need to do the same.

I turn back to my brother and strengthen my shoulders to steel. "You need to let me explain."

"That's why I'm here."

"Okay... Good." I nod, my head jerking back and forth as I sniff away the last remnants of tears. "Sebastian has a good reason for what he did. Our father isn't who we think he is. He's been trafficking—"

"I know."

My heart stops. My skin crawls. "You know?"

"Yeah." He holds my gaze, unrepentant, remorseless. "He offered to cut me in on the action after Richard was admitted to hospital."

There's a wealth of heartlessness in his words. Such cold, sterile detachment.

I shake my head, unable to comprehend what I'm hearing. "No." I place a hand over my mouth, attempting to bottle the effects of his betrayal. "You've been helping him? All this time?"

"Of course not," he snarls. "*Jesus.* Don't look at me like that. I said he *offered* to cut me in, not that I accepted."

"Why would you keep this from me? We tell each other everything."

"Do we?" He cocks his head in confusion. "Like assassination attempts against family members?"

"That was one thing, Cole. And it was *my* thing. I needed to cut him out of our lives."

"And this was one thing, *Keira*. One thing I knew you couldn't handle."

"But you still knew." Sebastian's hands find my waist, his

326

touch possessive. Protective. "And you didn't do a damn thing about it."

My brother takes a threatening step forward. "I think we're getting distracted from the real issue here, don't you? How long have you been singing to the Feds?"

Those hands on my waist tighten. "Since before you knew I existed."

Cole's brows rise as if impressed by the honesty. "Why? You had to know the consequences." He takes another step. "Something like this doesn't end well for you."

"Back off," I warn. "He had good reason. I would've done the same."

"In that case, you'll need to enlighten me, because I can't think of anything capable of justifying his actions."

I itch to blurt the information. The painful truth sits right on the tip of my tongue, waiting for permission.

But Sebastian needs to provide these answers.

He needs to... Yet he doesn't.

I turn, facing Sebastian as he glares at Cole.

"I can't say it," he murmurs. "I don't want him knowing about her."

"There's another woman?" Cole scoffs. "Keira, what have you gotten yourself into?"

"He knows." Sebastian meets my gaze. "And he didn't do a fucking thing."

The truth is a heavy weight against my heart.

Yes, Cole knows, but I have to believe there's a reason he kept quiet. He wouldn't knowingly allow for women to be tortured. He couldn't. Not when I've seen his compassion for my own torture. "Let me tell him."

"It's over." He kisses my forehead and drops his hands from my waist. "Your brother and I are going to go for a drive."

"*No.*" I grab his wrists. "I'll tell him."

He doesn't respond, just keeps glaring his fury at my brother.

I swing around. "It was his sister. His *only baby sister.* And our father took her."

Cole acknowledges the confession with the straightening

of his spine and the slight hitch of his chin. He understands family loyalty. And the heartache of loss. There's no way he can't empathize with Sebastian's situation.

"Now do you understand?" I plead. "You would've done far worse in his situation."

"Is it true?" He focuses over my shoulder, his eyes narrowed in scrutiny.

"Yes." Sebastian's hands reclaim my body, the heated palms searing my hips. "They manipulated her. Sold her. And eventually killed her."

"You're certain?"

His fingers dig into bone. "Yes. I'm fucking certain. I wouldn't be anywhere near your family if I wasn't."

I flinch, not expecting the rejection. In seconds Sebastian's arms are wrapping around me to lessen the blow.

"You know what I mean," he whispers in my ear. "I wouldn't have dared to betray your family if it wasn't for Penny."

I nod, because yes, I do understand. Venom flows through our family tree, and he isn't the type of man to shake branches.

He's here for vengeance. Not me.

We never would've found each other without his sister's death. And that hurts. It's brutal and punishing, and goddamn heartbreaking because I struggle to quit the selfishness to tell myself I'd give him up if I could change the past for Penny.

Cole nods. "I understand your situation. And can appreciate your motives. But unfortunately, it's time to deal with the consequences."

"If you can contemplate punishing him after everything he's been through, I don't want to know you anymore," I snarl. "I'm done. You can—"

"Keira," he warns.

"*No.* You would've done the same. *Actually,* you would've done far worse, and you know it."

"And I would've accepted my fate."

"I accept my fate." Sebastian steps around me, heading toward the door.

"No." I stagger forward to remain between them, placing a

palm on Sebastian's chest to hold him back, while holding up a hand of warning to my brother. "This ends now. We've all been through enough. There are no repercussions. It's over."

"Keira." Cole's eyes soften, his expression changing to one of derision. "He paid back our family by manipulating you. You may not see it, but you became the mark."

A wave of goosebumps flows down my back, and for a split second I believe him. "No." I shake my head. "*No.*"

I shove at Sebastian's chest to keep him at bay, then face my brother head-on. "Fuck you for thinking I can be easily manipulated."

"You've lived with what Richard did for years. Then all of a sudden you can't handle history?"

I storm forward, getting in his face. "All of a sudden I couldn't handle him looking at Stella the way he looked at me. My decisions regarding our uncle have never had anything to do with Sebastian. Or me. I was keeping your niece safe."

Cole snaps taut.

"I planned to kill him well before you made Sebastian my protector. And he had no say in what I did tonight. He's the one who tried to stop me." I glare all my fury at him. "Do you hear me? *He* tried to stop me. So I'm not the weak, defenseless woman who can be easily manipulated. I'm the one who will burn your house to the ground if you dare think about hurting him ever again."

My brother remains quiet, scrutinizing me while my heart beats a staccato through my entire body.

I know that look.

He's thinking. He's actually contemplating. The anticipation for his response becomes agony.

"Did you use her to get to my family?" He glides his attention to Sebastian, his expression impassive.

"I don't know."

I glance over my shoulder, wordlessly begging Sebastian to falsify an answer. It's clear he used me. I understand that. But our truth became far stronger than those lies.

"I never planned on getting this deep," he admits. "I was

ready to run the night you made me your bitch boy. Keira is the only reason I stayed."

"Because you thought you could manipulate the tumultuous relationship we portrayed?"

"No." His eyes harden. "Because I wanted to save her. From you."

"She's never needed saving," Cole grates.

"Tonight suggests otherwise. I saved her from your knee-jerk decision to walk into that warehouse without backup. *I'm* the reason she got out of there alive."

I swing back around to my brother. "He's the reason *you* got out of there alive. He risked his own safety to save us all. Doesn't that mean something?"

He doesn't answer.

"Cole, *please*, you need to let this go."

"What was your end game?" he asks. "What was the point of working with the Feds?"

"To shut down your father's operation. I wanted him behind bars."

"Bars won't hold him." Cole's lip curls. "You should've known that."

"He does now," I say in a rush. "That's why we've worked out a better plan. I want him dead, Cole."

"You're not working on a fucking thing," he snaps. "There's no *we* in this."

His eyes narrow on mine, and for the first time I see his disappointment. The emotion wasn't there when I was trapped in the warehouse, but now it stares back at me in stark clarity.

"If you have even the slightest inclination to keep this piece of shit alive, then you'll stick to the fucking sideline. You won't breathe a word of this to anyone. Not about Decker. Not about our father. And not about fucking Richard."

His words bear down on me, harsh and unrelenting. His anger is worse.

"You won't think about interfering with my plans for our father," he continues. "You won't even dare to ask to be involved. You will keep your thoughts and your relationship to yourself, and save your boy toy the pain of getting a knife in the neck. Do you hear me?"

I hear him.

I hear him too loud. Too clear.

The ultimatum repeats in my ears like a life sentence and clemency, all at once.

"Okay," I whisper.

"And if you upset her," he points a menacing finger at Sebastian, "even once, I won't kill you. You won't be that lucky. But I'll make sure you wish you were dead."

"Understood." Sebastian pulls me into his side with an arm around my waist.

We stand together, closer than we've ever been while my brother retreats toward the door.

"Wait," Sebastian calls out. "You need to know Hunt wasn't involved in this. He wasn't aware of my connections."

My brother pauses, his stance rigid.

There's no belief in his features. There's no dispute, either.

"He knew at some point."

"Two days ago," I interrupt. "When he beat Sebastian to a bloody pulp in an attempt to get answers."

Cole nods, his acceptance inconclusive, before he walks down the hall and out of view.

I remain in place, stunned. "What the hell just happened?"

"I don't know."

I stare into the hall as my mind does a rerun, trying to work out the puzzle. "Maybe he likes you after all?"

"No, pop tart." He steps into me, wrapping an arm around my neck, the other around my waist. "He doesn't like me in the slightest. He's only saving my ass to make you happy."

"Well, it worked." My chest burns, every nerve tingling beneath warmed flesh. "I'm so happy, Sebastian."

"Me, too. But what happened tonight is going to catch up with you pretty soon. The shock will be brutal."

I nod and snuggle into his chest. "I know. I can already feel it."

The memories hover on the periphery, fighting to be heard.

"You won't be alone." His hold tightens. "I've got you."

My eyes tingle with the threat of tears. I don't want to ruin this. I need our moment to remain with me a little while longer before the demons arrive. "Do you think we're capable of getting through a twenty-four-hour period without deceiving each other?"

He chuckles, the vibrations nuzzling my cheek. "God, I hope so. If you didn't pick up what your brother was putting down, I kinda need for us to get through a lot of twenty-four-hour periods if I don't want my dick blown off."

"How many do you think you can handle?"

"I'm pretty sure I don't want to lose this third leg of mine, which means you're stuck with me indefinitely."

"Why doesn't it surprise me that you're making jokes at a time like this?"

He blankets me with affection, the adoration seeping under my skin. "Because you know me, sparkles. You know me better than I know myself."

EPILOGUE
DECKER

"You're beautiful," I whisper.

No truer words have been spoken.

Keira is a vision before me in a sleek black dress, her hair loose and draped over her shoulders. She stands in front of her hallway mirror, her lashes dark, her make-up subtle. Everything about her is flawless, especially the way she smiles back at me with understated perfection.

"Thank you." She turns to me and bridges the space between us, her high heels tapping against the tile. "And you're utterly handsome."

Her arms slide under my suit jacket to hug my waist, accidentally bumping the gun lodged in the back of my pants. "Sorry. I'm still getting used to you wearing a weapon."

It's her brother's fault I've been unarmed. He demanded I hide my gun at home. To stow my only protection so the two of us could participate in a trivial game of chicken.

It was a power play. A reclaiming of his authority.

He also took away my cell and made two of his thugs shadow me.

And I understood the necessity.

I can also understand why he gave me back my freedom and my right to bear arms this morning.

"It's okay." I pull her into me and kiss her forehead. "Are you ready?"

"How can anyone be ready for something like this?"

I don't know.

Today, she lays her uncle to rest after suffering through days of turmoil pouring her secrets out to her sister. I've been with her through it all. I hugged her while her nightmares wreaked havoc and held her hand when she demanded Richard wasn't worthy of a church service.

There will only be a brief graveside vigil for a man who deserves far less.

I've stood by her through everything. I honestly haven't let this gorgeous woman leave my side. Half the time it's by choice, the other half is because she doesn't want to tempt her brother's itchy trigger finger.

But that fucker won't kill me. Not anytime soon.

Turns out, he's wrapped around his little sister's pinkie tight enough to cut circulation. Behind the charade of animosity, the two of them are thick as thieves. Cole wouldn't do anything to hurt her. So it all boils down to me treading the straight and narrow to keep this woman happy. Which is far from a hardship.

"Come on, guys," Sarah calls from the living room. "We're going to be late."

Keira stiffens in my arms, her slender body coiled tight.

"Don't worry." I grab her hand and entwine our fingers. "Life will get easier after today."

"Do you really believe that?"

"Yes." I shoot her a wink. "You know better than to think I'd lie to you."

She gives a half-hearted chuckle, and I know the apprehension in her features has nothing to do with me. The trust between us is unbreakable. Her fear comes from what she's about to face.

Not just the burial of her rapist, but the possible appearance of her father.

"We haven't heard a word from him," she whispers. "What if he doesn't show?"

"He will. You've said it before, he's not going to miss his brother's funeral."

"That's what I thought, but now I'm not so sure."

I squeeze her fingers. "It's out of our hands. Let Cole deal with it. I'm sure he's got it under control."

I lead her along the hall, only to have her pull me to a stop steps later.

"And you're okay with not being involved?"

"I'm fine."

"*Sebastian*," she warns. "Don't use that word."

I chuckle. "Okay, I'm not fine. But I'm dealing with it."

The intricacies of Cole's plan aren't at my disposal. He's kept the details a tightly held secret. Yet, this morning, he had the decency to tell me I'd have my vengeance before nightfall. That his father would be dead if today worked in our favor.

It was a murmured promise from my woman's brother.

A barely civil vow from the son of my sister's murderer.

It's all I have, and more than I need.

"Come on. If we don't get moving, we're going to miss the funeral."

The ride to the cemetery is done in silence. Hunter drives, I ride shotgun, while Sarah and Keira sit in the back.

Expensive sports cars and luxurious SUVs are lined up bumper to bumper along the narrow cemetery street. We park at the front, claiming our reserved space as a member of the notorious crime family.

"There are more people than I expected." Sarah unfastens her belt and scoots forward to peer through the windshield. "A lot of cars means a lot of witnesses."

Hunter cuts the ignition and scopes the growing crowd. "Torian isn't going to make a move at the funeral."

"You know what's going down?" I shoot him a questioning glance, which is quickly deflected with a look of caution.

"Everything will be handled after we leave the cemetery." Hunt opens his door and Sarah follows, both of them keeping their distance from Torian and Layla, who wait beneath a portable gazebo, Luca and Layla's husband standing one step behind.

I remain in place, not moving until Keira's ready.

"He's not here," she murmurs. "I can't see him anywhere. What happens if he doesn't show?"

"That's out of our hands. We've both known that for days."

She winces, her disappointment killing me. "You don't regret giving up on retaliation?"

"Not at all. That shit was tearing me apart. Besides, I got the better end of the deal when I walked away with you."

She sighs and rests her head against the window as she stares across at the gravesite. "It looks like they're ready to start."

I nod. "Yeah, the evil glare your brother is giving me is a great indication."

Her halfhearted chuckle fills the car. It's all the reward I need.

It's all I'll ever want.

She sucks in a deep breath and releases it slowly. "Let's do this."

She shoves open her door, and I rush from the car to meet her.

We walk hand in hand to the crowd that parts as we approach.

"I don't know half these people," she murmurs. "How could they all have cared about Richard?"

"I don't know. Business associates, I guess. Try not to think about it."

"Business associates would make it worse."

She's right. But as always, I'm not the best at comfort. Not in situations like this.

It's hard enough dealing with the constant prickle of the hair at the back of my neck. The vibe here feels wrong.

She pulls us to a stop at the front of the crowd, next to Hunter and Sarah, our position opposite the gazebo. It's her choice not to stand near her brother and sister, and I get it. She needs to do this on her own.

Her grief is far different than theirs.

The officiant steps forward, opens a thick, leather-bound book, and begins the proceedings.

I don't listen to a word he says. I'm too busy fighting disappointment.

I honestly didn't think Luther would miss his own brother's funeral. Keira had convinced me he would attend, despite all obstacles, in the face of all adversity.

Even though I've come to terms with being stripped of any role in his demise, the thought of him not being punished sits like a lead balloon.

But he's not here.

Torian's pinched face says he's not coming, either. And he'd know.

He has airport staff in his pocket. Cops on the payroll. His own men on the streets. If he hasn't heard anything by now, he never will.

I lower my gaze to the grass around my shoes and take solace in having Keira by my side.

She's the prize despite the losing hand. The peace to soothe the torment.

She reaches out, as if hearing my thoughts, and grabs the crook of my arm. Her fingers dig deep. Tighter and tighter, to the point of pain.

I shoot her a glance, wondering what the claws are all about.

"He's here." Her announcement is barely audible, yet the anticipation rings loud as hell in my ears.

I follow the angle of her vision to see her father striding forward from the other side of the cemetery, weaving in and out of gravestones in his flawless suit and tie with matching thugs flanking him on either side.

I've never seen the guy in person. Only in family photos in the restaurant or online. But it isn't hard to recognize him. He's an older version of his son. Broad shoulders. Stern face. The guy demands respect without saying a word.

Everyone remains still as he approaches, bringing a halt to the proceedings as he greets his eldest daughter with a hug. Then Cole with a handshake.

Keira bristles at the shared affection, and I can't help doing the same.

337

"It's all for show," Hunter murmurs. "Torian knows what he's doing."

I have to trust his faith because I have none of my own.

Cole is supposed to be kill the man before him. His own flesh and blood. Yet, here he is playing happy families.

I cup Keira's biting hand and squeeze. "Do you want to go over and see him?"

"No. It doesn't feel right."

"I don't think there's a right way to feel about this, honey," Hunter drawls.

"I know. But I thought I'd feel remorse at the sight of him." She meets my gaze, staring back at me in confusion. "And I don't. All I see is a monster."

"There's no rulebook here. And no judgment." I wipe the stray hair away from her cheeks. "You feel whatever you need to. It's the only way you'll get through this."

She crumples, her shoulders wilting as she nestles in front of me and wraps my arms around her waist.

Luther moves to stand between his children, his granddaughter before him, the goons at his back, when Torian inclines his head at the officiant to continue.

Adrenaline eats away at my veins while fabricated good deeds are recited to a silent crowd. We're painted a story of a man who never existed. A philanthropist. A devoted uncle and cherished brother.

Over and over the lies continue, twisting my stomach and making me livid.

But I'll have my peace soon.

The sweet taste of victory is on its way.

A few sobs ring out when the coffin is lowered a foot. Stella wails. People sniff.

I don't think anyone really cares except that little girl. She's the only one naive to Richard's actions and capabilities.

My heart breaks for her. Not only did she lose an uncle, she lost a fairytale, and one day the truth will come out to reveal a reality darker than her worst nightmares.

"I'd now like to call upon anyone who would like to place petals or sand in the grave as a personal goodbye." The officiant turns to the gazebo, offering the family the first opportunity.

Luther sidesteps Stella to move forward, away from his henchmen and toward the grave. He grabs a handful of petals as he passes, every set of eyes watching his movements. He scatters the offering, his actions delicate, then kisses his clenched fist and thumps it down on the coffin.

Keira jolts with the impact, her body trembling against mine.

There's a rustle of noise behind me, and a broad, middle-aged man bumps my shoulder to break through the crowd, his enthusiasm to throw sand on a dead guy outweighing his manners.

"Watch it," I mutter.

He ignores me and continues toward the grave. "Luther Torian?"

Keira's father scowls at the intrusion, openly hostile at the man stupid enough to call his name.

The stranger doesn't falter, his stride strong as he holds out a hand. "I'm Special Agent Anthony Easton, and you're under arrest for human trafficking," he clasps Luther's palm and retrieves a pair of cuffs with his left, "and solicitation involving minors under the age of sixteen."

Gasps break out in a chorus. Then whispers and growing chatter.

Keira freezes. So do I.

All of us—Hunt, Sarah, Torian, and Layla—watch in horror as the agent takes charge of the scene.

"You have the right to remain silent."

"No." Torian stalks forward. "*Stop.*"

Keira turns to me, her eyes pleading the same denial.

If Luther goes to jail, his crimes won't end. He will hire the best lawyers. He'll pay everyone and anyone to get him out of there. Then he'll disappear.

He won't go to prison.

He won't die for his sins.

He'll be free.

"What the fuck do you think you're doing?" Torian doesn't

339

shout, he seethes, the words holding enough venom to filter through the gathering.

The agent continues without pause. "Anything you say can and will be used against you in a court of law."

Luther's goons approach, but so do more unfamiliar men and women in the crowd, all of them pulling badges from pockets in a mass show of authority.

"Jesus," I hiss. They're everywhere. "That's the reason you didn't recognize half these people. They're all Feds."

Keira grabs my shirt, clinging to the material. "Do something. *Please.*"

Fuck. Her plea tears me apart, and there's nothing I can do.

I can't save her this time. I vowed I wouldn't get involved, and Torian knows I've kept my end of the deal. I won't lose her now. Not even at the expense of my revenge.

"We'll figure something out." Sarah places a hand on her shoulder. "This isn't the end."

The agent doesn't quit reciting the Miranda rights as he hikes Luther's hands behind his back and leads the silent man to the long line of cars.

"Everyone move," a woman shouts. "Make way."

"Anissa." Her name slips from my lips. That fucking bitch.

"Keira, you need to start making calls." Hunter hands over his phone. "Prepare your legal team."

"Why?" Her brows knit.

I lean close, placing my mouth near her ear. "This game is far from over. We both know he'll get out. And when he does, he needs to know you made every effort to protect him."

"I want to speak to Cole first." The device trembles in her hand as she stares at her brother now talking to Anissa. "What is she saying to him?"

"I don't know."

I'm not sure I want to. Not when the look on her face says she's enjoying the victory.

Keira starts toward them, and I follow close at her back, neither of us making it to Cole before Anissa saunters after the rest of her team.

340

"What did she say to you?" Keira demands.

"A lot of things." His lips press tight for a moment, his anger barely contained. "She has the impression we're going to be seeing a lot of each other in the future."

"She said that?" Sarah snarls from behind me. "She comes to your uncle's funeral, arrests your father, then lays more threats?"

That's Anissa—thirty percent cocky, seventy percent bitch.

"What are you going to do?" I hitch my chin at Torian. "Apart from the legal team moving into action, what's your plan?"

His jaw ticks, his narrowed eyes still focused on Anissa as she saunters to the mass of cars parked along the narrow cemetery road. "I'm going to give that woman exactly what she wants."

Please consider leaving a review on your book retailer website or Goodreads

Titles in the Hunting Her Series

Hunter

Decker

Torian

Savior

Luca

Cole

Information on Eden's other books can be found at www.edensummers.com

ABOUT THE AUTHOR

Eden Summers is a bestselling author of contemporary romance with a side of sizzle and sarcasm.

She lives in Australia with a young family who are well aware she's circling the drain of insanity.
Eden can't resist alpha dominance, dark features and sarcasm in her fictional heroes and loves a strong heroine who knows when to bite her tongue but also serves retribution with a feminine smile on her face.

If you'd like access to exclusive information and giveaways, join Eden Summers' newsletter via the link on her website - www.edensummers.com

For more information:
www.edensummers.com
eden@edensummers.com

Printed in Great Britain
by Amazon

82048715R00202